Mine

Kelly Florentia

S

First published in 2021

This edition published by Stylo Books 2024

ISBN: 9798873165445

Also by Kelly Florentia

The Magic Touch
A romantic page-turner, with a touch of magic.

No Way Back
An addictive romantic drama.

Her Secret
The sequel to No Way Back. A romantic thriller.

To Tell a Tale or Two…
A collection of contemporary short stories with a twist or surprise ending.

Prologue

North London, late August

I watch you sitting there chewing your thumbnail, staring into space. Your thick curly blonde hair is scraped back into a ponytail today. I like it. It suits you. Makes you look younger. You seem edgy though. Distant. Poor you. You've been through a lot lately. I get that. Which is probably why you've taken to the bottle. I know you have. I can see the tell-tale signs.

You'll never admit to it, of course. I know that too. You see, I know you inside out, better than you think. The slight tremor in your hand when you lift a cup to your mouth, those tired blue eyes, which you blame on staring at the computer screen all day long; those dry lips and dehydrated skin. It doesn't take a genius to work it out.

I want to tell you to slow down, but it's not my place. When you drop your head in to your hands, I almost feel sorry for you, knowing your fate. My tense muscles loosen and I exhale quietly. It's the drink that made you do it – deep down you regret it, hate yourself for it. I know you do. I can feel your angst like a mist on my skin, penetrating deep into my pores, giving me that sick twisting feeling in my stomach.

Sometimes, I wonder if you just lost your way, acted on impulse, and a part of me wants to cut you some slack. But I can't. The prospect of you getting away with it fills me with unease. Anyway, you're almost at breaking point now. I can't miss this opportunity. I pull out my phone and you suddenly jerk your head up and stare right at me, and for a horrible moment I think I've been rumbled.

Adrenalin soars through me and I stiffen, but then you pull something out of your handbag and carry on, almost as if I'm invisible. I give you one final indiscreet glare as you look at your reflection in a handheld mirror, pressing your lips together. You look so sweet and innocent standing there in your red Gap hoodie and blue skinny jeans. But you're a liar.

I know what you did and you have to pay. All I've got to do is figure out a way to get rid of you. For good.

Chapter 1

I smell the fug of stale perfume, alcohol, and tobacco in my hair the moment I rouse from sleep, ears still ringing from the pounding music, and I know, even before I open my eyes, that last night I did something stupid, something reckless, something I'm going to regret deeply. A feeling of dread courses through my veins. My skin feels tight and clogged with makeup, lips dry, lashes clumped together with yesterday's mascara. I can't even remember getting home last night, let alone climbing into bed.

I need to get up, get dressed, check my texts and social media, find out if I sent anyone any drunken messages, or posted any cringeworthy selfies on Instagram. I glance at my bedside table and panic starts to simmer in my stomach. Where's my phone? It's my clock. My alarm. My coach. My lifeline. I always keep it by my bedside table. Always.

Turning on my side slowly, I wait out a bout of nausea. I haven't felt this sick after a night out in years. I must be getting old. Or did I mix my drinks? Yes, I think I did. That must be it. I'll be fine after a shower; but as I go to whip back the duvet, terror charges through my body. I'm not alone. The sound of the toilet flushing feeds through my bedroom door, followed by the clamber of footsteps in the corridor and then the rattle of the doorknob. My heart is in my mouth. But instead of leaping out of bed and grabbing something heavy to protect myself, I just lay there, still as an artist's model. The door opens, there's a shuffle of footsteps and then I see him. A blurry figure, not my boyfriend, I'm single, in nothing but a pair of boxer shorts. I take a sharp breath but it catches in my throat and I almost pass out. My eyes close.

'Hey, are you okay?' he says in a well-spoken local accent. His voice is kind and caring. He doesn't sound like a murderer, although I'm not quite sure I know what a murderer sounds like. 'Lucy?' The man tilts his head to one side. I blink hard, forcing my clogged eyelashes apart and the fog lifts. I can see him clearly now – tall, slim, about forty, with short dishevelled chestnut hair, greying at the temples, light brown eyes, a ski-slope nose, wide mouth with thin lips. 'Hope I didn't wake you. I checked on you, like literally, five minutes ago and you were spark out.' Checked on me? Who does he think he is, my carer?

I gather the duvet tightly in my fists and pull it up to my chin. I'm not afraid of him. I know him, his name is on the tip of my tongue. Closing my eyes, a scene flashes in my mind – spinning, garish laser lights, his face glowing pink and then blue and then red – lips on mine, the taste of beer and cigarettes. I gasp and shudder under the bedcovers. I kissed him and, as he's in my flat half naked, I obviously slept with him too. I was dancing with him in a dingy club last night, but how did we end up in bed together? I don't even fancy him. I offer him a gormless smile but he just looks at me, nonplussed. I wonder if I'm having one of my lucid dreams again. I squeeze my eyes shut. Any moment now I'm going to wake up and he'll be gone. My eyes flicker open – he's still here. The sunlight, pouring in through the gaps between the shutters of my ground floor flat, have made horizontal lines on his face and broad hairless chest.

A humming sound fills my ears and I finally find my voice. 'What…how…' I go to sit up and the room swirls and bounces and I taste a bit sick in my mouth. I can't believe how hungover I am, that I can barely remember what happened last night. I didn't have that much to drink, certainly no more than usual – a few G&Ts and a couple of glasses of white wine. Probably prosecco. That's my usual Friday night tipple.

'Hey, hey.' Covering the tumbler of water with his palm, he lunges forward, stopping me short of falling out of bed, duvet still clutched at my throat. 'Take it easy, baby.'

Baby? Why is he calling me that? I'm not his baby. I try to speak but my mouth feels as if it's been lined with velcro. I can't believe I've been so stupid. I'm not still a bloody uni student. I'm a grown woman with a mortgage and responsibilities, the ink is barely dry on my divorce papers, yet here I am, in bed with a man I barely recognise. How did I let this happen?

Sinking my head back onto the pillow, I'm hauled back to yesterday afternoon like a rocket. I'm at my desk. It's almost 3pm. The girls in the office are chatting about their weekend plans. I'm catching wisps of their conversation. Nessa's going clubbing, Sam's taking the kids to the cinema, Hannah's staying home, she's too old to go out clubbing, glad her kids have flown the nest. Their laughter tears across the office, especially Nessa's because she's loud. I usually join in, but I can't this time, because I'm on a private call. Alison, my best friend, is jabbering down the phone – she's at Karen's, her mum, their new gardener is mowing Karen's lawn. They got chatting this time. He's fit and he's lovely and he's SINGLE. My perfect match. She'd go out with him herself if she wasn't married.

But I don't want another man in my life. I like being single again. Well, to a point. It does get a bit lonely sometimes and I do miss having sex, but it has its advantages too. I laugh at Alison's attempts to match me up with her gardener, throwing a glance at Gillian, my boss, who has just emerged from the loo, discreetly trying to adjust the visible knicker line beneath her too-tight navy skirt. When she clocks me, I say something to Alison about flights to Dubrovnik, jerking the mouse on the Travelicious logo mat, trying to look busy. I can feel Gillian's eyes on me as I frown at the cursor jumping around uselessly on my screen. I can't let her find out that I'm on a personal call. I'm already on a warning and I can't afford to lose my job, not now that I'm responsible for most of the mortgage repayment. I'm good at my job. I earn good money but I work hard. I've been top salesperson three times on the trot this year, which made our branch surpass all targets, and I've earned bloody good commission on top of my basic salary. However, gratitude isn't one of Gillian's strong points.

Thankfully, Alison gets it when I say, '*Is there anything else I can help you with today, madam?*' and chuckles, asks me if the old battleaxe is on the warpath, even though Gillian is only fifty-nine. I'm expecting Alison to tell me that Simon's working late again, ask if I fancy going round, but she doesn't. Instead she tells me that she's set me up on a blind date with her gardener – he'll be outside my office at six!

Before I can draw breath, a WhatsApp message pings through on my phone and then an image of Alison and Karen fills the screen. They're pouting at the camera, phone held at arm's length to ensure it's photobombed by the topless man in low-slung jeans, mowing the lawn – skin pink from the sun. I don't want to go to the pub with her fair-skinned gardener, he's not my type, but Alison can be very persuasive.

Then I'm sitting opposite him at The Fox and Hound. He's sipping a pint and doing an incredibly good job of looking interested while I attempt to induce him into a coma by droning on and on about how Andrew, my ex-husband, ran off with one of my old school friends. And then I'm walking a little unsteadily towards the exit of the pub.

The late August air is dense and humid. I'm tired. I've had nothing to eat since lunchtime and the wine has gone to my head. I know it's time to go home, but instead I'm climbing unsteadily into the back of a black cab; and then I'm in a hot sticky nightclub, laser lights spinning, techno music thumping – boom, boom, boom, vibrating through my body.

Someone is pulling me away from the bar, wresting the glass out of my hand, and then I'm on the dance floor – a sea of arms raised in the air, sweaty bodies jumping around crazily, stumbling onto me, or was I knocking into them? I can't remember. More shots at the bar, and then my arms slung around the gardener's neck, the glittering disco ball hanging over us, his face flashing with colourful shapes as I go in for a hot tongue-twirling kiss, and the rest is a blur.

Fear pierces through my skin and I stiffen under the bedcovers. Did my blind date spike my drink and take advantage of me? Did he have sex with me while I was semiconscious? But, no, I don't feel traumatised or anything. I'd have remembered something like that...wouldn't I? I narrow my eyes at the black TV screen mounted on the wall opposite my bed. I run a hand along my torso. Cotton. I'm not naked. No, he definitely didn't force me. I've just been very, very stupid. I glance up at him now, duvet pulled up to my chin. I want to ask him where our clothes are, how I ended up in my cotton nightie, but I daren't. My eyes dart around the room. There's a half-empty litre bottle of 7up on top of his brown corduroy jacket on the wicker chair, my black work shoes are strewn haphazardly by the patio doors, a grey damp bath towel is folded over the wooden bedstead. My face reddens – he must've taken a shower.

'Feeling better?' he asks, placing a mug and glass onto the bedside table. 'Thought you might need a couple of these.' He eases two paracetamol out of a blister back and places them next to the glass of water. 'Found them in the bathroom cabinet, swiped a couple for myself,' he says, as if I'm a drug dealer and he's just discovered my hidden stash. 'Great night, eh?' He winks, as Alison's words ring in my ears, *'Whatever you do, don't get pissed and sleep with him. I know you're feeling pretty shitty about yourself right now but drunken sex isn't the answer. He'll think you're a slag and won't want to see you again. This one's a keeper, Lucy, so please don't fuck it up.*

'Lucy?' His voice breaks me out of my reverie. 'Hope that was okay.' Silence. 'Taking the tablets, I mean. I've got a stonking head too. I'm not used to all-night benders.'

I nod quickly and my head feels as it's being repeatedly stabbed with a twelve-inch kitchen knife. Alison is going to kill me when she finds out I ended up in bed with her new gardener. It was only meant to be a quick friendly drink at the pub around the corner from my office, and that was only to keep her happy. I glance at his thick quads. Why is he still here? I want him to go, or at least put some clothes on. His nakedness is distracting.

'Last night was a bit crazy,' he admits, crossing the room. 'Can't believe how sick you were.' *Sick*? That's twenty-five-year-old Nessa speak. He must be younger than I thought. 'You're every bit as lovely as Alison said you were.' I'm about to retort with *'And you're every bit as easy to please.'* But as he opens the shutters and tries the lock, an alarm blasts in my head. Where did he find the key? I keep it in the middle drawer of my dresser. Has he been going through my things?

'Don't mean to sound rude,' he says, over his shoulder, fiddling with the lock. 'But this room is gasping for some fresh air.' I gaze around my chaotic bedroom, embarrassed, it looks like student digs. Housework isn't my forte, but I was intending on tidying up when I got in from work yesterday. However, fate and Alison had other ideas. 'Gosh, this lock,' he complains, through gritted teeth, shoulders shuddering. 'Is so…damned…' He yanks the handle up and down violently. I want to tell him to stop, that there's a knack to it, that he's going to break it, but I haven't got the energy. 'Open, you bugger!' More frantic yanking and muttering and then the doors fling open. Within seconds the room is flooded with a warm gentle breeze, lifting the stale fug of booze and manky socks.

'Make sure you drink plenty of fluids,' he advises, hands on hips like a warrior. I throw a reflex glance at his boxers. I'm sure he's got a semi going on. Well, if he thinks I'm up for round two, he can fuck right off. 'You need to replace all your electrolytes,' he adds. 'Sports drinks are good for replacing salts and potassium. Coconut water is great too.'

Hydration? Electrolytes? Is this man a gardener or a nutritionist?

He nods at the bedside table. 'I've poured you a mug of orange juice.' Oh, dear God, I'm imprisoned in my flat with a fitness guru from hell. 'It'll help top up your vitamin C levels.' I look up at him with a fainthearted smile. If I don't get some caffeine inside me soon I may commit a crime. I inhale deeply. Okay, Alison was right, he is lovely, but he's got to go.

I open my mouth to speak, when I spy a greasy box under the chair behind him, next to it a pair of brown loafers, each with a balled-up sock in it. The lid of the box is flung open and has two slices of limp pizza in it, the sight of it makes me heave. Turning swiftly, he follows my gaze.

'Uber Eats. Pepperoni with extra cheese. You said you were hungry.' I hate pepperoni. It always gives me indigestion. No wonder I feel sick. 'Anything else I can do for you?' he asks brightly. Yes, get the hell out of my flat and make the last twenty-four hours disappear. 'I can make you some toast if you like. There's half a loaf of white in the fridge, keeping the iffy milk and the Morrisons chicken tikka with rice company.' I was meant to have that ready meal last night, after tidying up, of course. 'Fancy some?' I look at him blankly. 'Toast, I mean,' he says. 'It's really no trouble at all. Might pop a couple in the toaster for myself. I'm famished after last night.'

I do a little, shaky movement with my head, meaning no, and my temples feel as if someone is piercing them with sharp needles. I really want to cry now. Why is this man, this stranger who has seen me naked on a first date, wandering around my flat like an obedient Labrador while I'm imprisoned in my own bed?

'Um…look,' I begin nervously. 'I don't usually…you know…with…Anyway, I think you should…' I nod towards the door. He half turns and then his face falls. And now I feel like a bit of a cow for wanting to chuck him out in his underwear without any breakfast. It's not his fault he's here. Obviously, I invited him in. Any other man would've legged it by now, yet here he still is, nursing me. 'Um… I'm sorry about last night,' I mutter, unable to meet his eye. 'Please help yourself to some toast and coffee while I–'

'Don't be sorry,' he interjects. 'I'm not.' Tears of shame sting the back of my throat. Why can't I remember anything about last night? 'Well, apart from when you were sick all over me in the back of the cab on the way home,' he groans. My face tingles. It wasn't Nessa speak when he said I was sick last night. I actually puked all over him. Great. I haven't been sick from alcohol in years. Karen will see the funny side, when I relay all later today, she's seventy-three going on twenty-five, but Alison will be mortified. I hope this doesn't mean he'll stop being their gardener. It took her ages to find one and he came highly recommended by one of the year 2 mums.

'You don't remember the incident in the taxi either, eh?' he asks, kindly. 'I thought you were going to kiss me again and then boom – all over my shirt and trousers. Talk about knocking back a bloke's confidence.' I have no recollection of this. But that's the least of my worries. I need to get this man dressed and out of my flat. I'm meeting Alison and Karen for our monthly pub lunch at twelve and I need to look reasonably presentable and coherent. 'Cabbie wasn't too happy,' he goes on, 'had to slip him thirty quid to keep him quiet.'

'I'm sorry for being sick on you,' I croak, then cough as if I've just taken a long lug on a cigarette, and then I remember that I did! I took a drag on one of his Marlborough Lights outside the club last night while we waited for our cab, even though I don't smoke, and almost choked to death. 'I'll…I'll pay for the dry cleaning,' I offer tiredly, 'and give you the thirty quid you paid the driver,' And then it occurs to me that he has no clean clothes to wear. I can't let him roam the streets half-naked. What will my neighbours think? My mind races. I'm sure there's an old pair of Andrew's trackie bottoms and a top lurking around somewhere. I stole a few of his items from the laundry basket before he left me, because they smelt of him. I used to cry myself to sleep, clutching his T-shirt, like a security blanket.

'Look, I want to get one thing straight. I don't usually…I mean…I…'

Smiling, he inclines his head and his light brown eyes crinkle at the sides. He's not bad looking, actually, in an ordinary, geeky, kind of way. The type you'd take home to your mother – not my type at all. Although I'm not quite sure what my type is, or if I've even got one. It's been so long. I've had a few disastrous dates since I split up with Andrew but they never progressed to a second date, and I was single for three years before him, celibate single. I don't sleep with men I don't know. And now I've had sex with a stranger. I look at the leftover pizza again, pepperoni curling upwards, cheese warped into the dried-out base like plastic, and feel the bile rising in my throat.

'Are you okay, Lucy, you seem slightly…restless.' Restless is a bit of an understatement. I've just made one of the biggest mistakes of my life. I'm mortified.

'Hangxiety, eh?' I look at him puzzled. 'You know, a cross between a hangover and anxiety. Hangxiety,' he repeats. 'It's a term people use when they feel… Oh, never mind. I'm quite surprised, actually.' Yawning, he raises his arms above his head and his skin stretches over his ribcage, and then a thought enters my mind. I wonder if there's a slim chance that we didn't have sex. I mean, if we were both pissed, we couldn't have, right? A flicker of hope flutters in my stomach, but as I slowly turn my head towards the pillow next to me, my heart sinks. It has an imprint of his head in it and a light brown curl. How could I have been such an idiot. 'A twenty-eight-year-old woman should be able to handle a Friday night sesh.' Shit. I lied about my age again. Drink always makes me do this. But knocking ten years off, what was I thinking?

'I'm in my late thirties,' I mutter into the duvet, 'you must've misheard.'

He looks at me, stunned, then says, 'Wow.' Ageist. Perhaps now he knows I'm much older he'll bugger off. 'You look great.' Or maybe not. Perhaps he likes older women.

I'm about to ask him his age when a phone bleeps, not mine, and the words dissolve on my tongue.

Reaching for the pizza box, he snatches his handset from beneath it. I scratch my hand under the duvet, peering at him curiously. What a strange place to leave your phone. He's obviously got something to hide. It's probably a message from his girlfriend, or wife even. I mean, how well does Alison know him? He's only been their gardener for a few weeks.

'You didn't come onto me,' he says, eyes not leaving his phone, 'if that's what's making you restless.' If that's meant to make me feel better, it hasn't. We still had sex. Probably unprotected and I'm not even on the pill. 'Unless you count snogging me in that club you insisted on going to after the pub,' he laughs, tapping out a message with his thumbs. Yes, that. The Quantum in Shoreditch. Nessa's haunt. She's always ranting and raving about how sick it is. Shit, she was there. We had shots at the bar. It's all coming back to me, albeit slowly.

I'd polished off my third glass of wine at The Fox and Hound when my blind date suggested sharing a cab back to north London, but there was no way I was going home. I was at that pinnacle stage of drunkenness where you feel invincible. My face reddens. I called him a boring old fart, asked him if his brown corduroy jacket belonged to his dad. I even had a feel of one of the leather patches on his elbow. I got a bit teary after that. Probably about my divorce. It's the usual drill, of late, after I've had one too many. I loved being married. Pity it only lasted twenty months. I was looking forward to having a family, buying a three-bed semi, getting a dog. Instead I was served with divorce papers and a save-the-date card to my ex-husband's wedding. Both of which flew through my letterbox eight days ago.

I sigh loudly, and my one-night-stand looks up at me briefly from his phone. Well, that was it then, what made me end up with 'hangxiety'. Let's face it, it isn't every day your ex-husband and childhood friend invite you to their prenuptials, is it? The heartless bastards. I had every right to get pissed and weepy with Alison's fair-skinned average-looking gardener.

It was that, wasn't it? I drag my teeth along my bottom lip thoughtfully, collecting remnants of dry skin and last night's lipstick on my teeth. My unwanted guest continues to text – tap, tap, tap. Tap. Tap, tap. Whoosh. I wish he'd bloody turn off the sound. I can barely hear myself think. I close my eyes, head throbbing, and then a trickle of dread crawls along my spine. It wasn't just the save-the-date card and my divorce that upset me last night. Something else happened – something dark and creepy. I'm pretty sure it was in the toilet cubicle of The Fox and Hound. Why can't I remember? Am I blocking it out? Alison once told me that some of her clients store traumatic events in their unconscious minds because they're just too painful to recall. Is that what's happening to me now?

I hear a low thud on my bed and my eyes snap open, his phone is on the pillow next to me. 'And then, of course,' he goes on. God, does he have to shout. 'There was that bedroom incident shortly after we got in,' he says, voice tinged with unease. Bedroom incident? For a horrible moment I imagine him filming us having sex. I shake the thought away. Of course, he didn't. I'm being ridiculous. He doesn't look the kinky type.

'You do remember that, right?' he asks. 'You were pretty full-on.' Okay. Maybe he is kinky, maybe he did film us having sex, and now wants to make sure I consented to it, in case I accuse him of anything. People make a good living from posting photographs and video clips on Instagram, don't they? But no, I'd never have agreed to anything like that. It's just not me. I'm safe, predictable, Lucy, with a dry sense of humour. The kind of person who can't sparkle without a drink inside them. Dread wraps itself around my neck and almost chokes me. I did have a drink inside me – several, in fact. What have I done?

With a sigh, he sits heavily on the edge of my bed. The mattress creaks. Holding his chin, he regards me carefully, as if I'm some sort of lost cause. I wish he'd just leave me alone. I stare at his sunburnt shoulders, and instead of being concerned about our kinky sex session, whether or not we used a condom, if I should take the morning-after pill, or get checked for STDs, all I can think about is why he didn't slap on factor 30 sunscreen before mowing Karen's lawn yesterday afternoon when he's so fair skinned. 'Er… you know.' He bites his top lip. 'That dream you had of being smothered. You were hysterical. I almost called 111.'

Closing my eyes, the scene flashes in my mind – a dark figure mounting me on the bed, his hand over my mouth and nose, that nauseating, familiar scent. I gasp and my eyes shoot open. I don't want to think about it. I can't.

'It's a recurring lucid dream,' I manage, blowing out a long anxious breath. He nods, gives my knee a good old shake, happy that I've remembered something.

'I only went into the kitchen to make you a cup of black coffee so that you can sober up. You must've fallen asleep because you ended up screaming your head off. By the time I shook you awake, you threw up again.' He gesticulates at the floor and I look down at the wet patch on the carpet, horrified. He must've cleaned it up. 'You said something about a smell?' Sandalwood. It reminds me of him. It will always remind me of him, no matter how many years slip by. 'You were terrified, Lucy, insisted you saw a figure by the patio doors, a shadow, or something. You even made me go outside to check.' I drop my gaze to his hand still resting on my leg and he moves it. 'It was a fox, by the way.' I nod, relieved. Yes, of course it was. My self-imposed adopted pet, who snoozes under a tree when it's raining, sunbathes on the lawn when the sun's out, and poos and wees all over my garden in-between. 'I chased it away,' he says, scratching a spot on his arm. Looks like a mozzie-bite. Andrew used to get bitten to death, they somehow preferred his skin to mine. 'Then locked the doors.'

'Yes, um, about that. Where did you find the key?' I ask, unable to control the accusation in my tone.

Incredulity flashes across his face. I've finally offended him, but I don't think I care. 'You unlocked it as soon as we came in, of course, said it was too hot, needed some air. Mind you, it was stuffy in here. You should think about getting a humidifier.' I don't actually recall doing this, but then I can't remember much about last night. 'Anyway, after I locked up you were out like a baby. It was boiling in here, so I stuck the fan on.' The whirring sound becomes audible again. 'You begged me to stay the night, said you were frightened in case Hannibal Lector turned up again.' He makes that slurping sound, but I don't react. It isn't funny.

'Anyhow, clothes are outside drying,' he explains, picking up on my vibe. 'So no need to foot you with a dry-cleaning bill. You fell asleep right after and I slept next to you on top of the bedding.' My eyes widen. Is he saying we didn't have kinky sex? 'Just for the record, you were a bit frisky.' Frisky? Me? Never. 'But I'd never take advantage of a woman who'd had too much booze. Besides, I don't do sex on a first date.'

He gets to his feet and I lift the duvet and peer into the darkness. I'm fully dressed in yesterday's clothes –my navy light cotton floral knee-length dress with side pockets. My entire body sags with relief. Alison did say he was a gentleman.

'Um…no…I didn't think that,' I lie, hauling myself up on one elbow and reaching shakily for the tumbler of water. 'It's just that I can't really remember much of…' I swallow the pills and they hit my stomach like golf balls. 'Um…what happened last night.' I accidently burp and a sour bitter taste climbs into my mouth. I give him a sharp look. If he heard me belch then he's pretending he didn't, which is pretty decent of him. I don't mean to sound ungrateful, but why is he still here, washing his clothes in my Bosch and helping himself to painkillers from my bathroom cabinet, hasn't he got a home to go to? I knock back the rest of the water, trying to dilute the golf ball sensation.

'Listen…um…' I pause. Christ. What's his name? Oh, yes. 'Freddie, I–'

'Teddy,' he corrects, and his lips twitch.

Damn it. I can't even get his name right. 'I'm sorry, Teddy. Still drunk,' I offer, rolling my eyes, and he gives me a *whatever* shrug. I wriggle up to a sitting position. 'Thanks for looking after me. I owe you a big drink,' I joke, kicking off the duvet. 'But I think I can manage now.' Pulling my blonde shoulder-length hair into a ponytail, I twist the curls in my hands and gaze at his shirt and beige chinos billowing in the gentle breeze on the clothesline outside. 'Your clothes should be dry,' I offer. 'Hope you don't mind but I've got a busy day ahead – need to freshen up and…' My phone throbs against my thigh in the pocket of my dress. No wonder I couldn't see it. I pull it out awkwardly – Alison calling. I grimace. I can't talk to her now, she'll want the post-mortem.

'It's okay,' Teddy says in a clipped tone, face darkening. 'I get the message. I should get going. I've a Salix to prune in.' He looks at his watch. 'Shit! I'm fifteen minutes late. Fuck, SHIT, bollocks.' And before I can say anything, he legs it across the lawn and pulls his shirt and chinos off the washing line. And as he hurriedly dresses at the foot of my bed, mumbling about trees and Mrs Burton killing him, my phone chimes with a message and last night's dark and creepy incident flies into my mind like a missile – the *text*! I bypass Alison's new message and quickly scroll through my texts with tremulous fingers, desperately searching for the one from the unknown number that beeped through last night while I was having a wee in the pub loos. Perhaps it was a mistake, or another dream. Mum and Kate, my sister, always laugh at the ridiculousness of my dreams, and I am prone to the odd hallucination. But no such luck, not this time.

I stare at the anonymous text in complete horror:

>I know what you did with your best friend's husband.

Chapter 2

'New bloke?' Andrew asks, moments later on my doorstep, as Teddy sprints across the road, stopping traffic in his haste, car horns blaring.

'To what do I owe the pleasure?' I say to my ex-husband, still reeling from the shock of the anonymous text. Who could have sent it? Who saw us? Is someone watching me? I quickly scan the tree-lined street, arms folded, and do a little shiver. Of course no one is watching me. The text is a hoax, a wrong number. It was meant for someone else, that's all. I return my attention to Andrew. 'Come to gloat about your wedding plans, then?' I sound bitter but I'm not. Okay, I am. Very. I head back inside.

I hear the click of the door latch as I leg it into the kitchen, pulling the bedroom door shut en route just before Andrew creeps up behind me. I don't want him to see how untidy my bedroom is. My inadequate housekeeping was one of his pet hates. He even mentioned it in his petition when he filed for divorce – unreasonable behaviour, apparently. What is he even doing here? The last thing I expected was for Andrew to saunter down the path as Teddy was rushing out, buttoning his shirt along the way. Of course, I can imagine what it looked like. I grin wickedly as I fill the kettle with filtered water from the jug, feeling a bit smug. I'm glad that Andrew saw Teddy leaving, glad he thinks we spent the night together.

'Good morning to you too,' Andrew retorts. 'You never were much of a morning person, were you?' Sliding his hands into the pockets of his shorts, he gazes around the kitchen wistfully. The way you do when you revisit an old school, or college, or the house you grew up in. 'Place seems much smaller,' he remarks, not unkindly. It's a gorgeous two-bedroom garden flat, but the entire place could fit into Jasmine's kitchen. Jasmine's family home is palatial.

'Yes, well, it's big enough for me,' I say, with a long sigh. 'So, are you going to tell me why you're here?'

I can feel his eyes on me as I move around the kitchen, squashing the empty orange juice carton ready for recycling, folding tea towels, putting things away. 'I was just passing. Thought I'd pop in and say hello.' We both know that's not true, but I don't contradict him. He helps himself to an apple from the fruit bowl on the table. The table we picked out together from Camden Market, ate breakfast and lunch at for almost two years.

'Have you lost weight?' he asks, before sinking his teeth into the apple. 'You look seriously unhealthy.'

I start loading the dishwasher. 'Do I?' I mumble, head in the machine. Is that why you ran off with my size-eight fake-boobed botoxed friend, I want to say. My ex-husband has been here for less than five minutes and he's already annoying the shit out of me.

'I'm not being funny, but I can see your bones through that dress. You should see your GP, get your bloods checked.'

'I've lost a few pounds,' I say dismissively, straightening up. 'Hardly anorexic.'

I've never been particularly overweight, but I did let myself go a bit after we got married. I went up a dress size. Or two. I suppose I slipped into complacency – too many cosy nights in front of the TV with a takeaway. It's what married couples do, or so I thought. I haven't weighed myself recently but, thanks to joining a gym, I can now fit into my size ten jeans.

'More than a few pounds,' he scoffs, through a mouthful of apple. 'You must be in love,' he says, and I'm sure I pick up a note of mockery in his tone.

'So, come on, what is it that's important enough for a home visit,' I ask dryly, ignoring his sarcastic remark. We usually discuss flat maintenance issues by email or text, so it's got to be something else, something more pressing. I turn on the tap and water pelts into the sink like bullets. 'Whatever's on your mind, can you please get on with it? I'm already running late.' I pump hand gel into my palm.

'Oh, come on, Lucy, don't be like that.' Behind me I hear the metal lid of the bin hitting the tiles – he's binning the core. 'I do still care about you, you know.' Soaping my hands, I roll my eyes, wishing he'd just leave, and then he says. 'Looks nice. Your new bloke.'

Turning to face Andrew, I grab the nearest tea towel and frown at him. Okay he's definitely after something. 'Polite,' he adds, pointing a thumb at the door. Then as he slips his hands back into the pockets of his grey marl boxing shorts, my eyes are drawn to his hairy legs. There's an aberration on his knee, probably a football injury, and he's wearing flip-flops. He never wears flip-flops. He hates flip-flops. I remember the time I bought him a pair from the hotel souvenir shop on our honeymoon in Crete. He refused point blank to wear them, said the camel toes gave him blisters and made me take them back. Yet here he is, standing in my kitchen, in flip-flops. Yellow ones.

'Ed, is it,' he asks, 'isn't that what he said?'

'Teddy,' I correct, eyes darting from Andrew's face to his feet. He's actually wearing flip-flops. 'And yes, he is very nice. Great, in fact.'

Andrew nods slowly, lips curved downwards. 'It was nice of him to stop and say hello, especially as he seemed in such a hurry. What is he?' Andrew peers into the garden. 'An accountant, doctor?' It occurs to me in that moment that I don't actually know much about Teddy Fallon, apart from what he does for a living, that is, but that's chiefly because I wouldn't stop talking about myself last night. 'Lawyer? Teacher? Lawn needs mowing, by the way.'

I take a sip of water as I gaze into the overgrown garden. Surprisingly, the paracetamol is kicking in. My headache's almost gone. 'He's a gardener, actually,' I say, although I'm sure my ex knows this. And I'm sure Alison told her husband that I had a date with their gardener last night. Simon must've mentioned it to Andrew. They're joined at the hip, those two. Always texting or whatsapping each other like a couple of teenagers. But my date with Teddy can't be the reason why he's here…can it?

'Seriously?' Andrew throws his head back and laughs. 'Sounds too posh to be a gardener. Why didn't you get him to sort your bush out? Oh, wait, he did.'

'Haha…very funny, Andrew.' I give him a tight smile. The kind that makes your face hurt. 'You're such a comedian. Anyone would think you were jealous.'

'As if,' he says, not looking at me, but I don't miss the pink tinge that sweeps over his face. Perhaps he thought I'd stay single forever, that no other man would ever want me. Damaged goods, he called me, if I remember correctly, before he walked out on our marriage.

Winding a loose curl behind my ear, I feel something hard and clumpy. I think it's a bit of dried sick. 'Look,' I say irritably, feeling an urgent need to jump into the shower. 'I don't mean to be rude but I'm in a bit of a rush. If I'd known you were coming I'd–'

'Sorry. I'll be off in a minute,' he butts in, sniffing. I hope he hasn't come here with a cold. My immune is in tatters. I can't afford to be off sick. 'Meeting Simon at the club for a game of squash.' I stiffen at the mention of his name. I wonder if Simon told him what happened. Shit, is *that* why he's here? But then why would Simon do that? He's the one who made me promise not to breathe a word about it, didn't want anyone finding out, so I doubt he'd go blabbing to Andrew. But clearly someone did find out – someone saw us. The anonymous text flies into my mind like a blinding flashlight – *I know what you did with your best friend's husband.* I push the image away.

'I thought you played squash on a Sunday,' I say absently.

I lean against the worktop and fold my arms, and Andrew follows suit. 'We usually do, but he said he'll be in Bath tomorrow.' Oh yes, that's right. Alison said they're going to check out Bath University for Oscar, stay over for a few days, take in the ambience.

'Speaking of which,' I say suddenly, straightening up. 'I really must get a move on. I'm meeting Alison and Karen for lunch in under an hour.'

He snorts at the mention of Alison's name, as if she were Satan. They've always had a bit of love:hate relationship. They've both got big personalities and have very different opinions and views on current affairs. But it was when she took my side over his when he left me that pumped him full of hatred. The ultimate betrayal in his eyes. Alison told me that they barely converse these days and when they do it's usually small talk.

'Well,' I say, glancing at my watch, 'Thanks for popping by then.'

'I'm glad you're seeing someone new.' Bit random. I raise my eyebrows, not bothering to correct him. 'God knows you deserve some happiness after…' He trails off, exhaling a long sigh of guilt.

Andrew's betrayal really hit me hard. I can still feel the pain twisting in my gut whenever I think about it, almost as if it'd only just happened.

I was meant to be going on an educational to Paris with Gillian, my boss, for the weekend, but, as fate would have it, our flight was cancelled at the last minute. It was gone midnight when the taxi dropped me off home. I unlocked the door as quietly as I could, took off my shoes, and tiptoed along the corridor so that I wouldn't wake him. I heard the groans coming from the bedroom the moment my hand was on the doorknob and my heart broke into a million pieces. I told myself that he was working out, even though it was gone midnight, that he was watching a sex scene in a film, that he'd caught the flu. But I knew he had someone in there with him. I hesitated for a moment, considered tiptoeing back along the corridor and quietly letting myself out, burying my head in the sand. I didn't, of course. I twisted the doorknob quietly and almost keeled over when I saw Jasmine riding him like a horse. Raged soared through my body, and for a moment I thought about grabbing the baseball bat, which he kept under the bed in case of intruders, and clubbing them both to death. I don't know how long I was standing there before Andrew saw me, sobbing into my hand, but when he did, his face blanched.

'Shit,' he said, throwing Jasmine off him, semi-erect. 'Lucy,' he yelled, one leg in his boxer shorts. 'Lucy, wait.'

I just about made it into the bathroom, locking the door behind me with tremulous hands before being violently sick in the loo. How could he do this to me? To us? And how could SHE? After all I'd done for her – welcoming her into my home, our lives. Andrew banged his fists uselessly on the door, calling out my name, as I retched over the bowl, and then, with my head lolling over the toilet, saliva dripping from my lips, I listened to them cluttering around, hurriedly getting dressed, their hushed voices outside the bathroom door, footsteps along the hallway, and finally the click of the front door latch.

It was one of the worst times of my life. But, despite it all, I thought we'd get through it. A lot of couples do. I loved him. We loved each other. I even convinced myself that it was my fault, that I drove him to it – I was working too hard, didn't invest enough time in our relationship, didn't give him enough attention, enough support, enough sex.

The next few days were a blur. Awkward chitchat, mostly. He kept saying how sorry he was, promised it was a one-off, told me it was me he wanted, me he loved. I believed him, for no other reason than wanting to. So you can imagine my surprise when I came in from work, two weeks later, and found him sitting in the dark staring at the wall. The curtains were open, the room dimly lit by streetlights. I could see the shadow and outlines of the TV, the coffee table, the scatter cushions we couldn't afford but bought anyway from John Lewis, the nutmeg three-seater leather sofa, his dark figure on the armchair. He was so still that for a moment I thought he'd just fallen asleep.

'Andrew?' I called out, shrugging off my winter coat, and he looked up at me. 'Why are you sitting in the dark?' I began to draw the curtains. 'Work was crazy busy. Gillian was a right moody cow today. Obviously, had the hump about something. Nessa reckons it's because she's not getting laid. Anyway, I got us a lasagne in for tonight and some garlic bread. M&S. Don't say a word. I know it's expensive but I did really well this month. We deserve a treat, don't we? Thought we could have it with that leftover salad in the fridge.' I flicked the light switch on and that's when I saw it. 'Going somewhere?' I frowned at his overnight bag between his feet. 'Oh, God, has something happened to your dad?' I asked, panic rising in my voice. His dad has emphysema, always in and out of hospital.

The silence that hung between us was unbearable. 'This isn't working out, Lucy,' he said at the black TV screen, face ashen, eyes dark. 'I'm not happy anymore. If I'm honest, it hasn't been right for quite some time, you must've noticed it too.' No. I hadn't noticed. Bar his one-night-stand, I thought we were happy. Yes, we had our ups and downs, but didn't every couple?

I looked at him nonplussed. 'What? Don't be silly, I…'

'You'll never forgive me for shagging Jasmine.' His fist tightened against the armrest. 'Jesus, you can't even look me in the eye most of the time.' He leapt to his feet and I took a step back.

'I'm sorry, I can't help it,' I said truthfully. 'But I'm sure that in time, I'll…'

Standing in front of me, his eyes searched mine anxiously. 'We don't quite fit, love, do we?' I shook my head, said we did. 'No, we don't. You're too negative, too cautious, you've no ambition.' I shook my head some more, eyes filling. 'You drink too much and you're always too tired to do anything. Apart from visiting your mum in Brighton, we hardly do anything together these days, and this flat is always in such a mess.' I followed his gaze – taking in the particles of dust on the TV screen, shoes piled in the corner of the room, newspapers and leaflets strewn haphazardly on the dining table next to an empty bottle of the previous night's wine. My eyes flit to the grey rug beneath the coffee table. The rug needed hoovering. Badly. I was meant to do it that morning but didn't get a chance. I was running late. Gillian wanted us in half an hour earlier for a staff meeting.

'I think it's what made me look elsewhere, to be honest.' He swallowed. 'I don't want this anymore. I'm sorry.'

I sobbed and I begged and I screamed, flung myself in front of the door so he couldn't leave, promised that I'd change. I'd stop drinking, keep on top of the housekeeping. I suggested a holiday, counselling. 'Alison can't be our therapist, obviously,' I cried, despairingly, 'but she could recommend someone. A colleague, or…' I went to touch his arm but he grabbed my wrist mid-air, immobilising me, eyes shut as if gathering strength. 'Don't make this any harder that it is, Lucy. My mind's made up.'

He let go of my hand and I stood out of his way, backing myself up against the doorframe. 'Are you moving in with her?' I asked icily, fresh hot tears filling my eyes. 'Jasmine?'

'Don't be stupid,' he answered, hand on the front door latch. 'I'm staying with Tony for a few days. You know, Sparky.' Tony the electrician. I'd met him once or twice. Nice man, single, with a habit of inhaling his phlegm and swallowing it. 'Until I sort myself out.' I nodded silently, believed him, consoled myself with silent platitudes – he'll be back in a few days – he just wants a bit of space – he'll miss me – miss us. But when the door closed I felt the click deep inside me, as if a switch had turned off my heart, leaving it in pitch darkness.

He didn't stay with Sparky, by the way, I found out from Ali that he moved in with Jasmine that very same night. It took close to a year to wipe Andrew out of my mind – for him to not be the first thing I thought of every morning.

'I'm really sorry, Lucy,' Andrew says now. 'About how things turned out between us. I never meant to hurt you.' I frown at him. There's got to be more to this visit than a late apology.

Narrowing my eyes, I look at my exhausted looking ex-husband, standing there looking pathetic in his designer sportswear and flip-flops. At five-foot-eight, he's not very tall, and he seems to have shrunk since we last met. Don't get me wrong, he's good looking, but he's no Tom Hardy. He was limping in a pair of football shorts and a number 9 shirt when I first met him at The Spaniards Inn in Hampstead five years ago. Kate and I were having a sisterly catch up in the beer garden, she'd come over to see me from Spain. The place was heaving, so when Andrew interrupted our conversation, pint of Guinness in hand, and asked if he could sit at our table while he waited for his friend, we agreed.

Andrew wasn't pervy, or anything. He sat there quietly, tapping away on his phone while Kate and I caught up with all the latest gossip. When I told Kate that I'd just split up with Paul, whom I met online, Andrew looked up at me and gave me a shy smile. It wasn't long before Kate got him involved in our conversation. Unlike me, she's a people person – can get chatting to anyone. Andrew was nice, friendly. He even got Simon to buy us all a drink when he eventually arrived. I thought Andrew had the most beautiful brown eyes I'd ever seen. But, if I'm honest, it was his uncanny resemblance to Freddie Mercury that did it for me, complete with buck teeth, short, thick dark hair and moustache. In fact, if he was wearing a white vest and a pair of Wrangler jeans, I'd have done the unthinkable and copped off with him that very afternoon. I'm a big Queen fan. His Scottish accent was another plus. I've always had a thing for Scottish men. But now? Now I can't work him out. Is he on a mission, or did the starkness of our divorce, the finality, stir something inside him? Make him want to see me – for old times' sake?

'The decree absolute came through,' I probe, and he nods, wordless. 'Ironically, on the same day you sent me the save-the-date card.'

He darts a look at me then, determined, and I notice that his eyes are a bit red. If I didn't know better I'd think he was suppressing tears. 'I swear, Lucy, I didn't do that on purpose.'

I shrug. 'I know. How could you have known? Anyway, it's over now. What's done is done. Everything happens for a reason and all that shit. You're marrying someone else. I'm seeing someone new,' I lie. 'I hope you'll be happy second time around.' I head for the lounge and he follows me, his flip flops flip-flapping against the soles of his feet.

'That's the thing, Luce, there's no real easy way of saying this.'

I shake my head and laugh as I fluff up the cushions on the sofa. I was right all along, he is here for a reason. And to think that I almost thought he was crying over the end of our marriage. I'm so gullible sometimes. I know why he's here now. It's obvious. It's because of the invitation. He doesn't want me at their wedding. Clearly, Jasmine made him invite me because that's what she's like, sick and twisted. And now he wants confirmation that I won't be going, probably terrified that I'll have a bit too much Dutch courage and make a scene.

'I won't be coming to–'

'We've got to–'

We've spoken at the same time. I look at my watch – I've got forty-five minutes to shower, slap on some makeup and get to East Finchley. I chew the inside of my bottom lip, tempted to ask Andrew for a lift.

'Go on,' I say, deciding against it. I'll jump in a taxi. You can always find a black cab on the highroad, day or night. 'You first.'

'Will you be coming to our wedding?' What did I say? I know him inside out. I sit down heavily on the leather sofa. He sits on the armrest, legs wide apart.

'Would you rather I didn't?'

He shrugs, tells me it's up to me.

'Why did you hand deliver the invite, Andrew?' I so wish he hadn't because then I'd have denied receiving it.

He rubs his eyes tiredly. 'Jas dropped it off, wanted to make sure you got it.' I bet she did. Talk about rubbing salt into the wounds. 'We've invited Simon and Alison too.' I give him a puzzled look. Simon's one of his oldest mates. He was best man at our wedding. Of course he's going to invite them, and of course I expect them to go. 'I didn't want to invite you, Lucy. It was Jas's idea.' He hisses loudly through his nose. 'She wants to bury the hatchet. Wants us to all be friends again.'

Nice try but we both know that's never going to happen. I'll never forgive her for stealing my husband. With her stunning looks, high-profile job, and all that money, she could've had any man she wanted, but she chose mine. Our friendship is over. Fact. Nothing will make me change my mind.

'Maybe now you've met someone else too, we can.' I stare out of the window silently. 'She misses you, Luce,' he offers softly, in an attempt to thaw me. But I just snort and roll my eyes. 'I don't expect you to come, of course,' Andrew reasons. 'It'll be humiliating for you.'

I raise my eyebrows. Typical Andrew – everything is about him. 'Don't flatter yourself.'

Getting to my feet, I look at the Newgate wall clock against the eggshell wall. 'Relax, Andrew, I won't be going. The card is in the bin. Now, if you don't mind I've got to shower and change and...'

I go to move but he grabs my arm to still me. 'Wait.' He looks up at me with those big brown eyes. There's a sheen of sweat on his forehead, his eyes are a bit dull, yellowy, nostrils red and veiny. A spit of acid hits my stomach. Is he ill? He's hurt me and he's an annoying little piece of shit, but I do still care about him. I take in the length of his body as he gets to his feet. He's a bit thicker around the waist, cheeks flushed – not ill then. Probably a late night. 'There's something else,' he says. I look at him, confused. And then out of nowhere a feeling of dread tears through my body and I have to hold onto the back of the sofa to steady myself. Simon *did* tell him, of course he has. Andrew's here to warn me, make sure I don't go blabbing to Alison, because, let's face it, I've got nothing to lose whereas Simon…

My heart picks up a little speed. 'Come on then, spit it out.'

'Jas is pregnant.' The slither of relief I feel is quickly followed by contempt. I don't fucking believe it. They've only been together five minutes. We were trying for a baby when I discovered he was screwing my childhood friend. It was my dream, my plan, my life. Mum had even started knitting a cardie and booties.

Tears sting the back of my throat and I know I've gone pink. 'Congratulations,' I mutter, unable to control the tremor in my bottom lip.

'Thanks.' He hesitates, pushes a hand through his brown cropped hair nervously and I notice that it's flecked with grey. He's only two years older than me, and yet, right now, he resembles a man in his fifties. 'That's not why I'm here.' A car swishes by outside, his mobile pings in his pocket. He ignores it. 'Jas and I will have to move out of the family home once the baby comes, buy a place of our own.' I frown. I'm sure they'll be very happy in their lush new home, but I don't see what this has got to do with me. 'I won't be able to keep up with the mortgage payment and…' he pauses. 'I'll need the money from the flat. My share, like.' My blood runs cold. No. Not my flat. Anything but my home. 'And before you say anything, I know I'm going back on our deal, but I've no other choice.'

When Andrew and I separated, we decided that I'd stay on in the flat for three years provided that he only paid 30% of the mortgage. We agreed that it was an investment. For both of us. Property prices in London were booming. Once the three years were up, we'd either sell, or I'd buy him out. That was the deal. He can't fucking backtrack now.

'If there was any other way, Lucy, believe me I'd do it,' he insists. We look at each other for a few moments. 'Anyway, it'll do you good to start somewhere new, somewhere fresh. You know it makes sense. You're a reasonable person. It's what I always loved about you.' He pauses but I just look at him, lips a thin line. 'We can't live with Jasmine's family forever. There's not enough room.' Six bedrooms and there's not enough room? Not to mention that her parents are away most of the time. 'So what do you say, hun?'

Hun? I don't think he's ever called me that. It's Jasmine speak. 'No,' I say sternly.

'What do you mean no?'

'As in not yes!'

'Well, I'm sorry, but it's happening,' he scoffs, hands on hips. I want to slap him so hard that it'll leave an imprint of my hand on his face for hours.

'I've got another two years left here,' I remind him. 'I'll buy you out then.' Realistically, I know that's unlikely. Unless I win the lottery, where am I going to get my hands on thousands of pounds in two years? But that's not the point. I'm not ready to move. And I don't believe he needs the money. I don't think he's doing it for the money. There's an ulterior motive. 'You can't go back on your word,' I warn.

Shouldering past him, I charge back into the kitchen, he follows swiftly behind me, all the while keeping up a monologue of how he has no choice in the matter, circumstances have changed, the mortgage repayment is killing him, half of it is his, why am I being such a selfish, vindictive bitch. My face is on fire. I open the window above the sink, then pace up and down my brand-new state-of-the art kitchen. We only had it fitted two years ago. I'm still paying for it now.

The bathroom, with the corner shower cubicle and freestanding bathtub, is practically new; the whole place, bar the kitchen, is parqueted. Proper parquet, not laminate. I can't give up my flat.

I can't breathe. I open and close the fridge door, run a tea towel across the worktop, flick on the kettle. I don't know what I'm doing. I can't lose my home. I won't let him take it from me.

'Look, calm down.' He's standing in front of me. The kettle starts to hum. 'I'm sorry to spring this on you, but what am I supposed to do? I'll have a wife and baby to support. Business isn't doing that well. I've lost five contracts this–'

'Stop it!' I cut in, covering my ears. 'Stop lying to me, Andrew. Jasmine's a partner in a law firm, for crying out loud, her parents are fucking loaded.' The Anands have a string of high-end restaurants scattered all over England, as well as an impressive property portfolio. And then it hits me. 'She put you up to this, didn't she?' I do a little hysterical laugh, taking a few hasty steps back. The kettle rumbles, water bubbling away as furiously as my brain.

Holding the bridge of his nose, Andrew exhales loudly. 'God, I was dreading this. Look, she doesn't even know I'm here.' Yeah, right. 'In fact, when I suggested selling she told me not to ask you, said we'd find another way, and that's the honest truth. She feels rubbish about what's happened.' And now he's lying to protect her. I feel sick.

'I can't lose my home, Andrew. Where're am I supposed to live?'

'Do what other people do,' he says coldly. 'Rent.' Am I being unreasonable? Yes, I think I am. But we had a deal. He can't go back on it now. 'Or move in with lover boy.' He gestures at the door with his head as if Teddy is standing behind it in a superman outfit and will whisk me away to his penthouse in Chelsea. 'It's your call.'

'You fucking bastard,' I utter quietly.

His dark eyes flash with anger. 'We're not the first couple to split up, Lucy. Stop blaming me for the breakdown of our marriage. You were impossible to live with.' The kettle roars, water spills from the lid and I realise that I've filled it to the brim.

'You're the one who had the fucking affair.' I scream to the backdrop of Spiros and Xenia rattling around next door. They must be having a late breakfast on the patio.

'Oh, not this again.' His face is on fire.

'In our bed!'

'I can't talk to you when you're like this,' Andrew says, raking a hand through his hair… 'Half of this flat is mine. You're not being fair.' I watch the steam rising from the spout of the kettle wishing I could jump into it and evaporate into thin air. He's broken my heart and now he wants to take my home.

'Please, Andrew, don't do this to me. I can't buy you out now. I haven't got that sort of money.' I throw my hands up, defeated. 'I'm up to my neck in debt. Just…just give me another year.' He rolls his eyes. 'Okay, six months…Andrew, wait, where are you going? We haven't finished discussing it. Andrew.'

But he's already in the corridor, flip-flops flapping against the parquet. I stay rooted to the spot, because I don't trust my legs to carry me if I barrel after him. 'I'll give you until the end of next month.' His voice echoes in the hallway. 'If you don't come up with the cash by then, this place goes up for sale.' There's a low groan from the kettle as it reaches its boil, then a click. It's over.

Chapter 3

Alison scrapes the last bits of apple pie and ice cream off her plate noisily. 'I told you Teddy was lovely, didn't I? When're you seeing him next?' I grin as she licks the spoon clean, pushing my own dessert around the plate languidly. I'm renowned for my sweet tooth but I somehow lost my appetite after telling them all about my date with Teddy Fallon.

Karen looks up briefly from her phone. 'I think he said he'll be round to do a bit of weeding next week.'

'Not you, you muppet.' Alison flicks a bit of her mum's blonde hair off her shoulder, while Karen frowns at her phone, irritated, batting her daughter's hand away. 'I was talking to Lucy.' Alison winks at me then mouthes, 'WhatsApp. Doesn't know what she's doing.'

'I can see you, Alison,' Karen says dryly, and we both snort, suppressing a fit of schoolgirl giggles. 'I'm seventy-three not ninety-three, so enough of the pathetic senile jokes, yes?'

The King's Arms is buzzing. I very nearly didn't come. Andrew dropping that bombshell practically winded me. After he sped off in a rage in his white van, I walked around my flat touching the walls and the surfaces, then sat down and had a little cry. I even picked up my phone and stared at Alison's number on my Favourites list. I was in no mood for socialising. But then I knew that if I rang and cancelled, Alison would want to come round, make sure I was all right, if I needed anything.

She might've even insisted on leaving the kids with Simon or Karen and staying over, like she did that time when I pulled a muscle in my ribs at the gym doing the Russian Twist. Because that's the sort of person Alison is – kind, considerate, unpretentious – the type of person who give you proper kisses where lips and skin make contact.

I look across at her now as Karen shows her something on her phone and the anonymous text swells in my mind. How could I keep this secret from her? It's massive. Why did I let Simon manipulate me into keeping quiet? Why was I so weak? I flick a glance at her. It's not too late. I could come clean now – tell her everything.

'So, come on, you,' Alison says, rolling up the sleeves of her dress. 'I think you've got some explaining to do.'

I immediately go red and fiddle with a Carlsberg beer mat. She can't know…can she? 'What do you mean?' I croak.

'When's the next hot date with Teddy the gardener?'

'Oh, right.' I sigh with relief, spinning the beer mat clockwise. 'We're not seeing each other again,' I explain, then pause as a student-looking waiter lifts some of the empties off our table, fringe falling in his flushed face. 'Not after that disastrous first date,' I go on as the waiter dashes off towards the kitchen, dishes stacked in his arms. 'Poor man couldn't get out of my flat fast enough.'

Okay, I know this isn't quite how it happened, but I don't want to give Alison any false hope. She's been trying to fix me up for months. So far I've had a date with her hairdresser Leon, who spent all evening criticising my hair and makeup, an ex-colleague of hers, whom she described as sex-on-legs, but failed to tell me that she hadn't actually seen him in fifteen years, by which time he'd turned into a sixteen-stone, balding, toothless perve who kept trying to touch my thighs under the table in Pizza Roma.

And then of course there was Darren, her good-looking successful neighbour. I must admit I quite liked him. He was tall and tanned and gym toned, with sea-blue eyes and cropped dark hair, flecked at the sides with grey. We'd say hello sometimes on Alison's doorstep, or over the garden fence in summer, and I'd gush. I accepted the date in a heartbeat.

He took me to an expensive restaurant in Hertfordshire. It was all going swimmingly, until he disappeared to the loo during our mains, returning ten minutes later, high as a kite with powder on his nose. I spent the rest of the evening listening to him slagging off his ex-wife – loudly. I thought the maître d was going to chuck us out at one point. And now there's Teddy Fallon. Teddy ticks all the boxes, and I know I probably sound picky but the spark just wasn't there.

I inhale a concoction of booze and barbequed meat. 'I don't think Teddy and I clicked, to be honest,' I say to Alison, nodding enthusiastically as Karen shoves her phone under my nose for my approval of a selfie of the three of us, taken at Oscar's seventeenth birthday party two weeks ago, even though I look like shit. I can't believe how Oscar has shot up in the last two years. He's almost as tall as Simon now. Oscar is by far Karen's favourite grandson. She's even started giving him driving lessons in her beloved car. It's not that she loves him more than the little ones, but I think because Oscar isn't Simon's biological son she's a bit…protective over him. She needn't be though. Simon, with all his faults, is a great dad to Oscar and treats him no different to Barney and Leah.

'Aww…you should give Teddy a chance,' Alison coos. 'What other man would keep vigil all night over a woman he's just met?' I do actually feel a bit bad about that, but you can't force yourself to fancy someone because they're nice. 'He looked smitten yesterday afternoon when I told him you'd agreed to a date.' Alison twists the stem of her glass and juts out her bottom lip. 'Even went a bit red. Poor Teddy.'

'I don't think he was that into me, Al, but thanks for being so lovely.'

'I'm sure he'll call,' she adds kindly. 'Look at you, you're so flipping slim and gorgeous.' Her eyes flit over my white Bardot knitted top and blue ripped jeans. 'I haven't been able to get into a pair of those since I had Oscar. Can't believe how much weight you've lost,' she groans, eyeing my half-eaten chocolate brownie. 'Just wait until you hit forty though, and your metabolism slows down.'

Alison's got bit of a complex about her weight. In fact, she spoke to me about it the very first time I met her, said it was the result of three pregnancies, as if she somehow had to justify it. But I thought she looked stunning, and at forty-two, she still does. My eyes flick over her low-cut red A-line dress. There's a diamond encrusted crucifix nestled between her breasts and her soft brown curls are tumbling over her shoulders. She looks stunning. Alison always shows off her assets with revealing tops and bright dresses. I often see men ogling her cleavage. And women. I'd kill for her boobs. I'd swap my average-sized breasts for hers in a heartbeat. Only God knows why Simon would look elsewhere, risk losing his family. Guilt finds its way into my stomach and twists.

'So, come on, then, tell us more about Teddy. What didn't you like about my classy forty-six-year-old gardener?'

'Forty-six?' I utter, stunned. 'I didn't realise he was older than me.' No wonder he didn't run for the hills when I told him my real age.

'Ageist,' she teases, taking a sip from her wine glass. 'It's not a problem, is it? Si's older than me.'

A zing of acid flies into my stomach at the mention of his name on her full red lips. 'Only three years,' I point out.

Gazing around the pub, I take in the colourful pumps on the long bar, two men at the table opposite staring at their phones, half-filled pints in front of them, the flashing fruit machine, anything to avoid eye contact with Alison.

'Anyway.' I give her a glance, then root around in my bag for my phone. Someone coughs. Music hums. I think it's Stormzy, or a similar-sounding grime artist. 'It's not the age gap,' I mutter. Age has never been an issue with me. I once dated a man twenty-five years my senior, twice divorced with three grown-up kids and five grandchildren. My mother almost had to go back on antidepressants when she found out. She even made an appointment with her GP. 'It's just that Teddy isn't my type,' I explain, looking at my phone. No messages, thank God. I slip it into the zip compartment and lean back in my seat. I was right, the anonymous text must've been a hoax, a wrong number.

'What is your type then,' Alison says dryly, giving me one of her looks. 'Short, stocky Scotsmen?'

I shake my head and laugh lightly. 'I don't want a boyfriend, Al. I like being on my own.' I stare at the men with the pints again and one of them, late-thirties, shaved head, short beard and glasses, looks at me as he takes a sip. Fuck. He thinks I fancy him. I look away quickly. 'I can go out whenever I want,' I continue. 'I don't have to worry about cooking, and I don't have to make reluctant compromises to keep the in-laws happy. I'm good.' Alison can't stand her in-laws, especially De, her mother-in-law, who never fails to have a passive aggressive dig whenever she visits, like droning on about how she lost all her baby weight almost overnight with her three, making acidic comments about the kids when they get a bit whiney, reminding her that Simon was a good baby, wondering who they've taken after. That sort of thing. But she still has them over for Sunday lunch every other weekend, without fail.

'I'm not asking you to marry him, for goodness' sake.' Alison shakes her head at her mother who is busy texting as if we were invisible. 'Although, he is a good catch and your biological clock is ticking away,' she adds, flicking a glance at my stomach. 'Just think, this time next year you could be holding a mini-Lucy or Luciano in your arms.' She squeezes my forearm, eyes sparkling, and whispers. 'Me and Si could be godparents.'

'*Alisssson,*' I groan, straightening my top self-consciously.

'What? You've always said you'd love a child of your own.' She exhales loudly. 'I just want you to be happy, sweetie, that's all.'

We lapse into silence. Karen continues to tap, tap, tap on her phone. I look up at the bar, digesting what Alison's just said. Pint man, who thinks I fancy him, is paying for another round of drinks with his card, phone in the back pocket of his jeans.

'Go on.' Alison nudges me on the arm. 'Go out with him, have some fun.' She's right. I'm pushing forty and single. Am I ever going to have my longed for baby, or has that ship sailed? 'I can't bear to see you looking so miserable,' Alison groans. If only she knew the reason why. I bat the image of me and Simon out of my mind. Pint man gives me a long lingering stare as he heads back to the table, wallet clenched between his teeth, and for a moment I wonder if Simon was right, if I do give off the wrong signals. But no, I'm being self-deprecating again, ridiculous. Of course I don't.

I square my shoulders and take a deep breath. 'You're right, Ali. I'll start going out more, especially now that I'm a fully-fledged divorcee,' I say determinedly, not meaning a word of it. How can I go out and have fun when all I can think about is Simon, the anonymous text, and the sale of my flat.

'Teddy's like my Si,' Alison drones, staring dreamily into the middle distance, glass in hand, 'Ordinary but reliable. The kind of man who grows on you. I still get tea and toast in bed every morning,' she beams. I feel sick. I wish she'd stop talking about Simon. 'Just tell me you'll think about it, hmm?' Leaning forward, she curls a few stray hairs behind my ear as if I were five, then wipes the corner of my mouth with her thumb, while Karen groans about the complexities of picture messaging and how you need a degree in physics to work it out.

'Bit of chocolate sauce.' Alison smiles, rubbing her thumb and index finger together. 'You're such a mucky pup.' Tears sting the back of my throat. I'm not sure if it's the booze, or because she's being so lovely to me, but I'm suddenly overwhelmed with a need to tell her everything, as if I've just swallowed a glass of truth potion.

I open my mouth to speak when she leans back in her seat, wipes her fingers on a serviette and says, 'Teddy might even turn out to be the love of your life, you never know – you might end up with a marriage as perfect as mine.' I want to tell her to shut up, that she knows nothing about her marriage, nothing about Teddy Fallon. 'Well, almost perfect. Simon can be a twat sometimes, I know.' He'd win twat of the year hands down. 'But he's my twat.' *Oh God, will you please stop, Alison. Don't make this any harder.*

'They broke the mould when they made Simon Maxwell,' Karen chips in, still frowning at her phone. 'Couldn't ask for a better son-in-law.' I look at her stonily, wishing I could grab the phone out of her hand, remind her that it's rude to text when you're in company, and tell her to shut the fuck up about her stupid son-in-law.

'Aww…thanks, Mum.'

'If Teddy turns out to be as good as our Si,' Karen adds, prodding the screen with a long red fingernail, glasses on the bridge of her nose. 'You'll be a very lucky girl, Lucy.' She throws me a glance and I force a smile. 'That's if you decide to go out with him. It's your call, lovely.' God, why are they so naïve? Can't they see past Simon's perfect husband persona?

'What?' Alison says as I regard her carefully. *Come on, Lucy, tell her. Get it over with. What's the worst that could happen?* 'You're having second thoughts, aren't you?' Alison grins. My heart knocks violently against my ribcage. 'I know what.' She puts her glass down. 'Why don't we all go out together? Me, you, Teddy and Si, hmm? That way you can have another look without any pressure. I'll text Teddy and set it all up, you don't have to–'

'No,' I cut in, curling a hand around her bare arm. 'Please don't. Look, there's something I need to tell you.'

Confusion flickers across Alison's face, pink and moist from the boozy lunch, and then she says. 'Ooooh, did you hear that, Mum?' Karen stops texting, finger in mid-air, and looks at me. 'Lucy's got some exiting news to share.'

I look at their expectant faces, lick my dry lips, take a slug of wine. My heart is beating so hard that I fear it'll rupture through my chest and knock them both out cold.

'Andrew wants to sell the flat,' I complain, bottling it. I can't do it. Alison's happy. I can't burst her bubble. 'Jasmine's pregnant and he wants to move from the family home. So, I've either got to come up with the money to buy him out, or put it up for sale.'

Alison gathers her eyebrows and looks at me worriedly. Karen immediately abandons her phone and start rubbing my back, asks if I'm okay, reminds me that Andrew and I had a three-year agreement and it's only been one, as if it's a bona fide legal contract.

'They didn't waste much time. Fucking tossers,' Alison groans, refilling my glass. 'What are you going to do, sweetie?'

I look at my loyal, sweet, kind friend through a mist of tears. 'No idea,' I take a mouthful of prosecco too quickly and the bubbles hit the back of my throat like a shot of sherbet. 'Sell up, I suppose. What choice do I have?

Alison bites her bottom lip. 'I could ask Simon if–'

'No,' I cut in. 'I'll sort something out.'

'He works in a bank,' she points out, 'it's his job.'

'No, really. I'm…'

'Oh, come on, Lucy, stop being pig-headed.'

'Alison,' Karen exclaims, picking up on my discomfort. 'How many times have I told you to stop interfering in other people's lives,' she warns, and Alison pokes her tongue out at her mum in mock rebellion. 'Let Lucy make her own choices, and put that thing to some good use, like ordering another bottle of wine.'

'Let me know if you change your mind.' Alison gives me warm smile, squeezing my arm. We fall into compliable silence for a few moments. I gaze around the bustling pub – a fruit machine chimes, muffled voices fill my ears, a man cries out, *'Are you fucking shitting me?'*

'He's too posh for me, anyway,' I say suddenly, breaking the silence.

'Who is?' they both say in unison.

'Teddy Fallon.'

'Yeah, you can't take 'im 'ome to your muvver, can ya?' Alison says in her best cockney accent. 'She'll fink you've lost yer nut.'

We all laugh, and then Karen says, 'Oh, for God's sake, how on earth does this thing work?' She holds the phone under Alison's nose, and while Alison shows Karen how to send a photo on WhatsApp, I nip to the bar for another bottle of fizz.

'Fifty-six-forty. Shall we call it twenty quid each with a tip?' Karen suggests, twenty minutes later as Alison shares the last of the wine between three glasses. 'None for me, love.' Karen covers her glass with her hand. 'I'm meeting Trevor at the golf club in half an hour for a drink.'

'New bloke,' Alison whispers conspiratorially. 'Fit.'

'I've been seeing him for about a month,' Karen says, giving Alison a sideward glance. 'Hang on, I'll show you a piccie.'

Karen scrolls through her photo album and as she shows us several photographs of Trevor, my phone pings with a text alert and then another and another. My skin prickles. I ignore it. It pings again.

'I'm sorry,' I say, to the hullabaloo of voices. 'I've got to get this.'

As I snatch my phone from my open handbag, Karen totters off to the loo in her two-tone navy and white heels while Alison announces she's going to ring Simon, find out what time he'll be home from the squash club – she's making spag bol, my favourite, will ask Simon to bring home a couple of bottles of that Californian Merlot we like. I murmur in approval, as I try but fail to unlock my phone with TouchID.

'Sounds great,' I offer, punching in my passcode. I've no intention of going, of course. I can't face Simon. It's too soon. I quickly open the messages app to the ruckus of glasses clinking, cutlery tapping against plates, a cash till chiming, and as I read the three new texts I feel the entire pub closing in around me. 'Oh God, no,' I murmur through my fingers.

'Everything all right, Luce?'

Swallowing hard, I look up at her from my phone, eyes wide, as she rummages through her bag, and then I imagine my phone in her hand, her startled expression, my hair in her fist and my head coming down hard on the wooden table.

I immediately lock my phone and try to regain my composure, smiling and nodding as she rants on and on about

Simon – he's not picking up, he's an arse, must be in the pub with that twat Andrew. I can hear Karen's voice now too. She's back from the loo, there was no paper, she'll have to hold it in and is livid, it's unhealthy at her age.

'Aren't they meant to check them on the hour?' Alison groans, looking around the pub as if a toilet attendant will materialise from the saloon-style swinging kitchen doors.

I go to put my phone in my bag, out of sight, as they discuss the dangers of holding in your wee and Tena pants, and then it lights up and buzzes in my hand, I look down at the screen and everything freezes. Karen and Alison are still talking. I can hear their voices but I can't decipher what they're saying. I look up at them as if in slow motion, mouth agape, behind them a waiter, in a white shirt and black waistcoat, dark hair tied at the back of his head in a knot, is balancing numerous plates in his hands, serving a group of tipsy middle-aged women. One of the women, blonde, heavy makeup, orange tan, says something to him and then throws her head back and laughs. I gawp at them for a few moments, feeling out of sorts, as if I'm watching the scene play out from the decorative cornice, framing the spotlighted high ceiling.

'Lucy will tell you. It was so–' Alison's voice is cutting in and out like a bad telephone line. 'You remember – hilarious – couldn't – Mum…tell…'

The room spins, plates clack, clack, clack in my ears. I grab ahold of the rim of the table. I think I'm going to pass out. I look at my screen again in horror, as if staring at it will make it disappear. 'Oh my God, no…'

Alison and Karen look at me worriedly. Shit. I said it out loud. Snatching my glass, I down the prosecco in one, and then I feel nails digging into my flesh. 'Lucy. Lucy, are you okay? Mum, she doesn't look well.'

'What's the matter, dear?' Karen asks. 'Do you think it was that fish, Alison? Is she allergic to anything?' Karen's on her feet now, waving at a waiter. 'Sorry, can we get a glass of water, please? Our friend's not feeling well. Probably something she ate. No, tap will do. Thanks.'

'I don't think she has any allergies.' Alison is on the edge of her seat, hand on my back. 'None that I'm aware of, anyway. Lucy?'

'Is she diabetic? That chocolate brownie she wolfed down was huge.' I didn't wolf it down. I left half of it. I'm not diabetic, anyway. I wish they'd stop fussing. I can't breathe. It's too hot in here. Why are their lips moving so slowly? What's that buzzing sound?

'Sheeeez nottttt diaaaaabetiiiic, Mummmmm.' What's happened to Alison's voice?

'Heeeeee's bringgggiiing yoooou a glaaaaass of waaaater, loooovve.' I glance up at Karen and stare at her for a moment, zombie-like, and then suddenly the kerfuffle becomes amplified, as if someone has released the pause button, and everything speeds up – people laughing, glasses clinking, cash tills pinging; one of the middle-aged women at the table behind us cries, 'It was so WEIRD.'

'No, I'm fine…' I mutter breathlessly, cold sweat beading on my forehead. 'Sorry…I think I just had a funny turn… got a bit dizzy for a moment, lost my bearings…from the um…alcohol…and a bit of tinnitus…from the music last night. God, it's so hot in here. Thanks.' I take the water from Karen's hand and, with a trembling hand, take a large gulp. 'Um…I'm okay now. I'm sorry if I scared you.'

'Phew,' Karen says, 'you had us worried there for a moment. Must've been the news about the flat – a delayed response. Stress affects us in such strange ways.'

‘Delayed shock,’ Alison pipes up. ‘Happened to one of my clients the other day after she confessed to having an affair with her brother-in-law,’ Alison explains, and I want to slit my wrists. She takes my hand and holds it between her palms. They’re soft and warm and comforting. ‘I had to make her a cup of tea with three sugars to get over it. Shall we order you a cup of sweet tea, flower? Mum, get that waiter with the funny ponytail back now. Your blood sugar may be a bit low,’ she says gently. I tell her that I’m fine, to stop worrying. ‘Oh, good,’ she says, sounding unconvinced. ‘You’re still coming over tonight though, aren’t you? About eight all right?’

Alison’s hand disappears into her small red crossover handbag. Swallowing back a silent holler, I glare at her inanely, as the teriyaki salmon I had for lunch spins in my stomach like a cartwheel. There’s no way I can go round to hers for dinner, not now.

‘Are you sure you’re okay?’ Alison rubs my arm. ‘You know, I think you might’ve had a panic attack. You’ve gone very pale, hasn’t she, Mum?’ Karen agrees, nodding, concerned, then Alison’s face darkens. ‘Oi, hang on a minute,’ she says ominously, looking at my hands. Adrenalin tears through my veins. My phone I didn’t lock it – she’s seen the picture message. She knows. I glance at the screen. It’s blacked out. Thank God for auto lock. I go to switch it off, but in my haste activate TouchID and it lights up again. ‘Were those texts from Andrew? Is he threatening you, because if he is I’ll… ?’ She goes to look but I pull my phone to my chest as if she’s about to snatch it from me. ‘Let me see,’ she demands.

‘No!’ I snap, shocked at own outburst, heart racing, mouth dry. ‘It’s private.’ I’m acting out of character, making them suspicious. Alison and I tell each other practically everything. But right now I’d sell my kidney to stop her and Karen from looking at my phone.

Alison exchanges glances with her mum. She looks a bit chastened, and I immediately feel like the worse friend in the world. I open my mouth to apologise, when Alison's lips curl into a wicked grin. 'They're from Teddy, aren't they?' She slaps the dark wooden table, sticky with ring marks and remnants from our lunch. 'I flipping knew he'd get in touch again. But not this soon! Blimey, he must be keen. Has he sent you something saucy? I know what a prude you are.'

'Oooh, Matron,' Karen says in a high-pitched voice. 'I bet it's a photo of him in his briefs. No wonder you don't want us to see it,' she hollers over the laughter and babble from the tipsy women at the table nearby. 'Or a sext,' she adds, 'or a nudie.' At this, the orange-faced lady with the heavy makeup looks round at her, drawn-in eyebrow raised, as if to say *Show me that phototext immediately*. I'm not surprised Karen's using text speak, she's more like our age than hers. 'He's a bit of all right, that Teddy, isn't he? I wouldn't kick him out of bed. Oh, excuse me,' she calls out to the Samurai-haired waiter. 'There you go, love. Keep the change.'

'Mum!' Alison slaps her arm. 'Teddy wouldn't send her obscene photographs. He's a gent. That's if it IS him and not that short arsed ex-husband of hers. So, come on,' she urges, 'put us out of our misery.'

They both look at me expectantly, big grins on their faces. 'Yes,' I lie, shaking my head firmly. 'They're from him. They're from Teddy. I've been rumbled.' I laugh feebly. 'I'll reply on my bus journey home. They are a bit…um…' I clear my throat. 'Sexy.'

After a bit of moaning and groaning, Alison and Karen grab their belongings. We're on our feet, gathering to leave, chairs scraping, purses clasping, jackets zipping, and as they shoulder their handbags and head for the exit, discussing tonight's dinner plans, I hang back and look at the image on my screen again, cold fingers pressed against my mouth. My lips are locked with Simon's. He's kissing me hard. I read the texts again and again and again until the words become a blur:

> *I know ur fucking Alison's husband.*

> *Uve got til weds midnight to own up.*

> *or she gets to see this!*

Chapter 4

The bus ride home is slow and painful. I can't get Alison out of my mind – everywhere I look I see her; every time I close my eyes, she's there, her lovely face flashing like a beacon. Alison's my closest friend and, if I'm honest, the only real friend I've got. I don't know how I would've got through the breakdown of my marriage, had it not been for her.

We first met at *The Black Olive* in Primrose Hill. I'd been dating Andrew for four weeks and five days. I'd already met Simon, several times, but was nervous as hell about meeting his wife. I'd heard so much about her, how she was this larger-than-life character, friendly, warm, full of confidence. All the attributes I lacked.

I imagined this perfect goddess wafting into the restaurant like a catwalk model, ordering something vegan and sipping sparkling herb infused mineral water whilst she analysed me over dinner, taking in my Matalan faded black jeans and pale blue H&M sweater, my lack of social skills, my tremulous hand as I took a sip of wine. I felt sick.

Andrew and I arrived first, which was a bit of a blessing because it meant I could have a swift one to calm my nerves. I managed two large glugs before the door swung open and Simon walked in, Alison behind him, wild haired, in a pair of black leggings and a crumpled white shirt dress. I could feel the heat radiating from her skin as she kissed me on both cheeks and apologised for being ten minutes late, her youngest was sick after a feed, she had to quickly change, didn't have time to iron.

I stared at her two-inch white roots with affection as she studied the menu, blue-rimmed glasses perched on the bridge of her nose. She was normal and funny and warm, and definitely not the self-righteous, arrogant therapist that Andrew had described.

We bonded over a fish meze and two bottles of *Othello*, a very dry red which you get used to after several sips, while Andrew and Simon put the world to rights. We've not looked back since. We're best friends. We're like sisters. We tell each other everything. Well, almost everything. You must understand that I'd never do anything to hurt her – not deliberately. I can't even begin to imagine my life without her in it. What happened with Simon was a mistake. An error of judgment made at a time that I was feeling very vulnerable. And a bit drunk.

The wheels squeak as the bus pulls up at a stop. People shuffle on and off. I close my eyes and Friday before last – the day it happened – manifests in my mind.

My divorce had just come through. I was a free woman. At last. I'm not going to lie, I did shed a little tear. Okay, I broke down and called all the confidants on my contacts list during my lunch break, apart from Andrew and Jasmine, obviously. I was expecting it, but the finality was overwhelming. Up until then I was the estranged wife. There was still that glimmer of hope, that chance that Andrew might get fed up with Jasmine and come home. The Decree Absolute made it so…so final. My marriage was officially over. There was no way back.

Alison was great, as always, spent half an hour consoling me on the phone as I sobbed into my M&S tuna and cucumber sandwich in the kitchenette of my Travelicious office.

‘I didn’t expect it to hit me so hard, Al,’ I cried, ‘I thought I was over him.’

Alison’s sigh crackled loudly down the phone. I could just imagine her face, bottom lip jutted, big blue eyes full of concern. ‘I’d suggest going out and getting pissed,’ she said, as I watched the hand of the cheap white plastic clock on the wall thundering towards the end of my break. ‘But Simon’s working late and I’ve got the kids. I’d ask Mum to come over and look after them but she’s gone away for the weekend – some yoga retreat in Devon, not that she practices, or ever will. Her neighbour’s an addict and wanted someone to go with, and you know what Mum’s like.’ I nodded as if she could see me down the phone. Alison has inherited her kindness gene from Karen. ‘And I can’t really ask Oscar, can I? He’s only seventeen, he’ll probably leave them to their own devices.’

‘It’s okay, Al.’ I wiped my snotty nose on my sleeve as Gillian appeared at the door like a phantom in a too-tight navy trouser suit, tapping her Fitbit watch. ‘I’ll be okay,’ I sniffed, snot running onto my lips. I’d better go. I’ve got to get back to work.’

There was another long crackly sigh down the phone and then she said, ‘Why don’t you just come round here after work? We can open that pricey bottle of champagne Jasmine gave me for my fortieth, celebrate your new single status as Lucy Harper at her expense.’ A Dom Pérignon Rose Vintage 2005, which cost an eye-watering three-hundred-and-thirty quid. I was with her when she bought it from Harrods for Ali’s surprise bring-a-bottle birthday bash organised by Karen and Simon. All I could afford was a bottle of Hendricks’s gin. Alison’s favourite tipple. I still felt completely inadequate when I handed it over though. Bloody Jasmine, she was always trying outdo me.

I accepted Alison’s invitation in a heartbeat because the alternative – drinking myself into oblivion in front of a muted

TV – didn't bear thinking about. The moment the clock hit 5.30, I switched off my computer and raced out of the Travelicious office on Dukes Street like a whippet on speed. An hour and a half later I was sitting in Alison's lounge.

We ate and we talked and I cried and we laughed, we drank champagne and I cried some more. At about nine thirty, when Simon arrived home, Ali put the kids to bed and we opened another bottle of wine and sat in the garden, lapping up the last of summer, leaving Simon and Oscar in front of the TV with PlayStation.

Once the second bottle was empty, Alison called out to Oscar to fetch another, but as her beautiful son appeared at the French doors all sleepy and tired, blond hair sticking up, bottle of red in hand, I looked at my watch and almost fell off my chair. 'Shit, Al, it's almost eleven thirty. I should get going.'

'No, stay!' Alison shouted. Alcohol always makes her talk loudly. 'It's Saturday tomorrow, you can have a lie in. Give it here, Oscar.'

I shook my head, got to my feet and swayed a little. I'd had too much. 'I really need to go. Mum's coming down from Brighton for the weekend and I have to meet her at Victoria Station at ten.'

'So, what shall I do with this?' Oscar asked, holding the bottle aloft.

'What's all this about another bottle?' Simon threw his arm around his stepson's neck, in mock strangulation fashion, and Oscar laughed as he tried to free himself from his loose hold.

'Come on, Luce,' Alison pleaded, 'One for the road. A lovely G&T. Simon, get the gin.' My poor friend could barely keep her eyes open. She looked exhausted. So, tempted as I was, I refused. I'd had enough anyway. I pulled out my phone to ring for a cab, but Ali wouldn't hear of it. 'Give her a lift home, Simon,' she demanded in a sergeant-major tone. I love the way Ali talks to Simon. How comfortable and confident they are around each other. I never had that with Andrew – he was way too sensitive for banter.

'Er...' He scratched his cheek, hand in pocket. 'BM's in the garage, in case you'd forgotten.'

Alison rolled her eyes. 'Take the Lexus!'

Simon cringed. 'Didn't get a chance to renew the insurance today. Sorry.'

And as they launched into an argument about insuring her 4x4, Oscar kissed me goodnight and I pulled him to me and hugged him tight, because he's the closest thing I've got to a son. Plus I was pissed. 'Goodnight, Auntie Lucy,' he said, when I let him go. 'See you soon.'

I smiled to myself as Oscar slinked off, pulled out my phone and scrolled for the Uber app. 'It's okay, Simon, I'll call a cab.'

'Oh, for the love of *Godddd*,' Alison huffed, 'Use Mum's Golf, Si. It's on the drive.' Alison rummaged around in her bag then threw a bunch of keys at him, which he caught like a top wicketkeeper. 'Doesn't like to keep it outside hers,' Alison said to me, 'after what happened the last time.' Karen's car got keyed on her driveway last year while she was away in Portsmouth with her cousin Meg, they had tickets for The Tina Turner Musical.

'Come on then, trouble,' Simon said, jerking his head towards the door, hands in pockets.

Outside, I buckled myself in and waved at Alison as we drove into the night. At the roundabout on Creighton Avenue, Simon crunched the car into second gear, all the while complaining about Karen's old Golf – why doesn't she buy a new car, it's not as if she can't afford it, who drives a bloody car with gears these days? Someone needs to drag her into the twenty-first century.

I laughed it off, and for the next five minutes or so, we drove in companionable silence, listening to Smooth Radio. When we turned into Alexandra Park Road, Simon harrumphed in exasperation, thrust a hand through his thick curls and slammed the air-conditioning on full blast, complaining that Karen's air-con system was shit, he was so bloody hot, had the day from hell; and I shrunk into my seat, wanting to disappear, feeling awful for dragging him away from his comfortable sofa.

Moments later, he glanced at me and said, 'Have you changed your hair?' His foot went down and we sped along Durnsford Road as if we were in the grand prix, his eyes flitting from me to the road. 'You look different.'

I'd had my highlights redone but that was weeks ago, and, quite frankly, I'm surprised he'd even noticed. 'No,' I said, touching my shoulder-length dark-blonde hair. 'Oh, wait, I didn't straighten it. Maybe that's it. I've got the windswept look.' I flicked my hair back theatrically.

Her grinned at me, slowing down at the traffic lights. 'It looks great. Suits you. You should wear it like that more often. You really are a pocket rocket, aren't you?'

'Yes, thank you, Simon.' I nudged him in the arm with my elbow. 'It's not my fault you're a giant.' Simon's always taking the piss out of my height. It's a thing. Five-foot-four isn't really short, but compared to his six-foot-two stature, I'm like a dwarf next to him in flats. Simon and I have always enjoyed good banter, so I thought nothing more of it.

The whir of the air con filled my ears as he took a sharp turn, and I did a little shiver. Karen's air con wasn't shit at all. I was flipping freezing. My toes felt as if they were going to drop off in my T-bar sandals, but I daren't complain, not after what he'd said minutes earlier. I'd have to just freeze my arse off, I thought, until I got home.

Wrapping my arms around my body, I stared out of the window at the houses as we stopped at a set of traffic lights, rubbing my hands up and down my arms, and then *Radio Ga Ga* filtered through on the radio. I'm not sure whether it was because it's one of my all-time favourite songs, or because I had a bit too much wine, but I turned up the volume and then we both started singing along, like Carpool Karaoke. Our voices getting louder and louder, drowning out Queen.

A car horn blasted, reminding us that the lights had turned green. Simon swore loudly at the driver behind us in the rear-view mirror, stalled, swore some more, then sped off with a jerk, face on fire, complaining some more about Karen's rubbish car.

On Alderman's Hill, Simon slowed down at a crossing, allowing a couple by, then accelerated before they even had a chance to step onto the pavement. Speeding along, I could feel his eyes on me.

'What?' I said, pulling the visor down and examining my face in the mirror. My makeup had been on since six that morning and as I'd spent most of the day crying my eyes out over my divorce, I wondered if my mascara had smudged. It had. I looked a mess.

Simon smiled, elbow against the window frame, fingers resting lightly on his mouth. 'Just for the record. I think Andrew's a prize prick. You're way better looking than Jasmine. I mean, is there anything about her that's real?' It was a catty remark but I liked it, liked that he was on my side even though Andrew was his best friend, liked that he was slagging Jasmine off even though we all knew she was gorgeous.

Simon took another corner sharply and I fell on him. A few things slid out of my bag. 'Oh, well,' I said, pushing the contents back in. 'He chose her. What can you do?'

‘I told him he was a bloody fool.’ Simon shook his head and his dark curls bounced. ‘Sex isn’t everything in a relationship.’

I gasped, shocked. ‘What do you mean?’ I said, jerking my head round to look at him. How dare Andrew discuss our sex life with Simon.

The indicator clinked as we turned into my road. ‘He reckons you were always way too tired for sex, so he had to look elsewhere.’

‘That’s bollocks,’ I snapped, pushing the strap of my bag higher on my shoulder. ‘Our sex life was perfect.’ It was twice a week and predictable, Wednesdays and Saturdays. Unless I was ovulating, then it was every night, which Andrew ended up dreading and described as a loveless, robotic chore. But I didn’t divulge this to Simon.

‘Yeah, to you maybe, but some blokes want it every flipping night. Andrew’s always been a randy sod.’ Eyes fixed on the road, Simon’s face suddenly tensed. ‘I’m lucky if I get it once a month.’ I wanted to cover my ears – too much information. I ignored his crude remark, and he yawned loudly and did a little quiver. ‘Ali’s always so bloody knackered – pretends to be asleep when I get into bed. Eyes tight shut like this.’ He closed his eyes and the car swerved.

‘Look where you’re flipping going,’ I yelled, annoyed that he wasn’t concentrating on the road, but mostly because he was slagging off my best friend. I wanted to say something, tell him off, but, under the circumstances, decided to let it go. He was tired. I was tired. It’d been a long day. I can’t tell you how comforting it was to see the familiarity of my road – the cars, the lights, the hedges, the wheelie bins.

‘Thanks for the lift, Si,’ I said as we pulled up outside my flat. ‘See you soon.’

The heat hit me like a hot steaming sauna the moment I stepped onto the tarmac and breathed in the moisture in the air.

A storm was imminent. I was glad. The garden needed it. Simon looked at me, smiling as I walked around the car, and I smiled back. I was grateful he was looking out for me, making sure I got home safely. I don't know why he mentioned his sex life to me. Perhaps it was to make me feel better about myself. Help me to understand that no relationship is perfect. He was a good mate, I thought, kind, caring, protective.

Then as I raised my hand to wave goodbye, miming 'goodnight', his dark eyes became like discs, 'Wait!' Leaping out of the car, he raced round to meet me, holding my phone aloft. 'Your oxygen,' he joked.

'Oh, bloody hell,' I said, taking the phone from his hand. 'It must've fallen out of my bag when you took that sharp corner.' I smiled up at him, feeling the hot engine thrumming against my leg. 'Good job you spotted it or I'd have been hammering on your door at three in the morning.'

He slipped his hands into the pockets of his tailored grey trousers. The top two buttons of his white shirt were undone, his red tie hung loosely against his chest. 'Where would we be without our phones, eh?' he groaned, scratching his five o'clock shadow. 'I'm not sure how we survived without them back in the day.'

I laughed lightly. 'Tell me about it. Night then.' I went to move but he leant forward to give me a peck on the cheek, like he'd done many times before. We went the opposite way, and then our noses brushed and then his lips were on mine, his big hands holding my face, his hot tongue parting my lips, the taste of whiskey, and, I was almost certain, the smell of weed in his dark brown curly hair.

For a second I hesitated, shocked. I couldn't believe what was happening. And then I pushed him off me violently and he staggered backwards, bile rose in my throat.

‘Fucking hell, Simon,’ I gasped. ‘What do you think you’re doing?’ And then we just stood there, in the middle of the street, glaring at each other, with this kiss, with this improper thing, just hanging there, sucking in all the oxygen around us. A car whizzed past, music blaring. ‘What’s wrong with you?’ I drew my forearm along my lips, feeling sick, spat on the ground to get his saliva out of my mouth, and then, out of nowhere, an eerie feeling of being watched prickled my skin. I glanced around me, the road was silent and clear, streetlights casted shadows on the parked cars along the kerb. My eyes flit to the flat above mine, the curtains were open in total darkness, Greta and Tamas were out; then at the house next door, curtains drawn, lights out, then as my eyes flicked to Spiro’s and Xenia’s on the other side, I glimpsed a figure of a woman ducking out of sight. Tall, slim – not Xenia. Maybe it was her daughter-in-law, Emma, or her granddaughter, Demi. It was dark. I couldn’t be sure, and quite frankly, I didn’t care. I couldn’t believe that my best friend’s husband had just tried it on with me. I had to get away, get inside, brush my teeth until my gums bled so that I could get the taste of him out of my mouth. ‘Go home, Simon, you’re off your fucking head.’

Then before he could answer, I sprinted to my front door, heart belting against my ribcage, tears of rage stinging my eyes. The drone of the engine died and a car door thudded. ‘Lucy, wait.’ And then Simon was standing next to me on my doorstep as I rummaged around in my bag for my keys.

‘Get lost, Simon.’

‘Lucy, I’m sorry,’ he gasped, ‘I don’t know what came over me. Let me just come inside. I can explain. I…’

‘No fucking way,’ I warned, pointing my front door key at him as if it were a six-inch kitchen knife. ‘You’re not stepping foot in this flat.’

Simon backed away, ran a hand over his face. 'I'm sorry,' he said at the ground. 'I read the signs wrong.'

I jerked my head up at him. 'Signs? What fucking signs? I'm not fair game now because I'm single, you know.' I pushed the key into the lock, furious. 'Go home, Simon, and sober the fuck up. You're pathetic. Alison deserves better.'

And then out of nowhere, his arm flew across my front door, blocking my entrance.

'You're not going to tell her, are you?' I didn't answer. 'Lucy, please don't do this.'

'Move,' I demanded at the ground. A cricket chirped. Behind me, the ruckus of female voices and drunken laughter shot to my ears. I swivelled my head round, following the racket. Four revellers staggered along the pavement, giggling and talking loudly, heels clicking. Simon waited until their voices faded before speaking again, as if they were spies who would record everything he was saying and report back to Alison. 'It'll end our marriage,' he admitted, coldly. 'She'll never forgive me.' Silence. 'I'm such a fucking dick.' His hand shot to his mouth and he looked at me, all teary eyed, fingers quivering. 'Lucy, please. Please, don't tell her about this.'

I looked at the Golf parked three feet away from the kerb, pushing the strap of my bag an inch further on my shoulder. 'How could you drink and drive, Simon? It's not even your car. What if we'd had an accident?'

'I've only had a couple of Merlots.' A couple of bottles by the look of it, I wanted to shout. 'We're named drivers on Karen's insurance anyway.' Rubbing his chin, he laughed nervously. 'It was a dumb thing to do,' he admitted, one hand loosely on his hip. Backing himself against the brick wall, he looked up at the black sky and sighed. 'I don't even know why I did it. I'm just under so much pressure at work – targets to reach. Our branch is underperforming. The company is making redundancies. My job's on the line. I don't know what I'll do if they let me go. We've got so many outgoings – the mortgage, school fees, holidays, the kids' upkeep. It's killing me, and Alison keeps spending like it's going out of fashion. I know she works too, but her part-time job at the clinic barely covers the monthly shop. Our outgoings are higher than our combined salaries. I just…it's…' And then to my utter surprise, he sat on his haunches and started crying. Right there on my doorstep. Big, loud, snotty sobs.

'Okay, okay,' I said quickly, looking around me. 'Stop fucking crying.'

He looked up at me then, brown eyes full of hope, thick eyebrows raised together like slashes. 'You won't say anything.' He clambered to his feet awkwardly, shirt hanging out of his trousers like a school boy. 'To Alison…or anyone else. Promise?'

I exhaled loudly. Alison likes spending money, she's generous, likes to live life to the full, but with a house on Creighton Avenue worth almost two million quid and Simon's well-paid job in the city, I thought they could afford it. I dithered. The last thing I wanted to do was destroy their marriage. I know first-hand what it's like to go through a divorce and I haven't even got any children. Simon and the kids are Alison's world. This would destroy her. But then, how could I keep something as serious as this from her? Let her live a lie? What if I wasn't the first? What if he had other women on the go? He'd already confessed to being sex starved. Surely, my friend deserve to know the truth? I owed her that.

'Lucy, I'm begging you. I love Alison…my kids…they're everything to me…'

'Then why are you behaving like a dick?'

'I don't know. I'm an idiot.'

I shook my head, looked at my feet. 'I don't know, Simon. I can't keep this from Alison. She…'

'If she leaves me I'll top myself,' he said suddenly, eyes wild. 'I mean it.'

I hesitated again. I'd recently read online that middle-aged men have the highest rate of suicide. What if he becomes one of those statistics? I didn't want that. I looked at him, standing there looking broken – was he having a mini breakdown? Yes, I thought, he was. 'Okay, okay,' I said, 'Let's just forget it.'

'Oh, Lucy, thank you.'

'But if I ever hear that you've hurt her.'

'No, I promise. This was a one-off. I've never been unfaithful.'

I shook my head. 'Right. Good. Go home, talk to Ali, tell her about the money problem. Sort your shit out.'

He nodded, lips trembling, then moved forward for a hug but I backed away. I watched as he left with his tail between his legs, I could almost see it curling around his sorry arse.

The engine groaned and hissed as he drove off into the darkness. I closed my front door and flicked on the lights. Convinced myself that I did the right thing. I thought it was done with. Over.

But someone was watching. Someone was waiting. Someone was out to get me.

Chapter 5

I take a glug of coffee from my polystyrene cup, then lift the lid off my gluten-free chicken and avocado salad. Café Americano is heaving today and the staff is rushed off its feet. I was lucky to find this tiny table right next to the loos. On a normal Monday I'd be wolfing down a homemade sandwich at my desk, washed down with a mug of builder's tea. But I thought I'd get away from it all today. Relax with a kindle read and a healthy meal prepared by someone else.

At the table in front of me, three officey girls are ravenously tucking into their Paninis, sharing anecdotes about their weekend, laughing, gossiping. I give them the thousand-mile stare as I spear a cherry tomato around with my disposable fork and pop it into my mouth. You'd have thought that forty-eight hours of silence from the blackmailer would have calmed me down, especially since I sent them a retaliating reply, saying I knew who they were and was going to the police. But their silence is eerie and unsettling, and Wednesday, the day they threatened to reveal all to Alison, is looming.

Returning my attention to my Kindle, I read a sentence from my novel, but the words won't sink in. It's as if they've been written in a foreign language. My mind wanders back to Saturday – Alison's disappointed voice when I rang to tell her I was too poorly for spag bol and Californian Merlot, after all. Her concern for my wellbeing, her texts that followed that evening, asking if I was all right. If I needed anything. I don't know how long I can keep lying to her. It's making me ill.

Alison and Simon get back from Bath today. Is that why the blackmailer set the deadline for Wednesday, to give them time to return, settle in? If it's who I think it is, then yes, I think that is why. Forking a piece of chicken, I shovel it into my mouth thoughtfully. The office girls howl with laughter. Am I wrong to take the blackmailer's silence for compliance? Should I risk it, or should I go to the police? Kate seems to think I should. Go to the police, I mean. My sister always does the right thing. She's the sensible one. Always has been. But can I honestly turn up at the station with a bunch of anonymous texts, a grainy photograph and a hunch? Really? What would I even say?

'Hello, officer. I'd like to report someone for harassment. Last Friday night, at about 11.30, my ex-husband's fiancée hid somewhere outside my flat in Palmers Green, took a photo of Simon, my best friend's husband kissing me, and is now blackmailing me with it. Obviously, she witnessed the entire thing and knows I refused Simon's advances, but, because she's sick and twisted, she's threatening to send that photo to Alison unless I admit to having an affair with her husband. I mean, why should I confess to something I'm not guilty of, would you? No, officer, I'm not, nor ever have been, having an affair with Simon. The idea is preposterous, sickening. I didn't reciprocate his advances, although in the photo it looks as if I did – as if we're kissing. The whole thing is a shambles. Do I have any evidence? Well, I did have a feeling that we were being watched at the time, and as I know she came to my flat that day, to drop off an invite, it places her at the scene. Everyone knows she's my nemesis. So, it must be her. Who else could it be?

I want you to take action, please. I want you to stop her from harassing me and, more importantly, I want you to make sure she doesn't send that photograph to Alison. What do you mean, that's not evidence. Look, firstly, she has all our contact details, and secondly, she knew that Alison and Simon were in Bath this weekend, which is why she set the deadline to Wednesday. Lawyers are clever. Methodical. They work things out. It's their job. Do you know that she stole my husband from right under my nose? Yep, and if that weren't enough, she's now making him sell my home, which we jointly own (long story), to destroy me completely. I don't know why she'd do such a thing, officer. Perhaps she thinks I'm still a threat, that my ex-husband will tire of her and come running back to me, but if I'm long gone – you get the picture. So, you see, she has a motive, hasn't she?

Yes, I'm sure it's her, officer. How many times? She's always been jealous of my friendship with Alison. I knew this, of course, saw the signs, but chose to ignore them. What signs? Oh, niggly things, snide remarks, a dig here and there, and she was always inviting herself over when she knew Alison would be there. Jasmine doesn't like me having other friends – wants me to herself. Always has.

We go back a long way, you see. We were inseparable at school. Joined at the hip. Classmates used to call us the terrible twins. Jas was so popular – studious, athletic, full of confidence. All the boys wanted to go out with her and all the girls wanted to be her. I felt privileged that she chose me as her best mate. I was, still am, if I'm honest, a bit of a loner; didn't have any other friends. The strange thing was, she looked up to me for some reason. Loved my dry humour, she said, and that I wasn't a brown-noser, like all her other mates. It might've been my sense of humour, who knows? Or, it might've been because I wasn't a threat to her. I mean, what boy would choose a wild-haired skinny girl with acne off the local estate over a voluptuous exotic middleclass beauty? That's right, no one.

Apart from Johnny White, that is. Johnny asked me to dance at the school disco then out on a date. We went to see a film at the local Odeon. He wasn't very good looking. Quite lanky with wiry, ginger hair and pale blue eyes. A five out of ten, at a push. But I quite liked him, he made me laugh. He was kind and gentle and funny. I thought the date went pretty well, but on Monday morning he dumped me and started going out with Jasmine instead. It only lasted a week. Johnny later confessed that Jasmine asked him out on the promise of going all the way, but she wouldn't even let him kiss her. Jas didn't fancy him. She was completely out of his league. She just wanted to take him off me. I didn't really care, to be honest. We were only sixteen, and our friendship was more important to me than five out of ten Johnny White.

Anyway, when we left school we lost contact, as you do, but then two years ago she sent me a friend's request on Facebook. I was one of those married women who used a double surname – Lucy Harper McLaughlin, so that old friends could find me. I was gobsmacked when she got in touch. I often wondered what'd happened to her. When she suggested meeting up, I said yes. I wanted to see her, find out how her life had panned out.

We met for lunch and literally just picked up from where we left off. Chatting, reminiscing, having a laugh. She told me she'd just moved back from Bristol, was staying with her parents in Hertfordshire. She'd just come out of a messy relationship with some Welsh bloke and was looking up old friends. I offered her a shoulder to cry on. After that, she practically lived round ours, and would often spend the night on our futon when we'd had one too many. I should've been suspicious, really, because she wouldn't leave the next morning. She'd spend the day wandering around our flat in a thong and flimsy t-shirt, titties jiggling around all over the place. Implants but good ones. Apparently, she felt so comfortable around us, said Andrew and I were like her second family. I know, more fool me.

The thing is, officer, I told her lots of things in confidence, things I shouldn't have said about my marriage. I'd moan about some of Andrew's annoying habits, like leaving his toothpaste gob in the sink – all he had to do was wash it away with warm water – never bothering to close cupboard doors, that really used to get on my tits. And why did I always have to tell him to fix something that was broken before he'd do anything about it? I mean he used the bathroom too; he knew that one of the spotlights on the mirror had come loose. It's still dangling off its hinges now. But I also told her how irritating his sister was, whom he adores, by the way.

Carol never did like me. I even heard her calling me lazy once when she stayed over, all because I had a lie in on a Saturday morning until eleven thirty. She actually stood outside our bedroom door and dissed me to Andrew. Quite loudly. I mean, what the fuck, right? And I might've mentioned, after a few too many vodka and tonics, that Andrew was a bit of a selfish lover. I don't even know why I said that because it wasn't even true. Perhaps, thinking back, it was to make her feel better about her divorce.

I mean, Andrew and I would have a quickie before work when I was ovulating but, if I'm honest, I was more impatient than he was. I didn't want to be late for work. Gillian, my boss, is a bit of a sergeant major. But despite my grievances, I wasn't unhappy, officer. I was just having a whinge. It was meant to be taken with a pinch of salt. It didn't mean I wanted a divorce. I loved him. He was my world. We were trying for a baby, for God's sake. How was I to know she was telling him everything?

Andrew and I began to drift apart, arguing more, just about silly things, really. Then he started telling me he was working late, sometimes not coming home until gone midnight. He fobbed me off with the excuse of an office building contract, and how they could only access the premises once the staff had gone home – he's a self-employed plumber. I believed him, of course. I even believed him when he told me he had a gig in Birmingham for the weekend. Why wouldn't I? We needed the money. We were trying for a family. He was my husband. I trusted him. I didn't once suspect that anything was going on between them. I trusted them both.

Anyhow, to cut a long story short, she stole my husband and now she's stalking me and taking photos, trying to destroy my friendship with the only friend I've got left. She's turning everyone against me, officer. This woman is dangerous. I've known her since I was eleven. I'm telling you, she'll stop at nothing to destroy me. Her name is Jasmine Anand. Please go to her office in Holborn and arrest her immediately.'

Taking a glug of lukewarm cappuccino, I laugh lightly to myself. They'll probably have me sectioned if I say all that, and even if they do believe me, what will they say when they see the photograph of Simon kissing me outside my flat? How can I prove that he came onto me, that I pushed him away, without a witness? They're going to think we're lovers. They may even arrest me for wasting police time.

So, no, I won't be going to the police. Instead, I'm going to take Kate's advice and come clean, tell Alison the truth. God, I could kick myself for not telling her right away, for ignoring my instincts. But it's not too late. Once I explain that Simon was drunk and depressed, because of their money problems, and that coming on to me was a cry for help, she'll get it. I'm certain. She's a therapist. Therapists aren't like the rest of us – they're like superheroes. They have this inner layer of compassion and understanding, even in the face of adversity. I mean, it's not as if anything actually happened. It only lasted a few seconds. We'll probably be laughing about it in the future. Okay, maybe that's a step too far, but Alison will come round. Eventually. I know she will.

I pull out my phone. Before I tell Alison, I've got to warn Simon. Prepare him for the backlash. Wrongly, or rightly, we had an agreement. It's only fair I should let him know, tell him about the photographic evidence that's emerged, about the blackmailer.

Pushing my barely touched salad away from me, I take a deep breath and dial Simon's number, and it rings and rings and rings. My heart thuds harder with each *brrrrr*. I think I need the loo. I cross my legs under the table, phone pressed so hard against my ear it hurts. Maybe this isn't such a good idea after all, maybe I should just tell Alison and let her deal with him. I mean, I've done nothing wrong. Kate's right, Simon isn't my friend. I don't owe him anything. I'm about to hang up when the phone clicks.

'The number you are calling is currently unavailable. Please leave a message after the tone.'

Bloody answerphone. I wait out the long beep, drumming my fingers against the table, sticky with coffee spills and crumbs, and then I say, a little too loudly, 'Hi Simon, it's Lucy.' A mature woman in a dark suit looks up at me from her sandwich.' I lower my voice. 'I…um…' My breath catches in my throat. I can't breathe. 'Um…' I shoot to my feet, clumsily slide my bag onto my shoulder and head for the exit, heat prickling my face. 'Can you call me back please, Si?' I ask, shouldering past a young guy in jeans and an orange t-shirt as he steps into the café. 'It's really important…I um…' Traffic rings in my ears. Christ, what am I supposed to say? I don't think I've ever rung Simon. I only took his number down for emergencies; and to text him on his birthday. 'Look, ring me, okay? We need to talk. Something's happened.'

I end the call and sigh with relief. Well, at least I've made a start. He's bound to return my call. I head back to the office, looking at my phone in my hand. The time reads 13:03. I'm three minutes late. Gillian will be furious. But I did the right thing. Once I've spoken to Simon, I'll go round to Alison's. Today, hopefully, straight after work, and come clean. Then we can all take it from there. I'm pretty sure Alison won't file for divorce over one kiss…will she? For a moment I imagine Alison clearing the mantelpiece with one fell swoop of her hand, thundering up the stairwell, pulling out Simon's Savile Row suits and ripping them all to shreds in a mad frenzy before hurling them out of the loft conversion window. I shudder as I walk through the revolving doors of the Travelicious building and my phone vibrates in my hand. It's him!

'Simon, hi,' I gasp, rushing along the plush foyer.

'What's up, trouble?' My stomach clenches at the sound of his voice. It's the first time I've spoken to him since he tried to snog my face off. I thought I'd be okay but I'm not.

'Did you get my voicemail,' I snap, without any preambles.

'No, sorry. Just got a missed call from you. This phone is shit. I've got to change it. Bloody hot, isn't it?' He sounds breathless. I can hear commotion in the background. I wonder if he's still with Alison and Oscar, if they're getting on the train at Bath station, or arriving at Paddington.

'Are you back? How'd it go?'

'Great. Oscar loved it. Got back this morning. I've popped out to Waitrose for a few bits. Karen's coming over for dinner with that new bloke of hers.' The sixty-something silver fox – she showed me photos of on her phone last Saturday – very handsome, very Richard Gere. 'A thank-you dinner for having Leah and Barns for a few days. Ali said she invited you too but you can't make it. Not like you to turn down a free meal.'

Bloody cheek. I'm not that bad. 'Have you got some sort of virus? You sound dreadful.'

'No, I'm fine, just exhausted,' I reply, waiting at the lift doors.

'So, you coming then?'

'No, I can't,' I say irritably. 'I texted Alison earlier. Nessa's coming over. Long story.'

'Oh right. Okay,' he says, sounding surprised. I hear him sniffing and then he says, 'Work Nessa? As in clubbing it all weekend Nessa?' He laughs, as if he knows I'm lying. I wonder if Ali thinks so too. If they discussed it. 'Or might it be a certain gentleman gardener?' I can almost hear his lopsided grin down the phone. The lift doors open. People shuffle out, shouldering past me as I stand there like an ornament.

'Listen, Simon, we've got a problem.' I move away from the lifts, lean my back against the marble wall and tell him everything. 'And now,' I cry, 'she's threatening to tell Alison about us.'

'Us?' he snorts.

'Oh, you know what I mean,' I hit back. 'About you and me. That day. About you kissing me.'

There's a long deep silence. 'Simon?...Hello?' I move the phone away and look at the screen, it's smeared with finger marks and sweat from my ear – we're still connected. 'Hello? Can you hear me?'

'Yeah...sorry. I'm just a bit shocked, that's all. Wow. I didn't expect this. How do you know it's a she?'

'Oh, Simon, it's Jasmine, isn't it?' I plonk my bag on a window ledge and stare out at the traffic. 'Andrew told me she posted one of those save-the-date cards through my letterbox that Friday. So that places her at the scene. She must've been texting in her car with the engine off, seen us, and taken a photo. Bloody technology. It's the sort of thing she'd do. She loves playing mind games. The stupid cow's out to destroy me.'

'Now, hang on a minute. Don't you think you're being a bit para? I know you can't stand Jasmine and I don't blame you after what she did to you, but I don't think she's that vicious. It's probably just some kid having a laugh. One of your neighbours, or something.' In my mind's eye, I see the figure lunging out of view at Xenia and Spiros's bedroom window that night. But no, their daughter-in-law or granddaughter have no motive. They haven't even got Alison's number. It can't be them.

'You don't know Jasmine like I do, Simon. She's ruthless, vindictive,' I insist. 'Just think about it for a moment – anyone else would've gone straight to Alison and told her what you did. Anyone without an ulterior motive, that is.'

'Okay, okay, I get the picture.' I can almost see him cringing. This is all his bloody fault, not mine.

'Only a person with a vendetta against me would set me up like this.'

Simon exhales loudly down the phone. 'I don't know what to say. You know Jasmine better than I do, I suppose. She is…' He pauses. '*Was* your friend. What a fucking mess. So, what do you want to do? I could have a word with Andrew. Fish. Perhaps I can get him to warn her off. Just give–'

'No!'

'All right, steady on.'

'Please don't say anything to Andrew. That might make matters worse. You know what he's like, he'll twist everything, make it seem like this is all my fault. I'm already in his bad books. He wants me to sell…'

'The flat,' Simon finishes my sentence for me. He knows. Of course he does. He's probably known for weeks.

'I'm being blackmailed, Si. I know it's Jasmine. I feel it in my gut. I can't just stand by and let her get away with it – ruin everything for me. So, I've come up with a plan.'

'Go on.'

'I've decided to tell Alison the truth.' I can almost feel his blood running cold. I close my eyes, mustering the strength for the backlash, for his refusal to cooperate. But instead I'm met with an eerie silence. I speak first. 'I'm sorry, Simon, I've no other choice. I can barely concentrate on my work. I can't sleep. I…'

'Whoa, whoa!' Simon yells. 'Slow down.' There's a crackling sound and the beep of the till scanner. How can he carry on with his shopping after what I've told him. His marriage may be about to fall apart. 'Okay,' he sighs loudly. 'I think you're right. We should tell Alison the truth. But look…' He pauses. I can hear him clucking his tongue. 'Let me do it. I'll explain that it was all my fault, that I lost it for a moment, didn't know what I was doing. You've been through enough anyway.'

I'm taken aback by his cooperation. I thought he'd put up more of a fight. 'Are you sure?'

'Yes, I'm sure. It's my mess.' He sighs, then I hear him swearing under his breath and then the sound of the automated machine, *'Please wait for assistance.'* 'I did this, Lucy. It's my bad, okay?' I nod firmly, as if he can see me, glad that he's agreed that it's the right thing to do. 'I'm going to fix this.' Another long sigh and more till beeping, followed by *'Do you have a Waitrose card?'* and then another beep. 'I promise. You don't have to worry about a thing.'

Behind me, the lift doors ping then I hear the sound of female banter, and then a thought flies into my mind. 'What if Alison thinks I've been disloyal though?' I say to Simon. 'You know, for keeping it from her for over a week?'

'Don't worry, Lucy, I'll make sure she doesn't blame you for any of this. I promise. I'll explain what happened, how I lost it, made you keep quiet.' Silence, and then. 'I should've listened to you from the start. To be honest, this is a bit of a blessing. It's been eating away at me since it happened. I need to confess – tell her how fucked up I am.'

I immediately feel the tension dissipate, almost as if I've had a couple of drinks. I was dreading telling Alison. My heart would race whenever the thought entered my mind. I was even considering taking one of the beta-blockers my GP prescribed for when I do presentations at work.

'Are you sure you don't want me to be there when you tell her? I can explain how it all got out of hand, that you didn't…'

His long sigh hisses down the line. 'Thanks, but I'd rather it was just the two of us.' I can hear the bustle of doors clanking and the beep of a car alarm. He must be in the car park now. 'Whatever happens, I'm going to take it on the chin. I've no other choice, really, have I? Not with that photo in circulation. Do you know any good divorce lawyers.' He laughs lightly.

'I'm sure it won't come to that,' I say softly. 'When are you going to tell her?'

'When's the deadline?'

'Wednesday midnight.'

'Right, today's Mondaaaay.' I can hear him clucking his tongue in quick succession. 'Alison's going to see her cousin in Kent tomorrow.' Fiona, Karen's niece. Nice lady – small, round, with kind grey eyes and four children under the age of ten. I met her at Alison's fortieth birthday party. David, Fiona's husband, and Simon don't get on, so Alison always goes to see them alone with the kids. 'The kids have been looking forward to seeing their cousins all week, so I can't tell her before that. I don't want to spoil it for them. So, it'll have to be Wednesday evening,' he says matter-of-factly, as if he's booking me in to repair my washing machine. 'When I get in from work.'

'Okay.' I frown, a bit miffed he's cutting it so fine. But at least he's taking responsibility for his actions. 'Text me when you've told her and I'll give her a ring. I want to discuss it with her too, reassure her.' I take a breath, then blow the air out slowly through parted lips. 'I hope she doesn't freak out too much. I'm really worried.'

'I'm sure it'll be fine. It's not as if anything happened,' he says, miserably.

'Good luck, then,' I say a little cheerily.

'Thanks,' he replies, 'I'm gonna need it.'

'You won't forget to text me afterwards, will you?'

'You have my word.'

I murmur a few parting platitudes, then as I go to hang up he yells, 'And, Lucy…'

'Yes?'

There are a few moments of silence. I can hear his ragged breath down the phone. I hope he's not going to bottle it.

'I really am sorry, you know. I mean it.'

Chapter 6

'You might as well knock off early, Lucy,' Gillian says, shuffling through some papers on her desk. 'It's almost five.' This is my boss's way of thanking me for working through my lunch hour. Wednesdays aren't usually busy but today was manic. Apart from trips to the loo, I was glued to my desk. I didn't even do the coffee run, even though it was my turn. Still, I didn't mind – keeping busy meant less time to worry about what will happen when Simon tells Alison the truth tonight. Last night she rang me from Kent.

When I saw her name flashing on the screen I froze, wondered if they'd returned earlier than planned, if Simon had told her. But he hadn't. Our conversation was very normal. Well, as normal as can be considering I was harbouring this secret. She did ask if I was okay a couple of times, must've detected something in my tone. I fobbed her off, told her I was stressed about the sale of the flat and work, and she believed me. The poor thing.

We talked about her trip to Bath and Oscar's application, about Kent and Fiona's new kitchen extension, about how much Barney and Leah enjoyed the beach but were missing their dad and big brother. Pretty mundane stuff really. But there was one thing she mentioned before she hung up, which made my insides ache – Karen and Trevor were going to babysit for them on Wednesday night so she and Simon could go out for dinner.

Simon's idea. A date night, she called it, then laughed heartily. My heart bled for her. He was going to tell her in a packed restaurant, the prick. Why couldn't he do it in the comfort of their own home? But then, I reasoned, it'll be harder for Alison to make a scene in public – perhaps, this way, it'll force her to sit there and listen.

I reach for my bag at the foot of my desk. 'Thanks so much, Gillian,' I say, gathering my things. Getting home half an hour earlier will give me time to shower, stick something in the microwave and down a couple of glasses of wine before I hear from Simon, although I doubt they'll be back before nine. 'It's been manic today, hasn't it?'

Gillian ignores me, frowns at a document that Josephine from admin has just put in front of her. 'You can go too, Nessa,' Gillian commands, scribbling on the document and handing it back to Josephine, without so much as a glance in her direction.

Nessa, who's been quietly googling how to apply eyeshadow perfectly for the last ten minutes, looks round at me with a start, eyes wide. 'Thanks, boss,' she exclaims. Throwing a glance at Hannah and Sam, who are busily taking calls at the adjacent desks, Nessa rolls her chair back. Like me, she worked through her lunch break.

'Is she off her head?' Nessa whispers, leaning towards me.

I inhale her peppermint chewing gum as she stuffs her mobile phone into her handbag hurriedly and snatches her jacket off the back of her chair, folding it over an arm hastily, almost as if she's afraid that Gillian will change her mind. Hannah looks up at me from her desk with a miniscule frown, confirming two seats to Paris into her mouthpiece.

'Must be,' I say in hushed tones, sliding an arm into my cream linen jacket. 'Or maybe she's in lurrrve.'

Nessa pulls a face, 'Eww…'

We giggle as we head for the exit to the milieu of muffled voices, the whir of the air-con, fingers tapping speedily on keyboards. Even though Nessa is quite a lot younger than me, we still get on really well and will often be found in the pub around the corner after work, mostly bitching about Gillian over a bottle of wine. I think Gillian must be related to Hitler somewhere along the line, but Nessa insists that she's of alien descent. I'm tempted to suggest a swift one now – start the anaesthetising process in preparation for Simon's text. But then I don't want to sound drunk when I speak to Alison. Nessa does make me laugh though. I couldn't ask for a better stable mate. And she's a bloody good sales agent too; the second highest commission earner. After me, of course.

'Oh, and, girls,' Gillian calls out as I hold the door open for Nessa. We both stop, as if she's pulled on a handbrake and look at each other, startled.

'I knew there'd be a catch,' Nessa hisses, jaw clenched. 'I bet we'll have to do one of those weekend travel fairs in Birmingham again. I fucking hate that pokey B&B with that fat pervy landlord.'

'Thanks for today, you did great.'

Nessa pulls a *what-the-fuck?* face, 'No problem,' we yell in unison, as Nessa ducks under my arm and scurries towards the open lift.

'Definitely in love,' I say, pressing the ground floor button.

Outside, we head for Bond Street station to the hullabaloo of traffic and the distant sound of Caribbean steel drums. Linking her arm through mine, we huddle together and I listen as she tells me all about her weekend – she met a hot boy on Friday night at the club after I left. He rang her the very next day. They went out for pizza on Saturday, sipped pints at her local in

Clapham on Sunday before going to see a movie at the Cineworld in Wandsworth.

'And I'm seeing him again tonight, Luce,' she hollers above the beautiful sound of the street performers. The quartet bang loudly on their drums and shake their maracas at us as I drop a handful of change into a battered brown fedora. I can barely hear Nessa's voice above the commotion.

'He sounds really nice!' I yell. 'What's his name?'

'Romeo.'

'Seriously?'

'Yeah, it's his real name. Sam thinks it's a sign?' I'm not surprised. Sam's our office cupid. Nessa grins at the crowd of commuters. The music dwindles in the distance. 'Hannah said she knew her husband was *the one* after three dates. Imagine that. OMG, Lucy, Romeo is SO fit. He's two years younger than me, twenny-free.' I raise my eyebrows. 'I know, but he's mature for his age. His dad's English and his mum's French. Can you imagine what our kids will look like? A quarter English, a quarter French, a quarter African and a quarter Norwegian. What a combo, eh?' I tell her that her children will be beautiful and she grins, squeezing my arm. 'I know it's only been five days, but I think I'm in love. Do you believe in love at first sight, Lucy?' I hesitate. If she'd asked me this question five or six years ago I'd have said yes in a heartbeat, but now…

'I'm the wrong person to ask, Ness,' I admit. A tall young hipster couple walk towards us, holding hands then raise their arms, making a garland for us to scurry under. I miss that new-romance buzz. That can't-keep-your-hands-off-each-other stage. I wonder if I'll ever feel it again.

'I'm a bit of a cynic when it comes to romance these days,' I say truthfully. It's not that I don't believe in love, per se, but I don't think it happens very often. I think people just 'settle for' or get used to being with someone, or simply don't want to be alone. I used to think Alison had the perfect marriage until her husband came onto me. Simon's face flashes in my mind and my stomach tightens. 'Maybe you should take things slowly, Ness, see how it goes, eh?' My eyes dart to the Queen of Time clock on the Selfridges building. It's just gone five. With any luck I'll be home by six thirty. Simon and Alison will be heading off to the restaurant by then. I wonder if he'll tell her during mains, or if he'll wait until dessert, or until the meal is over.

'You okay, Lucy, you've been a bit quiet all day?' Nessa asks kindly.

'Yes, I'm fine.' I paint on a smile and pull her to me. 'Bit of a rough few days, and I can't…' Then I swear I hear someone calling out my name. I look over my shoulder, stumbling over uneven paving in my haste, and Nessa's arm instinctively tightens around mine. There's no one there. Perhaps I misheard, or it was meant for someone else. I'm not the only Lucy in town. I return my attention to Nessa, pulling a lose strand of hair away from my mouth. 'What was I saying? Oh, yes…I can't believe how busy…' And then I hear my name again, only louder this time, as if the person is in closer proximity.

'Cy! Over here!'

We stop walking. 'Did someone just call you?'

'I think so…'

We crane our necks, searching for the voice in the throng. Impatient commuters brush past us, someone tuts loudly and calls Nessa a knob under her breath. As expected, fiery Nessa challenges the thirty-something stern-looking woman in a red suit with shoulder pads; and then, to my utter dismay, they launch into a tirade about street etiquette, ironically taking up the entire pavement. Jesus, this is all I need, Nessa having a fight in the middle of Oxford Street. I'm going to be late now.

I pull Nessa by the arm, tell her we're going to miss our train, but she shrugs me off and points a finger at the woman, yelling at her – she's not the effing pavement police, she should learn some effing manners. A few commuters stop and take in the floorshow, laughing, pointing. I think they might be tourists, or students, I'm not sure. I'm pulling Nessa away from the furious woman, who has pulled out her phone and is threatening to call the police, when a figure leaps in front of me and I gasp.

'Hi. I…I…I thought I'd…I'd…I thought I'd missed you.' Teddy Fallon looks up at me, breathless, hands on his strong thighs. 'I was…I was calling you from… across the street…down…down… there. Hello.' He lifts a hand languidly at Nessa, as the pavement-police-woman stomps off in a huff. 'Boy, you girls are fast walkers.'

Nessa gives me a look that says, *you sly fox*, then turns to Teddy. 'Helllllo,' she coos, her anger melting away like a snowflake. 'Vanessa, but everyone calls me Nessa.' Then she shifts her weight onto one leg and holds her chin. 'You look really familiar. Are you on the telly? No wait, it was on the internet. You're a vlogger, aren't you?' Narrowing her big brown eyes, she studies him. Teddy shakes his head, looking bewildered, goes a bit red. 'Oh, my gosh.' Nessa clicks her fingers. 'You were at the club on Friday, right?' Nessa never forgets a face.

Teddy nods and straightens, says he remembers her too. 'Vanessa, what a beautiful name,' he smiles, taking her extended hand, 'Edward Fallon, but everyone calls me Teddy.'

We all fall silent for a few moments. People buzz up and down the street. Traffic hisses. Teddy catches his breath while Nessa takes him in, eyes travelling down the length of his body. He's wearing a lose-fitting taupe suit and a pink cotton shirt, open at the neck. His hair is neatly combed to the side and he smells as if he's bathed in a pool of delicious aftershave.

Whoever he's meeting must be important; he's really made an effort. Gosh, I didn't expect to see him again. Talk about a small world. 'Teddy, what a lovely surprise,' I say, smiling. 'Are you here on business, or is it social?' I laugh lightly.

He gives me an incredulous look. 'What do you mean?'

'What brings you to smoggy central?' I'm sure he told me on Friday night, when he could get a word in, that he doesn't come into town because of the congestion charge. I even remember him calling the mayor a sadistic dick. 'Isn't north London your manor?'

'Yes, but I do venture outside the borders,' he says with a note of sarcasm.

Nessa's eyes flit from me to Teddy in quick succession, as if she's watching a tennis match at Wimbledon, and I suddenly feel awkward. I've got to get a move on. Alison is going to need me. I can't waste time standing around chatting.

'Um…well, anyway, it was nice…' I begin but then someone knocks into me hard and the strap of my bag slides off my shoulder. Teddy lunges forward and catches it, asks if I'm okay, then yells into the six-foot-seven, four-foot-wide bald man's back, telling him to watch it, mate. The man stops and turns, and Teddy takes a step forward, fists balled by his sides, daring the bald giant to retaliate; and for a moment I think he might. My stomach constricts. Jeez, what's wrong with everyone today? I can't cope with another altercation. I look up at the cloudless sky, pattered with white plumes, and remember Andrew calling them chemical trails, that the government is poisoning the population, messing with our minds. I poopooed his theory away, but now I think he may have been right all along. Looking at the man, I will him to go away, but he just glares at me, lips twisted, and then, as if by magic, he dismisses Teddy with a wave and melts into the crowd.

‘Blooming coward,’ Teddy mutters, thrusting a hand through his freshly washed-looking hair, face pink. ‘This is why I hate coming into town these days. Everyone is in such a bloody hurry.’

Nessa and I shake our heads in agreement, the knot in my stomach untangling. Teddy definitely isn’t a city boy. I can imagine him living on a ranch, surrounded by farm animals, four children, and a yogi wife who grows all her own vegetables and refuses to dye her greying hair. I offer Teddy a small smile, then look at my wrist even though I forgot to wear my watch today.

‘Anyway, have a great evening, Teddy. Pop in and say hello next time you’re passing, yeah.’ But as I go to walk away I feel his hand around my forearm.

‘Wait, what do you mean?’ he says in disbelief. Letting go of my arm, his eyes flit from me to Nessa, resting on Nessa worriedly, eyebrows knotted.

Nessa shakes her head, big silver hoop earrings swinging in her thick copper curls; then she shrugs, as if to say “nothing to do with me, mate.”

‘Look, I’m sorry, Lucy,’ Teddy says, palms up, ‘but weren’t we? I thought that…you haven’t forgotten, have you?’ Clearly, I have because I don’t know what the hell he’s talking about.

I scratch my head, shooting a glance at Nessa, who, in turn, raises her perfectly shaped eyebrows at me, chewing furiously. ‘I um…er…’ And then it occurs to me that I left work half an hour earlier today. Oh no, was Teddy making his way to see me at Travelicious? ‘Sorry, Teddy, was I meant to look up some flights for you? I can’t quite…’ And just at that moment a conversation we had at the pub on Friday night flies into my mind – he’s just returned from the bar with our second round of drinks. We’re talking about holidays. He’d love to go on a Mediterranean cruise but is strapped for cash. My cheeks burn.

I offered him a twenty percent family and friends discount if he books through me. Gillian is going to go spare. I've used that discount code on flights for Alison, Karen, my mum's friend Beatrice, Erika from next door but one, a lovely German lady who shares my love of books, and for Xenia and Spiros next door. Several times, in fact, they're always flying off to Cyprus. I'm not even sure I've any allowance left.

'About that discount…'

'Our date?' he jumps in.

Date? What date? I definitely didn't arrange another date with him. He's obviously confusing me with someone else. 'Our date?' I repeat, nonplussed.

'Yeah, you promised me a drink, remember?' He nods when he says this, as if I have amnesia. I shake my head – he's completely lost me. 'On Saturday morning. In your bedroom.'

Nessa, who's been quietly observing, as if listening to a suspense novel on Audible, takes a sharp intake of breath when he says *bedroom.* 'Sorry,' she murmurs, clamping a hand over her full red lips. I look at her in horror. What did he have to say that for? I know that look. She thinks I shagged him. I'll never hear the end of it. It'll be all round the office by tomorrow morning. I love Nessa dearly, but she's terrible at keeping secrets – especially juicy ones like this.

'Nessa, it's not…' I begin, then huffily twist my body towards Teddy, rubbing my temple. 'Look, Teddy, I–'

'When I woke you up, remember?' Teddy interjects. For the love of God, can today get any worse? I tighten my lips and give him a look. Nessa's chewing so fast, I fear her jaw will collapse.

Teddy looks at Nessa for clarification, as if she's my carer then back at me, 'You said you owed me a drink,' he insists, face pink. I didn't say that. This man is deluded. 'Your exact words were, if I remember correctly,' he says, '*Thanks, you're a star. I owe you a drink.*'

No, he's mistaken…I didn't…and then it hits me.

'Oh, yes, I did,' I admit, feeling my cheeks flush. But it was only a figure of speech. I didn't mean it. Teddy beams at me, pleased that I've remembered. 'But I didn't mean today, Teddy,' I explain, moving slightly to allow a good-looking man in a three-piece navy suit to walk past. 'I just meant one day.' As in never, I want to say.

But he doesn't seem to take the hint. He raises his arms as if I've won him in a prize draw, almost knocking out a young ponytailed woman with dark eyes and thick rectangular glasses. Reaching out, but not quite touching her, he apologises immediately but her face is tight and unforgiving. 'No time like the present,' he beams at me, as the tight-and-unforgiving lady shoulders past him, muttering, white cables hanging from her ears. I can't say I really blame her; we are hogging the pavement and it is rush hour.

I back towards a shop window, out of the way, trying to explain to a very confused-looking Teddy that there's been a misunderstanding. There's no way I can go out with him tonight. Alison is going to need me when Simon confesses. I've got to be there for her. End of. I look at Teddy and a trickle of guilt creeps into my veins. I do feel a bit sorry for him. But is it really my fault that he decided to be so spontaneous? Has he never heard of texting or phoning?

'I'd better go,' Nessa says, looking at her watch. 'I don't want to miss my train. I'm meeting Romeo at nine. I'll see you tomorrow, Luce. Nice meeting you, Teds.'

Teddy smiles at her and nods. But as she goes to leave, I snatch her arm. She can't leave me here with him. 'No, wait,' I cry. Nessa frowns, eyes flicking to the fistful of her double-breasted check blazer in my hand – Stella McCartney.

Ridiculously expensive. A gift from an ex-boyfriend. I let go and compose myself, clearing my throat. 'We've got that…that THING to do tonight, remember.' I squint one eye at her like a freemason but she shakes her head, confused. Oh, come on, Nessa, help me out here. 'For your mum.' I flutter my eye at her again as if there's something in it.

'Oh, yeah.' She nods vigorously, finally catching on, dark eyes shining. 'That birthday thingy…surprise…cake. Birthday cake!'

'Yes!!…That!' I give Teddy a nervous smile, but he's no fool.

Taking a step back, he holds up his hands in submission. 'It's okay – no problem.' A few lads in sharp suits belt past us, laughing loudly, leaving a trail of strong cologne behind them as they make a beeline for The Railway Tavern. Teddy swallows hard and his Adam's apple moves in his throat. 'I shouldn't have turned up out of the blue. It's just that. Well, I thought that…Oh, never mind.'

Sucking in my lips, I stare down at my navy heels, feeling awkward, then glance up at Nessa. The poor girl looks mortified.

'Bloody hell,' Teddy says, running a hand over his face, hand in pocket. 'This does all seem a bit stalkerish, doesn't it? I'm sorry. I'll go. Sorry, Lucy. Nice seeing you again, Nessa. I'm…' he hesitates. 'Sorry. Enjoy your evening, girls.'

'Nice…' Nessa begins, but he's gone. We watch as he snakes through a throng of commuters in haste towards the bus stop. 'You've got no shame, Lucy Harper,' Nessa hisses, 'Poor, lovely man.'

I snatch her by the hand and start walking. A bus horn blares, traffic hisses in my ears.

'I didn't have you down as being the love 'em and leave 'em type.'

'I'm not! We didn't sleep together, Nessa. You don't understand. It's complicated.'

Nessa looks over her shoulder, giving Teddy a wave as I drag her along Oxford Street, '*Phwoar*. He's got a nice arse. If you don't want him…'

'Nessa! He's old enough to be your dad. I thought you were all loved up with Leo, anyway.'

'Romeo,' she corrects, falling in line with me. 'Lucy, wait.' She snatches my hand to still me and her long nails graze my skin. 'I totally get that you don't trust men after what happened with your ex, but look at his little face.' I look round. Teddy is on the kerbside, waiting for a break in the traffic, wind blowing lightly in his chestnut hair.

'I hardly know him…I've got to…I must…'

'Did you meet him online?'

'No,' I hiss, 'he's Alison's new gardener and I–'

'Your bezzie mate Alison? Aww. He came all this way to see you, don't you think that's romantic? And he had a go at that bodybuilder who tried to bash you up, even though he was twice his size. You should start dating again, juicy Lucy. Show that pathetic Scotsman that you've totally moved on.'

'I can't…I'm not ready. I–'

'Can't, or won't?' she says at Teddy who's still waiting on an overcrowded pavement. 'He seems so nice. Like a keeper.' Alison's exact words. 'Don't let this one get away.' I open my mouth to protest but before I can speak, Nessa cups her hands around her mouth and yells, 'TEDS!' A few drunken looking tourists in colourful t-shirts and Union Jack top hats stop and look around, bewildered.

'Nessa,' I hiss, eyes darting everywhere, 'stop it. You're making a scene.'

But she ignores me. 'Teddy!' she shouts. The lights go red. The green man flashes. The pedestrian crossing beeps.

‘Shut up,’ I exclaim. ‘I’ve got to get home.’

‘TEDDY FALLON,’ she screams, and everyone turns around apart from him. ‘Bloody hell, Luce, is he deaf or summink?’ He’s about to cross the road, disappear from my life completely, when she sticks two fingers into her mouth and whistles loudly. Finally he turns around, flummoxed. ‘COME BACK,’ Nessa shouts, arms flailing in the air. ‘LUCY’S DYING OF THIRST.’

Chapter 7

Teddy rests his cutlery against the empty plate in front of him and leans back in his chair, he's absolutely stuffed, he tells me, couldn't eat another thing. I spear a few pieces of penne in creamy leek and pea sauce with my fork. I don't think I've ever seen anyone devour a plate of spaghetti carbonara so quickly. He must work up quite an appetite with all that gardening.

I check him out as I chew my pasta while he taps on the screen of his phone, eyebrows knitted in concentration. He's better looking than I remember, nice smile, warm, kind eyes. I'm not sure if this is because I saw him through a bleary-eyed hungover haze four days ago, or if he's just growing on me; and he smells bloody delicious too – Dior Sauvage, he told me earlier as the waitress seated us at a table for two, a gift from his mum last Christmas.

Clearly, Mrs Fallon has good taste, although I wish she'd suggested giving that crumpled shirt of his a once-over with the iron before he left home. It looks as if he pulled it off the washing line and threw it on in haste. Actually, no, on closer inspection it has the lines and creases of a new shirt that's just been unpacked. Either way, I expect, Mrs F had more pressing things to do, like prepare manifestos, or arrange committee meetings. She's a local councillor – Tories. Divorced his barrister father when Teddy was nineteen but kept the family name.

‘Fallon has more of a ring to it than Oakey, particularly as her first name is Carrie,’ Teddy said, as we studied the menus over large vodka and tonics, and we both laughed as if it was the funniest thing ever. I wondered then if it was her real name, or if he used that line as an ice-breaker with women. It certainly worked with me, because I felt completely at ease with him after that. I could almost feel the tension melting away, or was that the vodka? Maybe a bit of both.

I must admit, I’m not really into politics but his mother’s status has impressed me. Teddy has quite an interesting background. I’ve discovered quite a lot about him over dinner. He’s quite sporty, for a start, swims at the local pool twice a week, which didn’t surprise me given his athletic body; enjoys playing rugby and goes to the gym three mornings a week. Of course, this made me feel completely inadequate, so I bigged up my fitness regime, told him that I’ve got a personal trainer (I couldn’t possibly afford one), how I plucked up the courage to join a gym when my marriage broke down, even though I felt self-conscious, and now go five times a week (it’s closer to three. Okay, two).

It did the trick. I registered the look of approval in his eyes over his wine glass, before swiftly reminding me that he’s a fully-fledged member of the divorce club, almost as if he didn’t think I believed him when he told me on Friday night; perhaps he assumed that was the reason why I was reluctant to go out with him again. People are strange. I wish I could read their minds sometimes. Anyway, he has two boys, five and seven, who live in Whitstable with their mother. That’s where Lydia, his ex, is originally from. She moved back there when they separated so that she could be closer to her family, who live in Canterbury. He sees the kids every other weekend and doesn’t mind the long drive, enjoys motorway driving, finds it relaxing. Living in a four-bedroom detached house in Surrey was a dream, but Lydia cleaned him out when they divorced and he's now staying with his mum until he sorts himself out.

'So, where's Mum's?' I ask, shovelling another forkful of pasta into my mouth, whilst throwing a glance at my phone as it lights up – a Twitter notification, not my anticipated text from Simon.

'Cockfosters. She's got a nice little bungalow, leafy quiet road,' he replies.

I gasp, tell him it's a small world, I grew up in Southgate, went to Frogmore Comprehensive, not that far from where he's living now. The common ground seems to work its magic because he suddenly seems to open up to me.

'I probably shouldn't be telling you this,' he begins. A juicy bit of gossip. I lean forward in my chair. 'But Lydia had a violent temper. That's the reason why we split up. I stuck it out for as long as I could,' he confesses. 'You know, for the sake of the kids. But then one night.' He pauses, touches the edge of his plate. 'She just lost it. Pushed me down the stairs in a jealous rage.' I stare at him aghast, fork in mid-air. 'I know, shocking, isn't it? I spent a week in hospital.'

'Bloody hell, Teddy, she sounds like a maniac,' I say, feeling a bit stupid for fretting over a few mysterious text messages when other people have real problems. I push the half-eaten plate of pasta to the side, and instinctively reach out across the table and touch his fingers lightly. 'I'm so sorry,' I offer sincerely, 'it must've been horrendous.'

Teddy's eyes flick to my hand and I pull it away. I don't want to give him the wrong idea. Men aren't the same as women, are they? He might take my concern, my compassion for something else, like Simon did.

'It's okay.' Teddy rubs his face tiredly. 'Not many people know, so please keep it to yourself. I don't want the kids finding out – hating their mother.' A secret – one he hasn't even shared with his therapist employer. I want to hug him for trusting me more than Alison. 'Lydia was never aggressive around them,' he goes on. 'They're oblivious. She loves them to bits. They're her world.'

Elbows on table, he steeples his fingers and rests his chin under his thumbs. 'It was sporadic, anyway. Lyd was okay most of the time – just tetchy, but I could deal with that. Anyway, it's all done and dusted. We get on fine as mates. Well, most of the time.'

Straightening up, he leans back in his chair and starts folding the edges of a napkin, like origami. 'I try to keep on her good side to make sure I see the boys. I must admit, she's very good with visitation. I see them, more or less, whenever I want. I'm taking them on holiday next year with Mum. We're going to Portugal. One of Mum's colleagues has a villa out there, right on the seafront, with a swimming pool and everything.'

I'm quite astonished that he's being so reasonable, given his ex-wife's a thug, and, fuelled with several glasses of Cabernet Sauvignon, I don't hold back from expressing my opinion. 'I'm sorry, but Lydia sounds a bit unstable to me.' Teddy shrugs and takes a mouthful of red wine. 'Didn't social services get involved?' I ask. 'After she pushed you down the stairs, I mean. What with the kids and everything?'

He pauses for a fraction of a second, glass in mid-air, jaw clenched. Damn it, I shouldn't have asked him such a personal question. He's going to think I'm a nosey cow. Any moment now he's going to tell me to mind my own bloody business. I gear myself up to retract the question, apologise, when his face softens. 'I didn't report it,' he admits. 'I just told the hospital that it was an accident at work, fell over a wheelbarrow, forgot it was behind me.'

My eyes widen. How could he let her get away with something like that? I'm about to tell him that he's too soft, that

I would have gone straight to the police, especially if I had kids, when Mum's face flies into my mind, spiralling me into the past like a whirlpool. We're in A&E, I'm fifteen, she's lying to the doctor about her fall, egging me on to back up her story with one of her looks, letting Dad off the hook for dislocating her shoulder, for hurting her.

'I'm sure you did what you thought was best,' I say instead; no one knows what goes on behind closed doors, nothing is black and white. I've no right to judge Teddy Fallon. Besides, I don't even know Lydia, or anything about her.

'If I'm honest, it was more of an accident,' he says lightly, and I immediately get the feeling that he regrets telling me. 'She'd been to the pub with her mates, didn't come home until gone midnight. We were at the top of the stairwell, got into a bit of a spat, I asked where she'd been all night. Noah, our youngest, couldn't settle, wanted his mum, and things got a bit...well, heated. We had a full-blown slanging match and then she pushed me – didn't realise how close I was to the step and down I went.' He whistles and makes a diving movement with his hand.

'Fractured two ribs. She was really cut up about it afterwards – kept apologising, couldn't do enough for me. That really shook her up and things were good for a while. She even agreed to see her GP, you know, for some counselling.' I look at him, stunned. The poor man has literally been to hell and back. He holds my gaze for a few moments, as if he's trying to read me, work out what I'm thinking, and then he says, 'Oh God, I'm boring you with all this crap about my shambles of a marriage. Let's talk about something else.'

'No,' I insist, intrigued, 'go on. Was she ever violent again?'

Exhaling loudly, he fiddles with the serviette again. 'No, but the rows got worse, then she started accusing me of sleeping around.' He looks up at me sharply. 'I wasn't. I'm a one-man woman.'

'Man.' I laugh, and he looks at me blankly. 'A one-woman man.'

'Isn't that what I said?' He shakes his head, 'Sorry. Anyway, I couldn't put up with her jealous rages any longer. The relationship was toxic. I had to get out.' I nod slowly, lips curved downwards. 'But she's a good mum,' he adds hastily, nodding furiously at the napkin, which he's folded into a triangle. I stay silent, allowing him to let off steam, get it off his chest. 'Loves the boys to bits and I know she'd never hurt them. It was just me. I somehow irritated her, got under her skin.' I know the feeling. I had the same effect on Andrew. 'She was always so uptight.' He darts a glance at me. 'You know, the kids, the house, the bills, and work didn't help – all that stress.'

'What does she do?' I ask gently, folding my arms over the table.

'She's a teacher – science. Kids are both at school now and they have the same holidays so it works out well. Everyone likes her – the mums, the teachers, the pupils, she's popular. But they don't know the real Lydia, what she's capable of.'

I watch as he knocks back a glug of cabernet, and I'm not sure if it's the bitter tone of his voice, or the look in his eye when her name is on his lips, but I'm not sure he's completely over Lydia.

'Are you still in love with her?' I blurt, the words flying out of my mouth like a bullet before I can stop them. For a moment, everything seems to still, and he just looks at me, speechless, goes a bit red. Damn, why did I say that? What's wrong with me tonight? I'm not usually inquisitive. It's the drink. The stress of Simon and Alison. 'Teddy, I'm s–'

'Nah, not anymore,' he interjects. 'I was though, deeply, but it was never reciprocated. I don't think Lydia ever really loved me.' He sighs at the empty plate in front of him. 'I knew I was punching above my weight when I started going out with her, everybody said so. Mum even tried talking me out of it on the day of our wedding.' I raise my eyebrows. Wow, Mrs Fallon really is hands on. 'I know, but she meant well,' he explains, registering my surprise. 'She could see beyond. Mother's intuition and all that. I should've listened. Hindsight is a wonderful thing.'

An awkward silence hangs between us. Cutlery clatters against plates. Muffled voices amplify. This is getting a bit heavy. I'm about to change the subject, talk about something else when he says, 'I think she only married me because she wanted to have kids before it was too late. We're from different worlds. I didn't fit in with her circle, think Love Island, pool parties, skimpy outfits, fake tans.' I roll my eyes. I've never watched it but Nessa won't stop droning on about it at work. 'Exactly. It's ironic that I'm the one who walked out on our marriage in the end, isn't it? It was odds-on that she'd leave me.' He laughs lightly and I nod, smiling, waiting for a pause so that I can steer him off the subject of his ex-wife.

'So, your gardening busin–?' I begin.

'Jesus, I spent so much money on her,' he complains, talking over me, and I hunch into my shoulders. 'I took her and the kids to Dubai a couple of years ago. Cost me a bloody fortune, that did.' What an odd thing to say about your family, your wife, someone you loved at the time. 'Lydia's materialistic,' he explains, picking up on my vibe. 'Really into brands and labels. All my credit cards were maxed out.' I nod mutely – she sounds like a gold-digger. 'I even bought her a Louis Vuitton bag and purse from Selfridges once – no occasion, just to surprise her. I thought it'd make her love me.' He laughs nervously, making confetti out of the edges of the serviette. 'And it did, for all of five minutes.'

I don't know what to say. It's not my place and I don't know the whole story, but I think it's time we got the bill. I drum my fingers against the table. 'Well, I'm glad you told me. And don't worry, I won't say anything to anyone.' Leaning back, I take another small sip of wine, reciprocate a smile with a twenty-something dark-haired waitress as she breezes by our table, slim hips swaying in her black apron. I'm tempted to ask her for the bill, but perhaps I ought to wait until he suggests it. I don't want to come across as being rude.

'Alison knows about Lydia.'

I almost choke on my wine. 'Alison?' So, he did share his secret with her. I glance at my blank screen. Why hasn't Simon been in touch? It's been hours. Surely, he must've told her by now. A sense of unease filters through my body. Has he been trying to contact me; did I miss any WhatsApp notifications? Network coverage is a bit crap in *Bellissimo Ristorante*. I unlock my phone and scroll through the screens quickly, checking for any missed notifications – nothing.

The temptation to contact him bubbles in my stomach. I know I should wait for him to contact me, like he promised, but before I can stop myself, I type:

> *How's it going?*

I look at the text. No, that doesn't sound right. I delete it then as I go to type again Teddy says, 'Yeah, Alison's really easy to talk to, isn't she?' He gives me a lazy smile. 'Probably because of her job. That Simon's a lucky sod, isn't he?' I draw my hand back from my phone, deciding to wait it out. Simon probably hasn't told her yet, or maybe they're in the thick of it. 'They seem really happy together. Gives us old dropouts a bit of hope, eh?'

I nod mutedly. If only he knew. 'Alison's a rock.'

'Must be great to have such lovely friends.' He smiles, rolling up the sleeve of his pink shirt. 'Jesus, it's so hot in here.

Anyway, enough about me and my boring love life. Tell me more about Lucy Harper.'

I run a hand along the zip of my handbag, which is on the chair next to me, feeling the smooth metal teeth beneath my fingertips. 'Not much to tell really,' I admit, and then my phone pings and my heart stops. It's Simon. It's got to be. He's told her. My heartbeat accelerates. 'I'm sure I told you all you need to know last Friday,' I say absently, then as I go to grab my phone it pings again. It's definitely him. 'Sorry,' I say, snatching it off the table. 'I've got to get this. I'm expecting an important message.' It's him.

> U there?

> Alison knows everything

Oh, God, he's done it. Good. I text back hurriedly: *>Is she okay?*

I watch the bubble and three dots pulsating on my screen, he's typing.

> Will be

Will be? What the hell is that supposed to mean? I message back, index finger flying over the miniature keyboard: *>Out atm. Shall I ring?*

I wait and I wait, heart in mouth, but he doesn't reply. I'm about to text again when the bubble and the dots ripple along the screen.

>No, don't spoil ur eve. She's gone bed – migraine. Let her sleep on it.

'Oh God, no.' My heart cracks a little. Poor Alison. She must be feeling awful.

'Is everything okay, Lucy?' Teddy's snaps me out of my texting bubble.

My head jerks up and I look at him like a startled cat, for a moment I forgot he was even here. I'm about to tell him that it's work related, not to worry, when a female voice says. 'Are we all done here?' A tall young waitress with pale skin and mousy brown hair is hovering over us with a painted smile.

'Lucy?' he probes, ignoring her. 'Are you all right?'

'Yes.' I look up at the waitress, catching sight of her name tag pinned on her black and white stripy long-sleeved t-shirt – Megan. 'I'm sorry. It was lovely, big portions.'

'That's no problem at all. Would you like to see the dessert menus?' We both shake our heads, no. Megan picks up our plates. 'No problem.'

'I wouldn't mind another bottle of wine though,' Teddy says, looking at me hopefully. Another bottle, on top of this one and the large vodka and tonic aperitif. 'But if you've got to go…' He gestures at my phone. Megan shifts her weight onto one leg, glances at the entrance as the door swings open, smile waning.

I dither, look at my phone – 18:57. If we leave now I'll be home by eight thirty. Too early to go to bed. I picture myself sitting in my living room staring at the TV screen, worrying about Alison, wanting to ring but not being able to. 'Actually, more wine would be lovely,' I say, even though I know I've had enough, even though I know that one more glass will make me slurry, that I'll end up with a stinking hangover in the morning. 'It's just work,' I explain, slipping the phone into my open handbag. 'I'll deal with it tomorrow morning.'

Teddy's smile reaches his soft brown eyes. 'Another bottle then, please.'

'Yes, sir, no problem.' No problem must be Megan's favourite turn of phrase. 'I'll fetch another bottle.' I watch as she glides across the floor, phone in the back pocket of her black jeans, long plait almost reaching her waist, until she disappears down the winding stairwell.

'So, come on, tell me more about you. I know all about Andrew and Jasmine – bloody pillocks.' I raise my eyebrows.

He remembers their names. I'm impressed. 'But I want to know more about you…any brothers, sisters?'

'I hold up a finger, swallowing a sip of wine. 'One sister – lives in Spain with her boyfriend and baby son. My mum lives in Brighton. She moved down there when my dad passed away, always wanted to live by the sea. She's got a lovely home with a sea view. Adores it there.'

And now it's his turn to be sympathetic. 'I'm sorry. Losing a parent sucks.'

'Don't be,' I say stiffly, throwing a glance at a rowdy group of diners at an adjacent table who've just erupted in laughter. 'I didn't shed a tear when he died.'

Teddy puffs out his cheeks, eyes widening. I've shocked him. 'Tough childhood, eh?'

'Something like that.' And I'm not sure whether it's the wine, or because Teddy has been so upfront with me about his past, or because I'm feeling so wrecked about Alison, probably all three, but the next thing I know I'm telling him everything – Kate and I grew up with a monster of a father. A misogynist who wanted sons to keep the family name going but ended up with two girls instead. Constantly blamed Mum for giving him daughters. We were never good enough, strong enough, clever enough. He'd push our mum around, the odd punch in the gut, the occasional shove, once hard enough to dislocate her shoulder. But it wasn't just physical. Mum was a victim of, what we now call, coercive control – chipped away at her confidence with his acid tongue, day after day, year after year, until he finally broke her.

'Was he violent with you and Kate?' Teddy asks, once I've stopped talking.

I nod, take a sip. 'Yes. Well, not exactly. He used to.' I swallow, stomach knotting. 'He used to smother us.'

'What?' Teddy whispers.

‘He’d put his hand over us like this,’ I explain, palm against my face. ‘Then push us against the wall, or down on the sofa, and hold us there, suffocating us with his reeking hands. Sometimes…’ I pause, muster strength, ‘sometimes he’d do it while we were asleep. To wake us up for school, he’d say. Better than any alarm clock.’

‘Jesus.’ Teddy gasps, clearly shocked. ‘Didn’t your mum stop him?’

I nod again. ‘Tried to. Many times. He was an alpha male.’ I pause, take a breath. ‘A pillar of the community. But behind closed doors,’ I add a little loudly, and a forty-something man with longish blond hair looks round at me from the rowdy table, napkin tucked into the collar of his shirt and for a moment he morphs into my father.

Squeezing my eyes shut, I inhale the aroma of garlic and herbs, batting the image of my dad away. ‘He died in the line of duty.’ My eyes snap open. ‘He was a fireman. A proper hero.’ Teddy looks at me mutely, his face unreadable. He probably thinks I’m a crazy person, wishes he’d stayed home. ‘Anyway,’ I sniff, twirling my silver heart pendant between my fingers. ‘That’s water under the bridge.’

We sit in painful silence for a few moments. Teddy shifts awkwardly in his chair. I look around the restaurant, suddenly aware of background music. I think it’s Adele, and then I feel Teddy’s eyes on me, studying me beneath the flickering candlelight. I tap my index finger against the table – tap, tap, tap. The Gaggia machine rumbles. Someone’s phone rings. Oh God, why didn’t I just keep my big mouth shut? He’s going to try to psychoanalyse me now, want to help, be my hero. I’m so bloody stupid sometimes.

‘My uncle was a fireman,’ he says as his phone buzzes on the table. He picks it up, looks at the screen, then ignores it. ‘Always smelt of smoke, no matter what.’

I flash him a quick smile, grateful that he didn't probe me, patronise me. 'Mine used to drench himself in a horrid-smelling cologne to get rid of it. I still can't stand the smell of it.'

'That's understandable, our sense of smell is closely linked to memory, and sandalwood is quite a potent scent.'

I frown. 'How do you know it was sandalwood?'

'What?' He tops up our glasses with the last dregs from the bottle. 'You told me, didn't you? How else could I know?'

'Did I? When?' I've no recollection of mentioning it. It's not something I like to talk about. I rub the back of my stiff shoulder – the price of sitting in front of a computer all day.

'Um…Friday night, I think, or was it Saturday?' He holds his chin, narrowing his eyes. 'No, it was definitely Saturday. After you had that nightmare.'

'Oh, right…okay.' I can't remember much about Friday night, but I must've told him. 'Anyway, my dad loved it. I swear there was a half-empty bottle in every room.' His phone buzzes again. 'It's all he ever wanted for his birthday and Christmas. Mum used to buy him a bottle on Father's Day and say it was from us when we were little. Does Lydia do that for you?'

And then suddenly his face pales. 'Yeah? Um…' he murmurs distractedly, looking over my shoulder. 'Shit,' he mutters, 'I don't fucking believe it.'

I turn in my seat. A couple are tucking into their meals. A man is dining alone, face lit up by his laptop. Two women, mid-to-late-forties, are studying menus, glasses perched on the bridge of their noses. 'What is it? What's wrong?'

'Actually, do you mind if we take a rain check on that bottle of wine.' And before I can answer he grabs a waitress by the wrist, tells her to cancel the wine and bring us our bill right away. 'Sorry,' he says, flustered. He's on his feet now, shrugging on his jacket. 'I've just seen someone I know. One of

Lydia's school friends. I don't want her to see me. We didn't part on good terms.'

'Oh, right. Okay. I'll…um…' I get to my feet and start gathering my things as the waitress returns with the bill and a card payment monitor.

Glancing at the bill, Teddy slides his hand into the inside pocket of his jacket, frowns, pats the side pockets, frowns some more, then he thrusts his hands into his trouser pockets, the colour draining from his face. 'Oh, bloody hell!!! I left my damned wallet in my damned corduroy jacket.'

I'm not sure whether to laugh or cry. 'It's okay.' I smile. I wasn't going to let him pay for all of it, anyway. 'I'll pay. I owe you, anyway, for Friday night.' I look at the bill, gasp inwardly, then hand my card to the waitress. I'll have to sell a few more airline tickets this month.

And as the waitress taps away on the machine a voice says, 'Hey, I thought it was you.' Lydia's friend is standing in front of us, hazel eyes sparkling against her firm, tanned skin. I take a step back and tap my passcode into the card terminal, darting a look at Teddy. His face is on fire.

'Susanna, hi,' Teddy says, feigning surprise. 'Wow, you look great.' Leaning forward, he air kisses her on both cheeks.

The card terminal buzzes, then spits out a long strip of paper. 'Thank you, madam,' says the waitress, handing me the receipt.

'Long time, no see,' Susanna says, shooting a glance at me as she tucks her long blonde fringe behind her ear. She has a posh-ish west London accent. 'What brings you to smoggy London? I thought you were a suburban boy these days.'

'I am,' he says, forehead beading with sweat. 'I just had a meeting with…um…' He looks at me helplessly.

‘His solicitor.’ I thrust out a hand. ‘Lucy Harper. Wills and Probate.’ Teddy rolls back on the balls of his feet, hands in pockets, throwing me a look of gratitude.

‘Susanna Hawkins,’ she says warmly, then turns back to Teddy. ‘Jesus, I heard about what happened. Are you okay? Did you–’

Teddy doesn’t let her finish. ‘Don’t mean to sound rude but we’ve got a cab waiting outside. Lovely to see you, Souz, say hello to Tom.’

And with this he swiftly shepherds me towards the door, muttering in my ear – he can’t stand the sight of her, pretentious, nosey bitch, and as we reach the exit, I glance over my shoulder and just about manage to catch a glimpse of an incredulous-looking Susanna Hawkins returning to her seat.

Chapter 8

Big fat raindrops are splashing onto my shoes, leaving marks the size of plums on the uneven pavement. My head is throbbing. The air pressure before a storm often gives me a bit of a headache, but, thanks to that red wine, this one is bordering a migraine. I'm sure I drank most of the bottle. I berate myself for not listening to my instincts, for being such a people pleaser. I should've stuck to a glass of white wine with my meal instead of agreeing to a bottle of Cabernet Sauvignon. But Teddy's eyes lit up when he saw the Torres Las Mulas on the wine list, said it was one of his favourites and I didn't want to be a spoilsport. Cancelling that second bottle when he clapped eyes on that Susanna Hawkins woman was probably a blessing in disguise.

I turn into my road and a sudden gust almost blows me off the kerb, turning my brand new navy umbrella inside out. 'Christ,' I mutter as two figures in colourful clothing dash past me, jackets over their heads. 'This is all I need.' I fight against the elements, hair flailing in the wet wind, until it flips back with a thud. Holding my brolly like a shield in front of me, I notice that one of the metal stretchers has detached from the canopy and is sticking out like a weapon. Brilliant, that's another two quid down the drain. I make a mental note – don't buy brollies from the pound shop in future.

I hobble along, broken brolly in hand. It's hard to believe that the sun was drowning in a pink sky less than two hours ago, as Teddy and I headed for Bond Street Station in the sweltering heat, I with a jacket neatly folded over my arm and he puffing on a Marlborough Light. I think about tonight, about Teddy Fallon. Apart from the heated conversations we had about his ex and my dad, it was quite a pleasant evening. Certainly, much better than sitting in front of the TV with cheesy beans on toast, worrying about my problems.

We talked almost nonstop on our train journey home – just about mundane stuff – our favourite movies, music, where we've been on holiday. At one point, we got so engrossed in a debate about who wrote 'Bohemian Rhapsody', I said it was Freddie Mercury and he insisted it was Brian May, that I almost missed my stop. I was right, of course. He texted me whilst I was on the top deck of the 102, ten minutes ago, said he'd googled it.

I smile into the darkness of my umbrella as the rain spits lightly against the nylon. Alison was right too – Teddy and I probably are a good match. He's the best date I've had since my divorce. Perhaps, if I was in a better place, things might've been different. I hope he wasn't too disappointed when I simply said, 'See you around then,' as the doors slid open at Bounds Green Station and I hopped off. I don't even know why people say that, they don't mean it. I certainly didn't. My problems aside, I'm not sure I can take on a crazy ex-wife, two kids, and an interfering mother. I recall the look of astonishment on Susanna Hawkins' face when Teddy, quite rudely, stopped her talking mid-flow and ushered me out of the restaurant like a bodyguard. What was that all about? Why leave with such urgency? I'm not sure I believe that he didn't want her to see him because they parted on bad terms – she seemed delighted to see *him*. And why didn't he tell her that I was his date? Even if she is a friend of Lydia's, they're divorced. He's a free agent – can date whomever he pleases. Perhaps Mr Perfect isn't so perfect after all. Perhaps he has a secret of his own.

'Sakes, man,' says an angry voice, making me jump.

I look up at a young lad, rucksack on his back, pink bandana wrapped around his brown curls, big black wireless headphones covering his ears. 'I'm so…' I begin.

Sucking his teeth, he punches one of the pads away from his ear, and for a moment I think he's going to attack me. I pull my bag closer to my body. Grime music thumps from his earphones. 'Mind where you're going,' he groans, taking in the length of me. 'You almost had my eye out with that thing.' Nodding at the protruding rod of my brolly, he readjusts his headphones. Phew – just a twenty-something boy going on fifteen in a stroppy mood. 'It's not even fucking raining, man,' he groans.

I'm riled by his thuggish behaviour but he has got a point. I was lost in thought, not looking where I was going, didn't notice the rain had stopped. Stepping aside, I shake out my umbrella, mutter an apology, then shoulder past him and hurry along the road, head down. I really haven't got time for wannabe gangsters. I've got to get home, dry myself off and text Alison. Her painkillers might've kicked in by now. She might be up, wandering around the house fretting in her white fluffy bathrobe and faux fur pink slippers with the oversized bow – she loves those slippers, wears them all the time, even when she has guests. We were on our annual Christmas shopping jaunt, last November, when she spotted them in a shop window at Brent Cross. An eighty-five quid impulse buy she couldn't resist.

I rush along the pavement – almost there, almost home. God, I can't wait to get out of these work clothes and into my jim-jams. A droplet of rain dribbles off a branch and splashes onto my head, and as I jerk my head up I see a figure of a woman leaning against the wall beside my hanging basket – thumb on lips, strands of long dark hair glued to the sides of her face, mascara tears smeared on her cheeks, or is it from the rain? It might be. I hope it is, although my gut tells me it isn't.

'Alison?' I say urgently, pausing at the gate. But she continues to stare at her pink faux-fur slippers with the oversized bow, in a daze – she hasn't heard me. 'Alison,' I call out, pushing the gate open.

Alison jerks away from the wall, as if she were asleep and has woken with a start. 'Where the hell have you been?' she snaps, glancing at the time on her phone furiously. 'I've been waiting here for ages.'

I open my mouth to speak, tell her that I was having dinner with Teddy – he surprised me with a visit, I was reluctant to go at first, but it actually went quite well, until Susanna Hawkins turned up. But the murderous look on Alison's face tells me she's in no mood to talk about Teddy Fallon. She's obviously come round here to rant about Simon. They must've had a massive row. I wonder if she'll want a bed for the night. I do a mental browse of my chest of drawers – third one down – lilac bedsheets. Mum laundered and put them away when she last stayed over. I could make up the sofa bed in the spare room in no time at all.

'I'm sorry, Ali. Why didn't you message me?' My eyes dart to her car parked across the road. 'I'd have come home sooner.' Christ, how long has she been standing here, why didn't she just wait for me in the car, for heaven's sake? I drop my gaze to her clothes, clinging to her body, and realise that she's in her flowery cotton nightie. Shit, she's soaked through. I can see her nipples, no bra, and the outline of her knickers. She's going to catch pneumonia. I scramble in my bag for my keys, eyes darting everywhere. I've got to get her inside, dry her off and make her a hot drink. ‘Let’s go in, Ali. You’re going to catch your death.’

But as I go to push the key in the lock, she barges in front of me like a bouncer. I raise my eyebrows, flummoxed by her behaviour.

‘Tell me what happened, Lucy,’ she demands, bottom lip trembling.

‘Alison, I really think…’ I stop and search her big blue eyes, red-rimmed and teary, even her nostrils are sore from crying. I want to pull her to me, comfort her, but I’m still holding my wet umbrella. ‘Come in. I’ll make us a nice sugary cuppa. It’ll help with the shock.’

Stepping out of my way, she snorts with fake, almost hysterical, laughter, and I wonder if she’s been drinking. I sniff the air discretely but can’t smell anything, unless she’s been on the vodka. But no, she’d never drink and drive, she’s too sensible. Alison drives everywhere, even to the corner shop. And there’s the school run to consider. She’d never risk losing her license.

‘A cuppa?’ she says incredulously, and a woman walking by with a little boy looks round at us as she scolds him in a foreign language, red scarf tied tightly at her chin. The boy whines and drags his feet as she hauls him along the street by the hand, her voice growing louder and then fading as they disappear into the muggy evening. ‘That’ll solve everything, will it? Oh, why didn’t I think of that?’ Alison throws her hands up in the air, and I jerk my head back and look at her anxiously.

Clearly, I’ve said the wrong thing – my dearest friend is devastated and all I can do is offer her a cup of tea. Resting my umbrella against a bush, I rub my temple, head throbbing even more.

‘Alison, I know what happened.’ I pause, and then. ‘Simon texted me earlier. Let’s go inside and discuss it. How’s the head?' I give her a small smile but her face is deadpan. 'If it's any consolation, I've got a stinking headache too. What are we like, eh?' I offer, trying and failing to diffuse the tension. There are several moments of silence. Rain from the hanging basket splatters onto the paving slabs – tap, tap, tap, a car swishes by, and then I blurt, 'Oh, love, I am sorry.' She looks up at me sharply then, eyes filling. 'I don't want to use a cliché but you will get through this. Nothing happened. I promise you.' I take a step towards her but she backs away. I can't work out if it's hostility or devastation.

'Alison, I'm going to level with you,' I admit, hand out. She snorts when I say this and rolls her eyes. Okay, this isn't just about Simon, she's furious with me too. I chew the inside of my lip, hard enough to draw blood. It must be because I kept this from her. Damn it. I knew I should've told her myself. Why did I let Simon convince me otherwise? 'I think I know why you're angry,' I say quietly. 'But I can explain.'

'Can you?' She points her phone at me, stepping forward. We're a foot apart. 'Go on then. EXPLAIN.' Her eyes shine with adrenalin. 'Knock yourself out.'

'You'd better come in.'

'Now, Lucy!' A bit of spittle flies from her mouth and lands on my lips and under my right eye. I blink.

Discussing it in my doorway wasn't quite what I had in mind but it seems I've no other choice. Filling my lungs with the earthy fug of rain, I scan the area anxiously, almost as if I expect all the neighbours to be lining up with popcorn. But everything is still. Normal. Wheelie bins are aligned on the street like soldiers, ready for collection. Cars are parked in driveways. Curtains are drawn, shutters are closed. An ordinary Wednesday night – on an ordinary suburban street.

I return my attention to Alison, exhaling slowly. 'I'll start at the beginning, shall I?' Alison nods and I lean my back against the wall and tell her everything, while she watches me speechless, eyes like steel, lips a tight pout. The words roll off my tongue quickly – Simon dropped me off home, then as I rounded the car, he jumped out, I'd dropped my phone, he was returning it; I thanked him, went to move, but he leant forward to kiss me goodnight – we went the same way and then he pounced on me. I was mortified. I pushed him off, asked him what the fuck he thought he was doing.

'I told him I was going to tell you, Ali, but he broke down and cried like a baby. Begged me not to say anything. I think he was having some kind of meltdown.' I exhale loudly through my nose. 'I'm sorry, Al, but I thought it was the right thing to do at the time.' I wait for the tears, the frustration, the anger, but she just looks at me mutely. Sniffing nervously, I throw a glance at Gloria and Matthew at number thirty-six, who've just pulled up in their red Volvo. 'Say something then. Look, I don't know about you but I'm bloody parched. That Cabernet Sauvig–'

But as I turn my back and push the key in the lock, I hear the clank of car doors and the sound of hurried footsteps. I spin round and watch in disbelief as Alison heads for her Lexus in a half-walk-half-run gait, arms folded against her chest. Gloria glances at her briefly as she kicks the gate open, a box in her arms, while Matthew pulls out shopping from the boot of their car.

'Alison?' I barrel after her. 'Alison, wait!' Two high-pitched beeps ping in my ears. Matthew looks round at me and nods as he closes the boot, several Lidl bags in his hand, a huge pack of Andrex under his arm – I ignore him. 'Alison, wait!' I yell. 'Where are you going? We need to talk. Alison?' The door slams, the engine purrs. What the hell is she playing at? I rap my hand against her window repeatedly calling out her name again and again and again. The window buzzes down.

'Stay away from me,' she says, her words stinging like a hard slap in the face. The door of number thirty-six closes with a loud thud and I jump.

'Alison, what are you saying?'

'I thought we were friends,' she says at the street ahead. A dark cloud looms over us like a heavy balloon. In the distance I hear a crack of thunder. 'But you're nothing but a bitch,' she spits.

Everything inside me falls. 'Alison, no. I'm your friend. I…'

'I thought I could trust you with my life,' she whimpers at the steering wheel, lips wobbling. God, she can't even look at me. Why did I keep this from her for over a week? WHY?

I curl my fingers around the window frame and look at her pleadingly. 'I know I should have told you what happened right away and I truly am sorry.' There's a roar of thunder and then the clouds explode again. Rain is falling on my hair, my clothes, my skin. 'I own it. It was the wrong call but you must understand that it was for all the right reasons. It's backfired on me and there's nothing I can do. I'm still your friend. I still love you. You can trust me. Obviously, I don't want your marriage to end but we can't let a man come between us. Simon just had a meltdown, that's all – I could've been anyone.' She gives me a sharp look when I say this, lips a thin line. Fuck, I'm making it all worse. 'Alison, I promise I'll make it up to you. On my life, I thought I was saving your marriage by keeping quiet.'

'Saving my marriage? Ha, is that what you call it?'

'Yes, our friendship means everything to me.' Silence. 'Listen, I don't have to ever see Simon again if it makes you feel uncomfortable. You can come to mine, we can go out, we can…' But Alison just shakes her head, a mock grin playing on her lips, and then she revs the engine, face twisting in anger, almost as if she pressing her foot down on my throat, and I know in that instant, in that moment that this isn't about me not telling her – something else is wrong, something else has happened.

My mind goes into overdrive, like tabs opening uncontrollably on a hacked computer scanning all the files in my brain – she thinks Simon is in love with me. No, no, that's completely ridiculous. She's annoyed because I'm excusing Simon's behaviour instead of being furious with him. No, no, no, it's not that either. Oh, Jesus, what if he told her – in anger while they were spitting vitriol at each other, because Simon can be quite vicious when he's angry, that he's always found me attractive. But even he isn't that dumb, surely. Then suddenly the obvious tears into my mind like a bullet train and all the tabs shut down quickly in my mind – boom, boom, boom – only one remains open.

'Oh, God, he told you it was me, didn't he?' I whisper, hands clutching the window frame so tightly that my knuckles look as if they're going to pierce through my skin. 'He told you that I came onto him.' Alison shakes her head and laughs. Her phone, which has been lying languidly on the passenger seat starts ringing – Simon Calling. 'Didn't he?!!!' I yell. The phone stops ringing then starts again within seconds, buzzing uselessly on the passenger seat. She reaches out, turns it to silent, then flips it over, hiding the screen. 'You've got to tell me what he said to you, Alison,' I insist. 'He can't just go around spreading rumours about me. That's slander.' I can feel my heart hammering against my wet hands. 'Tell me! I've got a right to know. This isn't fair!'

'Fair? FAIR?' she screams. 'Andrew was right about you all along. You really are a self-righteous bitch. Everything is *allllways* about you. Well, this isn't the fucking Lucy show.' I look at her in horror – waiting for her to snap out of this madness, to come to her senses, admit that Simon has lied, that she doesn't trust him, never really has. The indicator clangs and I'm suddenly aware of a voice filtering from the radio, white noise, and then the DJ's words snap into my ears, '*You're listening to Heart London.*' And then the sensation of movement. 'Get away from the car, Lucy. I don't want to hurt you.'

Tears blur my vision. It's as if I'm looking at her through a kaleidoscope. 'No, no. Wait. It was all him.' I blink, clearing my vision, tears splash onto my cheekbones. 'I swear, Alison, hand on heart – whatever he's said to you, it's all lies. We didn't even kiss properly – no tongues. I promise you.' The engine roars. Oh God, what am I saying? Alison's face is scarlet. The vein on her temple is pulsating.

'He kissed you?'

'Yes.'

'And you pushed him off?'

'Yes. I swear.'

'Really? REALLY?'

'Absolutely, one hundred per cent. It was just a quick peck. His lips barely touched mine.' I know this isn't strictly true but what you don't know can't hurt you, right? She hasn't seen the photograph she never will, not now I've kept my half of the bargain.

Alison slams the car into Park and turns off the ignition. Thank Christ, she's ready to talk, but as I go to tell her that I'd never in a million years do anything to hurt her, or her family, she snatches her phone off the passenger seat, jabs at the screen manically, then shoves it under my nose. 'Recognise anyone?'

My legs give a bit as I recoil in horror, hands flying to my mouth. 'Oh, God, oh no.'

'Oh, yes,' she exclaims. The rain pelts onto the car like pins.

Bloody Jasmine. The double-crossing bitch. 'You weren't supposed to see that,' I gulp, voice shaking, unable to meet her eye, embarrassed by the starkness of the photograph, of how it seems, of what she must be thinking. Jesus, I just lied to her face. She'll never believe a word I say now. 'Where did you get that?'

'That's none of your business,' she says crisply. 'Correct me if I'm wrong, but it doesn't look as if he's forcing you, does it?' I stare at her mutely. 'DOES IT?' I shake my head to and fro, to and fro. 'Answer me!'

'NO.' I cry. 'It doesn't, but I did push him off. I promise you, on my life.' Alison snorts. 'On my mum's life then, my nephew's.' I pause, take a few breaths, push my wet hair, which has turned into corkscrew curls, off my face. 'I'm being blackmailed, Alison.'

Her face flashes with confusion. 'What are you on about?'

'The person who sent you that photo is blackmailing me.'

She looks at me as if I'm an idiot. 'It's from an unknown number.'

'It's Jasmine. Jasmine sent you that photograph. Andrew told me that she pushed the save-the-date card through my letterbox on the night Simon dropped me off home. She must've just left my flat as we pulled up. I didn't see her,' I jabber. 'But she obviously saw us – saw Simon kissing me and took a photo.' I exhale loudly. 'A week later, I started getting texts from an unknown number threatening to send you that photo if I didn't admit to having an affair with Simon.' Alison's face is on fire. 'But I'm not. I swear on my mum's life. Jasmine saw the whole thing. She knows what happened. She's trying to frame me, make me look like an adulterous. Bring me down to her level. Humiliate me. Destroy our friendship. Look, I'll ring her. Put her on loud speaker.' I go to open my bag but remember that I chucked it by my front door in my haste to catch up with Alison, because I thought it'd slow me down.

Alison looks at me, dumbfounded. 'Jasmine sent me this?' Alison gestures at her phone, which has now locked.

I nod furiously. 'I think so, yes.'

'Think?'

'Okay, I know she did.'

Alison pauses, and then. 'But why would she do such a thing? A professional – a lawyer. Risk everything she's worked for? Damage her career, just to get at you?'

'I don't know. Perhaps because she could. She's very, very clever and calculating.' Alison frowns, fingers tapping against the steering wheel – she's breaking. 'That's why she's a top lawyer,' I add for good measure.

'And you can prove this?'

'Well, no, not yet, but. Oh, Alison, please don't shake your head at me like that. Can't you see? Jasmine wants to turn everyone I love against me.'

'Oh, shut up, Lucy!' She buckles in. You're bloody obsessed with her.'

'No, wait…'

'You're a liar, a fantasist!' she yells. 'Stay away from us.'

My booms in my chest, cascading into my stomach. I think I'm going to vomit. 'Simon's the liar not me,' I scream. But Alison shakes her head. 'I'm not saying he's a bad person but he's desperate – he doesn't want to lose his family. I think he's having a breakdown, you know, because of the money problems.'

She looks round at me, eyes narrowing. I've hit a nerve. But, after a brief silence, she says coldly, 'What money problems? He's just had a flipping rise. I've never heard such nonsense in all my life.' I close my eyes. The lying bastard. 'Jesus, Simon warned me about this but I wouldn't listen.'

'Warned you?'

'He said you'd blame him – say that he's the one who tried it on with you. It's the obvious thing to do, isn't it? You're so fucking transparent, Lucy.' I open my mouth to speak but she cuts across me, pointing a finger, 'And before you say anything, I know all about you pleading with him not to tell me. Well, tough, missy. You lose. He chose ME. So you can take your gym-toned skinny arse and go fuck yourself.'

'You're making a big mistake,' I snap, voice all nasally.

'I think you'll find that you're the one who's fucked-up.' She turns the key in the ignition. 'Big time.'

'No. Wait. There's something else you should know.' I pause. Swallow. Alison gives me a cold hard stare. 'Simon said he'd kill himself if I told you. If you left him. And I think he meant it.'

Alison shakes her head in disbelief. As if I haven't just told her that her husband threatened to commit suicide. 'Admit it, Lucy, you've been caught out.'

'No, he's stitched me up,' I cry desperately, fingers cold with rain.

'Stay away from my family, you're poison.'

'No,' I shake my head to and fro, to and fro. 'You've got this all wrong. Why won't you believe me? Simon's lying. He's not the man you think. I…' The window buzzes against my fingers and I snatch my hands away before it closes. I'm holding onto the wing mirror, begging her to stop the car. In my peripheral vision, I see Gloria thundering towards me, calling Matthew for backup. 'Alison, wait,' I cry, but she puts her foot down, not caring if she mows me down, not caring what happens to me.

My elbow stings the moment I hit the tarmac, as if a knife has cut through my flesh, and I just sit there, a heap in the middle of the street and watch as Alison's Lexus tears into the night, wheels screeching, brake lights flashing. And then I feel a hand under my arm. Gloria is helping me up – firing orders at Matthew – she'll need an antibacterial wipe and antiseptic cream, there's a first aid kit in the glove compartment of the car. I look at her hands, streaked with my blood. Matthew is next to her now, face white, phone pressed against his ear, muttering something about reckless drivers and a criminal offence.

'Police, please,' he yells into the mouthpiece. 'Yes. A hit and run. The number plate is AL15…'

'No, please,' I cry, hobbling to my feet. 'hang up.' I pull his arm and the phone almost flies out of his hand. 'I'm fine.' Gloria and Matthew exchange worried glances. 'I know the driver,' I pant. 'It was my fault. It's all *my* fault.'

Chapter 9

I unscrew a bottle of Smirnoff and take a swig straight from the bottle, swallow, then neck another mouthful, not caring about my headache, not caring how it burns my throat, not caring about anything. I am a gullible, stupid idiot and deserve everything coming my way. Of course Simon was going to pin this on me; of course he was going to try to save his shambles of a marriage. I fasten the red cap back on the bottle of vodka tightly, eyes darting around the kitchen. Simon can't get away with this. I need to speak to him, make him own up. I thunder into the lounge on a mobile phone search, because I can't for the life of me remember where I last left it, but find nothing. I check the bedrooms, the bathroom – nothing.

Back in the kitchen, I open and close drawers, double-check all the worktops, the dining table – nothing, nothing, nothing! In a frenzy, I snatch a twelve-inch knife off the drying rack and slide it under the red toaster. It wouldn't be the first time it slid beneath it. I often chuck my phone onto the counter when I get in from work and make myself a cuppa, especially if I'm texting. The blade glides through, catches on something and flicks it out, a peanut, I think, then it flies out the other end, knocking a Tupperware container off the counter. The moment it hits the floor, the lid flies off, splattering a mixture of beetroot in balsamic and olive oil everywhere; a few specs shoot to my face like missiles.

I look down at my white linen dress, speckled with red dots and all I can do is stand there and sob. Why didn't I wrap the box in cellophane? I knew it had a dodgy lid. Why did I trust Simon? Why didn't I stand in front of Alison's car to stop her from leaving, like they do in the movies? We could've discussed it once she'd calmed down. I might've been able to convince her that I was telling the truth. But now, thanks to Simon and Jasmine and that incriminating photograph doing the rounds like a Trojan virus, Alison will go to sleep tonight believing that I tried to steal her husband from right under her nose. Me. Lucy Harper. Her best friend. How could she even think that? It's a bloody joke. I mean, come on, if I was carrying on with Simon, would I really stand there in the middle of the street and snog him like some lovestruck teenager, knowing that anyone could see us? A married man? Really? Alison knows how much the local community means to me. We're all like one big, fat happy family on Valley Gardens N13. I wipe my wet cheeks with the back of my hands, inhaling teary phlegm. I will vindicate myself, if it's the last thing I do. Prove to Alison that Simon is lying. All I've got to do is keep it together and think of a plan. *Come on, get a grip, you got this.*

Dropping to my knees, I swallow back my turmoil and quickly scoop up the beetroot mixture, using the blunt end of the knife as a shovel and my bare hand as a dustpan. My injured arm, bandaged lovingly by Gloria from number thirty-six, aches as I lob it into the bin and I let out a low groan. Then I stand there, staring around the kitchen for my phone, knife in hand like a serial killer, and my anxious thoughts start to manifest – Simon and Jasmine can't just walk away from this scot-free. They have to pay for the damage they've caused. *God!!!* Where's my phone?

Seething, I grab a fistful of my hair, close my eyes and retrace my steps. The last time I used it was when Teddy texted me on the bus about who wrote *Bohemian Rhapsody*. I grinned at his message, quickly typed *'I'm always right'* then slipped it back into… My eyes snap open – my bag. I dropped it by the bush when I chased after Alison and, in my haste to get rid of Gloria and Matthew earlier, to convince them that I was all right, that I didn't need an ambulance, or the police, or for them to call anyone, or babysit me until I'd stopped shaking, I forgot to pick it up. Fuck. It's still outside.

For a moment, I stand in the doorway, paralysed. I hope that lad with the pink bandana and curls hasn't nicked it. I could've sworn I saw him swaggering by in my peripheral vision as Gloria smothered antiseptic cream on my grazed elbow in the front seat of their Volvo whilst Matthew looked on worriedly, clutching the first aid kit to his chest. Christ. I've got all my credit cards in my purse and my PIN numbers are listed on the back of a Travelicious business card. Also in my flipping purse. He could clear all my accounts in minutes. SHIT! Adrenalin soars through my body as I thunder into the hallway, then as I yank open the door my heart stops. I'm not sure which one of us screams first but the combined high-pitched shrill is deafening.

'I didn't expect you to be standing there,' I mutter after a few seconds, heart in mouth.

Gloria swallows, hunching into her shoulders, hugging my handbag to her chest as if it were a new-born baby. For a few moments we stare at each other silently and I register the fear in her eyes, the same terror I'd see in my mum's eyes when Dad would tower over her, hand clenched into a tight fist. Surely, she doesn't think I'm going to hurt her…does she?

'Lucy, love, are you okay? You haven't…you didn't…' I follow her gaze to my hand and realise that I'm still holding the kitchen knife with crimson fingers. 'Anything stupid?' she gulps, and then her eyes widen so much that I can see the tiny veins in the whites. 'Oh God!!! I knew we shouldn't have left you alone. I told Matthew. That's it. You need to see a doctor right away. Libby, Matthew's first cousin once removed, mother's side, is a self-harmer. I'll just…'

Gloria goes to walk inside but I block the entrance with my arm and she flinches, and I immediately feel guilty. She's going to think I'm an ungrateful, cold bitch, now. 'Gloria, no, you don't understand,' I stutter. 'It's not what you think. I was just–'

But she's having none of it and clearly doesn't care that I'm being a thankless cow. 'Everyone says that, they start with self-harming and then–'

'No, it really isn't. I'm not.' I take a deep breath. 'I was just chopping beetroot, that's all.' An exaggeration of the truth, but I haven't got time to tell Gloria about the Tupperware with the dodgy lid on my worktop. I've got to get rid of her and ring Simon. 'I really ought to wear gloves.' I offer her a smile but Gloria continues to look at me carefully beneath her thin, dark brows. She doesn't look convinced. 'I promise you, Gloria, hand on heart. I'd never lie to you. I respect you and Matthew, you know that.'

Our eyes lock and we gawp at each other mutely for a few moments and then, 'Oh, thank God,' Gloria says, believing me. 'Beet stains. Of course. I can see that now. Ha. For a moment there…' Her hand flies to her chest. 'Phew! You should see our kitchen when I deseed a pomegranate. Matthew says it looks like a murder scene.' She laughs loudly and I wince. Gloria is one of the loveliest people I know but she has one of the most annoying laughs on the planet. Andrew avoided chatting to her at all costs, because she couldn't get to grips with his Scottish accent and kept laughing at everything he said. He even refused to go to their annual Christmas drinks do, so I had to go with Xenia and Spiros, and Erika from next door but one. Andrew marvelled at how Matthew must be some sort of saint for putting up with that unbearable cackle for twenty-five years. But then, Andrew knows nothing about true love. Nothing.

'We were just popping out and Matthew spotted your bag outside,' Gloria continues, 'what with it being yellow and all.' I look over her shoulder and wave at Matthew who is sitting in the Volvo staring at us, baffled. He gives me a small smile and a little awkward wave. Poor man must think I'm a certified lunatic. 'We didn't want anyone to steal it. What with all the crime around here lately. Bloody government and their cutbacks. When was the last time you saw a copper around here, hmm?' I open my mouth to reply but Gloria's on a roll. 'You do know that Mrs Hutchinson from number forty-two got mugged on her way home from the post office a few weeks ago, don't you.' I nod, it was in the local paper – eight-three-year-old pensioner mugged at knifepoint. I went round there with a cake, offered to do a bit of shopping for her, walk Manny, her black cockapoo. She was so grateful, bless her, even though I enjoyed every moment of walking Manny around the park. 'I mean, you've had such a wanky day, haven't you?' My lips twitch when Gloria says this. I don't think I've ever heard her swear before. She's always so twee, with her neat dark bob, minimal makeup, sensible shoes, and *White Stuff* frocks. 'Anyway, here you go.' Handing me my River Island bag, she turns and starts walking down the path. 'And if you need anything, you know where we are,' she adds kindly, securing the latch of the gate behind her. 'We're just popping out to see Matthew's mum at the care home – be about an hour or so.'

'Thank you, Gloria, you've done so much for me tonight already.'

'Nonsense. That's what neighbours are for. You've got beetjuice on your face, by the way, and in your hair too.'

I watch as they drive off, then slam the door, leg it into the lounge, and empty all the contents of my bag onto the grey rug, like a heroin addict in need of a fix, promising myself to jump in the shower and wash my beetrooted hair once I've spoken to Simon. My stomach tightens when I unlock the phone and look at the screen – five missed calls – all from Alison – all within seconds of each other – must've been when I got off the bus – didn't hear my phone ringing in my bag.

For a moment I hesitate, a question drilling into my mind – am I being hasty, acting in anger? Maybe I should sleep on it before ringing Simon. Sort my head out, plan what I'm going to say, make him listen, make him understand that he's got to tell Alison the truth. But then I say, 'Hey, Siri.'

'I'm listening.'

'Call Simon.'

'Which Simon? Simon Dentist – Simon Maxwell – Simon Head Knob at Travelicious.'

'Oh, for fuck's sake!'

'Uh-oh…I don't have a number for that.'

'Call Simon Maxwell,' I demand, exasperated.

'Calling. Simon. Maxwell.'

Circling the coffee table, I take another swig of vodka from the bottle, phone glued to my ear. It rings out and I call the number again and again and again, and then 'Sorry, the mobile phone you have called is switched off.'

'FUCK,' I scream, hurling the phone across the room. 'I hate you, you bloody arsehole.'

Squatting, I back myself against the wall, head in hands. Simon isn't going to answer my calls, is he? I picture him picking up his phone when it rings, seeing my name flash up on the screen, cringing, then switching it off. Wiping my teary face with both hands, I take a deep breath through one nostril, the other is clogged with phlegm, and give the black screen of the

TV in the corner of the room the thousand-mile stare, racking my brain for a solution. Simon's not going to get away with this, no way, and he can't avoid me forever. My leg jerks nervously. The landline. I haven't tried the landline. Oscar might pick up if they ignore it.

Scrambling to my feet, I cross the room to retrieve my phone, hoping it didn't break when I lobbed it across the lounge. It's already got a cracked screen from when it fell out of my pocket at Costa last year whilst visiting Mum in Brighton.

I'm on my knees, face pressed against the sofa, rooting around the side panels, it might've, if I'm lucky, slipped behind the seat. I pull out a green plastic lighter and look at it nonplussed. I've no idea how it go there or who it belongs to. I drop it onto the seat and continue searching, all the while thinking about Alison and what I'll say when she picks up. If she picks up. Judging by her earlier mood, she'll probably slam the phone down the moment she hears my voice.

I pull out a few coins and drop them next to the lighter. Maybe I should just go round there – she must be home by now. If they refuse to let me in, I'll threaten to have it out with them right there on their doorstep, outside their posh house, on their posh street, in front of all their snobby neighbours. Simon would hate that. He tries to act all cool and nonchalant, but deep down he's the kind of man who likes to keep up with the Joneses, cares about what people think. He'd sooner usher me inside than have me humiliate him in public. Their stupidly rich neighbours will have a field day. None of them really like Simon. Alison once told me, after one too many cocktails, that they think he's a pompous jerk-off and only speak to him to keep her happy. I can just see them twitching their curtains, or staring through the gaps of their shutters, G&Ts in hand.

I root a little more along the back of the seat and as I'm about to give up, my hand closes around my phone – thank goodness. I unlock it quickly and pull out the Maxwells' number. Their landline flashes up on the screen – *Calling Alison Home* Brrr…brrrr…Brrr…brrr…Brrr…brrr. It goes to voicemail and I hang up quickly. God, why aren't they picking up? Someone must be home. I run a hand over my face wearily, pick up the vodka bottle then put it down again. I've already had too much. I don't want to pass out. I'll give her fifteen minutes then try again – but what if she hasn't gone straight home? What if she's gone round to her mum's? An image of her Karen's smiling face, halo hovering over her head, flashes in my mind. Karen. Of course. Why didn't I think of her before? She's always liked me.

I pull out Karen's details from my contacts list. Karen's a good egg, impartial. I remember the time when Alison and I fell out a couple of years ago. The Maxwells had invited us round for one of their legendary summer barbeques in their ridiculously huge garden. They'd just had it landscaped and it looked like something out of Alan Titchmarsh's *Love Your Garden* with solar lights illuminating the lawn at dusk, a summer house, sculptures, bean bags for the kids, and brown rattan furniture – stylish, absurdly expensive.

It was a hot sticky humid day. The champagne and *Peroni* was going down like water, then Andrew told off one of the kids, I think it was Leah, she'd taken his phone out of his back pocket and stuck it in a pot plant. Alison was furious with Andrew for making Leah cry, and then with me for not telling my husband off, even though I did, albeit quietly. Alison got the hump and didn't speak to me for a week. Karen didn't take sides then; she even came round here for coffee and a chat, and, I later found out, she was the one who convinced Alison that she was being childish and petty, and she let it go.

I snatch the phone from its cradle and punch in Karen's number with trembling fingers, leaving my mobile phone free in case Alison calls back. Karen answers on the third ring, giggling, distant. She's not alone. 'Hello?' she says blithely, to the milieu of laughter and voices – she must be at her local. Wednesday night is quiz night. She never misses it. The moment I hear her voice I start crying.

'Oh, Karen,' I blub, 'Thank God.'

'Sorry, who is this please?'

'Karen, it's me…I'm…has…' I'm an incoherent ball slumped against the sofa, arm wrapped around my knees, snot dribbling from my nose and curving into my lips like a stream. 'Si… has… Alison…'

'Lucy, is that you?' And then I hear a man's voice and then, 'Turn the volume down, Trevor, I can't hear myself think.' Not at the pub then, just having a cosy night in with her new man, and now I'm about to ruin their evening. 'Lucy?' she says. But the tears have clogged my throat and I can't speak. 'Lucy, love, speak to me.' There's a pause, and then I hear her say quietly, 'I don't know. I can hear her breathing. I think she's drunk.'

No, I'm not drunk. Even though I've downed enough neat vodka to knock out a gorilla, I feel stone cold sober. There's a crackling sound and a murmur of voices. She's covered the mouthpiece, and then she says in a panicky voice. 'Has something happened to Alison? Lucy? Come on, love.' Karen sighs loudly into the mouthpiece. 'I don't know, Trevor. I'm trying to find out!' My heart sinks. She doesn't know. Alison hasn't told her yet, which is a bit weird because they tell each other everything. 'Are the kids okay? What's happened? Where are you? It's Oscar, isn't it? I swear that boy–'

'No, Oscar's fine, the kids are fine,' I cut in. 'Alison's fine,' I run the back of my hand against my snotty nose and swallow back the tears. 'Well, sort of.'

'Okay, love, back up a bit and take a deep breath. That's a good girl. Now tell me what's wrong and how I can help.'

Karen listens silently while I blabber on about recent events – the lift home, the kiss, the blackmailing texts, the photograph of Simon kissing me, Alison waiting on my doorstep, her cold harsh words piercing through my heart like arrows, how she almost mowed me down in the street with her Lexus in a bid to get away.

Karen doesn't say a single thing in response, not even a gasp or a sigh. I even have to stop and say *'Karen, can you hear me?'* a couple of times. 'And now Ali thinks that I tried to steal her husband. But I DIDN'T! Karen? Hello, are you still there?' She's definitely hung up this time. That's it. She hates me as well. Doesn't believe me. I look at my phone, her number is still on the lit-up blue LCD screen. 'Hello?'

There's a long hissy sigh and then, 'Oh, Lucy, what a bloody mess, lovely.' A warm glow washes over me when she calls me 'lovely,' because I know she's not angry with me.

'But you do believe me, don't you?' Silence. 'Karen?' I holler, eyes wide. 'I swear on my mum's life, on my sister's, on my nephew's, I…'

'Yes, yes, okay, Lucy, calm down, dear.' Another long sigh and then, 'I can't quite take it all in. Simon's a family man – loyal, decent. There must be some kind of misunderstanding, that's all.'

I shake my head to and fro, to and fro, eyes filling with fresh hot tears, she's not listening, she doesn't understand. 'Karen, he kissed me. There's no misunderstanding.' And then the doorbell shrills. I ignore it. I'm not expecting anyone, it's probably a parcel for upstairs. They're always ordering stuff online and are hardly ever home. On a normal day, I'd take it in for them but not today. 'You've got to help me get through to Alison,' I plead. The doorbell rings again, long and hard, followed by the rap of the letterbox. Whoever it is persistent, and then it hits me. 'Karen, wait, there's someone at the door. I think it's Alison.'

Dropping the phone onto the sofa, I race to the front door and wrench it open, 'Alison, I–' And then I stop short.

'I'm sorry to bother you.' There's a man standing on my welcome mat – small, stocky, bald, mid-sixties. He's deeply tanned and has an ID holder hanging from his neck. There's a bit of rain on his stripy shirt and neck. 'Is Andrew around?' he asks, hopefully. I want to slam the door in his face immediately. I haven't got time for cold-callers.

'Andrew?' I ask, as if I've never heard of him before in my entire life. I thrust a hand through my unruly mane, he looks at it, then his face pales. Fuck, the beetroot stains. I'm covered in them.

His lips twitch nervously, eyes full of apprehension, leaflet in hand. 'Mr McLaughlin? It's just about this survey on…' And then I'm no longer listening. The last thing I bloody need is a door-to-door market researcher.

I snatch the leaflet from his hand. 'He's not in,' I snap, and I'm not sure why I tell him this lie. Maybe it's because I want to get rid of him, or maybe it's because he's looking over my shoulder into the flat, as if he doesn't believe me. I don't want him to think I'm a woman alone. His eyes dart to my beetroot-stained hands. Or perhaps he thinks I've knifed Andrew to death and that he's lying in a pool of blood on my kitchen floor. 'But I'll make sure he gets it,' I say firmly.

And before he can reply, I slam the door in his face, without a hint of remorse, and race back into the lounge, hoping, praying that Karen hasn't put the phone down.

'Hello, Karen?'

'Yes, lovely.' Phew, she's still on the line. I can hear the TV in the background again.

‘I’m sorry about that, false alarm. Some salesman…interviewer.’ I look at the leaflet in my hand, ‘About housing, or something. Where was I?’ I pant, flicking the leaflet across the room. ‘Oh, yes. Simon kissing me and that bloody misleading photograph.’

‘But he told Alison that it was you who tried it on with him, is that right?’

‘Yes!’

‘Okaaaay.’

‘But you know it didn’t happen that way, right? You know me, Karen. We’ve been friends for years. You know I’d never do that to another woman.’

‘Obviously I wasn’t there, but yes, I know you’re a decent lass. I don’t believe you’d do that to our Alison.’ I close my eyes and mouth *thank God*. I even do the sign of the cross like Xenia from next door does whenever something goes her way. ‘Um…’ There’s a pause, Karen clucks her tongue, and then, ‘Look, I’d better speak to Alison. Get the full picture. I’ll call you back.’

‘Promise? ‘I say, getting to my feet, tears drying.

‘I promise.’

‘And you will try to convince her, won’t you?’

‘I’ll do my best. Now–’

‘And you’ll tell her that I’d never do anything to hurt her.’

‘Of course, just leave it to me and I’ll see what I–’

‘And you’ll phone me right back?’

‘Yes!’

‘Tonight?’

‘I’ll phone you as soon as I’ve spoken to Alison. I promise.’

My mobile phone rings. I glance at it hopefully – Nessa Calling. She’s probably anxious to find out how it all went with Teddy. ‘Okay, Karen. Thanks, I’ll be waiting.’ And as I go to end the call, that’s when I spot it, poking out from under the coffee table. I cover my mouth as bile rises into my throat. Someone's been in my flat.

Chapter 10

A lick of caffeine dances under my nose as I lean back in my seat, taking in the formica tables, shiny coffee machine and glass display unit of the greasy spoon, tucked away behind Farringdon Underground Station – poky, indiscreet, the kind of place you'd meet your lover.

The plastic red clock hanging on the white wall on top of sweltering black tiles reads six twenty-five. We've been sitting here for eleven minutes, and, because his phone hasn't stopped vibrating with messages since we arrived, and because he hasn't stopped replying to them, neither of us has spoken a word.

I clear my throat, throw another glance at the clock for effect. 'Are you going to be on that all evening?'

Simon continues to type, ignoring me, thumbs flying all over the lit up screen, and I sigh in exasperation, exchanging a half smile with a lady who briefly looks at me as she turns the page of her paperback, dark glasses perched on her head. The sun has scorched her big arms and face, lines cut into her sunburnt décolletage and meet at her cleavage like road intersections. I stare at the book in her hand stupidly, the title swimming in front of my eyes.

What the hell am I doing here? I shouldn't have come. This was a mistake. But as I reach for my bag on the chair next to me, Simon drops his phone onto the table, tears a sachet of sugar and pours it into his white cup, giving me intermittent glances beneath furrowed brows, and I sit back, dropping my hands into my lap.

'You look rough,' he says eventually, sighing long and hard through his nostrils. Yes, so would you if you'd been up all night worrying yourself half to death. It's not every day your friend accuses you of trying to steal her husband and then almost mows you down in the middle of the street in front of your neighbours. I touch my bandaged arm beneath my purple long sleeved t-shirt. It's healing well, thanks to Gloria, hardly any pain left at all.

I stare into my untouched cup of tea. It's strong and dark and rich. Just how I like it. I want to take a sip but my hands won't let me. I look down at them, trembling in my lap.

'I didn't sleep well,' I admit, wrapping my hands around my tea to stop them from shaking. A distraction mechanism Mum taught me, which she picked up during her cognitive behavioural therapy sessions when Dad died. It's supposed to make you feel grounded. It works – most of the time.

I squeeze the cup, feeling the warmth against my skin. Simon glances at it, pouring another sachet of sugar into his cup and I wonder if he's noticed my tremor, but then he says, 'You can't just turn up at my office like this, you know.' His spoon clatters as he stirs. 'It's not on. If Alison–'

Something inside me roars when he says her name and my hand flies up like a buckler, stopping him mid-sentence. 'Don't, Simon…' I bite down hard on my lips, forcing myself to remain silent. How dare he treat me as if I'm some sort of bunny boiler, as if I'm in the wrong? I've lost the trust and respect of my best friend because of him; my reputation is in tatters. Pressing my fingers firmly against the Formica table, as if it's about to take off, I watch him like a wolf, pulse knocking in my throat, vibrating in my stomach and ribs.

I want to leap across the table, snatch him by the lapels of his grey tailored jacket and shake him, call him a lying bastard, tell him that because of his stupidity, his lies, his cowardice, my life is in chaos. I may even be in danger, if yesterday's finding is anything to go by. I swallow back the words and they sting my throat like thorns. I don't want him to get up and leave. I need him to sit here and listen, help me.

'It's not as if you left me with much choice, Simon, is it?' I retort, rubbing a blue pen mark off my hand with my thumb. I sat on the floor after I ended the call with Karen, doodling, waiting for her to ring me back. She didn't. 'If you'd answered my calls, we could've sorted this out like mature adults and I wouldn't have accosted you outside your office like a flipping stalker.'

At half five on the dot, I raced out of the Travelicious building and jumped into a black cab, hoping to catch Simon on his way home. Twenty minutes later, I stood in the lobby of his plush office building, looking around me wildly. I knew he finished work at six and that his office was on the fifth floor, but hadn't a clue how I was going to get through the barriers and to the lifts. But then, as luck would have it, a kind man with short dark curly hair, caramel skin and kind brown eyes, asked me if I wanted him to buzz me through. I jumped at the chance, but as he swiped his card and the barriers swung open a man cried, 'Madam, you can't just walk through. Who're you here to see.' I spun round, panic surging into my chest and wrapping itself around my throat, and just then I saw Simon going through the revolving glass doors. 'Madam!' the faceless man yelled, 'Can I help you?' But I was gone.

'So,' I say now. 'Why did you ignore all my calls?'

'I wanted to pick up, talk to you, but Alison's been watching me like a hawk and I can't take personal calls at work.' Liar. You could have called me in your lunch break. 'I was going to ring you tonight.' I watch him carefully as he leans back in his seat and drapes an arm along the back of the wooden chair, slipping a smile at a pretty dark waitress as she bustles around the tables in a white apron decorated with the day's colourful dishes. Lying must be like second nature to him. 'What do you want from me, Lucy?'

What do I want? I want you to call Alison right now and tell her the truth.

I swallow hard. 'Firstly, I want you to explain why you lied to me. Why you set me up,' I say, unable to restrain the indignation in my voice. 'For crying out loud, Simon, I thought you were better than this. I honestly used to look up to you.' The dark-haired waitress glances up at me as she wipes down a table, then exchanges a conspiratorial look with Simon, and I wonder if they've got something going on. He almost frogmarched me to this place when I leapt in front of him as he tried to cross the road outside his office building earlier, even though we passed several cafés on the way. I spy her from the corner of my eye – about 5'7, long hair tied back, slim but full in all the right places – could quite easily be a model. Maybe she is. Are they lovers, grabbing every opportunity to see each other? Is he cheating on Alison with her? I shake the thought away. I'm being ridiculous. She's half his age for a start off and, with her sultry Italian dark looks, far too gorgeous for him.

'Now, hang on,' Simon protests, leaning forward. 'I didn't lie to you. I told you that Alison knew everything, that's all.'

I purse my lips, swallowing back expletives that are sprinting up my throat. 'That was a misleading text,' I say through gritted teeth. 'And then filling Alison's head with all these lies about me coming onto you. I mean, what the fuck were you thinking? That I wouldn't find out, that she wouldn't tell me?'

‘Will you keep your voice down?’ Simon exclaims, eyes darting around the café, nostrils flaring. ‘People know me around here.’ Then he looks at my phone on the table. ‘Is that on record?’

‘What?’

‘Are you recording this conversation, because if you are then–’ He goes to stand up but I snatch the phone up, unlock it and hand it to him. I watch, fingers against lips, as he flicks through the open apps, closing them down as he goes along, berating myself for not thinking of such a cunning plan. If I’d recorded everything I’d have had him by the balls and this nightmare would be over. Satisfied, he hands the phone back to me.

I look at him expectantly. ‘Well?’

‘It wasn’t my fault,’ he begins, and I roll my eyes. ‘I was going to tell Alison the truth, exactly how it happened.’

I look up at him sharply. ‘So what stopped you?’

‘You’ve got to take some responsibility for this mess, Lucy. You were going to kiss me too, remember.’ He blows on his coffee, takes a sip, grimaces, then reaches for the silver sugar holder.

I stare at him in disbelief as he pours another sachet into his cup. This man is deluded. A complete fantasist. ‘Yes, on the cheek,’ I snap, unable to control my incredulity. ‘A friendly goodnight peck.’

He takes a slurp of coffee. ‘If you say so.’ He groans. Oh God, I hate this man so much. I think he actually believes his own lies. ‘Oh look, I’m sorry.’

We sit in silence. Crockery clanks, Italian voices hum, an old Beatles track drifts from the radio; I think it’s ‘Eleanor Rigby’, one of Mum’s favourites. ‘Listen,’ Simon says, ‘I…um…’ He scratches the side of his neck and I notice that it’s red. I’m not sure if it’s an abrasion from his starched collar, or a love bite. Maybe he and Alison had a lot of making up to do last night. 'I was mustering the courage to tell Alison the truth – explain how the pressure of work was getting to me – that I felt we were drifting apart – both wrapped up in work, the kids, the house. I had a wobble and you were there, friendly as always…' He pauses, lips tightening, fingers drumming against the table. 'Do you want me to tell you what happened, or are you just going to sit there and sneer?'

Shit, I didn't even realise I was pulling faces. I suck in my lips and put on my best poker-face. 'Go on, I'm listening.'

He gives me a long hard stare. The sultry waitress brushes past our table, he looks up at her darkly until she's safely out of earshot then says, 'I was in my office having a couple of cognacs, you know, for a bit of Dutch courage when I heard Ali's phone tinkle with a message in the lounge. I was secretly pleased, thought it must be one of her mates, or Karen, expected her to be texting for ages, give the booze time to kick in. But then the next thing I knew she was towering over me at my desk, waving the phone in her hand, making threats, accusing us of having an affair. I thought she was going to hit me,' he says indignantly, and a tiny imp in my heart does a little Floss dance, because I so wish she had. I so wish he was sitting in front of me now with a black eye.

Grimacing, Simon leans forward, fist clenched near my teacup, looks me straight in the eye and whispers, 'Why did Alison get to see that photo, Lucy, hmm? You said you had it under control, you said the blackmailer gave you a deadline, which we were adhering to.'

I tell him that it *was* all under control, that Jasmine stitched me up. 'She was probably going to send Alison the photograph regardless,' I reason, inhaling a concoction of his stale aftershave and sweat. 'I should've known better.'

Simon doesn't take his eyes off me as he loosens his stripy tie and unbuttons the top of his pink shirt, revealing several more red marks from his stiff collar – not love bites then. Shrugging off his jacket, he rolls up his sleeves. 'I've never seen her like that, Lucy. Poor kids were terrified; seeing their mum lose it like that. I had to bribe them into the garden with a trip to Legoland.'

Simon rests his hairy arms on the table and my eyes are instantly drawn to the blue face of his silver watch. It's new. A Breitling. So much for being broke. Lying piece of shit. 'So, what happened next? What stopped you from coming clean? It was the perfect opportunity to tell her the truth, squash it, but instead you chose to lie.'

Reclining in his seat, he tilts his head back. 'No, it wasn't like that. I tried to explain, got to the part where we went the wrong way, our noses brushed, blah, blah, blah, and she blew up. Wouldn't let me finish. I couldn't get a word in. She was out of control, Lucy – thundering from room to room, screaming that she was going to fucking kill you, accusing us all of mislaying her car keys, swearing, banging things, slamming doors. I tried to stop her from leaving, pleaded with her to sit down so we could talk about it, but she was out of the house like a fucking whippet with a rocket up her backside.'

He pauses, glances at a man pulling out a chair at the next table. 'I didn't know she was coming to yours. She said she was going to her mum's.' *Bollocks*! If Alison thought I tried it on with her husband and threatened to kill me, why would she be going round to Karen's for tea and sympathy? 'Quit with the eye rolling, Lucy, it doesn't suit you. Look, I'm trying to be honest with you here.' Honest. Really? 'I swear on my kids' lives, if I knew Ali was on the warpath, I'd have warned you at least.' I hesitate, that part might be true. He wouldn't use his kids as pawns – whatever I think of him, he is a good father.

'But Alison said you blamed me, told her that I came on to you.'

He shakes his head at the table. 'I didn't.'

'She even told me that you said I'd blame you, turn it around.'

'No.'

'Lied.'

'No!'

'That I made you promise not to tell her. That I wanted you.'

'Jesus, this is worse than being on trial.' He laughs at the ceiling, shaking his head. 'No, that's not true. I didn't say any of those things. Alison just came to her own conclusions.'

Narrowing my eyes, I focus on the swirly writing of the *Today's Specials* chalkboard against the wall, visualising Alison in her plush lounge, smiling when a text pings through on her phone, crumbling when sees the picture message, charging into the study with the red walls, huge maple desk and green Chesterfield sofa, accosting him, accusing him, wanting answers. A natural response to seeing a photograph of your husband locked in a kiss with your best friend. I'd have reacted in the same way – I did.

I glance back at Simon – he's looking at his phone, typing again. I tap my fingers against my cup irritably, sighing for impact.

'Soz,' Simon says, looking at me briefly. 'Ordered some headphones for Oscar – those Beats Solo Pro Bluetooth ones in all those bright colours. All the rage, apparently.' Yes, they are. I've seen them advertised on TV – very smart, expensive. Oscar's going to love them. I told you Simon was a good father. 'They're arriving today. Just letting him know to keep an ear out, cos I'm running late.'

I leave him to it and mull over what he's just told me. What he's basically saying is that Alison took one look at the photograph and believed what she wanted to believe, is in denial. But why would she think that? It doesn't quite ring true. Anyone who looked at that photograph would think that kiss was consensual. If anything she'd think we were having an affair. There's only one way she'd think otherwise.

'Okay, I'm all ears,' he says, locking his phone.

'Simon. I can understand how Alison jumped to the wrong conclusion,' I lie, 'got angry, came to mine to confront me in haste. But why didn't you just tell her the truth when she got home?' He looks at me aghast, phone in hand, but I plough on. 'Once she'd calmed down?' My words hang in the air, unrequited; someone's phone starts ringing, an alarm goes off in the street. 'You still can if–'

'Sorry, no,' he barks, dropping the phone onto the table with a loud thud. I look at his handset as if it deliberately launched itself onto the table to make me jump. 'She'll leave me – she's made that quite clear.' He glances over his left shoulder to make sure no one's listening. 'I can't risk losing my family,' he hisses, fist on the table. 'Oh, come on, Lucy, this is my life we're talking about, my livelihood. Do you want to see me on the streets? Oscar, the kids to grow up without a father?'

No, of course I don't. But what about my life? My relationships? My reputation?

'I'm sorry it's turned out like this,' he whispers, leaning forward. 'If I could turn back the clock I would. But, look, at the end of the day, you and Ali are just friends, aren't you, you can find another drinking buddie.'

I shake my head at the cup of tea in front of me, swallowing back the tears as I tug at a loose thread on the rim of my pale blue dress. Alison is like family to me. I'm not going to lie, I get on better with her than I do my own sister. Kate has even complained to me about it once or twice. Ali and I are thick as thieves. We share everything, apart from husbands, that is. It's only been twenty-four hours and I already miss her.

Looking away, I discretely swipe the corner of my eye with my index finger. I don't want Simon to see me crying, but he's not even looking at me; he's too busy exchanging smiles with the sultry young waitress who is taking an order at an adjacent table. But Simon's right, isn't he? I am just a friend. Who am I to stand in the way of Alison's happiness? I don't want to break up her family. I don't want her to be unhappy. Oscar and the kids adore Simon. I don't want to take their father away from them. If this kiss was just a blip, a one-off like Simon claims, and God knows I hope it was, although I'm now not entirely convinced, then maybe I should take it on the chin, for the sake of my friend's happiness.

'Someone broke into my flat yesterday,' I say numbly, slurping my lukewarm tea.

A plate smashes in the background, someone swears loudly and Simon pulls a face, wincing, as if he misheard me. 'What? Were you burgled? Jesus, did they take anything?'

'No, that's just the thing.' I reach into my bag as he pops a bite-sized biscotti into his mouth, a freebie, and starts crunching loudly. 'Nothing was taken, nothing was moved, but they left this behind.' I hand him the photograph that I found near the coffee table last night as I ended my call with Karen – the photograph of me and him kissing.

'Shit,' he whispers, holding the 6x4 glossy print with both hands. 'This is the first time I've actually seen it close up. No wonder Alison went loopy.' He studies it carefully, eyebrows furrowed. 'They didn't use a flash, for obvious reasons, and it was taken from afar and then zoomed in and cropped. It's quite dark and fuzzy. Jesus, why would someone go to the trouble of actually printing it out and leaving it in your flat? They could've been rumbled by your neighbours. The stupid bellend.'

'They weren't,' I say coolly. 'I asked them all today – no one saw anything suspicious.'

'This person certainly has balls.' His eyes flit from me to the photograph in quick succession. 'Still, they've done their worst – Alison knows. Game over.'

'For you,' I exclaim. 'But what was she doing creeping around in my flat and leaving photos to freak me out? This isn't over, Simon, not by a long shot.'

Simon purses his lips and gives me one of his faux sympathetic looks. 'Do you still think it's Jasmine?' he asks, sticking a finger into his mouth. 'Love these almond biscuits but they don't half stick to your teeth.'

I shrug, squeezing my bottom lip between my thumb and finger. 'Yes, pretty much, but I've no proof.' I sigh. 'Jasmine is very conniving. It's just the sort of thing she'd do, but would she go this far?' I pause as Alison's words ring in my ears – *Risk everything she's worked for? Damage her career, just to get at you?* 'I don't know, Simon – maybe. If she was desperate.' I scratch my cheek. 'Who else could it be? Who else would want to hurt me like this?'

'What did the police say about the break-in?'

'I haven't reported it.'

He looks at me, horrified. 'Please tell me you're joking.' I shake my head. 'Seriously? Can I ask why?'

'There was no break-in.' His face is a mixture of confusion and incredulity. 'I think I left the back door open.' I go to take a sip of tea. 'I can't remember. Stop looking at me as if I'm some kind of nutjob, Simon. I've had a lot on my mind lately. I didn't do it on purpose.'

Simon nods at the biscotti on my saucer. 'Do you want that?' I shake my head, tell him to help himself. 'Thanks, I'm bloody starving.'

We lapse into silence. Simon picks up a laminate menu and starts reading it, I check my phone for any missed calls or messages, while Rick Astley promises to never give us up, and never let us down from the radio behind the counter. I'm about to reply to a text from Nessa when Simon's phone vibrates and lights up on the table. Sucking his teeth, he frowns at it, dislodging the remnants of the biscuit with his finger, glances at the counter over his shoulder, or is it the clock? I'm not sure. Then turns the phone face down on the table. Acid gushes in my stomach. It's another woman. A scene flashes in my mind like an erotic clip from a film – he's snogging the gorgeous sultry waitress in the hot kitchen behind the counter, trousers around his ankles, her slender legs wrapped around his waist, saucepans flying, hips thrusting, voices groaning, breaths quickening, and then, 'If you left the back door open, it could be anyone.' Simon's voice breaks me out of my trance.

Tapping the photo against his lips, he narrows his eyes. 'We could do a process of elimination, figure out who it could be.' He gives the photo a few more taps and wrinkles his nose. 'We can eliminate our families for a start – Alison was home with the kids, Karen was on that yoga retreat.' I give him a look. I can't believe he actually entertained the idea. He's sick. 'What? Don't you want to do this properly?'

'Go on,' I say, stiffly.

'Whoever took this photograph was either already in the area, or following you. One of your neighbours. What about Zainab?'

'Xenia,' I correct.

'Xenia, yes, or that flowery woman across the road with the crazy laugh.' How does he know about Gloria? Andrew must tell him everything.

'Definitely not Xenia, or the lovely people at number thirty-six.'

'That eastern European couple upstairs look a bit dodgy.' I'll add racist to his list of flaws too.

'Don't be absurd,' I say, rubbing the back of my neck. 'My neighbours are compassionate, trusting people. We all look out for each other.' A rarity in London these days. It's one of the reasons why I don't want to move. 'That only leaves Jasmine – she's the only one there that day.'

Simon tuts. 'You can't be certain. She could've dropped that invite off at any time of the day.' He pulls his chair in as a group of officey looking people assemble at the table behind us. The café is starting to fill with evening diners, chairs grind and squeak against terracotta tiles, a cacophony of voices thrill in my ears. We should leave. They're going to need the tables, and I'm fighting a losing battle here with Simon. He's never going to tell Alison the truth about what happened. I'm going to have to find another way, track down the blackmailer.

'She might've dropped it off on her way home from a night out.' I know I'm clutching at straws, but my auntie Stella has always told me to go with my gut feeling because it is almost always right, and I just know that it's Jasmine. 'Jasmine often sees her girlfriends on a Friday night. It's a thing. We used to do it.' He looks at me mutely, lips parted. 'You and Jasmine.' I close my eyes briefly. 'You and this person can't get away with this.'

Pausing, I shake my head at a blonde lady's back with stripy highlights. 'The blackmailer knows what happened that night and I'm going to find out who it is and prove my innocence. Clear my name.' I don't want to hurt Alison but she needs to know what kind of man she's married to and I can't let him slander my name. People gossip, news travels fast. I don't want to be pointed at in the local pub, snubbed by my neighbours, labelled as a husband snatcher, an adulterous.

Getting to his feet, Simon buttons his single-breasted grey jacket – he wants shot of me, fast. 'Good luck with that,' he says, straight-faced. 'You're gonna need it. Yo, Vincenzo, thanks,' Simon yells, lifting an arm, then he turns to me and says, 'Pongs a bit, doesn't it?'

I get to my feet too, photo in hand, sniffing the air while Vincenzo, a round man with thinning white curls and a deep tan, waves at us from behind the counter and yells, 'Ciao, guys, have a great evening.'

'I wouldn't go as far as that,' I say. 'I think they're frying fish.'

'I mean the photograph.' He takes it from my hand and sniffs it. 'It's got a bit of a whiff. Like cheap aftershave. Here, smell.'

I inch forward, inhaling deeply, and as the woody scent of sandalwood soaks into my lungs, everything dims. I go to lean on a chair to steady myself, miss it and stagger forward. A chair topples over, my cup and saucer fly off the table and crash somewhere near my feet, tea splashes everywhere, voices gasp, and the room is spinning like a merry-go-round.

Faceless people have turned in their seats. A few are standing up. I can hear Simon's voice, asking me what's wrong. Vincenzo is standing next to him, jabbering in an Italian accent – what did I eat – they've got a five-star rating for hygiene on TripAdvisor – maybe it's something I had for lunch – should he call an ambulance?

'No,' I manage. 'I'm…I'm.' I feel a hand on my shoulder. It's Simon's. I shrug him off like an awkward drunk and stagger forward, handbag swinging from the crease of my elbow.

‘Leave me alone. I’m fine. I just need…I need…some…some air. I can’t…I…’ I gaze at the green exit sign swaying in front of me, and as I go to move, the puke surges into my chest, and this time I can’t keep the sickness at bay.

Chapter 11

The crunch of a handbrake startles me and my eyes snap open. 'We're home,' Teddy announces, engine still running. I'm laying back on the reclined seat in his Ford Mondeo feeling hot and clammy, mouth dry and dusty. The window is rolled down but instead of a fresh breeze, warm air is coming through.

Feeling almost jetlagged, I take a deep breath through my nose, inhaling a concoction of mud and foliage drifting from the tools in the back of the car. The small space feels asphyxiating, even though we drove home with all the windows open. Teddy's idea in case I threw up again. He said the fresh air would do me good. It has. He also made sure he talked to me all the way home, in case I fell asleep and choked on my vomit – firing questions at me quicker than I could answer – what's my favourite colour – what books did I read when I was little – how many GCSEs have I got – what about A levels – do Kate and I look alike – do we have similar personalities – vanilla or chocolate – cats or dogs – what was my first job – question after question after question. My ears were bleeding. I wanted to tell him to stop but I daren't complain. When we reached Muswell Hill he quietened and my eyes closed but then he shot off again – about giving his mum a lift to the GP in the morning – her cholesterol levels are raised, the doctor needs to up her statins, her car is in the garage and their GP is a few bus rides away; his mother doesn't do buses, or walking.

I sit up a bit too quickly now and the seatbelt locks, immobilising me.

'Let me help,' Teddy says gently. Leaning across me, he unbuckles my seat and winds my chair up, so close that I can feel the heat radiating from his face, the scent of him – pine deodorant, sweat and tobacco. I'd take that smell over sandalwood any day.

I think about the photograph as I gather myself. Simon asking me to sniff it, the nauseating smell sucking the life out of me. Jesus, even the thought of it is making my stomach swirl. What kind of maniac would let themselves into my flat and deposit a photograph under the coffee table, sprayed with the only scent that makes my insides want to sprint out of my mouth? Someone who knows me very well, that's who. I can count the people who know about my sandalwood phobia on one hand – my sister, Kate, Mum, Andrew, Alison. And Jasmine. I don't need to tell you who my money's on.

I take a deep inhalation and Teddy looks at me. It's a good job he showed up when he did, or I'd still be curled up against the wall on the pavement outside Vincenzo's of Farringdon.

'You okay,' he asks, and, with a small smile, I tell him that I am, thanks to him. Satisfied, he proceeds to give me a lecture on healthy eating and the importance of replacing nutrients and minerals after throwing up violently, and I sit and listen quietly, nodding whenever he pauses.

Poor Teddy, he looks like how I feel. I'm sure he would've run for the hills if he knew what was in store for him tonight. I hardly know him really, but I can tell that he's a good man. A nice person. Who else would have done what he did for me tonight? Teddy's got a good energy, and that's a very important attribute, according to my psychic aunt Stella. She spotted Andrew's negative energy immediately and told him so over Sunday lunch at Mum's on the very first day she met him. Mum and I choked on our wine. Andrew was mortified. Went bright red. I didn't blame him. It was harsh and judgemental, but that's what Aunt Stella's like, says it how she sees it. I jumped to his defence, of course, and Aunt Stella and I spent the rest of the weekend giving each other the silent treatment. But she was right all along, wasn't she?

Aunt Stella would love Teddy Fallon though, and I know that if she met him she'd tell me to give him a chance, say he'd make an ace boyfriend, husband material. The kind who'd hold your hair back while you were spewing up in the toilet after a night out, empty the dishwasher and tidy up before you even got out of bed, take the bins out without being asked twenty-six times, assemble Ikea furniture without moaning and groaning and throwing all his toys out of the pram; the kind who'd be lovely and charming to your mum and psychic aunt Stella. I bet Lydia, Teddy's ex, is kicking herself now, letting him get away. I watch him as he revs up the engine and peers at the speedometer. His hair is gelled back today and he has a five o'clock shadow, which actually quite suits him – makes him look a bit rough and rugged. Can someone really grow on you in seven days? Someone who isn't even your type?

He revs the engine again, says something about spark plugs, then switches it off. 'You sure you're okay?' he asks suddenly, clearly feeling my eyes on him.

I quickly drop my head and stare at the RI gold fob hanging from the strap of my handbag, dismissing all thoughts of a romance with Teddy Fallon. I'm in a very dark place at the moment. I feel lost, alone. I miss that intimacy you can only share with a partner. The isolation is sometimes deafening. It's not just the sex. I miss cooking for two, sharing meals, exchanging glances when something funny or stupid or amazing happens on the telly. But starting a relationship now wouldn't be right – or fair. On him or me.

'Yes, I'm fine. I'm just a bit hot,' I reply, then as I fan myself with my hand, the stench of puke on the sleeve of my cream jacket makes my stomach spin like a gyroscope. Oh my God, I didn't think I had any vomit left in me. My face burns as I clumsily reach for the door lever.

'I'm sorry,' I pant, retching. 'I need to get out.'

Swallowing back the sickly sourness in my throat, I start pulling the metal lever but it won't budge. I yank at it with urgency, the beige interior closing in around me. Jab, jab, jab. It must be stuck. Panic swells in my stomach and bolts into my chest. I feel trapped. I can't breathe. Jab, jab, jab, and then I hear a thud like bullets and the door opens. I let out a puff of relief, heart whacking against my ribcage like a squash ball, and it is only then I register that Teddy switched the ignition back on and released the central locking. It all happened so swiftly.

'You're making a habit of being my knight in shining armour, aren't you?' I say breathlessly, the sickness now choosing to park up in my stomach. 'How many times have we met? Three? And I've been sick on two of them. What must you think of me.'

Teddy turns in his seat, one arm draped over the steering wheel. 'No, not at all. I think…' he hesitates, looks out of the windscreen, as if he's not sure if he should deliver the next line, and, judging from his facial expression, I'm not sure I want to hear it. I really can't take any more knockbacks this week. 'I think you're a very intelligent and strong woman, actually,' he says finally. Strong? Intelligent? I think he needs to have a lie down. 'We all have our off days. Our ups and downs, and you've been through so much in such a short space of time.' I do a miniscule frown, does he know? Surely, Alison hasn't told him already. 'What with the divorce and the affair.'

I shake my head. Glad that Alison hasn't been slagging me off to her gardener. Teddy's being very kind but I can tell by the look on his face that he doesn't mean it. I bet he wishes that I hadn't answered his fifth call outside Vincenzo's of Farringdon forty minutes ago.

My phone started ringing the moment I stepped out of the café, Simon's hand firmly under my right elbow as if escorting his ninety-eight-year-old deluded great aunt, Vincenzo on his heel, asking if I was okay, if he should call me a cab. Simon dismissed him, lied, told him I'd had one too many, because that's the sort of man that he is; and then he just stood there like a useless twat, hands in pockets, face etched with pity, or was it disgust? Probably both.

I steadied myself against one of the tables outside and searched for my ringing phone in my handbag, gasping, strands of hair in my mouth, cold sweat on my nape and back, while Simon rambled on about having sick on his trousers, being late and missing his train. By the time I pulled out my phone it stopped ringing. But through a mist of pained tears, I registered four missed calls from Teddy Fallon, and then it lit up again, as if by magic – Teddy calling. I almost cried out with relief when Teddy said he was in the area and did I fancy dinner, because I had no idea how I was going to get home. There was no way I could risk it on the underground with nausea on the warpath, and I'm not sure a cabbie would've allowed me into the back of his car covered in spew. However, having almost emptied my internal organs on the tiled floor of Vincenzo's of Farringdon, dinner was the last thing on my mind. But I accepted a lift home in a heartbeat and before I knew it Teddy's Ford Mondeo came tearing down the street like a scene from a superhero movie.

'Look, I know it's none of my business,' Teddy says now, 'but…well, do you want me to come in? Just to talk, I mean, nothing else. I can tell that something's wrong,' he says kindly. I focus on his thumb gently caressing the steering wheel – his nails are clean and clipped and very clean for a gardener. I like a man who takes care of himself. Andrew only showered when I had a go at him and often wore the same underpants all week. 'I'm a good listener,' Teddy offers kindly. 'Or we can just sit and watch rubbish TV if you like.'

'Um…' I blink furiously, a habit I had as a child, which infuriated my father enough to show me the back of his sandalwood scented hand on occasion. I outgrew it after he died, but it occasionally returns to haunt me, usually when I'm under a lot of pressure, or when life gets a little complicated.

I mull over Teddy's offer. My plans for tonight was a lonely night in with a TV dinner washed down with that leftover wine in the fridge, then nipping to the offie for another bottle. I could really do with a bit of company, and, if I'm honest, I am a bit afraid of going into my flat alone after what happened yesterday. What if Simon's right, what if it isn't Jasmine? What if the intruder is waiting for me inside this time? I could ask Teddy to come in until I search the place, make sure I'm safe. But then should I really confide in a man I barely know? He is the Maxwells' gardener. He really likes them. They're his employers. He might not even believe me when I tell him what happened. No one else seems to. Even Karen has blown me out. Teddy might just get up and leave – not want to get involved. But what if he does believe me? I'll have someone on my side then. Someone to fight my corner. He might even have a word with Alison for me. Satisfied, I reach into my handbag for my keys, then as I look up to say "Yes, that'll be lovely," I catch him glancing at his watch.

'No,' I snap, returning my attention to the contents of my handbag. 'I'll be fine. You get yourself home.' Of course he doesn't want to spend another moment with me. What was I thinking? He was just being polite and thoughtful. I mustn't take advantage of his kindness.

‘What?’ I’ve shocked him. He’s gone red. ‘No, I really don’t mind. I–’

I don’t let him finish. ‘Why the hell does everything always end up in the bottom of my fucking bag?’ I feel my cheeks sting as I rifle through my bag for my door keys, blinking some more. God, he’s going to think I’m a total nutjob. He’s been so kind and lovely to me and I’ve just been a burden. ‘Found them,’ I say, waving the keys in my fist at him. ‘I’ve taken up enough of your time. Thank you so much for coming to my rescue – again.’ I wait for him to respond, to say that I’m being silly, that of course he’d like to come in and keep me company, but he just looks at me, lips curved downwards, eyebrows drawn together like slashes. I bet he’s delighted that I threw him that get-out-of-jail card.

Feeling stupid and pathetic, I swallow back a fresh bout of tears, but as I dangle a leg out of the car, the engine dies and I hear the zing of a seatbelt flying into its socket. ‘No, come on,’ Teddy insists. ‘I’m coming in. You look like you need a friend tonight.’

‘I’ll be fine,’ I lie. ‘Go home. Your mum’ll be worried. You’ve got an early start.’

‘Lucy,’ he says indignantly. ‘I’m not five, you know.’

‘But you must be starving,’ I protest. ‘I’m warning you now, there’s no food in the flat. I don’t even think I’ve got any milk.’ I know I haven’t got any because I used the last of it this morning to make a cup of tea, but I’m too ashamed to admit it. ‘And besides.’ I gesture at my clothes. ‘Look at me, I’m a complete mess. I need to shower.’ I point at my hair. ‘Wash this mop. Run while you can.’ I laugh lightly.

‘You look great.’ He’s being kind again. I smile but as he reaches out for my hair I freeze. I hope he’s not caressing any dried vomit. ‘You always look lovely. I love your golden curls.’

‘I straightened it this morning,’ I give it a flick for misbehaving, and his hand drops onto the gear stick. ‘I hate it.’

‘Got caught in the rain this morning, eh?’

‘It was the steamy café and the heat, actually. Long story.’

He smiles warmly when I say this. ‘You see, that’s what I love about you, you don’t care about how you look.’

I pull a face, just for a fraction of a second. ‘Thanks. I think.’

‘No, what I meant was, most woman would be mortified if they got their freshly styled hair ruined in a smoggy café. Lydia refused to get out of the car if there was a downpour.’ Teddy stares ahead wistfully. ‘Unless I ran alongside her with an umbrella; and God help me if a drop of rain landed anywhere near her head.’

Leaning closer, he pushes a few loose strands off my face, then his gaze drops to my lips. Bloody hell, I think he’s going to kiss me. Oh God, please make him stop. I really don’t want this, not just because of my vom breath, but because I just don’t, not here, not now. I pull the strap of my bag higher onto my shoulder, breaking the moment, and he sits back, curling his hands around the steering wheel, grimacing into the footwell. I hope I haven’t offended him, but I don’t care if I have. If he read the signs wrong, like Simon did, at least he’s got the message now and knows that there’ll be no sex off me tonight. Or any night. Not that I think he wants to sleep with me. Why would he? Jesus, when did I turn into this paranoid freak? He’s been nothing but a gentleman from the onset and I’ve been nothing but a pain in the fucking arse.

‘Look, Teddy, thanks for giving me a lift home.’ I’m itching to get out of the car now but I don’t know what to say to him. So, we just sit there in awkward silence, staring ahead, as if watching a film. A cyclist blinks by, a flash of yellow and blue. Across the road, a young woman unloads shopping bags from the boot of her car then disappears behind a huge tree. I wonder if it's the exact spot where Jasmine spied on me and took that incriminating photograph, or if she was, as I suspect, parked up in her car further along the road. I gnaw the inside of my bottom lip. If she were hiding there now, snapping photos of me and Teddy, we'd look like something out of a dependency group – a therapist and his patient. I've barely slept these last few days. I've been living off crisps, toast, tea and Xenia's apples from her tree in the garden, which she swung over the garden fence in an Asda bag for life.

The clank of the door opening makes me jump. 'Sorry, I'm coming in and I'm not taking no for an answer. Come on. You look like you could do with a hot meal inside you. I'll order us a takeaway while you freshen up. I've got Deliveroo on speed dial.'

Chapter 12

I catch a flicker of a stocky man in a white helmet and the back of Teddy's head at the front door as I pad into the living room, towel drying my hair. My mind was so full of that sandalwood-spritzed photograph and what happened with Simon earlier that I didn't hear the doorbell go in the steamy bathroom as I dried myself off and hurriedly threw on a pair of old joggers and t-shirt.

Chucking the wet towel onto the sofa, I lift my phone off the coffee table and amble into the kitchen for some clean plates and cutlery. Has Alison or Karen tried calling me? Texting? Whatsapping? No. There's just a lone voicemail notification from Mum, which makes my stomach tighten. I still haven't returned her missed calls from yesterday morning. I haven't been ignoring her on purpose. It actually slipped my mind. The poor woman will be climbing the walls. Mum's a worrier, a gene she kindly bestowed on me. Kate's more like our late father – nerves of steel, strong, confident.

I press play and Mum's gruff voice filters through the handset. *'Lucy, it's your mum.'* She pauses for dramatic effect, as if the answerphone will greet her with glee. *'Why haven't you returned my calls?'* she demands. I can hear voices in the background – the TV, I think. *'I've only rung you twenty-nine times!'* There's a long-drawn-out sigh, or is it a drag on a cigarette? *'I hope everything is okay. I'm a bit worried.'* A bit worried in mum language is 90% worried. I picture my petite mother sitting on the edge of her green retro fabric armchair, hair in pink rollers, one arm folded under her chest, ciggie in hand. '*Or, maybe you phoned the landline and I was out. Did you?*' she asks hopefully. Mum has a habit of asking questions in a voicemail. Another long drawn-out sigh – definitely a lug on a fag. *'I was out with Linda Hunter, you know, from number sixteen. Oh, don't ask, Lucy. It was a last-minute thing. She had a gift card from her birthday last January that was about to expire. Didn't have anyone else to go with. I know I said I'd blown her out since she made those acidic comments about my thinning hair and old age jowls, but...'*

As Mum continues to give me a monotonous commentary on her afternoon tea at The Grand Hotel with her friend Linda whose husband left her for a man, I notice that the table has already been set, which I find slightly weird, but in the nicest possible way. I take in the knives and forks, neatly placed on green Ikea napkins, two plates, the ones with the gold rimmed edges. I usually reserve those for guests. I bet Teddy's ex didn't lift a finger around the house when they were married. Blimey, he's even pulled out that half bottle of Chilean Blanc I was saving for a sesh later on and filled two glasses. I was wondering where I'd put those crystal goblets. They were a wedding gift from Andrew's aunt Peggy. Tall stemmed and elegant with a design of two hearts entwined. Royal Daulton. Pricey. Andrew looked them up on Google because he wanted to take them back for the cash equivalent, but I wouldn't let him. Aunt Peggy is loaded. She and her husband Ron own half of Edinburgh. It occurs to me as they glint under the spotlight that we never actually used them. I thought Andrew nabbed them when he left. Funny how Teddy came across them so easily.

'ANYWAY, Lucy.' Mum's voice goes up an octave, as if she knows I'm not listening. 'I know you're busy, love. I just want to know if you're okay. I haven't heard from you in days, so unlike you. Ring me when you get this, lovey. Love you. Bye.' She says the word 'bye' in a whisper. Mum and I always say goodbye to each other at least four times before we hang up, our voices growing smaller and smaller, until they become a whisper. Kate and I do it too. It's a Harper thing. I end the call and smile at my screensaver – a selfie of me and Mum on Brighton Pier, blonde curls blowing in the wind, heads together, arms flung around each other. Maybe selling up and moving to Brighton isn't such a bad idea. What have I really got left in London, apart from my job?

'Hope you like Thai.' Teddy bustles in, white plastic carrier bag in hand, filling the kitchen with an aroma of delicious spices. My stomach rumbles. It's my favourite takeaway. A man after my own heart.

Over dinner, Teddy tells me more about his boys. They stayed over for a few days while Lydia went on a spa break with her mates. Carrie, his mother, loves them to bits, cooked them their favourite meals and bought them lots of pressies to take back home, she even popped in a scented candle for the ex-wife. Carrie's a kind woman, non-judgemental, fair, leaves her blue jacket in Parliament before she comes home. The apple doesn't fall far from the tree then. He loved doing all the dad things with them, kicking a ball around in the park, taking them to the cinema, scoffing junk food – all the things their fitness-freak mum won't allow.

'At least you and Lydia are civil with each other and she lets them stay,' I reason, biting on a spring roll, and he agrees.

When I ask to see a photo of his kids, his face lights up and before I know it two lads in P.E. kits stare back at me from his mobile phone. I pinch the screen to get a better look, gasp, tell him they're the spit of him, with their dark eyes and brown hair, which results in my forearm being squeezed so tightly that I fear he'll cut off my blood supply.

It isn't long before we slip onto the subject of my vomiting session at Vincenzo's of Farringdon. And because he's so kind, because he seems so trustworthy, because I'm desperate to share this secret with someone other than my sister, I risk it and blurt out everything, bar the break-in and the fragranced photo, because I don't want to overload him with information, and I don't want to spook him. Teddy nods and sighs and murmurs in-between mouthfuls of Pad Thai and sips of wine. By the time I've finished talking, he looks almost as exhausted as I feel.

Contrary to my expectations, he isn't full of wisdom and hasn't got the answers I was hoping for, nor does he suggest having a word with Alison, despite my heavy hinting. I don't blame him. He probably doesn't want to get involved, risk losing the gardening gigs. Alison might sack him if she thinks he's a busybody and Karen will follow suit. I'm just bloody delighted that he believes me. The devil in me even does a little fist pump when he tells me that he's only met Simon once but didn't like him, got bad vibes, seemed shifty and sneaky. We both agree that Alison is blinded by love and is too good for him.

'Don't worry, Lucy, the truth always comes out in the end. Alison's a great person. You'll be friends again in no time once she finds out what a knob she married.' I love his optimism but I doubt that'll happen. 'But you really ought to report all this to the police. Blackmail is a serious offence,' he insists, and I feel my face go pink. Imagine if he knew about the break-in and the photograph, he'd march me to the nearest station himself. 'I'm sure there's a law against harassing someone anonymously via text too.'

I shake my head at the plate, pushing a few red peppers around. 'They might want to question Alison if I report it. I don't want that. Besides, I doubt they'll take me seriously, especially once they see the photograph.' I wish people would stop telling me to go to the police and come up with something more useful. 'I'm pretty sure it isn't an offence to send someone annoying texts from an unknown number. Google's advice was to block the caller, which I haven't done – yet.' I look up at him for a reaction but he just carries on eating. 'I want to see if Jasmine sends me anything else,' I go on, scratching my cheek. 'I want to catch her out. Even clever lawyers can let their guard down sometimes, and she is partial to a few glasses of red and the odd sniff of coke.'

Teddy inclines his head as if to say, *your call* as he wipes his mouth with the green napkin. 'If you've got a hunch that it's Jasmine, why don't you confront her?' he asks casually, and I almost spit out my mouthful of rice.

'I can't just turn up and accuse her of blackmail without any proof,' I say, swallowing. 'She'll probably throw me out, and Andrew will do his flipping nut. That's the last thing I need right now, especially as I want to hang onto this place.' I look around the kitchen, as if it's my birthright.

'I'm sure it won't come to that,' Teddy reasons.

'You don't know Andrew. He's got a short fuse.'

Teddy twists noodles around his fork thoughtfully, and then his face lights up. 'Hey, I know what. Why don't you tell Jasmine you've decided to put the flat on the market and want her input, put her in a good mood?'

'But I haven't.' I take a glug of wine.

'Yes, I know that, but you could just pretend, so you can get your foot in the door, sweeten her up.'

My cutlery clashes against the plate. 'You mean LIE?' I cry, as if I've never lied to anyone in my life before. 'It was lying that got me into this mess in the first place. If I'd gone to Alison from the beginning and told her what Simon did we wouldn't be having this conversation now.'

Teddy spears the last strip of beef and swishes it around his plate, soaking up all the gravy. This man certainly has an appetite. He polished off most of food himself, whilst I nursed a bit green curry and rice. Despite my earlier pangs of hunger, I lost my appetite the moment I sat at the table. I push my plate away and fold my arms.

'It'll only be a white lie. If you can convince Jasmine that you're no longer the enemy, she might crack and confess. She might even tell Alison what she really saw.' I want to hug him for saying this, for believing me, for being on my side. 'Do you want that?' He nods at my plate, I shake my head, tell him to help himself. 'Once you get a confession, you can say you've changed your mind about the sale,' he says, pouring my leftovers onto his polished plate. 'Or that you've raised the money, after all. That your great aunt in Cheam came up with the cash.'

'I haven't got a great aunt.'

'Luccccy,' he groans, clearly exasperated by my lack of cooperation. I stare at my empty plate, smeared with green creamy sauce as he wolfs down my leftovers. 'Make something up. Anything.' His chair scrapes against the tiles as he gets to his feet. 'Come on, I'll wash up then make us a coffee.' Coffee? I was hoping he'd nip out for another bottle of wine.

Sighing, I mull over his suggestion as he crosses the kitchen and puts the dishes in the sink, all the while keeping up a monologue of how I should be vindicated, it isn't fair, Simon can't get away with it – Teddy hates morons like him who take advantage of women.

Maybe Teddy Fallon is full of wisdom, after all. Leaning forward, I cross my arms over the table. I suppose I could go round to Jasmine's tomorrow. She works from home on Fridays. Alison told me that her parents are away, and Andrew will be unblocking someone's loo. The house will be empty. I file my nail against my tooth thoughtfully, then leap to my feet, dismissing the idea. Teddy's being naïve, he doesn't know Jasmine, doesn't realise what she's capable of. She'll never admit to what she's done, no matter what I say.

With a heavy heart, I stack the takeaway cartons, giving Teddy a sad smile as he rolls up a sleeve of his denim shirt. Bless him. I know he's trying to help and I am grateful for his input but his idea is completely flawed. It'll never work. Then as I pinch the wineglasses between my thumb and two fingers, an idea flies into my mind like a rocket and I do a little involuntary gasp. What if I go to Jasmine's but instead of trying to get a confession out of her, I look for evidence instead, like the phone she's been using to blackmail me with and the sandalwood cologne she sprayed on that bloody photo. There's a good chance she's hidden them somewhere together. Teddy shoots me a look, eyebrows knitted, and I realise that I've been still for ages, glaring at the microwave on the worktop, posh glasses pinched between fingers, empty containers in hand.

'What's wrong, have you got cramp?' Teddy says. Cramp? Seriously? I give him a weak smile, tell him that I've decided to take a few days off work, which isn't a lie, and was wondering whether to call Gillian, my boss, in the morning, or just send her an email tonight, and he nods, smiling, says it's a splendid idea, then squeezes green liquid into the sink and turns on the taps.

'These are bit delicate,' I warn, placing the glasses onto the worktop.

'No problem.' He throws me a lopsided smile. 'I'm good with delicates.' And I get the feeling he's talking metaphorically.

I grab a tea towel, and as Teddy hums the theme tune to *Tipping Point* under his breath, my masterplan plays out in my mind like a movie trailer. I arrive at Jasmine's, full of confidence, the moment she sees me she tries to slam the door in my face but I manage to hook my foot between the door and frame like a loan shark. I say I've come in peace, that I forgive her for taking my husband because it's led me into the arms of my soulmate, not true, but Teddy's right, a white lie won't hurt. I can even take a selfie of me and Teddy before he leaves tonight to make it look authentic. Then I lay it on thick, tell her that I miss her, and now that I'm settled with someone new I hope we can be friends again, and she nods, stands aside and lets me in.

My mind starts reeling as I buff a wineglass down until it squeaks, one idea stumbling over the other excitedly while Teddy continues washing and humming. Once Jasmine and I are settled in the Anands' hi-tech celebrity style kitchen. I'll tell her that I've decided to sell the flat, get her in a good mood, like Teddy suggested, and then I'll call the anonymous number discreetly while she's brewing coffee, and listen out for it ringing in the house. If it's switched off, and I imagine it will be, I'll make out I need the loo and go on a hunt to find the evidence.

'You seem suddenly chirpy.' Teddy gives me a sideward glance. 'What's up?'

I pop the gleaming glass onto the worktop. 'I've decided you're right,' I enthuse. 'I will go and see Jasmine.' I can't share my genius plan with Teddy because if I tell him I'll be snooping around her house looking for evidence he might try to put me off. Teddy's got that stiff law-abiding air about him. An old-school kind of person. You know the sort I mean – honest, conscientious, does everything by the book, but would report his neighbours to the council for noise pollution in a heartbeat. Teddy grins and goes a bit red, tells me that it's the sensible thing to do. See what I mean?

'I'll pop round tomorrow morning,' I say cheerily, elbowing him out of the way. 'Let me finish the dishes, you put on the kettle.'

'Now, that sounds like a plan.' Teddy grins, brushing past me. 'Do you want me to come with?'

'Oh God, no. I can handle Jasmine,' I laugh lightly feeling strangely calm as the warm suds caress my skin. I run a sponge over a plate. Behind me, I hear Teddy cluttering around making the coffee, the clank of mugs, the hiss of the cutlery drawer. I smile at the soapy water. I'm glad Teddy's here keeping me company and offering friendly useful advice. Glad I've got someone fighting my corner.

A sharp noise startles me and my head snaps up. Outside, the security light comes on. I catch sight of a ginger tail before it disappears over the fence. I smile into the soapsuds; a tin rattles along concrete, tarp flaps against scaffolding from the adjacent house, they're doing a loft conversion, and then I remember reading about Storm Nigel hitting the south on Twitter this morning. I hope none of my fences come down. I hear the low thud of the fridge door behind me.

'We're out of milk,' Teddy announces, and I go stiff at the sink. The security light goes off. The garden darkens. WE'RE? As in US? Me and him? I hope he's not getting too cosy. I do like him and he's definitely growing on me. But I don't want a relationship. Perhaps I need to make that perfectly clear. Nip it in the bud. I open my mouth to speak when he says, 'I'll just pop to the corner shop and get some for you.'

'No, please, you've done enough for me already.'

'Don't be silly, that's what friends are for.'

Phew. Friends. I rinse a fork, head down, so that he can't see that I've gone pink. It was a figure of speech, of course it was. A slip of the tongue.

'We haven't got the luxury of a corner shop, I'm afraid,' I say over my shoulder, rinsing the last dish. 'Don't worry, I like black coffee.'

'Nonsense. I'll drive to a petrol station. What if you fancy a bowl of Cheerios in the morning, hmm?'

'They're my favourite. You must be psychic.'

'I knew you were going to say that,' he says and I laugh – kind and quick witted too. 'I saw them in your cupboard when I was looking for the wineglasses.' He grins, throwing on his brown corduroy jacket.

'Ah, that explains it then.' I smile.

'Won't be a mo.'

'Semi-skimmed,' I call out as he heads for the door, 'and just a pint. I'm doing a big online shop tomorrow.'

'Okey-dokey.' Teddy's Doc Marten's clamour in the hallway.

Okey-dokey? That's the kind of thing Mum would say. I slide the plate onto the drying rack, fingers dripping with suds, and just then I catch sight of his mobile phone on the worktop.

Drying my hands quickly, I snatch the phone and barrel after him. 'Wait! Your–' The door slams and the words die on my lips. I reach for the lock, I could still catch him before he drives off. I turn the latch, his phone buzzes in my hand. I look down at it, eyes wide – *Alison Calling.*

Taking a few steps back, I gawp at the phone stupidly as it rings and vibrates in my hand. Why is she calling Teddy at nine in the evening? Brrr…brrrr… Surely, she's not that desperate to get her grass cut, he only did it for her last week. Brrr… Did he tell her he was seeing me tonight? Brrr…brrrr… Is he her SPY?

Brrr…brrr… Is that why he's here, to get information out of me? Brrrr…brrr… BRRRR! I stare down at the phone as if it's a deadly virus. I should answer it. It's kismet. I could speak to Alison. Explain. My heart belts like a squash ball – thud, thud, thud. Swallowing hard, my trembling thumb hovers over the screen hesitantly. What's the worst that could happen if I answer it? She'll just hang up, right? I can live with that. My hand is shaking, blood is pumping in my ears. Filling my lungs, I go to press *Accept Call* when it stops ringing. 'Shit,' I say out loud. There's a ruffle and I jump and then the door flings open.

'Sorry,' Teddy says, all red and jolly and flustered. 'Left my…oh.' He stares at the phone in my hand. A missed call alert buzzes through. I look at him and my blood runs cold – how the hell did he let himself in?

Chapter 13

'You've got to be flipping kidding me,' Kate says, as I sashay along the path to a waiting taxi, phone glued to my ear. 'He's going to think you're a bloody psycho.' My sister isn't one to mince her words but this time she has got a point.

Poor Teddy went pale when I accused him of being Alison's spy last night, but when I insisted that he had a copy of my key cut, broke into my flat and left that photograph, spritzed with sandalwood to freak me out, he had to sit down. But what was I supposed to think? How was I to know he picked up my door keys instead of his own from the tall table by the front door? Normal guests carry their keys in their pockets.

Kate's laughter merges with the clunk of bottles and cans. I look round quickly, giving the metal gate a push with my free hand. Spiros, my neighbour, is chucking a shedload of empties into his recycle bin. I'm about to shout out *Good morning, Spiros*, when his wife's voice filters through the hallway and he responds to whatever she said in Greek with, '*Nehhhhhhhh.*' Xenia has taught me a few Greek words and I know that Neh means yes. But Spiros has dragged it out to show his annoyance. He shuffles towards the door in his brown slippers with the velcro straps and navy dressing gown. He hasn't seen me.

'Hang on,' I say to my sister, jamming the phone between my jaw and shoulder. 'I'm just getting into a cab.' My black stilettoes, the only pair of killer heels I own because I'm usually in kitten heels or flats, feel as if they're lined with an army of needle bashers. I steady myself against the open gate, slip off my right shoe and wriggle my toes. For a moment I consider legging it back in and throwing on my leopard print converse shoes, but no, Jasmine's quite tall at 5 foot 8, and I don't want her to look down on me, in any shape or form. Foot pain is a small price to pay for making the right impression. I want to look confident and in control when I confront her at her front door in my snazzy black wide-legged trouser suit and pale blue blouse, complete with sunglasses perched on my head – all Primani, but she's not to know. I'm dressed to kill – metaphorically speaking. I'm not planning on doing her in and burying her within the grounds of her family's seven acre estate…although.

The cab driver revs the engine, my cue to get a move on. I slip my sore foot back into my shoe. A cyclist dings his bell as he swishes by in bright clothing, warning me to stay back. Isn't cycling on the pavement a criminal offence? At the junction ahead, he does a U-turn. I give him a look as I close the gate behind me, and then he leaps off his bike, swings it around and unbuckles the strap of his helmet. I truly hope he's not going to confront me about stepping onto the bloody pavement. I square my shoulders, ready for battle, but then, with a small smile, he pushes my neighbour's gate open. Glancing over my shoulder, I spy Spiros at the door, waiting for him. I recognise him now from the photo on their mantelpiece. It's Kiki. Xenia's good-looking nephew. The one she's been desperate to fix me up with.

The taxi driver revs his engine again and I quickly open the car door, looping back into my conversation with Kate. This is no time for eye-candy.

‘So, why did Alison called Teddy at nine in the evening, then?’ Kate asks.

‘Lucy Harper, booking for twenty-seven The Heath, Brookmans Park,’ confirms the driver in a foreign accent, and I nod and give him the thumbs up.

‘Karen’s fences collapsed in the storm last night,’ I say to Kate as we pull away from the kerb, ‘and Alison wanted to book him in before he got any other jobs.’ Alison doesn’t do nine to five, her tradesman are on 24/7 callout. ‘And then, of course, I was forced to tell Teddy all about the photograph incident and intruder after all that upheaval. And it made everything ten times worse.’

Teddy insisted that I rang the police the moment I showed him the photograph that I accused him of leaving in my flat. I had to pull his hand away when he picked up the phone to dial 999.

‘But I think I’ve redeemed myself with Teddy,’ I say, ‘He rang just before you did, asked if he could store his equipment in my garden overnight, needs the boot space for some gardening posts he’s buying to fix Karen’s fences. No, his mum hasn’t got a garden. Well, she has but it’s all in the front of the house. He’s dropping it all off while I’m at Jasmine’s and picking it up in the morning. It was the least I could do.’

The driver takes a corner sharply, darting a glance in his rear-view mirror as if we’re on the run, and I slide to the right. He must know a short cut. The line crackles in my ear. ‘Look, I’m gonna have to go, Kate, you’re breaking up.’

‘Okay.’ Kate sighs. The volume of the car radio suddenly increases and a woman’s voice blasts from the audio system. ‘*Two men were arrested on suspicion of...*’ I press the handset closer to my ear. It’s hot. ‘Let me know how it goes with Project Jasmine,’ Kate demands. I agree and as I’m about to say goodbye, she quickly adds, ‘And don’t let that slut sweet-talk her way out of it. The woman's a maniac. She should be locked up.'

'I won't,' I say indignantly, rolling my eyes at the taxi driver in the rear-view mirror, as if he's my accomplice.

There are a few moments of silence and I wonder if we've lost connection because we haven't done the goodbye-turning-into-a-whisper session yet.

'Kate? Hello?'

There's a crackle and then a long exhalation. 'Just be careful, Lucy,' she says softly, and I get the feeling that she doesn't approve of what I'm about to do. But she needn't worry. I've worked out my plan to the very last detail. 'If she breezed into your flat and left that photo, you don't know what else she's capable of, do you? A lot of professional people are sinister.' Silence. 'What about that GP who sexually assaulted his female patients, or the one who murdered them with a lethal injection. I know you were besties at school but that was over twenty years ago, people change.' I don't answer. I want her to stop talking, to stop being negative, she's putting me off. 'If you want my opinion I don't think you should go.' A pause and then: 'But I know you will anyway. Just promise me that you'll get the evidence you need and get the hell out of there, okay?' Kate warns. 'Then go straight to the police.' I grimace and shake my head. What does she think Jasmine is going to do, lock me in the cellar and feed me rats' tails for twenty years? 'OKAY?'

'Yes, Miss. Okay!'

'And there's no need to be sarky. I'm just concerned. Right, I'll speak to you later then. Bye.' And with this she hangs up, without even doing the whispery farewell routine.

Twenty minutes later, we pull up outside the Anands' six-bedroom detached house and, as expected, everything inside me tightens.

'We're here, madam,' the driver announces.

I look up at the Georgian-style mansion, squinting at the sun, and without warning a flurry of warm memories dive into my mind – Jasmine and I singing along to the latest George Michael CD in her bedroom, using hairbrushes as microphones, playing cricket in her garden with her cousins and siblings, laughing because she can't bat a ball to save her life; giggling and slightly pissed fifteen-year olds necking her parents' vintage champagne straight from the bottle while they're at work, and then, much later, dropping her off in Andrew's white van after rescuing her from a disastrous date with a sex-starved creep whom she met online who looked twenty years older and three stones heavier than his profile picture. I can still see his beady eyes checking me out as I stormed into the pub and blatantly lied about a family emergency, still feel his sweaty palm in mine as he stood to greet me, taking my form in hungrily. Beady Eyed Perve knew that Jasmine and I weren't sisters, any fool could see that; she's darker and prettier and much better spoken than I am, but I didn't care. I just wanted to get her away from him, protect her.

Breaking out of my reverie, I shuffle forward on the leather seat awkwardly. 'Thank you,' I say to the driver. 'I was…um…wondering if…' The driver fiddles with his phone, disinterested. 'If you could…um…do me a favour.' He gathers his thick brows, eyes on his phone. I suppose I should take that as a *no*, but I plough on hopefully. 'Would you mind waiting?' More frowning, deeper this time. 'For about five minutes.'

He pivots in his seat stiffly and looks at me, as if I've just asked him to drive me to Scotland for free, then as he opens his mouth to protest, I pull out my purse and his dark, almost black, eyes shine. 'In case they're not in.' I curl a strand of hair behind my ear. 'And could you reverse the car a bit too. I don't want them to see me arriving.' He looks at me, unsmiling, and I can tell that he thinks I'm an idiot. 'It's um...' I give my hair another curl behind my ear, even though it hasn't moved an inch out of place. 'Bad luck to see a guest arriving in their religion.' And now I don't even know what I'm saying. 'They're very spiritual.'

The driver's expression says: *'Are you fucking serious?'* His lips part but before he can speak I stick my arm between the gap of the two front seats, twenty quid aloft. 'Sure, miss, no problem.' He whips the note from my hand, shoves the car into reverse and back we glide.

When the cool air slaps my face, a cocktail of questions spill into my mind and I hesitate. What if Kate's right, what if I'm walking into a danger zone? What if I get the door slammed in my face, because, let's face it, I'm not going to hook my foot in-between, am I? I'm no gangster. Jasmine might ring Andrew to come home if he's nearby. Andrew will go mental, and if he thinks I'm harassing his pregnant girlfriend, he might even call the police. For a moment I imagine being escorted off the premises by a young WPC, driven home in a panda car in shame and served with a restraining order. I'll get a criminal record. I shudder, batting the thought away. It won't come to that.

I focus on the sound of my heels clattering against the pavement for distraction as I head for the house – clickerty clack, clack, clickerty, clack, clack. My feet burn in my pointy shoes. Clickerty, clack, clack; clickerty clack clack. I'm almost there. I can see the curve of the two-way driveway, the navy double doors with the white pillars on either side. Clickerty, click, clickerty click. Then as I go to turn into number twenty-seven, the door suddenly flies open. A figure steps out. Backtracking quickly, I throw a glance at the driver over my shoulder, like a deer in headlights. He gives me the thumbs up, indicating that he's on standby. I think he's expecting me to get back in. Moving forward slowly, I peer over a hedge. It's Andrew. He's on the doorstep looking haggard, holdall in hand, frowning at his phone. I look at my wrist – 10.05. Why the hell is he still at home? Andrew's a stickler for punctuality, never takes a day off work, even when he's got man-flu.

I jump as an ambulance siren screams in my ears, lights flashing. Andrew looks up absently as it zooms past and my stomach flickers. I duck out of the way. Shit, he's seen me.' I'm on my haunches, backed against the hedge. Cars swish up and down the street. A car door thuds, the engine of his white van thrums. I'm safe. He hasn't seen me. I look at the driver again, who is blatantly craning his neck to get a better view, mouth hanging open. He must think I'm mad.

Turning up the collars of my jacket, I straighten up, slip on my sunglasses, then pull my phone out of my bag, turning my back on the Anand mansion, so that the driver can think a call is coming through. I even shake my head and shrug for effect. Pressing the handset to my ear, I dip my head. Andrew must not see me. It'll ruin everything if he does. There's a crunch of wheels against tarmac, then the familiar cranking and rattling of his diesel engine as he takes off in the opposite direction.

Once Andrew's van becomes a white dot in the distance, I push the strap of my bag higher onto my shoulder and make my way down the hundred-foot drive. I glance at my watch – almost ten past. Jasmine should be up and brewing coffee at her Lavazza. That's if she's not suffering from morning sickness.

I'm standing in front of the huge double doors, slightly breathless, finger hovering over the doorbell, and then I suddenly freeze. What if her parents are back? What if Jasmine's not even home? What if… I take one last lungful of breath. *Come on, Lucy, you can do this.* Then as I go to push the doorbell, a feeling of dread washes over me and everything darkens. What if Jasmine catches me snooping around her house? Will she call the police? Will I get a criminal record, lose my job? I look at my hands, they're trembling violently, my arms tingle, my legs feel like lead. With a shaky hand, I touch my forehead. I've come out in a cold sweat. What's happening to me? I've had panic attacks before but this is off the scale. Am I having a heart attack, a stroke? I look around wildly. The exit swims in my vision, as if it's a mile away. I can't go through with this. Dad was right; I'm weak, pathetic. Andrew was right; I'm damaged, broken. What made me think I could carry off this ludicrous plan?

My pulse picks up pace and starts thumping in my ears – lubdub, lubdub, lubdub. I've got to get out of here before anyone sees me – lubdub, lubdub, lubdub. I take a few awkward steps back. Above me, a bird squawks, and as I look up I see it, staring at me like a huge evil eye. Oh no, they've fitted a security camera in the doorway- lubdub, lubdub, LUBDUB. Is Jasmine watching me now on her laptop like big brother?

Turning, I hurry along the paved driveway, breaking into a semi-jog, legs like jelly. I look at my watch. I'm not going to make it. The driver will have gone. I'll be stuck here for ages waiting for another cab. I decide very quickly that the only chance I've got of getting back to the waiting taxi in time is to make a run for it barefoot. Steadying myself against the back of Jasmine's Porsche, I go to pull of my shoe and in my clumsy, panicky haste, my bag slides off my shoulder, landing by one of the wheels before I can catch it. 'SHIT,' I say out loud, and then, with a glance over my shoulder, squat and start stuffing everything back inside, blinking furiously, hands shaking, breath quickening, sweat beading at my hairline. I chuck in the last item, an old lip gloss, face ablaze, pull off my right shoe and then…

'Lucy?' I freeze, shoe in hand, eyes squeezed shut. Oh God, no. Please, no. There's a shuffle of footsteps and then, 'I thought it was you.'

Getting to my feet, I turn around slowly, one foot on tiptoe so that I won't look like a midget next to her, and then I'm face to face with my nemesis, and I know, without a shadow of a doubt, that there's no way back. Not now. Not ever. I have to see this through to the bitter end.

'Hello, Jasmine.'

Chapter 14

It's been so long since I last saw Jasmine that I've almost forgotten what she looked like. I'm not sure what I was expecting, if I'm honest. I suppose I was secretly hoping she'd be a mess. A rough pasty version of herself, given that she's up the duff and has probably been spewing her guts out all morning. Jasmine always had a bit of an icky stomach, even on school trips she had to sit in the front of the coach with the teachers and a sick bag.

But now she looks vibrant, fresh; has a glow about her that I've never seen before. Her sultry brown eyes sparkle against her healthy looking mocha skin. Gone is the middle parting with the nineties-style strands framing her pretty oval face, and in its place is a high ponytail and a thick shiny fringe that starts at the crown of her head. It suits her. It's taken years off her. I look at her stomach for evidence of a bump, but it's covered in a loose-fitting running top, which she's worn over Lycra leggings and high-tech purple and orange trainers. Probably Sweaty Betty, she loves their stuff.

Jasmine speaks first. 'What a surprise.' She tugs at the sleeve of her t-shirt and does a little quiver. The hairs on her arms are standing on end. September has brought the chill of autumn with it. It's hard to believe how warm and humid it was yesterday. Or perhaps seeing me on her doorstep has sent a cold shiver up her spine.

I give her a tight smile, heart returning to its natural rhythm. Not a heart attack or a stroke, thank God. A massive, very, very scary panic attack. 'How did you…um,' I croak, then hesitate. This isn't how I imagined it would be. Jasmine was supposed to be alone for a start, not waving Andrew off on the doorstep looking like she's just stepped off the front cover of Women's Running magazine. I expected door slamming, tempers flaring, police calling. This warm friendly demeanour has thrown me. I try to swallow but my throat is dry. 'How did you know I was out here?' Then I point over her shoulder. 'Ah. You saw me. On that.'

Jasmine follows my eyes to the CCTV at the front door. 'Oh, no. That's been on the blink for ages. Whole system is a shambles. Mum's been moaning at Dad to get a new one fitted but you know what he's like.' Yes, I do, tight as two coats of paint, despite his millions. 'I was just coming down the stairs and saw someone standing by my car from the lobby window.' She glances at her Porsche lovingly. 'It's new. Only had it a few weeks.' I know this. Alison told me. But say nothing. I smile at the car and nod approvingly. 'Anyway, er… if you're looking for Andrew, you've just missed him.'

'Actually I was…' I suck my lips in and look at my pointy black shoes peeking beneath the flare of my wide-leg trousers, and I suddenly feel ridiculous. What possessed me to dress as if I was going to a court hearing on a Friday morning? 'I'm…' I want to tell her that I'm here to talk about the sale of the flat, like Teddy suggested, that I want her thoughts, input, but the words have gone into lockdown at the back of my throat. I shake my head. 'Actually, yes, I was hoping to catch Andrew. I wanted to talk to him about the flat. It's not important. I'll ring him later. Sorry to have bothered you.'

I make to leave when she says. 'Don't be stupid. You're here now. Why don't you come in? I'll order a cab to take you home. We can have a coffee while you wait.' She waves a hand, as if there's been no bad blood between us, as if she didn't steal my husband from right under my nose, as if she hasn't been stalking me and sending me anonymous blackmailing texts, didn't break into my flat and leave that smelly photograph that almost made me shit myself, isn't carrying my ex-husband's baby inside her, hasn't stolen my life.

'But I…' I point aimlessly over my shoulder. Jasmine knits perfectly shaped eyebrows and leans forward, shifting her weight onto one leg and begins to scan the drive.

'Is someone waiting for you?'

The perfect excuse. Why didn't I think of that? I might still catch the taxi if I get a move on. I'm sure he'll be happy to drive me back home, a double fare for him, plus a big tip. The thought of being back in my cosy flat in my loose-fitting clothes and slippers sends a warm rush through my body. 'Actually, no there's no one waiting,' I say, deciding against it. I've come this far. I won't get this opportunity again. I've got to get inside the house and search for the evidence I need to implicate her. 'A taxi just dropped me off. Coffee would be lovely.

Jasmine pours freshly brewed coffee into Orla Kiely mugs, then takes a pew opposite me at the breakfast bar. 'I heard about your fallout with Alison,' she says, curling a slender manicured finger around the handle of her mug. My stomach tightens into a fist. Alison didn't waste much time. I picture them on the phone for hours gossiping, slagging me off. 'Simon told Andrew,' Jasmine clarifies, taking a sip from her flowery cup, and the fist in my stomach unclenches. Alison didn't tell her. 'If it's any consolation, I don't believe a word of it.' No, that's because you know the truth. I blow on my coffee. 'Shit, that Simon really gives me the creeps, you know.' Jasmine does a little shiver and I frown. I wonder what she means by that. Did he try it on with her too, or is it because of what she saw him do to me? I take a sip. It scalds my lips but I'm too wound up to register the pain.

I open my mouth to speak, to find out why he creeps her out when she shifts forward in her seat and says, 'Oh, let's just talk about something else, shall we? I'm sure it's the last thing you want to discuss with me. It's none of my business.' Giving me one of her widest smiles, she puts the mug down on a wooden coaster and reaches for the tongs and a clean plate. The Anand home is full of coasters – Anaya, her mother, chases people around the house with them whenever she has visitors – she's got ring mark phobia. Mind you, this place is fully kitted out in expensive furnishings. I look around the huge luxury kitchen with its slick white handleless units, marble butler's sink and silver Miele appliances. Andrew must feel right at home here; he always reprimanded me for marking all our Ikea furniture. I don't care. Life's too short for coasters. I can ring mark all my furniture to my heart's content now. One of the perks of being single.

Jasmine places a huge croissant dusted in icing sugar in front of me before sitting back down, and I thank her, even though I know I'm not going to touch it. 'Look, Jasmine,' I say, inhaling a waft of sweet buttery pastry.

'I know why.'

We've spoken at the same time.

'Go ahead,' I say, running a finger against the rim of the plate, 'you first.'

Jasmine takes a deep breath in through her nose, rubbing her lycra-clad thighs, and her perfectly rounded fake boobs rise and fall. 'You don't know how long I've been waiting for this moment,' she admits and my eyes twitch. This is it; she's going to confess. I'll get my life back. My friend back. Everything will return to normal. 'I can't begin to tell you how very sorry I am…' she falters, voice breaking. Come on, Jasmine, don't bottle it now. I follow her eyes to the spotlights. Two have blown. 'What I did,' she pauses, swallows. 'Well, it's unforgiveable.' Bloody right it is. You've turned my life into a living nightmare. But instead of anger surging through my veins I feel a light relief. Any moment now it'll all be over.

The whiff of my deodorant dances under my nostrils as I sit upright and straighten my blue blouse in readiness for her confession. I'll ask her to hand over the phone and SIM, then insist that she calls Alison now and tells her the truth. If she refuses then I'll threaten to go to the police. 'I shouldn't have slept with your husband. I truly am sorry,' she blurts and my head jerks up. Not a confession, a bloody useless apology for stealing my husband. A single tear spills from her eye and curves along her petite nose. I wonder how hard it was for her to squeeze it out so convincingly.

Wiping it away quickly with the back of her hand, she flashes me another big smile. 'I don't know why I did it,' she admits, sniffing. I cover my mouth with my fingers to stop myself from screaming *LIAR*. 'I think I was just jealous,' she says with a little laugh, dabbing her nose with the back of her finger.

Dear God, is she seriously suggesting that she ruined my marriage out of pure jealousy? 'Jealous? Of what?'

'Of YOU.' Jasmine throws a hand out, taking in the length of me. 'Of your relationship. Of how things panned out so well for you, yet for me…' A pause and then. 'I know it's no excuse.' No, it isn't. You destroyed my life. What is she going to say next, that it was a mistake, that she wants to call the wedding off, that she doesn't even love Andrew? 'I lost all my confidence after my divorce and just went for the first bloke who showed me a bit of attention. I wanted to be wanted – fancied. You do understand, don't you?' I don't answer. Instead I stare at the shiny black splashback tiles above the counter as an image of her on top of Andrew, of them having sex in my bed flashes in my mind – bedpost knocking, mattress squeaking, hot sweaty naked bodies, the sickening fug of lust.

'It was only supposed to be a one-night stand,' she says, breaking me out of my sickening reverie. If that's her attempt at making me feel better, she's failed miserably. 'We weren't meant to fall in love,' she whispers, and I feel as if I've been punched in the head. 'I'm so sorry.'

The room spins and I have to touch the edge of the worktop to steady myself. God, what am I doing here? Why did I come? Why am I in the same room as the woman who stole my life? I want to leave but I can't move. I continue to stare at the splashback tiles as she whines on and on about Andrew, her words like hard slaps across my face – he means the world to her, they're soulmates, kindred spirits. I want her to stop. I want to cover my ears with my hands and sing lalalalalala to block out her voice. Why is she doing this? I didn't come here today to pick the scab of an old wound and watch it bleed uncontrollably.

'I know you'll never forget this and I don't blame you,' she gulps. 'You've every right to be bitter. I'd be.' More fake teary sniffing. 'But if you could find it in your heart to forgive me…I…' Forgive her? I want to punch the granite worktop so hard that my knuckles will bleed and need stitches. I can feel her eyes on me as I study my chipped nails, watching me, trying to gauge my reaction. Second-guessing people is what she does, isn't it? It's her forte. I stay silent and she sighs loudly, realising she's wasting her time.

‘We all make mistakes. Let’s just put it all behind us,’ I say in a clipped tone, not meaning a word of it. I’m never going to forgive her, but I don’t want to alienate her. I’m here to do a job and I want to see it through.

Jasmine tears off a piece of kitchen towel and blows her nose hard enough to burst a blood vessel. ‘Thank you, Lucy. You’re a much better person than I am.’ That’s the only sensible thing she’s said today. ‘It means a lot,’ she sniffs. We’re silent for a few moments. Birds tweets in the garden. A car door thuds outside. ‘About the invite.’ Rub salt into the wounds, why don’t you? I was wondering when we’d get round to discussing her wedding. ‘Andrew said you won’t be coming.’

I exhale loudly through my nostrils. ‘Bit below the belt, Jas, inviting me. Don’t you think?’ I say, and we both laugh, almost like old times.

‘When I saw you outside, I thought that’s why you were here.’ I frown at her over my coffee cup. ‘You know, to have a go at me for sending you an invite.’ And then, pressing a hand on her chest she says. ‘But I swear to God, Lucy, that was never my intention. I told Andy not to invite you.’ Andy? He always hated being called that. ‘But he just went ahead and posted it through your letterbox anyway.’ I scratch my chin and look at her carefully. Andrew definitely told me that she hand-delivered that card. Why is she lying? Does she know I’m onto her? ‘Stubborn old Scotsman,’ she snorts, rolling her eyes.

I decide very quickly not to challenge her. She obviously doesn’t want me to know that it was her who pushed that card through my letterbox. ‘So, why did you then? Invite me, I mean? It’s not like you to take orders, especially not from a man.’ I take a sip of warm coffee. It is a good blend. Jasmine knows her coffees.

‘Andy convinced me that an invite would reignite our friendship. I do miss you, you know.’ Bullshit. Jasmine doesn’t care about anyone but Jasmine. 'He said you'd moved on, were over what happened. He even suggested that you'd get offended if we invited everyone but you – Alison and Simon are coming, obviously. Andy thought it'd be cruel to leave you out.' I raise my eyebrows. 'Exactly. He forgets I know you better than he does.'

Biting her bottom lip, she cups her hands around her mug, elbows on table, then says, 'I mean, technically, he's the one who cheated on you, isn't he? He was married. I was single.' The mistress, I want to correct, but bite my tongue. 'It could've been any woman.' I look at her pitifully. But it wasn't any woman, Jasmine, was it? It was you – my friend – my childhood buddie. And now I can't sand the fucking sight of you, yet have to sit here and pretend that I'm fine with it all when all I really want to do is tell you to fuck off. I swallow back my angry words and take a deep breath. I don't want her to throw me out, not until I've found what I'm looking for.

'Well, Andrew's…' I pause. 'Andy's right about one thing,' I say, feigning nonchalance. 'I have moved on. I'm seeing someone new actually.' I stare dreamily into my coffee cup for effect then glance up to see her reaction. Her eyes light up. Bingo. 'Early days but I really like him.' Reaching out, she squeezes my arm and annoyance courses through me. I want to slap her hand away but instead, I stiffly cover her hand with mine, forcing a smile.

'Seriously? Wow, that's fantastic, Lucy!' I'm surprised Andrew didn't tell her that he saw Teddy leaving my flat half-naked last Saturday. Not like him to hold back juicy gossip.

'I can show you a picture if you like.' And before she can answer, I whip out my phone and wave the selfie I coaxed Teddy into taking with me yesterday evening, under her nose, even though he wasn't keen, even though he said he hates having his photograph taken, even though he made me promise not to show anyone because he looks awful in it.

'Wow.' Jasmine takes the phone from my hand. 'Not your usual type,' she says smoothly, eyes flitting from me to the phone. 'Bit geeky.' I want to punch her for knowing what my type is, for knowing me so well. 'But he looks really nice.' She pinches the screen to get a better look at him and then a notification flashes up – *How's it going?* Shit, it's from Teddy. Jasmine tilts her head to the side as another message flashes up and her eyes shine – *Need a lift back?*

'You look really cute together,' she trills and I know she's reading the notifications. 'All, right, all right, keep your hair on,' she laughs as I tear the phone from her hand. 'Oh, please tell him to pick you up, Luce. I'd love to meet him.'

'I can't,' I fib. The last thing I want to do is put poor Teddy through a Jasmine Anand grilling. 'I've got to go into the office this afternoon.' I don't. I've taken compassionate leave – emailed Gillian last night – told her someone had broken into my flat (true) and ransacked the place (not true but it was the only way I could get paid leave). Her reply was short and tetchy –*Sorry to hear that, Lucy. Hope you're back with us soon. G.*

Jasmine nods, giving me a once-over, checking me out, and I thank God that I wore this suit after all. 'I bet you wouldn't give Andrew a second look now,' she says and I frown. What's that supposed to mean? 'Theoretically, speaking,' she clarifies, sensing my confusion, and I agree, tell her Teddy and I are a perfect match, that I've never been happier.

We talk about Teddy for a while. I tell her he's Alison's gardener, how she set us up on a blind date last Friday, that it's only been a week but I'm already smitten – he's great around the house, sensitive, kind, intelligent. All true apart from me being smitten but right now I'll say anything to make her believe that I've moved on and am no longer angry with her.

Smiling, she shakes her head, convinced, so I swiftly move on to the sale of my flat, as per our plan.

'Oh, are you moving then?' Jasmine picks up her cup. 'You haven't touched your croissant. They're freshly baked. Lena picked them up for me this morning from the local bakery.' So she still gets her poor old housekeeper to do all her chores for her. Nothing's changed.

I smile, apologise, tell her that I had a big breakfast, even though I only had a cup of tea. 'Yes, I've decided to put the flat on the market,' I lie. Teddy would be so proud of me. 'That's why I'm here. I was hoping to discuss it with you and Andrew.'

'Aww,' she coos, draining her cup. 'You love that flat.'

'Hmm, well…' I stretch my back. I've never been a fan of this bloody barstool. 'I want to make a fresh start, somewhere new. You need the money now, what with the house move, the ba–'

'Money?' she cuts across me. 'House move?' She puts her cup down.

I look at the door as if Andrew is standing behind it. 'Now that you're looking at new properties.' I look at her stomach. 'Because of the baby.'

'Baby?'

For goodness' sake, why is she repeating every single word I say like a parrot? 'Um… yeah, Andrew said…' I cringe. Her three months probably aren't up yet. Andrew being desperate to get me to sell the flat must've told me behind her back. 'Sorry, I must've got it wrong,' I say quickly. 'Crossed wires.'

But it's too late to backtrack. Jasmine looks mortified. 'What the hell do you mean, crossed fucking wires?' And finally, the real Jasmine emerges, claws and horns and fangs. 'What has he been saying about me?' she spits.

I stare at her mutely, shrinking into my shoulders. Oh no, what've I done?

Chapter 15

'I'm not up the duff, if that's what you're thinking,' Jasmine says furiously. 'At least, I bloody well hope not. Shit, why the hell did Andrew tell you that? Fucking dick.' So it's Andrew when she's pissed off with him.

'No, he didn't,' I insist, mouth dry. 'I just assumed.'

She looks at her stomach. 'Are you suggesting that I'm wearing this baggy top to conceal rolls of fat?' Silence. 'ARE YOU?' she demands and I jump. Brilliant. Now she thinks I'm insulting her. 'Because if you've come here today to make me feel like shit, Lucy, you can leave. I mean, I have apologised to you. Hell, I even helped you find your soulmate. You'd never have met Eddy if it weren't for me. What more do you want from me?'

'Nothing,' I say in a panicky voice and I don't correct her version of Teddy's name. 'I'm sorry. Come on, Jas, you know me, that's not what I meant.' *God, please don't let her chuck me out.* 'It's just that I know you've always wanted to be a mum, and what with the shotgun wedding and everything…' I falter. Her face twitches – she believes me. 'In fact, you look as if you've lost weight since I last saw you.' She doesn't, she looks the same but I need to calm her down.

'I *do* go to the gym five times a week,' she says begrudgingly, pushing her half-eaten croissant away from her.

Clearly, she doesn't want me to know about her pregnancy, so I don't push her. 'About the flat,' I say, swiftly moving on. 'Andrew said you both want out, for personal reasons, obviously, so I've decided to agree to the sale. Andrew can get his share and I'll be out of your lives forever. It's only fair. Fresh start.'

'Lucy, you can sell the flat if you want to. I'm not going to tell you what to do, but I know nothing about it. What has Andy told you?' I don't respond. Is this a trick question? You never know with Jasmine. 'My parents are away most of the time, they've been in India for the last three months. We've got this big house to ourselves, complete with housekeepers, swimming pool, cinema room. Why would we want to move? I haven't a clue why he spun you that line.' She taps her fingers against her mouth thoughtfully. 'But it's got nothing to do with me. Perhaps he needs the money for his business. He hates asking me for money. Or maybe you pissed him off.' She laughs. 'You know how spiteful he can be, like a flipping school bully sometimes.' Spiteful isn't a word I'd use to describe Andrew – quick tempered, yes, spiteful, no. 'But he knows he's met his match with me.' She nods for emphasis. 'I'm not another Lu…' The words die on her lips.

'Lucy?' I say dryly.

'Maybe you should discuss it with him again.' She gets to her feet. 'You're right, you must've got your wires crossed. Pity you didn't turn up five minutes earlier. He literally just walked out the door a few minutes before you arrived.' If only she knew I was hiding behind the bushes. 'He's gone to see his parents for a few days – Mum's a bit poorly. But you're welcome to come back when he returns.'

'In Edinburgh?' I shrill. Their house is like a castle. I used to love staying there during holidays and Christmas. Andrew even took me to the Edinburgh Fringe Festival a couple of times.

'Oh, no, they sold that place about six months ago.' Gathering the plates, she crosses the room, asks if I'd like another coffee.

'Yes,' I say, a little too eagerly and she gives me a look. I need to get her rattling cups and fussing over the Lavazza, so I can get up those stairs and look for evidence. 'Taxi's going to be another twenty minutes.' I glance at my watch absently and she murmurs in agreement. 'Another coffee would be great.'

'They downsized to Clacton-on-Sea, wanted to be near their daughter and grandkids.' Carol, Andrew's sister. The one who hates me. 'A house came up for sale right next door, so they snapped it up.'

'Lovely,' I say, disinterested. 'Um... is it okay if I use the loo?'

'Sure,' she replies over her shoulder, 'you remember where it is, don't you? First on your left.' Bloody hell. I didn't even consider the downstairs cloakroom. How stupid.

At the door, I hesitate. 'Actually, do you mind if I use the one upstairs, need to do a number two?' I cringe inwardly as I say it.

'Eww,' she laughs, spooning coffee into the machine. 'Don't forget to open a window.'

Hurrying past the pair of gold growling Versace cheetahs, I feel for my phone in my pocket to make sure it's there, even though I only slipped it in a few minutes ago. My heels click and clack against the marble floor, echoing throughout the majestic hallway, each agonising step taking me closer to unravelling the truth.

Eight minutes later, having rifled through the cupboards and drawers of the office and spare rooms, I'm standing in Jasmine's bedroom, hands on hips, looking around madly. It's just as I remember it – clean and tidy and elegant, with ivory furniture, fitted mirrored walk-in wardrobes and a thick shag-pile cream carpet. Above me, a contemporary raindrop crystal chandelier sparkles. An oil painting of Jasmine on graduation day hangs against the chimney breast above her dressing table, adorned with perfumes and makeup; the rest of the beige walls are bare. Jasmine's always been minimalistic. I was right about the mobile phone, by the way. It's switched off. I dialled the number outside her parents' room, which was locked. But I doubt she'd hide it in there. Mrs Anand always takes the key with her. It has to be in Jasmine's bedroom – it has to be.

I quietly open her wardrobes and check the pockets of all her designer gear and expensive handbags, but find nothing, I do the same with Andrew's wardrobe – nothing. Next, I tackle the chest of drawers, rifling through each one quickly – still nothing. I creep around the king-sized bed with its crisp white bedsheets, squishy pillows, pale blue duvet and stitched velvet tiger-yellow throw, which has been stylishly turned down and looks amazing.

I crouch by Andrew's bedside table. There's a book about cars, a remote control, a pair of reading glasses and a framed photograph of the two of them taken at The Shard in London, smiling at into the camera stupidly. I pick it up and study it. It looks like a selfie. Bastard. He never had a picture of us on his bedside table when we were together. Replacing it where I found it, I rummage around in his sock drawer – nothing.

Crossing the room, I kneel down by Jasmine's side of the bed, curling my hair behind my ears. There's a roll-on deodorant and a tube of hand cream neatly placed on her bedside table next to her iPad, and an oval grey alarm clock with luminous numerals. I slide open the drawer as quietly as I can, keeping an eye on the door, and root around wildly. God, I can't believe I'm doing this. A Nasofan spray, lots of knickers, a pair of ivory Beats Solo headphones, and, I gasp, a dildo! I pick it up as if it's been dipped in a vat of germs and study it inanely. It's huge and black and shiny. Jasmine has always had a high sex drive. No wonder Andrew prefers her to me. We only had straight sex, mostly the missionary, and it was usually over in minutes.

My knees creak as I get to my feet, and then I just stand there, rubbing my chin, feeling hopeless. The house is massive, the mobile phone and cologne could be anywhere. It's probably under the floorboards, knowing Jasmine. I ought to get back downstairs before she gets suspicious. I tiptoe towards the door, cringing as the floorboards groan beneath me.

On the landing, my eyes are drawn to the bathroom at the end of the long wide corridor; the door is ajar. It's my last and only hope. My feet almost cry out with relief as I slip off my shoes and I leave them outside the bedroom door. I listen out for any movement from downstairs. There's a kerfuffle of crockery and the faint sound of music, she must've stuck Spotify on. I'm about to negotiate my way to the bathroom when the landline goes off followed by quick footsteps in the hallway and then Jasmine's voice, 'Oh, hello, Mum.' Good. This means I'm safe for the next five or ten minutes.

The bathroom smells of an infusion of mango and flowers. The air moist. There's a damp towel hanging off a grey Laura Ashley chair. Someone must've just taken a shower – probably Andrew before he left for Clacton-On-Sea. I bet Jasmine makes him shower every day. He won't like that. I notice that the toilet lid is up and there's pink liquid spilling from the rim, smearing the bowl, and the faint smell of peonies. Lena was here early this morning.

I bypass the chair and slide open the top drawer beneath the gleaming double sink with gold lion head taps. If I'm honest, I always found them ostentatious and scary. The Anands love a bit of bling. It's in their DNA. I root around the fluffy towels. I do the same with the second drawer, jam-packed with *Molton Brown* products. Next, I open the bottom drawer, the biggest of the three, and dig around behind two folded white towelling dressing gowns. Honestly, it's like a posh hotel in here. No wonder Jasmine doesn't want to move. As expected, I find nothing.

I stare at my reflection in the huge mirror above the sink. A haggard middle-aged neurotic looking woman looks back at me. What the hell have I become? What am I even doing here? Am I mad? I brush myself down and stand upright. *Get a grip, girl, you can't give up now.* The last port of call in the tall cabinet next to the double shower cubicle. But as I go to move something catches my eye, stopping me dead. Gleaming under the spotlights, next to the ostentatious hot tap, is my engagement ring. The ring I searched for high and low. The ring I thought I'd lost. Or could it be a similar ring? Surely, Andrew didn't palm Jasmine off with my cast-off.

I whip it up and study it under the light spotlight; definitely mine. It even has that tiny scratch from when I almost lost it down the sink just after we got engaged. My face burns. The fucking tight bastard. No wonder I couldn't find it. I wouldn't mind but I put fifteen hundred quid towards it, which Andrew promised to give back but didn't. I hardly wore it after the sink incident but that's not the point. It's mine. I slip it into my jacket pocket. I'll flog it online. I could do with the cash. He can fork out for a new one for Princess Jasmine. It's not as if he can't afford it now.

I tiptoe along the tan tiles, past the double shower as quietly as I can. The cabinet opens with a click and I'm faced with a box of toothpaste, two bottles of Listerine mouthwash, spare toothbrushes, several Clarins products, a can of hairspray, a tube of Anusol cream and a few packets of painkillers – ibuprofen, co-codamol, paracetamol, and, I gasp, a packet of Microgynon – the same birth control I always used. I pull out the blister pack and count right up until today. My hand shoots to my mouth. She's on the fucking pill. She's telling me the truth. She isn't pregnant. Why did Andrew lie to me?

'Found what you're looking for?' a voice says.

I spin round, startled. Jasmine is standing in the doorway, balancing my shoes on two fingers, face like thunder.

Chapter 16

'Jasmine…' I mutter, contraceptive pills in hand. 'It's not what it looks like.' Jasmine has caught me going through her things, snooping around in her house. The worst case scenario has just happened. How in God's name am I going to get out of this one? *Come on, Lucy, think. THINK.* I inch forward. 'I…I had a funny turn, and was…was just looking for some meds.'

Jasmine's glare intensifies, lips a thin line. Right, she doesn't believe me. Of course, she doesn't. She's an intelligent woman. A lawyer. Dropping my shoes by the door, her eyes flick around the bathroom. Oh dear God, the ring. What possessed me to take it? If she realises it's missing I'll be done for. And what will I say, that it accidently fell into my pocket? My heart knocks hard against my ribcage, breath quickening. I'll tell her the truth, say that it's mine. No, that's a terrible idea, she might not believe me, get angry. I'll deny any knowledge of it – call her bluff. No, no. I can't say that. What if she calls the police – they'll frisk me – find it – lock me up.

Shifting her weight on to one leg, Jasmine crosses her arms and fixes with me with a long hard stare. I know that look – she's about to attack. Her lips part, 'Where is–'

'Vertigo!' I blurt, before she can finish. 'I had one of my attacks – everything was spinning. I felt so…so sick. I tried to call you but you must've been on the phone. I could…I could hear voices.' Jasmine's face flickers with concern. A good sign.

It means she hasn't noticed that her ring is missing. I stagger towards the sink and stand in front of it, hands on either side of the bowl, blocking her view.

'I remembered that your mum had balance problems too, and I thought these were…' Raising a hand, I shake the blister pack at her. I say shake, but it's more of an involuntary tremor. 'Stemetil. The packaging is…um…the same, I think.' Jasmine knows I've suffered from Labyrinthitis since I was a teen. I have no idea if the packaging is similar but it's worth a shot. 'I'm really sorry, Jas. I didn't think you'd mind.'

Jasmine eyes me quizzically. I hold my breath, inwardly chanting, *please believe me, please believe me.* But the murderous look on her face tells me she's having none of it. Sniffing the air, she cracks her knuckles, eyes narrowing, and my insides twist. She knows I've taken the ring. Any moment now she's going to push me out of the way, discover that it's missing and confront me, make me empty my pockets like she did when we were twelve and couldn't find her diamond-encrusted watch with the brown leather strap that her parents bought her for her birthday. It was beautiful and blingy and expensive, and I wish my mum had been able to afford to buy one for me too, but I didn't steal it. Sadly, Jasmine never did find out who did.

'Know what, Lucy?' Yes, I do. I'm a thief. I've stolen your ring, even though it is actually mine. I close my eyes. Swallow. 'You're the only person whose shit smells of roses,' she says, coldly. My eyes snap open. 'Those pink skid marks.' She jerks her head at the toilet bowl, 'are quite remarkable, don't you think?' Relief slithers through my veins. The toilet. She's spotted that it hasn't been flushed. 'So, do you want to tell me what you were really doing up here because…'

'False alarm,' I snap, 'I've been constipated for days. Jasmine raises an eyebrow. 'I really wouldn't lie about something like this, Jasmine. Please…just… get out of my way,' I say warily, holding my stomach. 'I've got to call work, tell them I won't be able to…' Brushing past her, I stagger in a zigzaggy gait, as if I'm about to faint. It works.

'Come on, love,' Jasmine soothes, believing me. 'I've got you.' I feel her hand slip around my waist. 'Think Mum keeps the Stemetil in the loo cabinet downstairs. Give me those.' Snatching the contraceptive pills from my hand, she chucks the box hastily into the sink, then picks up my shoes, and my heart almost leaps out of my mouth. 'Pop your arm around my shoulder. That's it, and take your shoes.'

And with this, she escorts me out of the bathroom and down the majestic stairwell, with the floor-to-ceiling lobby window; I smile gratefully when she hands me two Stemetil pills from the cabinet in the downstairs loo; allow her to slip on my shoes for me as I gulp down the pills with a glass of water; thank her when she helps me into the waiting taxi like an invalid; reciprocate her air kisses and agree to stay in touch before she closes the passenger door for me; hate myself as I wave back from the cab when it pulls out of her drive, knowing that the evidence is still inside her house, knowing that I failed and she won – again.

A sudden piercing shrill fills my ears. My eyes snap open. Someone's at my front door. *Brrrrrrr!* I glance at my clock on the bedside table – 11:31. Shit, I slept through the alarm. *Brrrr.* It had better not be that survey guy again looking for Andrew, or those Jehovah Witnesses from last week with their big smiles and all the time in the world at their disposal. The doorbell shrills again, long and hard this time, followed by pounding on the front door. *Oh, go away!* I keep very still, duvet pulled over my nose praying they'll disappear. It's not that I'm anti-social, per se, but I'm not in the right frame of mind for visitors, not after last night's session. I feel like shit. I listen out for the doorbell again but everything is still – silent. Good. They've gone.

With a deep inhalation, I follow a tiny spider along the coving. It's quite fast for a little thing. I'm not afraid of spiders – never have been. Shifting position, I notice that my calves have that tingling feeling I usually get when I overdo it on the treadmill, but I haven't been to the gym all week. I shift again. Hannah, from work, told me she had something similar a few weeks ago, kept her up all night. I think she called it restless legs. She was googling the symptoms but had to shut the page down quickly when Gillian sauntered over. Gillian is such a bloody sergeant major, won't let us use the computer for anything that isn't work related.

I shake my head at the tiny spider who is halfway across the ceiling and then a thought flies into my mind and I almost cry out – Gillian is the only person who rings the bell then raps her knuckles against the glass panel. Could it have been her just now? She only lives a couple of miles away in Southgate. It wouldn't be the first time she'd popped round with a work-related issue – dropping off some paperwork, picking me up en-route to a meeting or the airport in a taxi. But there's no reason for a visit today. Unless… I clamp a hand over my mouth. Unless she's here to check up on my non-existent burglary. Shit, shit. SHIT!

Kicking the duvet off, I sit upright and swing my legs around the mattress and everything in the room sways. I didn't have time to respond to Gillian's short tetchy email yesterday morning because I was too busy stressing about going to Jasmine's, and then it slipped my mind. I imagine her on my doorstep, thick bob framing her heavily made-up face like a yellow helmet, crimson lipstick bleeding into the fine lines around her mouth. The doorbell goes off again and adrenalin soars through me. It's definitely her and she's not taking no for an answer. It rings again – one long burst, *Brrrrrrrrrrrrr,* followed by two tiny rings and then thump of the letterbox. Christ almighty, she must be furious if she's looking through my mailbox.

Grabbing my dressing gown, I quickly slide my feet into flimsy white slippers, which I nabbed from a posh hotel in Cornwall during an educational last year and head for the door. Excuses fly into my mind like arrows, skimming past each other in their haste for priority as I tie my belt into a knot. I'll feign surprise, deny any knowledge of an email, say that I've been too tied up with the insurance people to look at my messages, the underwriters are giving me grief, refusing to payout. She'll soften if I tell her that because I remember her saying that she had a two-year battle with her brokers when her house got burgled a few years ago. I'll even pretend that my GP has prescribed drugs to help me sleep. Lay it on thick and hope to God that she believes me, because there's no way I can afford to lose my job.

Oddly, I can't see her familiar silhouette through the glass door panel; perhaps she's leaning against the wall outside. A Gillian thing, as if she's rushed off her feet and hasn't got time to dither at the front door.

Breathing into my hand, I inhale to make sure I don't smell like a brewery before reaching for the latch. I must've necked half a bottle of Bacardi last night. Maybe more. I don't know. I just wanted to block everything out. I shouldn't have gone to Jasmine's. I shouldn't have taken the ring. It was a stupid, stupid, stupid thing to do.

I wrench the door open and peer outside – nothing. How odd. Gathering the lapels of my dressing gown, I pull them tightly to my chest and tiptoe onto the stone porch, feeling the coolness of the slabs beneath my flimsy slippers. My eyes dart up and down the street. Whoever was furiously hammering on my door has disappeared without a trace.

Pleased that Gillian isn't lurking on my doorstep, I amble back inside, heading for the kitchen. I plan on spending all day in bed with my phone. I'll reply to Gillian's email first, she always reads her messages, even at the weekends. I'll tell her I'll be back in the office first thing on Monday morning, then I'll text Teddy. Apologise for waking him up last night and blabbing down the phone. God knows what I told him. I can barely remember. I got blackout drunk on rum and Coke and passed out on the sofa, woke up with a start at about one o'clock from a loud thud outside, a fox, probably, knocking over a pot in the garden, then stripped naked and crawled into bed. I just hope I didn't mention the ring. I honestly wouldn't have called if I'd known he was in bed, but what adult sleeps at nine o'clock?

In the kitchen, I spy about half a pint of water through the kettle gauge. It's been boiled to death and I know I'm going to get some scaly bits in my coffee but I don't care. I flick on the switch, the blue light ignites, the kettle groans, then as I lift my L initial mug off the drying rail, I hear the sound of footsteps, followed by light tapping. I freeze, listening, eyes darting from left to right. Perhaps it's the agent showing potential tenants around the house next door. Xenia told me that the old lodgers are leaving at the end of the month, going back to Albania. Satisfied, I go to move when I hear it again, a hollow noise coming from the depths of the flat – rap, rap, rap, like knuckles against a door, then the doorbell again – *Brrrrrr.* Heat spreads throughout my body. Gillian is back. She must've gone to the Costa on the High Street for one of those soya cappuccinos with no sugar, giving me ten minutes to sort myself out in case I was still in bed. Something she's done before.

Racing to the front door, I see a woman's shadowy figure moving out of sight. 'Gillian,' I say in a raspy tone, yanking open the door. 'I was in the show…' The words die on my lips as I stare into empty space. She's gone. A light wind snaps at my legs and bare chest as I step outside and scan the area once again. An empty crisp packet rustles by the gate. A car door clunks and I jerk my head round. Matthew from number thirty-six gives me a quick nod as he dashes towards his car, unlocking it from a distance. He's uncharacteristically dishevelled today – unshaven, grey hair sticking up like a parrot. I'm about to call out to him, ask if he saw anyone hanging around outside my front door, but then his engine rumbles and he pulls away from the kerb quickly. If I didn't know him better I'd think he was trying to avoid me.

I press my back against the door and it closes with a low thud. How strange. I definitely heard knocking. I stand very still, head cocked, listening. The faint soundtrack of a TV filters through the ceiling, the kettle ruffles and hisses from the kitchen. Could it have been the couple upstairs, they're always coming and going? Or a courier delivering an item for next door who got fed up of waiting for me to get out of bed and buggered off.

Convinced, I go to move but then I hear it again – rap, rap, rap. Acid leaps into my stomach – the noise is coming from inside – someone is in my flat. My hands shoot to my mouth. They will kill me. I will die without fulfilling my dream of becoming a mother. No one will report me missing for days. My internal organs will start to decompose before my body is discovered, because that's what happens to a corpse after a few days, I saw it on one of those real-crime documentaries once. Blinking the thought away, I tiptoe along the green and white oriental runner in the hallway, pulse belting loudly, amplifying in my ears – whoever is in my flat is here to hurt me.

'Hello?' I call out with a shaky voice. 'Who's there?' Silence. 'Jasmine, is that you? Stop mucking around.' But everything is still. Silent. All I can hear is my ragged breath and the kettle ebbing to a boil then clicking off. 'Right that's it, whoever you are, I'm calling the police!'

I slowly and carefully check every room, including the bathroom. The flat is empty. I'm safe. I'm not going to die. At least not today. Inhaling deeply, I pad back into the kitchen, heartbeat slowing as if it's been turned down by a dial. The noise must've been coming from outside the building. I rub my tummy and the tie of my dressing gown loosens. I do feel a bit ropey after last night's rum and Coke binge.

Filling a glass with tap water, I knock it back in one and flick the kettle on again, even though it's only just boiled. Another one of Andrew's pet hates. I mimic him in a silly voice, *'You've boiled the fuck out of that kettle. Stop wasting electricity.'*

I pull out a pint of semi-skimmed and close the door with my elbow. One of the pleasures of being single is that you don't have to answer to anyone. I can boil the kettle all day long, leave the lights on in every room and spend all day in bed watching boxsets on Netflix. Although, if I'm honest, I do miss being in a relationship. I miss waking up next to Andrew in bed, a snoring mound beneath the duvet, mouth ajar; going to the pub on a Sunday afternoon and reading the papers over a pint; snuggling up on the sofa watching TV, exchanging glances whenever someone says something funny, or silly, or ridiculous.

Sighing wistfully, I glance at the orange blackout roller blind on the back door as I spoon coffee into a mug straight from the jar. It's faded and a bit frayed at the edges. Teddy said he'd put a new one for me if I wanted – something cheap and cheerful from B&Q to brighten the place up, make it desirable for potential buyers, because, let's face it, my days here are numbered.

I smile to myself, then as I screw the cap back onto the jar of Nescafé, I see a flicker of a shadowy figure behind the back door and my breath catches in my throat. It wasn't a courier. It wasn't the couple upstairs. It wasn't the agent showing the flat next door. Someone's in my garden! I open my mouth to scream but the only sound I hear is the jar smashing against the ceramic tiles and then the wail of a siren outside – an ambulance, or maybe a police car. I can't tell the difference.

'The police are outside,' I cry, voice breaking, grateful that the siren went off at the right moment. The shadow darts out of the way. It's the blackmailer. I know it is. They're going to make a run for it. No, no, I can't let them get away. This may be the only opportunity I get to find out who's behind all this. I snatch a metal ladle from the shelf and negotiate my way around slivers of glass and coffee granules, ladle held high. The figure reappears at the door, face pressed against the window, hands on either side of their face. I take a step closer, eyes wide, heart galloping. There's no way they can see me through the blind.

'Lucy?' A woman's voice, followed by more tapping. 'I can see you.' Jesus Christ. So much for the 'blackout' blind. It really does need replacing. I drop the ladle onto the worktop and take a step back. 'Lucy.' Rap, rap, rap. 'It's me. Emma.' Emma? Who the fuck…and then it hits me. It's Xenia and Spiros's daughter-in-law. The smug florist with the perfect life. What the hell does she want? Smoothing down my mop of hair self-consciously, I tighten the belt of my dressing gown, concealing my nudity. I can't let Emma see me like this. I'm a complete mess.

Backing up against the fridge, I inhale the aroma of coffee wafting from the spill. If I keep very still she might go away.

‘Lucy, are you okay? Lucy?’ More thumping. ‘Please, open the door.’ Rap, rap. ‘Okay, stay where you are. I’m calling the emergency services.’ I clamp a hand over my forehead. God, I’m sweating. An ambulance? Is she for real? There’s nothing wrong with me. I can’t let her call the paramedics out for a don’t-want-to-let-anyone-in attack – she’ll be wasting NHS money. What’s wrong with this woman? Surely, she can see that I’m on my feet, walking around. I inch sideways along the length of the worktop, avoiding fragments of glass and coffee granules.

‘Fuck,’ Emma mutters, sighing loudly. ‘I’m going to be late.’ I hear a shuffle of footsteps. I think she’s leaving. Phew. She knows I’m safe. Of course she does. It’s obvious. I could be wandering around in the kitchen listening to music on my headphones for all she knows. She was just being overdramatic. ‘Hello, yes…ambu–’

‘Emma, NO,’ I cry, and with two long strides I’m at the back door.

Chapter 17

'Sorry,' Emma gasps, all flustered and pink. 'I didn't mean to startle you. I tried the front door but there was no reply. Your curtains are drawn and as it's almost…' She throws a glance at her smart watch, taking in my dressing gown en route, it lights up. 'I thought something might've happened to you,' she says with a slight grimace, clearly thinking better of reminding me that it's almost midday and I haven't bothered to get dressed. 'I'm sorry. I panicked.' I go to speak but she talks over me. 'Harry's always telling me off for thinking the worst. Oh, God, I hope I didn't wake you!'

I give her a tight smile, eyeing her watch. It has a large square face and a white sports strap. I'm sure it's an Apple. Probably the latest version, knowing Emma. I wonder what it feels like to have it all – the looks, the money, the perfect husband.

'No, just having a lazy day off,' I lie. 'Well, I say that but I've got a million things to do,' I add hastily, rolling my eyes and laughing lightly, hoping she'll take the hint, tell me why she's here and bugger off. I'm in no mood to be judged by Emma Georgiades today in her designer jeans and tailored navy jacket and expensive Apple watch.

'Phew,' Emma says, her face matching her scarlet kitten heels. I take in the redhead on my doorstep quickly as she babbles on nervously about people living on their own – I should get a dog, something intimidating like a German Shepherd. Her mother owns a Rottweiler. Tilly, a big old softie, but daunting all the same. 'Mum still has to lock her in the kitchen whenever my sister visits.' Emma giggles. 'Well, my half-sister – same dad. Tessa's terrified of dogs. The last time we were there, Tilly ate Mike's steak dinner off the worktop while we were all watching *Tipping Point* in the front room.' She laughs and I laugh too, because it is a funny story, even though I've no idea who Mike is. A brother? Stepdad? Uncle? Lodger?

I nod and hmm as Emma carries on talking about the increase in burglaries and knife crime in London – the government is ruining our city with their cutbacks, destroying our NHS, her poor husband works all the hours God sends, he can barely survive on his nurse's salary, it's a good job they've got the florists. I shake my head and smile, saying nothing. I don't want to encourage her. I want her to leave. But she just keeps babbling on. She's much chattier than I expected – pretty in an ordinary way, green eyes, a sprinkling of freckles over her nose, minimal makeup and a splash of lip gloss. She's taller than me by a few inches too, probably about 5'7, I'd say, lean and athletic looking. A runner. I've seen her turn up in her running gear a few times. Once wearing a race number on a MIND charity shirt. I notice that her neck and chest, exposed at the V of her white t-shirt, is covered in red patches. The kind you get from anxiety, I'm guessing, because they weren't there a few moments ago. Emma pauses, grins, and I realise that she's expecting a response, but I haven't a clue what she just said.

'Anyway, I'm here now,' she says kindly, realising I haven't been keeping up with her commentary. 'My mother-in-law asked me to… Shit, you're shaking. Are you okay?' Taking a step forward, Emma squeezes my hand, and her silver hoop earnings swing against her curls. 'God, you're freezing. Are you sick? Shall I call a doctor? Oh, you poor thing, and all alone too. It's a good job I called round, eh?'

No, Emma, it isn't, and I wish you'd just tell me what you want and go away. I've got to email Gillian and text Teddy Fallon.

'I'm fine,' I say in a raspy tone, flexing my cold hand. 'Cold water from the tap.' Her gaze sweeps around my kitchen floor and it takes all the strength I have not to roll my eyes, because now I've got to explain why it's splattered with shards of glass and instant coffee. 'I was making a coffee then heard all this banging and…' I stop short as a horrible thought flies into my mind and I almost fall down the three steps leading onto the patio. The siren I heard a few minutes ago, was it an ambulance? Has something awful happened to Spiros or Xenia? They're in their eighties. I stare at her agape, willing them to be okay. 'Are your in-laws okay?' I ask accusingly, as if she's tied them up and locked them in the garden shed.

'Yes, they're fine.' Emma waves a freckled hand. Her fingers are long and thin and milk white. 'Kiki's just taken them to the airport to pick up their cousins Taki and Vasoulla.' Kiki, the good-looking nephew I bumped into yesterday morning. 'Xenia just asked me to drop this off to you before I go. I was doing a bit of tidying up for them.' Emma picks up a long pink box that is propped against the wall behind her. I don't remember ordering anything online. 'Postie said there was no one in yesterday.' No, there wasn't. I was at Jasmines' playing private detective. Badly. 'So, Mum took it in for you. It needed a sig.' She pauses but I don't say anything. 'Anyway, she asked me to make sure you got it.'

'It's nice of you to help them out with the housekeeping,' I offer, taking the box from her arms, surprised that it isn't as heavy as I'd imagined. I negotiate my way around a few shards of glass, coffee granules crunching beneath my feet, and pop it onto the worktop next to the ladle.

'It's only a bit of dusting and hoovering,' Emma admits, 'nothing major.' I can almost smell the soft leather of her burnt-orange bag as she pushes it further up her shoulder. I know it's expensive because it's embossed with *Mulberry England* in gold where the drawstring leather cords meet at the bottom. 'I usually do it after work but…' She grimaces, does a little spitty thing whilst pulling something invisible out of her mouth. 'I eat my own hair, very nutritious,' she jokes, and I smile, warming to her. Actually, she's quite nice, friendly, normal. 'What was I saying? Oh, yeah. Xenia's cousins are staying with them for two weeks and she wanted the house spick and span before they arrived. Mum was a bit anxious about your parcel, thought it might be important.' Emma rolls her eyes, but in a nice way, an endearing way. 'You know what she's like.'

I decide very quickly that Gillian's email and Teddy's text can wait. 'Look, why don't you come in, Emma, I was about to have a coffee. Kettle's just boiled.'

Backing down the steps, Emma lifts up a hand, and I can tell that she's not the kind of person who intrudes. 'Got to get to work. Ruby's opening up for me today and I can't leave her on her own for too long,' she says, as if I've known Ruby for years. 'We've got a big order going out – a funeral.' I grimace. 'I know but you do get used to it. Ruby's got the spirit of a twenty-year-old but she is in her nineties. She only does a few hours a week for me, can't stand being stuck in her retirement flat day after day.'

'Oh, I see.' Cleans for her elderly in-laws and offers lonely pensioners jobs, Emma's not the up-herself diva I imagined her to be after all. 'Is it just the two of you at the shop then?' I ask politely, slipping my hands into my pockets.

'Michele does four days a week.' Michele? Clearly, Emma's got a habit of expecting people to know the names of all her family and friends. 'But she doesn't start until twelve during the summer term, because of the kids. Her mum childminds but she can't get to hers before eleven.' It's official – Emma is a saint. We nod knowingly and exchange wide humourless grins, the kind you give when you've exhausted all topics of conversation.

'Right,' she says finally, adjusting the strap of her bag again even though it hasn't moved an inch. 'Better get going. Look after yourself, Lucy, and hope you get some gardening done. Met Office said it'll be chucking it down this afternoon.'

I follow her eyes to Teddy's gardening equipment stacked neatly by the fence – a fork, spade and a rake, a pair of worse-for-wear gloves, a sack of compost, a tub of weed killer and a tub of homemade patio cleaner.

'The gardening stuff isn't mine,' I clarify, 'They belong to my new b…' I almost say boyfriend but stop myself. 'My friend. He's a gardener. He's very good if you ever need one, does patio cleaning too. Only uses organic stuff.'

'I do my own landscape.' Emma smiles, slipping her hands into the back pockets of her blue jeans. Of course she does, she's a gardener, owns a florists. How silly of me. 'Watch out for foxes if you're leaving that compost out overnight though. They love tearing into bags. We've got lots where we live. I'm always finding their rubbish on our lawn. Bloody pain, but what can you do?'

'Oh, I love foxes,' I say, stepping into the garden. 'Don't laugh, but I feed them sometimes – leave them food outside. Used to drive my ex mad.' I do a little laugh that makes me sound like a soprano. Emma's phone pings. She pulls it out and reads the text, screwing up her eyes – she must wear glasses.

'Right, I'd better dash,' she says, slipping her phone back into her bag. 'Michele's running late.'

I smile at her. 'Thanks for bringing the parcel over.'

'No problem, and sorry about the Freddy Kruger incident earlier. I didn't mean to scare you.' She's funny as well as kind. I like her now.

I watch, smiling, as Emma steps onto the shared driveway, securing the latch of the metal dwarf gate behind her, and as I turn to go back inside a thought enters my mind. 'Emma, wait.' If Emma cleans twice a week for my neighbours after work, she might be the figure I saw ducking out of the way at Xenia's bedroom window the night Simon kissed me. 'Um…I know this is a long shot but were you around Friday before last? I…um…' I finger the hair behind my ear. 'Got a lift home from a friend and…I…' Confusion flashes across her face, and for a moment she morphs into a younger version of Julianne Moore. 'It's just that I thought I saw someone at the bedroom window next door and I…Oh, never mind.'

Emma's hands fly up. 'I'm sorry, Lucy. I didn't mean to snoop.' A flutter of hope dances in my stomach. I was right, it was her. 'I was making the bed and I heard voices and I thought…' She inhales deeply, looks up to the sky. 'You're going to think this is so weird. I thought my ex-husband was following me.' Emma pauses, takes a breath. 'Sounds crazy, doesn't it? Harry said I'm being paranoid. I mean, Carl doesn't even know where we live and he's been living in Spain for years.'

Ex-husband? I didn't realise she'd been married before.

'Carl was a bit rough with me. Well, I say a bit.' Raking a hand through her long thick hair, she holds it at the top of her head and looks at me pointedly. 'He used to beat me up. Broke a chair over my head the last time I saw him and left me for dead.' I suck in the air noisily, shocked by the brutality but also of her starkness – she barely knows me yet she's shared such an intimate piece of her life.

'I kept forgiving him, giving him one more chance. Until the chair incident. I even blamed myself for his violence – thought I made him do it, because I irritated him so much. I am a bit chatty.' I smile when she says this. There's nothing wrong with chatty. It's a good attribute. 'I know. You must think I'm a weak pathetic fool.' She exhales loudly. 'People wonder why women put up with it but they don't know what it's like. The lies, the promises, the coercion, and, dare I say it, the love. Yes, strange as it may seem, I loved him. I thought I couldn't cope without him.' She shrugs. 'I was trapped.'

Stepping forward, I touch her arm. 'God, no, of course I don't think you're weak.' I can smell her perfume – sweet, floral. 'Quite the contrary, actually.' I hate myself for judging her so harshly in the past. Now all I want to do is hug her. But I don't. It'd be too much. Emma doesn't strike me as a touchy-feely kind of person. I move my hand away. Poor Emma. Andrew used to shout lots but he never hit me – not once. But I know first-hand what it's like to live with a bully. My dad was a monster when he was bladdered, and he wasn't much better on the rare occasions when he wasn't. 'Emma,' I say softly, 'I'm so sorry. It must've been horrific.'

'It's okay, Lucy. It was a long time ago. I've got Harry now.' She pauses, turns her wedding band around on her finger, and I wonder if she's unhappy in this marriage too. If something's wrong. But no. Harry's such a lovely gentle man. Although, who knows what goes on behind closed doors. I shake the thought away. I'm not going to ask her about her marriage. It's none of my business. I should go inside. Let her get to work.

'Anyhow,' I begin, backing away. 'I'd better…'

'It wasn't just the violence,' Emma says suddenly. 'I had to put up with all his affairs too.' She scratches a red blotch that's just appeared on her jaw, eyes fixed on mine. 'I mean, Carl was a ruthless pig, but I don't know how those women slept at night. Most of them knew he was married.' The accusation in her voice hangs between us like a huge bitter mist. 'One of them was his flipping P.A,' she says, anger sliding into her tone like acid. 'They were having an affair on our bloody honeymoon.' Blimey, Carl sounds like a right tosser. But where is she going with this? Why the sudden need to share her past with me?

'Emma, is there anything you want to tell me?' I say carefully. What exactly did she witness from the bedroom window? Did she see the kiss? Emma doesn't know the Maxwells but her in-laws do. We all had a barbeque together a few years ago when I was still married to Andrew. Could she be accusing me of something here? I go to speak when, out of nowhere, a feeling of dread courses through my veins and my face singes. Emma has met Simon and Alison. Once. Briefly. She turned up on the day of the barbeque with Harry, came round the back into our garden and stood not far from where she's standing now. A family emergency, Harry told us, and my neighbours had to leave before dessert. A chill jaunts along my spine and I stand up rigid. Does she think I'm having an affair with Simon? That I'm one of those women she's just described?

'Actually, yes, there is something, Lucy,' she says crisply, and I know I'm right – she thinks I'm fucking my friend's husband.

'Go on,' I say, folding my arms.

'It's about what I saw that night from the bedroom window.'

See, what did I tell you? Adrenalin powers through me so quickly that I almost levitate. 'Emma, what exactly did you see?' If she saw us kissing then surely she must've seen me pushing Simon off too.

‘I don’t want to cross the line, Lucy,’ Emma says. I tell her it’s fine, urge her to go on. ‘Only if you’re sure.’

I nod furiously. ‘Yes, I’m sure, Emma. Please!’

‘Okay, well, I saw you having a disagreement with some bloke on the street.’ Some bloke? Not Simon then. So, she didn’t recognise him, didn’t witness him kissing me, forcing me? ‘I heard loud voices. Is he a boyfriend? Was he breaking up with you?’

I shake my head. ‘No, not a boyfriend.’ Should I tell her, confide in her? She does seem trustworthy. ‘Um…It’s complicated,’ I reply. There’s no point in telling Emma, she didn’t see the whole scene play out. Unless she was standing there for longer than she’s letting on. Unless… ‘Did you see him trying to kiss me, Emma? Did you?’

Emma’s green eyes widen. ‘God, no! Was he trying to force you? You poor thing.’ She puts a hand on my back. Kind and thoughtful too. I like her even more. I thought she was punching above her weight with Harry but I was wrong. ‘I’m not sure if I should be telling you this but…’ she hesitates, bites her thumbnail. ‘I’m sure Mum won’t mind. I know all about your ex-husband running off with your best friend. Please don’t be angry. Xenia wasn’t gossiping, or anything. In fact, she was slagging them both off. She really is fond of you, you know.’

I’m not angry with Xenia for telling Emma. Why should I be? It’s common knowledge around here. Everyone knows what a shit Andrew is. ‘I saw your ex a few times. Short chap, good looking. Reminded me a bit of Freddie Mercury.’ I smile, agree, tell her everyone says that. ‘Find someone who’s kind and thoughtful; someone ordinary who’ll take out the bins for you and make you cups of tea. Someone reliable you can snuggle up with on the sofa and watch TV’ I feel a slight shiver – she’s just described Teddy Fallon. ‘I know what you’re going through, Lucy. If you ever want to talk, here’s my number.’

Fifteen minutes later, after sweeping up the glass and coffee debris, I make myself a cuppa and begin to unpack the package on the worktop. Emma surprised me today. I pull a strip of perforated cardboard off the pink box. It goes to show you that you should never judge a book by its cover. She seems like such a lovely lady. I think we found some common ground today. Both divorcees. Both been shat on by men from a height. We could even be friends, and God knows I could use one right now.

I tear off more cardboard and glance at Emma's business card on the worktop. I might give her a call next week, ask her round for a drink. I open the box, the doorknocker raps in the background, but instead of going to see who's at the door, I stand there staring stupidly at a bouquet of white flowers wrapped in cellophane and tied with a silver bow. Who on earth are they from? It's not my birthday. The doorbell rings – *Brrrrr*. They must be from Teddy. A thank you gift for storing his gardening equipment. He didn't have to do that, the daft fool, it's not as if he's made of money.

I go to pull the card out of the tiny white envelope when the doorbell rings again, long and hard this time. I drop the card back in the box. It rings a third time – *Brrrrrrr*. 'Oh, all right, all right!' I yell, 'keep your hair on, I'm coming.'

I see two dark shadowy figures behind the stained glass panel. Oh, please not the Jehovahs. I run a hand through my springy curls. I'll tell them that I'm late for work and to call back another time, accept the leaflet, promise to read it and bin it the moment they leave. But as I yank the door open, my face falls. Two humourless police officers – a man and a woman – are standing on my welcome mat.

'Lucy Harper?' says a woman with rosy cheeks and a blonde ponytail.

'Yes, that's me.' How do they know who I am? Acid swishes in my stomach. I hope they haven't come with bad news.

'Sorry to bother you, Miss Harper. I'm PC Jacobs and this is my colleague PC Michaels. We'd just like to ask you a few questions about an incident that happened yesterday.'

I frown, wrapping my dressing gown around me tightly. I'm not sure what my rights are but I don't want to break the law.

'What incident?' I query, arms folded, eyes darting up and down the street behind them. 'I've only just got out of bed. Has there been another burglary?'

'No,' PC Michaels says. In my peripheral vision I see Teddy rushing down the path behind them. 'It's in connection with an incident that took place at Miss Jasmine Anand's yesterday.' I stiffen. The ring. Jasmine's discovered it's missing, of course she has, it was only a matter of time. They've come to question me, arrest me, take me into custody. 'This won't take long. Can we come inside, please?'

Chapter 18

'Why did you lie to the police?' I ask Teddy, closing my front door behind him. Teddy looks as confused as I feel.

'Shit, did I lock the car? I can't remember?' He opens the door and points his key fob at his Ford Mondeo and the orange lights flash.

'If they find out you're lying,' I warn, as he steps back inside, 'you could get done.' I shot Teddy a look when he told PC Jacobs he was with me all night. I'm sure she picked up on it because she gave me a long hard stare before returning to her notes.

'They won't find out,' he says airily. 'I was home all night.'

'Alone?' I retort, unable to control the accusing tone in my voice. I don't know why but I'm not sure I believe him. He seems shifty, nervous. And why is he avoiding my question: why did he lie to the police?

'Yes.' Turning away, he drops his car keys onto the tall table in the corridor, then spins round and straightens his white polo top, face flushed, smile forced. 'Most of the time. Mum came in at about tenish, but there's no…'

'For God's sake, Teddy.' Brushing past him, I open the living room door and am instantly greeted by a fug of stale air. My hand twitches on the doorknob. I want to close it immediately but Teddy is standing so close behind me I can hear him breathing. The lounge looks like it's been ransacked.

I'm glad I showed the constables through to the kitchen earlier. My eyes sweep around the room. There's a mug of ring-marked cold tea on the coffee table next to a half-eaten curry with rice, the remnants congealed against the plastic container. A bottle of Bacardi is on its side by the armchair. A bottle of cola next to it. I quickly lift two scatter cushions off the floor and chuck them on to the sagged sofa, covertly giving the bottle of rum a kick before Teddy spots it.

'I just wanted them to stop questioning you, that's all.' Teddy's eyes swish over the mess but he says nothing. 'You looked really uncomfortable.' He goes to the window and twitches the net curtains. 'Why are they still outside?' Then his voice goes up an octave. 'Did you see the way they were watching us just now?' When the police left, I helped Teddy carry his gardening stuff to the car. He's right. The police didn't take their eyes off us. 'They were looking at that bag of compost in my arms as if it were a dead body. I almost felt as if it *was* when I chucked it into the boot. Mum said thanks for letting me store the stuff in your garden, by the way.'

I pick up the half-eaten curry and mug, amble towards him and peer over his shoulder. The police car is still there, parked across Spiro and Xenia's drive. Spiro's would blow a gasket if he saw it. You'd think the police would know better, set an example, but most of them think they're above the law. 'You needn't had stepped in. I wasn't uncomfortable.' I was. Very. I was thinking so much about Jasmine's engagement ring and what pathetic excuse I was going to give them if they questioned me about it that I barely took in what PC Jacobs was saying. 'I didn't need an alibi,' I insist.

Teddy whips his head round. Our faces are so close that I can smell an amalgamation of coffee and tobacco on his breath. 'But I thought…' he mumbles, his gaze drifting to his car parked outside my house.

'You thought what?' I look at him expectedly, but instead of explaining, he rubs his mouth, watching me worriedly. Come to think of it, he looks as if he hasn't eaten or slept in days, and I'm sure I get the whiff of campfire on his clothes. 'That they suspected me?' I snort. Then I open my arms wide, curry in one hand, mug of tea in the other, and swagger like a yob ready for a fight. 'Crazy ex-wife throws acid on new girlfriend's brand new Porsche in a jealous rage,' I say in a newsreader's voice. I laugh and look at him, waiting for him to join in, but his face is deadpan. Surely, he doesn't think… 'Oh, no. Oh, no, no, no.'

'You don't understand. And it was paint stripper not acid. At least that's what the police said. It's just that…Lucy, wait, where are you going?'

'Jesus!' I yell, voice echoing in the corridor, 'what do you take me for?'

He barrels after me, feet clambering in the hallway. 'You've got it all wrong. I'm not blaming you.' He could've fooled me. I see him in my peripheral vision as I bin the curry and turn on the taps. 'Come on, don't be like that.' And now he's telling me how I should feel. How dare he. How bloody dare he. I give him the silent treatment as I stare stonily in to the sink, hair falling in my face, taking out my anger on the coffee cups. 'You're right. I'm sorry. I shouldn't have lied to the police. It was a dumb thing to do. I thought I was helping. Epic fail, obviously.' He points two fingers at his temple and makes a whooshing sound as I fold a tea towel angrily and toss it over the watermarked tap.

'That's not even funny, Teddy.'

'I'm sorry.'

'Oh, stop apologising.'

'Okay. Sorry. I mean… I'll go outside now, they might still be parked up. I'll tell them I got it wrong, got the dates mixed up, or something. That I had an all-nighter – was confused.'

He goes to move but I stop him. ‘Leave it.’ I don’t want them to start on him now too. ‘It’ll only make matters worse.’ I throw him a weak smile. ‘I know you were only trying to help.

‘You sure?’

I nod, rubbing my forehead, and he lets out a sigh of relief. ‘I can’t believe you actually thought I had anything to do with last night though.’ A cold chill ran through me when the police told us that someone had poured paint stripper on Jasmine’s new Porsche.

Teddy looks at his loafers. ‘You should’ve told them about Alison and the texts,’ he says. ‘About being blackmailed.’

‘Why?’ I shrug. ‘It isn’t relevant. There’s no connection.’

‘Still, they might’ve looked into it. Tracked down the assailant. God,’ he says to the kitchen tiles, shaking his head, ‘I wonder who vandalised Jasmine’s car? What a shit thing to do.’

‘Yes,’ I nod, filling my lungs. He’s right but to be honest, I was just relieved that they didn’t come here to question me about the stolen engagement ring. ‘It was cruel. I’m no fan of Jasmine’s but no one deserves that. She loves that car. Hopefully, they’ll catch whoever did it.’

Teddy curves his lips downwards, inclining his head. ‘Very unlikely,’ he says, pulling out a chair at the table. ‘Police said there were no witnesses and if her CCTV isn’t working then there’s no chance.’

The hairs on my skin prickle. ‘What makes you think their CCTV isn’t working?’

He looks at me, bewildered. ‘Isn’t that what you said?’ He’s lying. I didn’t. Why would I? ‘Last night when you phoned me?’ I shake my head and his eyebrows rise and fall. ‘You said that you thought she’d seen you loitering outside the house on their CCTV, but then denied it when you questioned her, said something about it not working properly.’ I twist my lips to the side. Did I? I might've when I was relaying the story to him in a fit of fury.

'I'm sorry, Teddy. Yes. Yes, I did tell you. I'm not thinking straight at the moment. Sorry.'

Teddy smiles, nods, and we lapse into silence, and then, 'Someone keyed Lydia's car outside our house once. We never did find the culprit. Lydia was sure it was Jordan Harris's mother – revenge for getting her thug of a son excluded for beating up one of the other boys. Poor lad needed medical attention. Blood everywhere.'

'Oh, God, how awful. So, what did you do?'

'Got it repainted at the garage. The police were bloody useless.' Teddy picks up an empty glass of water, tilts it to the side, sniffs it, then puts it down. Shit. He must've seen the bottle of Bacardi. 'Lydia left it a few weeks and then went round there one night and did the same to Mrs Harris's new Ford Fiesta.'

'Are you kidding me?' I drop into a chair next to him. 'That's horrible.'

'Lydia was no pushover.' He pulls a fork out from the utensils holder and turns it around in his hand. 'An eye for an eye doesn't even scratch the surface. She's a very vindictive woman.' I'm disliking her more and more, even though I've never met her.

'But what if it wasn't even the school mum?' My eyes flick to three days' post piled on the table. Teddy shrugs. 'Lydia might've vandalised an innocent woman's car. She could've lost her job if someone saw her. Ruined her career.'

Teddy scoffs. 'There's no way Lyd would've got caught,' he says, as if Lydia is invincible. A flicker of pride sweeps across his face and an unexpected, unwanted, shot of jealousy powers through me. 'My ex-wife is many things but stupid isn't one of them.' No, but I can think of a few other choice adjectives to describe her.

'Yes, but they do catch them sometimes though,' I insist, sifting through the post – bills, junk mail and more bills. My heart sinks. 'And once they speak to Jasmine they'll get a clearer picture, I'm sure.'

'Yeah, that. Bloody hell. Why can't they find her? I thought the police could track down anyone these days with GPS.' The police told us that Jasmine wasn't answering her door this morning, after one of the neighbours called them out because her car alarm was going off all night, and, according to PC Michaels, she wasn't answering her landline and her mobile phone appears to be switched off.

'Yes, that is quite weird, isn't it?' I frown at the gas bill as I tap it against the table. I must remember to go online and go paperless. 'What did PC Michaels say, the number isn't recognised?'

'Unavailable,' Teddy corrects.

'Perhaps she forgot it at home, or it's out of juice.'

'Hmm…' Teddy groans, and I can tell that he thinks there's more to it. But there isn't. He doesn't know Jasmine. It wouldn't be the first time she took herself off without telling anyone. She's probably booked herself into a lux spa for a few days to unwind. Alison and I went on one of those mid-week breaks with her once in Oxford. Probably the most relaxing three days I've ever had, although I didn't have any of the treatments because they were too expensive.

'She's only been gone one night.' I stretch my back. 'She's hardly on the missing person's list,' I point out, rubbing the side of my neck. I'm getting too old for passing out drunk on the sofa. 'Want another coffee?' Teddy shakes his head. I get to my feet and flick on the kettle. 'Like I told the police, she's probably in some swanky hotel having saunas and facials.' I spoon coffee in to a mug. 'Bit weird that she didn't take her car though, she usually does.'

'Well, if you say so,' Teddy sighs, looking into the hallway as if he can see the police car a mile away and hear everything they're saying. 'I didn't like the way they were questioning you though, especially that woman officer with the implants and trout lips. She had that accusing tone. I thought she was a strip-o-gram when I first saw her on your doorstep.'

I laugh lightly, grinning at Teddy as I pull out a carton of milk from the fridge. 'Relax,' I say, unscrewing the top and giving it a quick sniff. It's a day past its use-by, thanks to Teddy not checking the date when he picked one up from the corner shop the other day. I hope the police officers don't get sick. 'They're only doing their jobs.'

I won't lie, I was a bit miffed when PC Jacobs started questioning me about my whereabouts yesterday evening and my connection to Jasmine. But I was upfront about it all, told her we were good friends, until she had an affair with my husband, that there'd been some bad blood between us but it was water under the bridge now. I was there yesterday morning to discuss the sale of this flat, which I jointly own with my ex-husband. The PCs nodded and I thought that was the end of that. But when PC Jacobs pulled out my Travelicious ID card and said they'd found it by Jasmine's Porsche everything darkened. I didn't even realise it was missing. Did they think I had anything to do with the damage to Jasmine's car?

It was only when she smiled and handed it back to me, saying that they were returning my property that I could breathe again. They believed me when I explained how I must've dropped it when I leant against her car to shake a stone out of my shoe yesterday morning. Maybe because it was true. PC Jacobs even laughed about the stone in the shoe thing, said how annoying it is.

I toyed with the idea telling them what happened with the ring after that. I mean, if PC Jacobs resonated with me about the shoe incident then perhaps she might understand how I reacted when I discovered that my ex had stolen my engagement ring and given it to his new fiancé. But as I braced myself, they stood, thanked me for my time and the moment was gone.

'I hope they don't come sniffing around here again.' Teddy's voice breaks into my thoughts. 'Once they speak to Jasmine, I mean. No doubt she'll be pointing the finger at you after yesterday's impromptu visit, especially as it didn't go to plan.' I swallow hard, not meeting his eye. I must've told him everything last night, but I'm pretty sure I didn't mention the ring incident. 'That's if they ever find her.'

'Stop being so melodramatic, of course they will.' I take a sip of coffee, grimace, then splash more milk into it. 'It's not the first time something like this has happened. The police are always being called out to the Anands'. Jasmine's had eggs thrown at her windows, scratches on her car, threatening tweets, not to mention death threats. She's got enemies. She's ruthless. It comes with the job, I guess. But she's a tough cookie – she can take it.' I take a glug of warm coffee. 'It's probably some hoodie that she sent down for stealing.'

'Or someone with a vendetta against her,' he suggests, an accusing tone slinking into his voice.

I frown at him over my mug. 'You don't still think that I had anything to do with it, do you?' He opens his mouth to speak when there's a clatter at the front door and our eyes slide towards the hallway. 'Probably a flyer,' I offer, returning my attention to him.

'Jasmine betrayed you to the highest degree.' Teddy hesitates, swallows. 'Taking revenge would be a natural response for anyone.'

Annoyance powers through me. 'Yes, maybe. Not my style though.'

'No, not in your normal state. Alcohol, on the other hand, can make us do things we wouldn't normally do. It's a fact and…'

'And what?' I snap. 'I took leave of my senses? I only had a couple,' I lie. 'I can handle my drink, you know.'

His sigh is long and hard. 'You can't remember, can you?' I look at him as if to say, *What the fuck?* 'You said you hated her, that she's ruined your life.'

'I do. She has. But I'd never deliberately hurt her, damage her property. *Jesusssss*!!'

'I'm not suggesting that for a second but…you did say something else.'

I exhale in exasperation. 'Go on.'

Teddy rubs his lips and hisses through his nose. 'You said that someone needed to teach her a lesson and that you wished she was…' He pauses, rubs his lips some more. 'Dead.' My eyes widen. I've no recollection of saying this but then I was quite pissed – passed-out-on-the-sofa pissed.

'It was a figure of speech,' I say through clenched teeth, not admitting that I was too drunk to remember saying it. 'I haven't killed her and buried her in Highgate Wood if that's what you're suggesting.' I know he doesn't really know me well, but what does he take me for, a fucking psychopath?

Teddy tuts loudly. 'Of course you haven't bloody killed her. It's just the car…' he falters. 'Look, I'm sure you're right. It's probably some kid with a chip on his shoulder and Jasmine's having a mud bath in a spa somewhere. I'm not judging you, Lucy. We all have bad days. I'm only looking out for you.' His eyes slide to the empty glass that he sniffed out. 'Do you know that alcohol can stay in your system for hours?'

That's it. I've had enough of his accusations. I slam my mug down and brown liquid sloshes onto the table. 'Get out!' I shoot to my feet.

Teddy looks at me, horrified. 'What? Why? What've I done?'

'You obviously think I'm still drunk and don't know what I'm doing or saying,' I yell. 'And just for the record, I didn't go anywhere near Jasmine's car last night. I was here drowning my sorrows like a pathetic, lonely saddo, because my life is so fucking shit right now. Satisfied?' I glare at him but he just looks at me, clearly mortified by my outburst. 'Why don't you ring the bloody police, hmm? Tell them you suspect that I did it. That I've killed Jasmine.' I go to move but he grabs my arm to still me.

'Lucy, will you please just let me finish?' he says quietly, hand still curled around my forearm. 'I was going to say that if Jasmine had a drink yesterday, she might not have taken the car, didn't want to risk losing her licence. Alcohol stays in your system for a few hours but a breathalyser can detect it for up to twenty-four. I'm guessing Jasmine knows this, being a lawyer.'

'Oh. Right. Okay. I didn't know that,' I mutter, chest heaving. I look at him beneath furrowed brows. I can see his heart beating through his white polo shirt. 'Yes, you might be right. Jasmine is quite sensible. But I think you should go. I need some space.'

Teddy runs a hand over his face, exhaling loudly. 'If this is because I questioned you about Jasmine's car, I'm sorry. My bad. It's just that…' I give him a sharp look, eyes filling with tears. 'Okay, okay, I'm going.' I watch as he walks towards the door and then suddenly he stops and spins round. 'Just for the record, I do really like you,' he says, one hand on the doorframe. 'A lot.' He goes to leave again and then, 'Actually, fuck it. It's more than that. I think I'm falling for you.'

An unwanted burst of delight swells in my chest and my face tints, even though I don't believe in love at first sight, even though I know it's mad, that he can't mean it. Can he…?

Teddy walks towards me, takes my face in his hands, and brushes away my tears with his thumbs. 'I really mean it,' he says softly, as if he read my mind. Leaning forward, he presses his forehead against mine, our noses brush. I can smell his gorgeous cologne through my teary phlegmy nose. 'I wish I could…' But before he can finish I kiss him. He hesitates at first, goes to pull away, but I haul him back and then I feel his hot tongue in my mouth. We kiss hungrily, wildly. Then he suddenly stops and holds me at arm's length, chest heaving, breath ragged.

'What's wrong?' I pant.

'Are you sure you want this?' he asks, eyes hungry with lust.

'Oh, come here.' I take a handful of his polo top and pull it out of his black chinos.

Eyes not leaving mine, he yanks off his top and chucks it on to the worktop. The sight of his smooth skin and strong muscles makes me stir. I untie my dressing gown quickly and let it drop to the floor. God, what am I doing? He takes in the length of my naked body as I move forward and fumble with the buckle of his trousers. My skin tingles as I unzip his flies, feeling his arousal against my wrist.

Parting my lips with his tongue, he lifts me off the ground and I wrap my legs around his back as he carries me clumsily across the kitchen. I hear the crash of objects hitting the floor as he clears the table with one fell swoop of his arm – metal utensils, yesterday's post. A glass breaks, but I don't care.

Drunk on lust, I tug at his boxers and he pulls them off and kicks them across the room with his foot, planting hot kisses along my neck and collar bone. My lips find his again, our teeth clatter in our urgency, hungry for each other, tongues entwined. I arch my back, aching for him, and as he pushes himself inside me, I close my eyes and really hope that I'm not going to regret this.

Teddy throws a glance at the worktop as he zips his trousers and pushes a hand through his messy hair, face red and glossy with sweat. 'What's this?'

'What? Oh, the flowers,' I say breathlessly, tying the belt of my dressing gown and feeling a bit awkward. Did I really just have a quickie on my kitchen table with Teddy Fallon? A man I've known for only a week? It's insane. Wait until I tell Nessa at work on Monday. She'll be thrilled – want all the details. Sex is her favourite topic of conversation. 'Aren't they from you?'

'God, no. I'd never send you white lilies.' Teddy says, catching his breath. 'They're funeral flowers.' He pulls on his polo top then plucks the card from the box and slides it out of the tiny envelope.

'What does it say?'

Teddy swallows hard then looks at me and the colour drains from his face.

Chapter 19

‘They’re from Andrew?’ I walk towards Teddy gingerly, still feeling a bit high from the spontaneous sex. 'Seriously? That’s outrageous. He’s never sent me flowers before. What does the card say? What are you doing? Give it to me.’

‘I don’t think you should read it,’ Teddy warns as I try but fail to snatch it from his hand which is aloft and out of reach.

‘Come on, Teddy, stop messing around.’ I tickle his side but his muscles tense and he grimaces. He really means it. Surely, he doesn’t feel threatened by Andrew now we’ve had sex. What does it say? Possibilities flutter around in my head – he misses me, he’s sorry he left me, wants me back. But no, he loves Jasmine, they’re getting married, everything’s booked – he’s spoken to Jasmine and he’s had second thoughts about selling the flat, is sorry for messing me around – the flowers are a peace offering.

‘Lucy, I know you’ve only known me a week but please trust me on this.’ Teddy’s ominous tone tells me that I’m wrong on all counts and the way he pauses and looks at the ceiling, Adam’s apple moving in his throat, makes me think that it’s something quite sinister. ‘You’ve had a tough few days. Why don’t you go and stay with your mum for the weekend? Get away from it all.’

‘Get away from what? You haven’t had enough of me already, have you?’ I laugh lightly. ‘Give it here.’

'The sea air will do you good.'

'What? Are you kidding me?'

'Just think, fish and chips on the pier.'

'No! Come on, Teddy. You can't forbid me from reading it.' I snort. 'I'm not five.' I manage to yank his arm down but he whips it quickly behind his back before I can snatch it, and then I'm circling him like a dog on heat, trying to wrestle the card out of his hand.

'They say it'll be lovely and warm this weekend.'

'I'm not going to Brighton. I've got tons of stuff to do here.'

'I'm sure your mum would love to see you.'

'Mum hates surprises.'

'Lucy, stop it, you're going to tear it. Ouch. Fuck!'

I take a step back, panting as he examines his hand. I've scratched him. 'I'm sorry. Are you okay?'

He sucks the pink mark on his wrist even though I can clearly see it isn't bleeding. 'I'll live,' he mumbles frowning at the scratch. Our first fight. The honeymoon period didn't last long.

I thrust out a hand, exhaling loudly. 'Just give me the card, please.'

Teddy hesitates, rubs his hand then holds out the crumpled card. 'I'll drive you to Brighton myself,' he pleads, snatching his hand away before I can take it. 'I've no jobs on today. We could be there in a few hours if you get a wiggle on.'

'I want to read the card,' I demand. He really is starting to piss me off now. 'I mean it, Teddy, that's enough.'

But instead of handing me the card, he pulls out a silver zippo lighter from his pocket, lights it and holds it under the card.

'Don't you dare,' I say indignantly, blood rushing to my face.

'If you calm down. I'll let you read it. But only if you agree to go to Brighton.'

'This isn't up for negotiation, Teddy,' I warn. He won't burn it. He's just winding me up, surely. 'Give. Me. The. Goddam. CARD.' I go to grab it out of his hand. The flame licks the corner, glows orange, shrivels to ash and blackens. He flicks the lighter again, it sparks. He flicks it again and again and again but this time I manage to pull his arm down. Then as I try to snatch it out of his hand, he squeezes it in his fist.

'For fuck's sake,' I scream, 'just because you've fucked me doesn't mean you own me now.' And then everything stops. It's as if someone has hit the pause button. He looks at me, stunned. My face reddens, shocked by my own outburst. I shouldn't have said that but I can't unsay it.

'Jesus,' he whispers, after a few moments, 'is that what you really think? I wasn't going to burn it. I was just trying to spare your feelings. Here. Take it. But don't say I didn't warn you.' It was a low blow, I know, but I had to do something before he accidently cremated that card. What a stupid stunt to pull, anyway, not to mention dangerous. I snatch the crumpled card from his hand, unfurl it and read it silently, inhaling a fug of burning smoke.

Pack your bags and leave, WHORE. No one wants you here. Don't even think of going to the police. Mammy must get lonely by the seafront.

My hand flies to my mouth. I think I'm going to vomit. 'My God, who would do such a thing?' I look up at Teddy who now has his hands on his hips and is shaking his head.

'I did warn you,' he says, pushing a hand through his dishevelled chestnut hair. 'God, you're a stubborn woman.'

'It's just so…so…' I read the card again as if for the first time. 'So evil.' My lungs feel dense. It's as if invisible hands are squeezing me by the throat.

'Listen, don't worry. Andrew's just trying to scare you into selling up so he can get his mitts on the money from the sale of this place. Bloody spineless prick.'

I look up at Teddy, bewildered. 'Andrew? But it isn't even signed,' I hear myself say, then throw a glance at the pink box on the worktop. 'There's no business card, no address on the package. Nothing. It isn't even his handwriting.'

'So, you're a handwriting analyst now, are you?' Teddy retorts, and my head snaps up. His face is red, glistening with sweat, brows knotted, jaw tight. Well, this is a side to him I haven't seen before. Is this what happens after you have sex with someone? After you let your guard down? We stare at each other speechless for a few moments, and then his face softens.

'Oh, come here.' Teddy pulls me to him and I bury my head in his shoulder, inhaling the fug of Dior Sauvage, smoke and sweat. 'I'm sorry for snapping at you. I'm just worried that's all. I care about you, Lucy.' He sounds like he means it but how could he? I know we've had sex but we hardly know each other really. Unless he means it in a philanthropic way. He's a kind man, that much I do know. He told me that he helps out in soup kitchens when work is quiet; he even showed me photographs on his phone with the other volunteers, all in Christmas jumpers and red bobble hats. Maybe he thinks I'm a victim, that I need saving. Maybe I am.

'It's obvious that your ex is spying on you,' Teddy points out. I frown up at him, hands resting on his chest. Why is he so convinced they're from Andrew? There's no evidence to suggest it. 'What if he means it? What if he accidently on purpose hurts your mum? I think you should go to Brighton, make sure she's safe. Today.' I pull away from him, rake my hands through my hair then let them rest over my ears. I don't want to hear any more. I wish he'd stop accusing Andrew. He's starting to sound jealous. 'Pack a bag with a few things and I'll drive you there myself. Just for a few days until all this blows over.'

'Blows over?' I rub my forehead, staring at the card, as if I've misread it, missed something. 'Andrew wouldn't hurt my mum. That's if he is the blackmailer, which is very unlikely. It's Jasmine. It has to be. That's why she's gone into hiding. She's never liked my mum, always used to call her names when we were little, teased me about her mental health issues, and now, because she knows she's the most important person in the world to me, she's using her as bait.'

'Whoever it is has got to be stopped. This is getting out of hand. We need to find out who's behind it all.' Teddy pauses, and then, 'I wasn't going to say anything until I was sure, but I was speaking to one of my clients yesterday, Alan, a techno geek, and he reckons he can trace any number from a mobile phone.'

'Seriously?' My eyes widen. This is the best news I've had in days. 'I thought only the police could do that.' I googled it to death. You can't trace a number on a pay-as-you-go sim that hasn't been registered. But the police have other methods – something to do with GPS and the handset. 'Is Alan an ex-copper?'

'I don't think so, no. He may need your phone though.' I want to run to my bedroom, snatch it off the bedside table where it is charging and give it to Teddy immediately. 'He was in a bit of a hurry yesterday, but told me to give him a bell this afternoon so we can discuss it in more detail. He'll want a few quid for it, of course, upfront, and it'll take a few days to sort out.' I tell him that's fine. I'll meet the costs, so please hire him. 'Once Alan gives us a location, an address, we can go to the police.' I nod and Teddy's eyes shine with adrenalin. 'This has got jealous ex written all over it.' It isn't Andrew but as Teddy is hell-bent that it is, I stay silent. I don't want to put him off. I need techno Alan to find out who the blackmailer is. I need to know if it's Jasmine.

'Okay, so you're happy to go ahead, yes?'

I shake my head, agreeing. 'If you could do that, this will all be over and we can carry on with our lives.'

'I promise you, I'll do my absolute best. I'll ring him later today. Now, pack a bag.'

'What? No. There's no way I'm going to Brighton now. I need to stay here and work out a plan, see if the blackmailer gets in touch again. If they are watching me then they'll know I've only just received the flowers.' I pace up and down the kitchen, finger in mouth. 'God, I wish Alison was still speaking to me,' I say. 'She'd know what to do.' I stop walking and round on him, grabbing his arm. 'Do you think I should call Karen?'

'Alison's mum? What for?'

'She might be able to give me some impartial advice.'

Teddy snorts. 'Karen? She's hardly Miss Marple. I've always thought she was a bit…' He makes inverted commas with his fingers. 'Eccentric.' I let go of him and narrow my eyes, taking in his frame indignantly. 'You know.' He does a funny whistle. 'Away with the fairies. I don't think she knows what day it is half the time.' I pull an incredulous face but he leans against the worktop and picks at his nail. 'Tried to pay me again today when I went back to sort out that fence I put up yesterday afternoon.' I frown. I didn't know he'd gone back to Karen's today. 'One of the brackets came loose,' he says dismissively, registering my confusion. 'A five-minute job. Jesus, some people are so gullible.'

'Karen's an intelligent woman,' I hit back, defending her. 'You do know she's a member of Mensa.' Silence. 'Hmm, thought not. Don't be so harsh to judge. But you might be right.

It's probably not a good idea to get her involved.' I pause, stare into mid-air and then, 'I know what I'll do. I'll ring the estate agents on Monday morning, get them round here to do a valuation then put the flat on the market. If the blackmailer is watching me then they'll see the sign go up, that'll throw them off the scent, give techno Alan a chance to trace the number. What do you think?'

Teddy throws his hands up in the air. 'I don't know, Lucy, do whatever you want.'

We fall silent, and then he says, 'Speaking about the sale of the flat, how come Jasmine didn't know anything about it? Why didn't Andrew tell her?' Andrew again. God! Although, Teddy's got a point. Jasmine looked genuinely surprised when I told her Andrew wanted to sell the flat. And he did lie to me about the pregnancy too, which was odd. Maybe the pregnancy thing was to hurt me. He knew how much I yearned for a baby. I was even secretly hoping that I was pregnant when he left me. When I was three days late I bought a test, praying that it'd be positive, willing to be a single mum, go it alone. I sat on the loo and had a little cry when 'Not Pregnant' lit up on the screen.

'I don't know, Teddy. He must've had his reasons,' I say, batting the thought away. 'Jasmine thinks he might need the money for his business.' Slipping the card into my dressing gown pocket, I squat, and pick up the objects that flew off the table during our sex rampage, an impish smile playing on my lips. 'He's a very proud man – wouldn't want to ask Jasmine for a loan.'

'Okay. If you say so.' Teddy sighs, exasperated, clearly he's had enough of trying to be my superhero. 'But I wouldn't rule him out, Lucy. If he's desperate to sell the flat he might be in serious debt.' Teddy's legs swish in my vision as I carefully pick up a few shards of broken glass, then I hear the ruffle of cardboard and the rustle of cellophane. He's opening the box.

‘You never know what people are capable of until the shit hits the fan.’

A spit of acid flies into my stomach. The ring. It was pure desperation that made me do it. I should tell him, be upfront. I’m sure he’ll understand once I explain how it happened, that it wasn’t planned, that my emotions just ran away with me, and then there was no going back. But as I turn to face him he gives me a lopsided grin that reaches his warm eyes and says, ‘Not everyone is as kind and honest as you, you know.’

‘Andrew isn’t cruel,’ I hear myself say, bottling it. I press my foot against the bin pedal and it flies up, hitting the tiles. My confession will have to wait. ‘He’s just sarky and thoughtless.’ Throwing the glass into the bin, I turn and walk towards the box of flowers on the worktop. ‘Andrew’s not a gangster, Teddy. He wouldn’t hurt anyone on purpose.’

I touch a white petal poking out from the top of the cellophane, feeling its smooth, velvety flesh between my fingers. *Who sent you flowers?* I jump slightly as Teddy wraps his arms around my waist and rests his chin on my shoulder. Closing my eyes, I inhale the scent of lilies as we spoon-hug, savouring the moment. I’d forgotten how good it feels to be held, wanted. ‘Penny for them,’ Teddy murmurs.

‘I just want everything to go back to normal,’ I whisper.

‘What are we going to do with you, eh?’ Teddy asks softly, cheek on mine. ‘Not a bad word to say about anyone. I wish my ex was as compassionate.’ I feel his warm sigh on my skin. ‘Andrew’s one lucky bastard, but you know him better than anyone and if you say he isn’t vindictive, I believe you.’

I smile sadly as I look down at the heady bouquet, glad that Teddy trusts my instincts. ‘They are lovely though, aren’t they? Shame to bin them, really.’ I sigh, running a hand along the cellophane. ‘They don’t look cheap. I might pop them round to Gloria and Matthew’s later, a thank you for helping me out the other day. I'll say they're an unwanted gift, that I'm allergic to lilies, or something.'

Teddy murmurs in agreement but as I go to close the box, I suddenly remember the time when Andrew had a spat with one of his clients. Some stuck-up couple in St Albans, according to Andrew, an accountant and his princess wife – filthy rich. He'd fitted a bathroom suit for them. It was a tricky job. The tiny tiles pattered with white lilies were a pain in the arse to put up. It took him two weeks to finish. But then the owner said his wife found a scratch on the bath, which Andrew vehemently denied doing. The snooty accountant refused to pay him point blank. That night, Andrew snuck round to his house and punctured one of the tyres on his wife's Range Rover. The man owed him two grand but still. It was a bit much. I couldn't sleep for weeks after that. I kept expecting the police to hammer our door down and take Andrew away – naked in handcuffs.

'I've just had another thought.' Teddy's voice makes me jump. 'Does Andrew do drugs?'

I pull out of his embrace and rub the back of my stiff neck. 'Drugs? No,' I say dismissively. 'Only a bit of weed now and then.' Then a scene locks in my head. We're at Jasmine's. It's Halloween. I'm dressed as Morticia Addams and I'm looking for Andrew the vampire. I can't find him. I'm weaving through a sea of hot sweaty bodies, glass of fizz in hand, searching for him. In the hallway, one of the guests, Priya, I think, Jasmine's sister, tells me she last saw him in the kitchen with Jas. I'm standing by the kitchen door, their backs to me, watching them sharing a joke. I can see Andrew's gelled-back black hair against the high satin collar of his cape, and Jasmine's long black ponytail and latex cat-suit. When she clocks me, she almost chokes on her champagne, then, wiping her wet lips, she tells me to take my husband away, that he's pissed and leading her astray. Andrew sniffed and dabbed at his nose when he turned round. He was high as a kite that night and we had the best sex ever.

I bite the flesh of the inside of my bottom lip. Were they doing cocaine? I know Jasmine dabbles occasionally. She tried to do it round ours once but I told her point blank, 'No coke in the flat.'

'Oh, lighten up, Luce,' she'd retorted. 'It's no different to knocking back several glasses of rum and Coke. Only without the hangover.'

Has Jasmine turned him into an addict? It's an expensive habit. Is that why he's desperate to sell the flat, does he owe people in low places money?

'Hang on a minute,' Teddy says, breaking me out of my reverie. 'That last sentence, read it again.'

I pull the card out of my pocket and read it out loud, '*Mammy must get lonely by the seafront.*'

'Who calls their mother Mammy?'

'I don't know. Isn't it an Irish term?'

'It's Scottish too.'

'I don't think so. Andrew's never…' And then another scene bolts into my mind like a meteoroid and my knees give a little. Andrew and I are in Edinburgh visiting his parents. We're about to go out shopping. It's freezing, minus three. I'm shrugging my coat on and Andrew is winding a scarf around his neck, then as he closes the door behind us he yells, "See ya later, Mammy."

I suck in so much air that I'm almost sick.

'Lucy, I don't want to influence you but all this stinks. It's your call though. If you're sure it's not Andrew, that's fine, and if you think your mum is safe alone in Brighton.' He holds his hands up. 'That's fine too. You can stay put and see what happens next. It's entirely up to you. I'm only trying to help.'

I look at Teddy in horror, fear seeping into my veins. 'You don't think he means it, do you? About hurting my mum?'

Teddy sighs. 'Do you want to risk it?' I shake my head firmly. 'I'll get my car keys.'

'I'll pack a bag.'

Chapter 20

Forty-five minutes later I'm sitting in my living room staring morosely out of the window, holdall by my feet, jumping whenever a car drives by in case it's Teddy. He said he was popping out for some fuel while I threw a few things into a bag. But he's been gone ages. It's only a five-minute drive. I look at my watch. I wonder if he's changed his mind. Done a runner. I wouldn't blame him if he has. I have a vision of him heading for the petrol station, Magic on the radio, and thinking it all through – the danger, the implication, the risks, and then just putting his foot down and driving home to his mum's smart bungalow in Cockfosters with the garden at the front. I'll probably never hear from him again. I bat the thought away. He wouldn't do that to me. He's too decent. We've had sex and he doesn't strike me as the love 'em and leave 'em type. He must be stuck in traffic. I forgot to tell him about the roadworks at the triangle. That's what's holding him up. Of course it is.

'Alexa,' I say loudly and the blue light glows. 'Is there traffic at the triangle?'

'Sorry, I'm not sure about that.'

'Alexa, is there traffic near the triangle in Palmers Green?'

'Sorry, I couldn't find what you're looking for.'

'Alexa, has my new bloke done a runner?'

'Sorry, I can't answer that. But I do have a skill you might like – It's called 'Something Nice.' Wanna try it?'

I'm about to tell Alexa to piss off when my phone buzzes in my pocket and my heart almost stops. I pull it out quickly and look at the screen – *Editor's Picks – Who killed the sex symbol? Plus more great reads.* A news notification – not Andrew with another threatening text, not a message from my mum replying to the overly cheery voicemail I left her half an hour ago saying that I'm on my way to see her. Surely, she must've picked it up by now. I press my fingers against my lips. I don't want to turn up on her doorstep unannounced. Mum doesn't cope well with surprises. It might set her tick off – the one where she flicks her head to the side repeatedly – the one which breaks my heart whenever it happens – the one my ruthless father inflicted.

I tell Alexa to play *Queen's Love of my Life* on Spotify and within moments I'm swathed in Freddie's haunting voice. I allow the song to fade into the background and scroll through the texts from Unknown Sender. If they are from Andrew then surely I'll detect his tone. I was his wife, for goodness' sake. I know him inside out, or at least I thought I did. I read the texts one by one to the backdrop of Freddie's voice. God, they seem more threatening than ever. Maybe Brighton isn't such a good idea. Maybe I should go to the police after all. Hand over my phone, the box of flowers and the card, and tell them everything. Let them do their job instead of playing private detectives with Teddy.

But then what if Teddy's right? What if Andrew is jealous of my new relationship? What if he's got himself into serious debut? Doing drugs? He did look a bit weird last Saturday when he came round to see me – restless, irritable, kept sniffing. Did he see me and Simon that night? Did he take that photograph? Is it possible that my ex is stalking me, blackmailing me, trying to scare me into selling up? Freddie Mercury's voice slices through me. Shooting to my feet I command Alexa to STOP!

The music stops and I stand there, breathless, sweat tickling down my spine. If Teddy's right and Andrew is spying on me, then he'll know if I go to the police, won't he? My eyes flick to the window quickly. Is he out there watching me now? Lying in wait? No, I'm being paranoid. *Calm down, Lucy, and get a grip!* Andrew's in Clacton-On-Sea. Jasmine was very adamant about that. My finger finds my mouth. There are other ways to keep a tag on someone. He might've put a tracker on my phone for all I know. He's had plenty of opportunities to do so. Or perhaps he's paid someone to follow me. A private detective. It's not as if he can't afford to hire one. My breath catches in my throat. If Andrew means what he said on the card, he could be in Brighton before the police catch up with him. My poor mum's blood pressure will go through the roof if her turns up on her doorstep. She might even have a heart attack, or a stroke.

A car horn beeps and I jump. It's Teddy. I grab my bags, double check that everything is locked and, with one quick look in the hallway mirror, pull the door behind me, belt down the path and slip into the seat next to Teddy. His car is warm and smells of musk and spices.

'Got everything?' Teddy says as I secure my stuff in the footwell, and I nod, throwing a glance at him. He looks different somehow, cleaner, fresher, hair slicked back neatly.

I scratch my head. 'God, this is mental. I feel like we're Thelma and Louise. Well, Thelma and Louis.' Teddy frowns. 'Oh, you know what I mean. Yes! Let's do this. I'm ready.'

'Sure?'

'Yup.' I look at him and he gestures at my legs.

'You do realise you're only going for a couple of days, not a fortnight,' he says wryly and we both look at my bulging holdall between my feet.

I give him a look as I yank the seatbelt across my body, and then I remember the note I wrote for Spiros and Xenia. 'Oh, wait,' I cry as the seatbelt flies back into its socket with a crash. Lifting my bottom off the seat, I pull a piece of paper from the back pocket of my jeans. 'Forgot to drop this off next door.' Teddy frowns at the paper in my hand. 'Just a note to let them know I'll be aware for a few days.'

'Can't you just leave it?' Teddy huffs. 'I'm sure your neighbours won't even realise you're away.'

I laugh at that. Xenia is more in tune with my itinerary than I am. 'No, Sunday is koupes day.'

'What day?'

'Koupes. They're a Cypriot street food made with bulgur wheat, mincemeat and lots of different herbs.' Teddy screws his face up. 'I'm not explaining it well. They're yummy. Xenia pops a few round to me and I have them for lunch. She'll freak out if I'm not in. Won't be a mo.'

'Call them later, traffic will be…'

Teddy's voice dies as I slam the door and run down the path, just missing a collision with two kids tearing along the pavement on their bikes. I push the note through the gold letterbox and hope to God that my Greek Cypriot neighbours can read my sprawl. My hand wouldn't stop shaking as I quickly scribbled on a notepad earlier – *Gone to see my mum in Brighton. BBS. Pls keep an eye on my flat. Love, Lucy xx.* God, why did I write BBS? They won't know what it means, they might panic. Pressing my forehead against the white double-glazed door, I claw at it longingly, wishing I could push my hand through the letterbox, retrieve the note and write it all out again neatly in capital letters, with the 'Be Back Soon' in full. English isn't their first language. A car horn honks – *beep, beeeeep!* Teddy's getting impatient. I spin on my heel and rush towards the waiting car, telling myself that Emma or Harry could read it for them if they have any trouble understanding my writing, or even their nephew, Kiki, when he drops them off later today.

Teddy's checking his phone as I clamber back into his Ford Mondeo, then as I go to close the door I hear my phone ringing in my bag. This had better be Mum telling me she's just got in and noticed my missed calls. I don't even know why I bother leaving her voicemails, she never listens to them. I rifle through my bag for my handset, one leg in the footwell, the other dangling out of the car.

'We'd better get a move on, Lucy,' Teddy warns, slipping his phone into the inside pocket of his brown corduroy jacket. 'Sat nav says traffic is starting to build up on the M25.' My eyes flit to his face and then I spy him peering at the dashboard, then at his watch. 'Can't you leave that for now and buckle in?' he says. 'You don't want to get fined for not wearing a seatbelt.'

'Just a second. I think it's my mum…returning my call…' I mutter into my bag, praying that I'll see 'Mum Calling' on my screen when I pull out my phone. 'My mum's a bit…jittery. She'll want to know why I've suddenly decided to go and see her. Mum even gets panicky when she's watching contestants on game shows. She sometimes cries if they lose. I've got to put her mind at rest. I need to speak–'

'At least close the door so we can get going,' Teddy interjects with miniscule irritation, and I feel as if we're an old married couple embarking on a road trip. He turns the key in the ignition and the diesel engine rumbles. 'Lucy, did you hear me?' he says, but all I can do is stare at my handset. 'Is it your mum? We'll never get there at this – what's wrong?'

I shake my head. It stops ringing then buzzes with a missed call alert. 'Three missed calls,' I utter, unable to hide the shock in my voice. 'It must've been going off while I was getting ready to leave. I can't always hear my phone when it's in my bag.'

Teddy's eyes are like discs, his hand tightens around the steering wheel. 'From the Unknown Number?' I shake my head. 'Jasmine? Oh, God, not Andrew?'

'No,' I murmur, swallowing hard. 'They're all from Alison.'

Chapter 21

'Alison?' Teddy says finally, clearly as surprised as I am. 'Wow.'

'I know,' I say, chewing what's left of my thumbnail. 'I never thought I'd hear from her again.'

We lapse into silence, punctuated by the low rumble of the engine and then the sudden whoosh of wheels against concrete – a blink of a yellow tricycle and a woman yelling 'Christopher,' in the distance.

'What do you think she wants?' I ask nervously as Christopher's mother dashes by with a child in a stroller, ponytail swinging, phone glued to her ear. Teddy stares after her, face ashen. Hardly surprising given that he's been dragged into the drama of two women he barely knows.

'There's only one way to find out.'

Ring her back? Is he insane? The idea fills me with trepidation. I don't think I can speak to her now, not without knowing what she wants first. Staring ahead, I continue to chew my nail frantically as my brain spins like the reels of a slot machine, faster and faster and faster and then it hits me.

'Jasmine must be back.' I bark, spittle flying from my lips. 'She's spoken to Alison – told her about her car and about…' I pause, fill my lungs. I can't tell him about the ring, not yet. I wait for a reaction but he just revs up the engine, eyes on the dashboard, face unreadable. 'They think it was me, don't they?

That I vandalised Jasmine's car.' I jabber on. 'Don't you agree?' *Vroom, vroom.* 'They're ganging up on me now.' *Vrooooom.* 'Jasmine will tell the police. I'll get questioned again, accused.' *Vroom, vroom.* 'Oh, will you please stop that,' I snap, 'I can't hear myself think.'

'Sorry.' The engine dies. 'I was just checking the revs. They seem a bit…' He pauses. 'Go on, you were saying.'

'I think Alison wants to question me about the Porsche. Try to catch me out. Jasmine must've told her that I was there yesterday morning, acting suspicious, going through her things.' More frantic nail biting and staring ahead. 'Fuck!' I bet Jasmine's told her that she thinks I stole her engagement ring too, which I suppose I did. 'Oh, God,' I murmur, dropping my head in my hands. I'm a thief.

Teddy looks at me worriedly, hand on my forearm. 'Relax. You're overreacting.' Silence. 'You haven't done anything wrong. Let them think what they like.'

It's easy for him to say, he doesn't know the half of it. 'You don't know what Jasmine's like.' I shake my head at Mrs Dench from number forty who is on a stepladder trimming her hedge. 'Jasmine sends innocent people down. It's her job.' I should tell him about what I did. About…the ring. After all, he's in it up to his neck now too, after lying to the police. Doesn't he deserve to know? Don't I at least owe him that?

'Teddy, I did a–'

'Don't–'

We've spoken at the same time. Teddy hisses loudly through his nose, eyes on the dashboard, and then, 'Don't let Alison get to you. If we leave now we could still be in Brighton by four thirty.' I look at Teddy, cold fingers pressed against my lips. He looks shattered – eyes dark and puffy. Guilt skims along my spine and I sit up straight. What am I doing, dragging this poor, innocent man into all this? Am I taking advantage of him, using him? I've always hated selfish spongers and now I've become one. I suddenly feel like the worst person in the world.

'What do you want to do?' Teddy asks wearily, throwing me a fed-up glance. He's had enough. I bet he'll never want to see me again after today. I've blown it with him before it even began.

Focusing on the red Mini Cooper that's pulled up in front of us, I exhale loudly. 'I suppose you're right. I'll have to ring Alison back and…'

Teddy sighs. 'Yes, that is an option. But it'll only hold us up. Unless you're happy to have the conversation while we're driving.'

'What if I lose reception? My phone isn't reliable and this is important.' I sigh at two lads getting out of the red Mini, sharing a joke as they cross the road. Mrs Dench's hedge trimmer buzzes in the distance. 'If I don't call Alison back she'll keep ringing until I pick up. I know what she's like. I mean, she's already called me three times in the space of five minutes.'

Teddy nods. 'I know. I'm just worried about being stuck in traffic on the M25 on a Saturday afternoon, that's all.'

I look at my front door longingly. I've been running away from problems all my life. Maybe it's time to stop. Perhaps I'll give Mum another call – ask her to come to me instead. I'm off until Wednesday now, anyway. I texted Gillian just before I started packing, asking for a few more days off. Her reply was razor sharp:

That's fine, Lucy. But you'll have to take it unpaid or as holiday leave. Regards, Gillian.

'Actually, you're right. I think you ought to go home and ring Alison,' Teddy suggests kindly. 'You won't rest until you've spoken to her, will you? I can run you to Brighton tomorrow morning if you like. Go early – avoid the traffic.'

That's the most sensible thing I've heard all day.

I cup his cheek and he kisses my hand. 'What would I do without you, hey?'

Filling my lungs with an infusion of Dior Sauvage and foliage, I go to open the door and that's when I spot it. 'Where did you get that shirt from?' He's wearing a smart white shirt with tiny yellow and blue flowers under his brown corduroy jacket. My eyes skim his body. 'And those blue jeans?' I'm not observant as a rule, but even I noticed that he was in a white polo top and black chinos when we had sex on my kitchen table earlier.

He looks at me wordless for a few moments, almost as if he hasn't registered what I've said, and then. 'I popped home to change and pick up a few things.' That's why he was late coming back. Teddy jerks his head towards the rear of the car and I turn in my seat. There's a black holdall on the backseat. 'It was meant to be a surprise,' he says.

I look at him agape, phone clutched so tightly in my hand that it hurts. 'Surprise?'

'I've booked a B&B in Hove for a few nights. I haven't got any jobs on until Thursday morning – Mrs O'Connor wants her patio jet washed.' The colour drains from my face. I hope he's not suggesting what I think he is. This trip is for my mum's welfare. 'A friend of mine moved there six years ago,' Teddy clarifies. 'Richard Jarvis. We were at Uni together. Thought we could catch-up over a few pints while you check on your mum. Only thirty quid a night. Richard knows the landlord. They're members of the same golf club.' My shoulders slump. He meant a single room for himself not a shag fest with me. 'Was going to suggest giving you a lift back on Monday or Tuesday, depending on when Alan traces the mobile phone number; save you faffing about on the trains.' Teddy gives me a sad smile, throwing a glance at the dashboard again. 'But if you've changed your mind about going, I'll ring and cancel. I'll only lose one night's deposit.' Then his face drops. 'You okay? You look like you've seen a ghost.'

'Don't cancel,' I say, suddenly changing my mind. 'Let's go. Alison can wait.'

'You sure?'

'Definitely. This is more important.' I turn my phone to silent and slip it into my open handbag. But as I hug the leather to my chest, an alarm bell shrills in my head. 'Isn't it your turn to see the kids this weekend?' Pissed as I was last night, I do recall him mentioning it during our phone call.

'Change of plans,' he says miserably. 'Lydia called this morning and cancelled.' No wonder he looks so rough. 'It's her parents' wedding anniversary. They always throw lavish parties at their mansion in Canterbury. Apparently, they've hired a magician and set up archery for the kids in the garden, and a disco for later.' A disco? I haven't heard that turn of phrase in years, apart from when my mum threatens to go to one. 'Lydia's taking the kids there for the weekend. The whole family's going and she doesn't want them to miss out on all the fun.' I nod slowly. I suppose it makes sense. 'Claims she messaged me about it last week and followed it through with a phone call today because I didn't get back to her.' I can tell by the tone of his voice that he thinks she did it on purpose – to punish him for leaving her. What a cow. 'So, I'm at a bit of a loose end, anyway.'

Poor Teddy. He was really looking forward to taking his kids to The Tower of London, even bought the tickets online to save queuing.

'I'm sorry,' I offer, giving his arm a light squeeze.

'It's okay,' he says despairingly. 'I'm used to it. I'm shattered, to be honest.' He rubs his eyes with the heels of his hands. 'A few days by the sea would be a real tonic. Don't worry, I won't get under your feet, or anything. Although, dinner would be nice one night if you're free. I'd love to meet your mum.'

'What did I do to deserve you?' I smile. Karma really has been kind to me lately, at least where romance is concerned. 'But you don't have to stay in Brighton, Teddy. I can jump on a train on Tuesday. Honestly. Save your money. You'll need it when work dries up. Winter's only around the corner.' I pause and then, 'Actually, why don't you just drop me off at Bounds Green Station? I could jump on a train to Brighton from Victoria.'

'Absolutely not,' he insists.

'But…'

'Ah…'

'I can…'

'I won't hear of it.' Leaning forward, he kisses my forehead, working his way down to my lips. 'Anyway,' he whispers, rubbing his nose softly against mine. 'Richard Jarvis is really looking forward to seeing me now.'

A lift back would be nice. I could even spend a bit more time with Mum instead of rushing back on Tuesday morning. We could go to The Lanes, or have lunch on The Pier. We haven't done that in ages. Closing my eyes, I can almost hear the waves lashing against the shore, the squawk of the gulls, the aroma of sea air, me and Alison dipping our legs in the foamy freezing ocean, Mum and Karen yelling at us from their deckchairs as if we were five. My eyes snap open.

'Well, we can't let Richard Jarvis down, can we?' I say, and Teddy laughs lightly.

'Did anyone ever tell you how amazing you are?

Leaning back in my seat, I buckle in and as he turns the key in the ignition I feel my phone vibrating in my bag. I look ahead as Teddy faffs about with his seatbelt and the sat nav all the while giving me a running commentary of his weekend plans – a meal out tomorrow night with Richard and his wife Wendy, a few pints at lunchtime with Richard on Monday, dinner with me and Mum in the evening, if we're up for it, maybe even squeeze in a round of golf on Tuesday before we head back. I umm and ahh distractedly as the phone continues to buzz insistently against my tummy. I'm not going to answer it. Alison will have to wait until I'm ready. Teddy crunches the car into first gear, the indicator clangs, then as he goes to release the handbrake, I yell, 'Stop. Wait.'

'What is it?'

I pull my phone out. 'I'm sorry, Teddy, I must…' I stare at my screen – Missed Call from Nessa Work. 'Sorry,' I mutter, voice thick with disappointment, 'I thought…'

The engine dies, Teddy's seatbelt flies over his shoulder. 'You were hoping it was Alison, weren't you?' We both sigh loudly. 'Let's go home.'

I nod, wordless, open the door and dangle a leg on to the pavement. 'Sorry for messing you around, Teddy. I'll make it up to you. I promise.'

'You don't need to apologise to me. I'm right here for you, remember. I'm on your side – always.' I nod like an eight-year-old child. 'I'll make us a cuppa while you phone Alison, and if she gets all heavy, I'll step in if you like.' I don't like. I'm not a little woman. I can fight my own battles, but I know he means well, so I say nothing. 'Come on,' he says brightly.

But as I got to pull the door lever a thought enters my mind. 'What do you mean, if Alison gets heavy?'

Teddy leans back in his seat. 'Actually, I've a confession to make.'

‘Confession?’ My heart picks up a little speed. I’m almost as bad as my mum when it comes to surprises. ‘Spit it out.’ Teddy’s face darkens and I know instantly that there’s something he’s not telling me. Something’s happened. Something bad. I can feel it. Why is he looking at me like that? Why isn’t he answering my question? ‘Teddy?’

‘The thing is…I haven’t been entirely honest with you about Alison,’ he admits. All the hairs on my body stand on end. He’s keeping secrets from me. Already. Lying to me. I knew he was too good to be true. ‘But before you say anything, I only kept quiet for your sake, because I know how fragile you are at the moment.’

My anger liquefies into pure panic. ‘Please, if something’s happened to Ali, or the kids. Oh my God, it’s Karen, isn’t it?’ I remember Alison telling me that her mum had to see a specialist recently, a cardiologist, something about her heart not functioning properly and a pacemaker. ‘She hasn’t had a….’ I cover my mouth. I can’t say the words. ‘Heart attack?’

Teddy’s face creases with confusion. ‘What? No. Karen was getting ready to go for a run this morning when I was round there securing her fence.’

‘A run?’ I doubt that, given her heart condition. She was probably going for a long walk. The doctor told her to take gentle exercise every day.

‘She was in her marigolds shifting pots around on the driveway when I arrived. I offered to help out but she wouldn’t hear of it. Shoved a hammer and nails in my hand and practically frogmarched me into the back garden. Strange woman.’

That doesn’t surprise me. Karen’s very independent. Doesn’t like asking anyone for help. Not even Alison or Simon. It was nice of Teddy to offer though. ‘What is it then?’

He looks at me for a few moments, then starts clucking his tongue. 'Simon and Alison have split up.'

I gasp. 'Split up!!? When? Why?'

'Just let me finish please, Lucy,' he says in a patriarchal tone, and I hunch into my shoulders. 'She found something on his computer…' I open my mouth to speak again. 'Uh.'

'But–'

'Uh…uh…' He puts a finger to his lips. This has obviously become our 'thing' whenever he wants me to shut up. 'Alison checked his history and found a significant number of porn and dating sites.'

'Porn,' I repeat loudly, and a smartly dressed elderly man walking his aging dog pauses and looks round at me stiffly, and then, with a small smile on his thin dry lips, he tips his trilby at me. I don't recognise him but I give him a little wave anyway. 'Poor Ali…' I sigh, gazing absently at the old man and his dog shuffling along the pavement and then, 'Hang on a minute.' I look round at Teddy sharply. 'How did you find out, did Karen tell you this morning?' Bit out of character. Karen's usually such a private person.

Teddy shakes his head, tells me he heard it from the horse's mouth. 'I was booked in to work on Alison's garden on Monday. But she called last night, after I spoke to you actually, and cancelled. I could tell she'd been crying. I asked her if everything was okay and she fell apart – told me the whole story.'

'Jesus.' I puff out my cheeks and blow. 'I don't believe it. No, well, I do. Simon's a piece of fucking shit. Obviously, I'm glad Alison's found out what her husband's really like, but that doesn't mean that I'm not gutted for her. I was in her shoes not long ago, and believe me, there's no worse feeling than discovering that your husband is a lying cheating prick.' It's official – all blokes are bastards. Apart from Teddy Fallon. I rub my lips, trying to process everything. 'So, that's why Alison is dying to get in touch with me. She obviously wants to apologise for wrongly accusing me. Patch things up.' I picture us sitting in the pub – me, Alison and Karen having a tearful reunion over a few bottles of prosecco.

'Jesus, why didn't you tell me all this before, Teddy? It's good news,' I say, glancing at him. 'In a way,' I add hastily. 'Not for Alison obviously. But for me it…well, I've been vindicated, haven't I? Alison must know now that Simon tried it on with me. That I was telling the truth all along. She must be feeling awful. I'll forgive her, of course. I mean, I can understand why she reacted so harshly towards me, especially after seeing that picture message of me and Simon, and then hearing all his lies. I'd have probably done the same thing in her shoes.'

I nod furiously, wanting to believe my own cliché. 'No one wants to believe that their husband is cheating on them. No one wants the fairy tale to end.' I square my shoulders. 'It's all falling into place now. Once we find out who's been blackmailing me, we can put it all behind us and try to get back to some kind of normality,' I insist. 'And if we don't have any luck with techno Alan, maybe Alison can help. She's good at stuff like that. Problem solving – probably because of her job. Therapists have to…'

Teddy's sigh is long and audible. 'Lucy, it's not that simple.'

'I'll ring her back now,' I go on, ignoring him, 'and we can go to Brighton tomorrow, like you said, with a clearer head.'

'You don't understand.'

'I'll pay for your B&B deposit.' I root around in my bag for my front door keys.

'Lucy…'

'I'll ring Mum first – in case she's picked up my voicemail – and tell her there's been a change of plans and I'll see her tomorrow instead. I'm sure she'll be safe for another night. Andrew won't go round there if I don't go to the police anyway.'

'No, you–'

'Andrew won't hurt her, Teddy. He's just trying to–'

'Lucy, STOP.'

I jerk my head round at him, keys in hand. 'There's no need to shout.'

'I'm sorry. I didn't mean to.' He inhales deeply. 'Look, Alison isn't calling to make up with you.'

'But you just said…'

'She found some random number on Simon's phone and some…some texts.' He flicks his hand out, eyeing a young woman, dressed as an eighties Madonna who is dropping a leaflet through my letterbox. 'She tried calling the number but it's unavailable. Whoever it's registered to has closed the account.'

'And your point is?' I flick a glance at the Madonna lookalike with mild irritation as she leaves my flat without closing the gate behind her. That Staffie from down the road will rock in and poo on my path now while its owner natters on her phone in her pink tracksuit and garish yellow trainers.

'She's convinced it's you. That you're the other woman.'

I draw my breath in quickly. 'What? She can't…No…'

'Said you've been having an affair for months.'

'Please tell me you're joking. I don't–'

'I tried to tell her otherwise but she wouldn't listen. 'She even apologised for setting me up with you. Warned me to stay away – said you're dangerous – poison.' I look at him agape. 'I'm sorry, Lucy, I didn't want to tell you like this but you forced my hand. She doesn't want to make up with you. She's on the warpath.'

Chapter 22

‘Come on, let’s get you inside,’ Teddy says briskly. ‘I’ll stick the kettle on while you ring Alison. You two need to talk. Sort this out once and for all.’

He pulls the door lever and goes to climb out of the car but I grab his forearm. ‘You don’t…’ I close my eyes briefly, swallow. ‘You don’t believe her, do you? I’d never…I haven’t…’ Tears sting my eyes.

‘Of course not, baby. It’s pure drivel.’ He cups my face with his hands. They’re warm, clammy and smell of cigarettes. ‘Why would someone as gorgeous as you be interested in a middle-aged married twat like Simon?’

I frown at Teddy. It isn’t about looks. It’s about morals and ethics. ‘I’d never steal another woman’s husband,’ I insist, and he smiles warmly, tells me that he knows, that I’m one in a million. ‘Do you think she knows about Jasmine’s car, then?’

Teddy shrugs, sighing through his nostrils. ‘I’ve no idea. She didn’t say anything. She was too busy ranting on about you and her husband.’

A ball forms in my throat and I swallow hard. ‘And what did Simon say?’ I twist the metal clasp of my red Gap hoodie between my fingers. ‘Did he tell her we were having an affair? If he’s said any more lies about me I swear I’ll–’

‘Actually, he said nothing’s been going on between you two.’ Teddy looks at me pointedly. ‘That he just wouldn’t go there.' I raise my eyebrows. 'I know. In his dreams right?' he says at two women walking by, arms wrapped around each other, heels clicking against the pavement. 'Simon told Alison that the texts are from a woman at work, a widow, I think she said, who took his kindness for something more. Apparently he was just being kind, trying to let her down gently. But Alison doesn't believe him. What are you doing?'

I switch my phone off and fasten my seatbelt. 'I don't want any more interruptions,' I say. 'Come on, we don't want to get stuck in that pile up.'

'But don't you want to…' He looks at my front door. 'Speak to Alison?'

I shake my head. 'No, not now. Let's go.' I pull down the sun visor and almost cry out. 'Look at the state of me,' I sniff. I open the glove compartment. 'Got any tissues?' There's a bulk of serviettes right in the centre, the kind you nab from McDonald's or a Costa. They are wedged between a notepad and a bag of Haribo sweets. Teddy turns the ignition on, the engine rumbles. But as I go to pluck out a serviette a few things fly out with it and land by my trainers in the footwell. 'Sorry,' I offer. 'I hope I haven't broken anything.' The blood rushes to my head as I bend forward and pick up a few items with one hand, then root around under my seat for the rest, to the backdrop of Teddy's impatient voice telling me to leave it, it's okay, he'll tidy it all up later.

Straightening up, I blow a strand of hair off my hot face. 'I think this is the lot.' I hand him the items in my hand – a white adapter, a neatly folded white cable secured with an elastic band, and a white mobile phone, not his usual one, this one is smaller and scratched, grubby, finger-marked.

'What's this?' He frowns, turning the phone around in his hand, then looks at me. 'Is it yours?'

'Mine?' I say incredulously but he just stares at me. 'No. Why would it be mine? It's in your car.' He continues to look at me, yet through me. It can't be… No, of course not. I'm being silly. What would Teddy's motive be? He hardly knows me. And, anyway, that picture text from Unknown Sender was taken a week before I even met him. It isn't Teddy. It's Andrew. Or Jasmine. I haven't ruled her out yet, even though Teddy thinks it can't be her because she's the obvious suspect and wouldn't be that stupid – not with her high-profile job at risk. I push the accusing thoughts out of my mind and straighten up in my seat. Teddy continues to stare at the phone in his hand in bewilderment. 'Teddy? Are you okay?'

At the sound of his name he snaps his head up as if awoken from a trance. 'It looks like Max's old one,' he says finally, his smile returning. His eldest son. That makes complete sense because he told me he bought him a new Huawei phone off Amazon a few weeks ago and is now worried because Max has access to social media. 'I'll take it round on my next visit,' he says, panic creeping into his voice. Perhaps he'll get an earful off Lydia for losing Max's handset.

'Oh, wait. There's something else by my foot.' I hand him a long plastic tube, eyes not leaving his hand as he slides Max's phone into the inside pocket of his jacket. *It's not him, Lucy. Stop being an idiot. It's impossible. He's one of the good guys, remember. Don't scare him off with your hang-ups. Get a fucking grip.*

'Ah, my battery booster. I've been looking for that for ages.'

I smile, nod, settling in my seat. I press on, changing the subject. 'Anyway, what did you say to Alison, when she told you she regretted setting us up on that blind date?'

Leaning across me, he chucks the charger back into the glove compartment and snaps it shut. 'What do you think? he asks wryly, turning the key in the ignition. 'Hard to believe that she was begging me to go out with you a couple of weeks ago.' He frowns at the speedometer and revs the engine. That's not what Alison told me – she said he was really keen from the get-go. I was the one dragging my feet when Alison rang me last week at Travelicious to tell me she'd set me up on a blind date with him.

'Practically forced me to take your number and address,' he goes on. 'She even made me wait until she grabbed a pen and paper.' Yes, that part must be true. Alison always writes everything down in longhand – isn't a fan of sending personal information via text, not since her phone was stolen and hacked a couple of years ago. We all received a picture message of an erect penis the size of a large cucumber along with several photographs of Alison from her deleted folder, looking pissed. The hacker managed to use her credit card that was stored on her phone too; raked up a bill for two and a half thousand pounds.

Tilting my head back on the headrest, I sigh. Teddy's the only good thing to come out of all this. But the trouble with me is that I often don't think I deserve good things, and always find a way to mess them up. Don't feel worthy, thanks to my dad. Alison always scolded me for being negative, said I was blocking positive energy – something to do with the law of attraction. But I've got Teddy now. A good thing. I mustn't let him go and I mustn't have negative thoughts about him.

'And the ironic thing,' Teddy's voice again, 'is that now we're finally an item, Alison's trying to break us up.' He laughs lightly, shaking his head as he turns on the radio. 'You're My Best Friend' by Queen fills the small space and we grin at each other stupidly. 'Talk about serendipity.'

And as we pull away from the kerb, a small satisfied smile plays on my lips. I'm glad Alison set us up – glad that he's still here despite everything – glad he's on my side. I give him a sideward glance as he looks from left to right before turning on to the High Street, humming the song under his breath, eyes on the road. We don't know each other well. We don't know each other at all. But I've got a really good feeling about Teddy Fallon. I think he might even be the one.

Chapter 23

Teddy's so engrossed in his phone, thumbs flying over the screen, that he barely acknowledges me as I slide into the seat next to him on the duck-blue carousel. I accidently elbow him on the arm as I unzip my Gap hoodie, shrug it off and chuck it over my bag on the seat next to me. He sways and frowns but doesn't look up from the screen. Must be something really important. Probably a work gig. Most of his appointments are arranged by text, or perhaps he's messaging his mum to make sure she's okay. They're always texting each other, those two. There's no doubt that he's a mummy's boy. It's always, Mum said this and Mum did that. I'll definitely have my work cut out for me if this goes any further. If I fall deeper.

'What do you fancy eating,' Teddy asks, once he's stopped tapping. 'Burger and chips, or what about a sausage roll? There's a Greggs over there, you could try that vegan one you were harping on about.' I mentioned that Twitter went into meltdown when it was first released, not that I wanted to eat one. He locks the phone then chucks it onto the Formica table and yawns, stretching his arms above his head, revealing a bit of flesh above the belt of his jeans.

'Or how about an M&S chicken mayo?' he suggests, folding his arms and doing a little shiver. My aunt Stella always says that someone has walked over my grave whenever I do that. Used to frighten the shit out of me when I was little. 'You can't beat their sarnies, can you? Mum swears by them.' See what I mean? I quickly take in all the eateries in the heaving service station – Burger King, Costa, Greggs, M&S Simply Food, West Cornwall Pasty Co. We've stopped for a loo break, because I almost wet myself in the car forty-five minutes into our two-hour journey, but also for something to eat, because Teddy's tummy was making gurgling noises that sounded like a dodgy radiator. I thought it was a loose exhaust pipe to begin with, that's how bad it was.

I look at him, elbow on table, chin in hand, and he reciprocates my gesture, smiling warmly. I read somewhere recently that copying someone's posture means that they really like you. I give him a smile and he holds my gaze with those mesmerising brown eyes of his, almost as if he can see through me, feel what I'm feeling, know what I'm thinking.

'What?' I grin, crossing my arms on the table.

'You've got such a gorgeous smile, that's what.' My cheeks tingle. I'm not used to compliments. 'And lovely teeth,' he adds, elbow on table, fist under chin. 'I've always thought that. You're perfect.'

I run my tongue along my small but straight teeth self-consciously. 'You're not so bad yourself, Mr Fallon.'

'I want to know everything about you,' he breathes, staring dreamily into my eyes. God, he's got such lovely eyes. 'What are you thinking right now?'

I straighten up, breaking the moment. I need to get to Brighton, make sure Mum is safe. My love life will have to wait. 'That I could murder a cup of tea,' I say, unzipping my handbag.

'Tea it is, then – a dash of milk, leave the teabag in, a spoon of sweetener.' I raise an eyebrow, tell him that he already knows me so well, and he bends forward and kisses me on the lips, sliding a hand under my t-shirt and caressing my ribs with his thumb. My skin tingles. The chemistry between us is electric. I push him away. I want to be romantic, especially now we've taken our relationship to the next level, and I will be – just as soon as he rings techno Alan and gets the Unknown Sender's number traced. Then we can put all this behind us and concentrate on us. 'Anything to eat?' I shake my head as I pull out my phone. I'm too anxious for food. 'You've got to eat something,' he says, taking in the length of my body as if I've lost a stone overnight.

'No, I'm fine. Honestly.'

'At least have a pastry. We've still got an hour's drive – longer if there's traffic. What about one of those lemony muffins, you like them, don't you?' I've got a packet of them in my cupboard. I bought them when Mum stayed over recently. They're *her* favourites. He must've spotted them. I power up my phone and wait for it to light up. 'What're you doing?' He folds his arms on the table in front of him. 'I thought you decided not to ring Alison.'

'I'm not ringing Alison. I just want to see if Mum's returned my call,' I smile, glancing up at him briefly. He doesn't look convinced. 'Muffin would be lovely.'

'Oh, I see,' he croaks. 'Um…' He inches closer, clearing his throat, and peers at my screen, almost as if he doesn't believe me.

'You okay?' I say, turning the phone slightly from his prying eyes. Not that I've got anything to hide but I think he should respect my privacy. 'You look a bit peaky.' My screen finally lights up. I look at the little white battery on the top right-hand corner – thirty-nine percent – that won't last me very long. I wonder if Teddy's portable charger is fully loaded. I punch in my passcode and wait for my phone to buzz with voicemails or messages but nothing happens.

'Look,' Teddy says crisply, 'if Alison rings again–'

'Stop worrying,' I interject, 'I told you, I won't say anything.' Teddy spent the first half of our journey pleading with me not to tell Alison that he betrayed her confidence when I next speak with her – to feign surprise, let her do the talking, allow her to explain what happened between her and Simon. If she doesn't mention it, then I'm to keep schtum, because she might, just might, have discovered who the 'other woman' is, and changed her mind about me. Plus he doesn't want her to think he's a snitch, which, of course, is the real reason he wants me to keep quiet. And I will.

'It's just that I don't want to lose my job,' he affirms, 'not with winter around the corner.' My point proven. 'These two gardening gigs have been a godsend, Lucy. Mum said it's karma. Payback time for all the shit I've been through. Karen's even asked me for some quotes to redesign her landscape.' He leans in closer, I can feel the warmth of his proximity, the hum of chatter from nearby tables. 'Alison hasn't texted then?'

I pull the phone away. 'No,' I say a little louder than intended, and the woman at the next table, late twenties, long mousy hair, no makeup, looks round at me, still holding her partner's hand; and then, with a miniscule frown, goes back to their conversation. 'Perhaps she's got better things to do,' I go on, 'like finding out who her husband's really fucking behind her back.'

Teddy raises his eyebrows and goes red. 'Right, I see,' he says. I think I've shocked him. Although, I'm not sure why, he has heard me swear before. Perhaps he's used to a more eloquent woman. Lydia is from a middle-class background – a privately educated, uni-graduate – parents are both consultants. I think the mum works at Moorfields Hospital, or is it the dad? I can't remember. But I'm not going to put on any airs and graces. If Teddy wants me, he'll have to accept me as I am – a soon-to-be-thirty-eight-year-old divorcee from a working-class background with more hang-ups than a cold caller. And who swears. Occasionally.

I locate Mum's number in my Favourites list and press the phone to my ear. 'I don't understand why she hasn't returned my call,' I say, changing the subject. 'I hope nothing's happened to her. Oh, it's ringing.' I enthuse, his cue to get a move on with those drinks and cakes.

Teddy grips his knees. 'Right. A cuppa and a muffin it is then.'

I nod and he smiles, eyes crinkling at the corners. 'Oh hi, Mum, it's me.' I cover the mouthpiece and whisper, 'Blueberry muffin, if they've got any. What do you mean who's me?' I say into the mouthpiece, 'Lucy. Your daughter!'

I roll my eyes and Teddy laughs, miming 'Won't be a mo.'

Leaning back in my seat, I watch Teddy striding towards Pret a Manger, arms swinging by his sides, as Mum goes into one – why didn't I tell her I was coming down today – she was at Tesco, could've bought something in for tonight, has only just retrieved my message and was about to call me – I must be some sort of witch, must've taken after my aunt Stella. I try to get a word in but she just talks over me in typical Mum style, and as I continue to listen to her ranting with a smile on my face, Teddy's phone flickers with a message. I automatically glance at it, catching the first line before it disappears.

WhatsApp

> *Where the hell are you?*

Shit, it sounds like an irate customer that he's let down. I hope it wasn't because of me. I hope he wasn't lying about not having any jobs on until Thursday. It flashes up again and I lean forward, curiosity tiptoeing into my mind, and this time I catch the name of the sender too.

WhatsApp LX

> *U do realise UR risking everything.*

I frown at that – not a customer then. And then another flicks through:

> *a woman, no doubt. Can't believe I trusted U again.*

And another before the screen goes black:

> *the kids r in bloody bits!!!!*

My stomach clenches like a tight fist. It's his ex-wife. I thought Lydia and the kids were spending the weekend at her parents' mansion. Why did he lie to me? Another woman? What's that supposed to mean, isn't he allowed to date other women? And then it hits me like a spear through the heart. He's still bloody married, isn't he. I look up at Teddy putting in our order with the barista, hand in pocket, laughing, joking, as if he hasn't a care in the world, and then everything seems to decelerate. It's as if someone has hit the slow motion button.

Mum is still talking, something about getting a fish and chip supper from Tony's down the road, and watching *Some Like it Hot* on BBC2. But instead of responding, all I can do is watch Teddy ambling towards me, two cups in a cardboard holder in one hand, two white paper bags in the other. He bumps into a red-haired woman and she looks up at him, flutters her eyelashes, apologises, and he smiles without even breaking his stride. But not in a pervy way. In a kind, *I'm with someone else* way. He's within earshot when I say, 'Okay, Mum, gotta go. Yes, in about an hour. See you soon. Love you too. Bye.'

'Jeez.' Teddy slides back into the seat next to me. 'That barista couldn't understand a word I was saying. They didn't have blueberry, so I got you…' Then, with a hand through his hair, his face falls. 'What is it? Was that Alison on the phone?' His jaw tightens. 'Did you ring her?'

I shake my head and he follows my eyes to our phones lined up next to each other on the table like soldiers. 'Is your mum okay?' And just then his phone lights up and belts out a rock tune. *LX Calling.* He looks at it and says, 'Shit.' He's gone pink. Any moment now a big red blotch will appear on his neck, which I've a sudden desire to wrap my hands around.

'Aren't you going to answer it?' I say crisply, folding my arms. 'You don't want to keep Mrs Fallon waiting.'

Chapter 24

We stare at each other in agonising silence to the hullabaloo of chatter, cash tills bleeping, a child wailing, their screams tearing from their lungs to my ears like a missile. I've been such a fucking idiot. Why did I trust a man I barely know? Why did I have sex with him, initiate it?

Teddy drags his bottom lip between his teeth, drumming his fingers on the table – tap, tap, tap, tap. I know he's trying to come up with a good excuse but he can't. He's been caught red-handed. There's nowhere to run. I can see his heart beating beneath his fitted shirt. God, what is it with these men, why isn't one woman enough? If it weren't so tragic, I'd laugh.

'I can explain,' he says finally, swallowing hard.

My eyes dart to the third finger of his left hand resting on his thigh. I'm sure I can see a ring mark, a hint of different skin tone. Why didn't I notice this before? I bet he's got his wedding ring stuffed in the inside pocket of his jacket, or in the glove compartment of his car. I bet his heart almost tore from his chest while I was rummaging around in it earlier looking for a tissue to blow my nose. No wonder he was hurrying me up, getting frustrated. No wonder he leant across and snapped it shut for me. I imagine him slipping his wedding band off in the car outside my flat, then sliding it back on again as he walks down the garden path of his beautiful home in a leafy suburb of north London, huge bouquet of guilt flowers in his arms for his unsuspecting wife; mother of his children. I bet he doesn't even live near his mum, let alone with her. What a fucking creep.

I shake my head at him, sucking my lips in and biting down hard as I gather myself to leave. I'm a stupid, stupid fool.

'Wait, Lucy, please…let me explain.' Teddy's phone rings again. 'Oh, fucking hell.' Snapping it up, he leaps to his feet. 'Stay where you are,' he commands, pointing his finger at me. 'We need to talk – Hello? Can you hear me? Yes, of course it's me. Who else did you expect to answer my phone? Oh, very funny – ha-ha, you're such a comedian.'

On the edge of my seat, I jiggle my leg nervously, eyes on Teddy, willing him to give me a good explanation when he gets off the phone, willing him to magic all this chaos away. I don't even think it's because I really like him, although I do. It's just that I don't think I can cope with being mugged off by a man again. But who am I kidding? He won't be able to placate me – he can't. And how the hell am I going to get to Brighton now? I look around me wildly, a young lad in a blue polo top stuffs crisps into his mouth. An old lady in a purple blouse and mop of white hair shuffles by, hands visibly shaking, while a mature lady steers her carefully to a nearby seat. They look like a mother and daughter outfit. I need to get to my mum. My eyes fill. I don't even know where I am.

'Oh, you really are something!' Teddy blasts down the phone, and the woman with the boyfriend at the adjacent table looks round again. Furrowing her thin brows, her eyes flit from me to Teddy in quick succession, and then, eyes resting on me, her expression softens. She thinks I'm in a relationship with a bully. It's written all over her face.

'What do you mean…?' Teddy shrieks. 'Will you just let me speak…No, of course not. Listen. What? No. I… Look, if you're going to talk over me then…' He glances around him frantically, face hot and pink, neck covered in red blotches.

The woman at the table leans forward and says something to her partner and he looks up at Teddy, dark eyes like bullets, one hand balled on the table. Teddy hesitates, looks at me pleadingly and then raises a finger and mimes, *'one minute'* before marching off towards the wall-to-wall window, one hand covering his ear as if he can't hear what she's saying. *Oh, don't you fucking dare, Teddy Fallon. The real reason you've dashed off to take that call is because you don't want me to hear what YOU'RE saying to your WIFE!*

Anger charges through me like a steam train, burning in my chest. I've had enough. I'm not wasting any more time on him. I don't want to hear his lame excuses. I owe him nothing. I've been stitched up – taken for a ride. Tricked by a married man. I can't believe I fell for all his lies.

I shake my head at him as he paces up and down, phone to his ear. Jesus, how could Alison have set me up with a married man? She can't have known, surely. Unless…unless she's only just found out herself.

Shouldering my bag, I take a large gulp of unsweetened lukewarm weak tea – he couldn't even get that right – then hurry towards the exit, phone in hand. I locate Alison's number without breaking my stride, bashing into bodies in my haste. I glance briefly at two faceless people, mumble an apology, then shuffle around a couple with rucksacks on their backs the length of their bodies. We go the same way and I knock into someone else as I change direction.

'Watch where you're bloody going, stupid bitch,' a woman yells. But I don't even bother looking round. I stare down at Alison's number in my Favourites list, adrenalin powering through me, heart thudding against my ribcage. *Come on, Lucy, ring her. What are you waiting for?*

'Did you say a swear word?' someone says. I look up sharply. There's a grey-haired bearded man, late fifties, in baggy jeans and glasses, towering over a little girl of about seven or eight. They're standing in front of me by the sliding doors.

'No, Daddy,' the little girl says. She pushes her glasses up the bridge of her nose, and my stomach stings. She doesn't look frightened, but still.

'Are you sure?'

'Yes, I'm sure. Can I have crisps and a chocolate?'

'You can have one or the other.'

'But I want both,' she wails.

'No, you're having one,' he insists calmly.

I smile to myself and return to my phone, their voices melting into the background. Just a dad and his princess having a little domestic. With a deep heartfelt exhalation, I tap on Alison's name. Within seconds, User Busy, flashes on my screen. I press redial with a trembling finger. I can't breathe. I need to get out. I need to find a way to get to Brighton. I can't even call anyone to pick me up, no one's talking to me. I wonder if cabbies pick up from motorway service stations. I negotiate my way around the ranting little girl and her father, as she yells, 'You're not the boss of me, Daddy. Stop telling me what to do.'

'Yes, I am,' I hear him say as I slip through the automated sliding doors and out into the fresh air. I'm about to call Uber when my phone vibrates in my hand – *Andrew Calling.* Wow, they're all coming out of the woodwork today. I stare at the vibrating phone in horror. *Drrrrh. Drrrrh.* This must be important. Andrew hates talking to me at the best of times. *Drrrh. Drrrrh.* Is he still angry with me for refusing to put the flat on the market, or has Jasmine told him that her ring went missing after my visit? *Drrrh. Drrrrh.* It can't be anything else, can it? Teddy practically convinced me that Andrew's the blackmailer but now I'm not so sure. I think Teddy was just being jealous. *Drrrh. Drrrrh.* The phone stops vibrating. Missed Call. Then lights up again – Andrew Calling. *Drrrh. Drrrh.* I slide the bar to Accept Call.

'Lucy, can you hear me?' I can't believe how good it feels to hear his familiar gruff voice.

'Yes, Andrew. I…' I look from left to right, motorway traffic screaming in my ears. 'You're not going to believe this but I'm stuck on a motorway. Well, in a service thingy. I don't know where I am. I was with Teddy. You know, that man you saw at my flat last Saturday – long story. We've had a blazing…' I pause. I don't want to tell Andrew what happened. I don't want him to gloat. 'A disagreement and now I don't know how to get home.' I walk towards a sea of cars, the colours blurring into a kaleidoscope. 'Is there any chance you could pick me up? I wouldn't ask but–'

'I've just come off the phone with Alison,' Andrew cuts across me. 'I know everything. *God*, Lucy, how could you? What's wrong with you?' How could I what? What does he mean he knows everything? What's *everything*? Did Alison tell him I'm sleeping with Simon, or has Jasmine told him it was me who stole her ring, that she saw me do it? I'm too wound up to ask, and, quite frankly, right now I don't care.

'Andrew,' I blub, ignoring him. I wonder if he's back from Clacton-on-Sea. If he'll pick me up. 'I need a lift to…'

'Where's Jasmine?' he barks.

'Jasmine? How am I supposed to know?'

'I know that…' The phone crackles as I walk along. He's cutting out. 'Capable of…' Crackle, crackle. 'Bloody…car…stripper,' crackle…hiss. 'Psychopath…' My insides collapse. That I wrecked the Porsche. And now he's calling me a psychopath. That's it now. I'm finished. They all think I'm a bloody maniac.

'Andrew, you're cutting out. I can't hear you. Listen to me. I had nothing to do with Jasmine's car. Do you hear me? I swear I…' But he just keeps talking over me.

'Crazy bloody…' Crackle. 'Weirdo.' Sputter. 'Flat…money.' So, I was right, this is about the flat – about the money. Creep.

'Andrew, listen, about that–'

'Brighton,' he cuts in. 'M23…' How does he know I'm on my way to Brighton? Is he following me? I look around me anxiously, searching for his white van. 'Just wait until…' Crackle…hiss… 'Get my hands on.' I feel my blood run cold. Get his hands on who? Me? My mum? Crackle…chhhhrrr… '…sick fuck!!' he screams into my ear and I have to pull the phone away.

Fury charges through me, my eyes fill. 'You bloody BASTARD!!' I shriek. 'How dare you speak to me like that after what you and that bitch did to me.' Spittle flies from my mouth and latches to the side of my top lip. 'I should've bloody killed you both when I had the chance!!'

He goes silent, almost as if he's hung up, but I can still hear him breathing. God, why did I just say that? I must apologise. Immediately. Say it was a figure of speech said in anger. But I don't. Instead I stand there, phone pressed against my ear. Two men walking by give me a look. One of them nudges the other as they hurry along, behind them the ranty little girl with the bossy dad, skips along behind her father who's talking on the phone, taking a bite out of a chocolate bar whilst swinging a large packet of crisps in her other hand. Did I really just say I wanted to murder Andrew and Jasmine? Andrew will think I've hurt Jasmine now, as well as vandalising her car. But I'd never…

Closing my eyes, I move the hot phone away from my ear and take a deep breath, and then I say, 'Andrew, I don't know why I said that, I didn't mean it.' I take a few more deep breaths, steadying my belting heart. 'It's just that you keep pissing me off.'

'Lucy, for fuck's sake,' he says softly, his voice suddenly much clearer. 'What's happened to you?'

'Andrew, I want you to listen to me very carefully before we lose connection again. I don't know where Jasmine is and I had nothing to do with damaging her car. I'd never do that, you know me. And before you say anything, I will sell the flat. You obviously haven't spoken to Jasmine yet but I went to see her yesterday morning, to see you both, actually, but you'd already left. We need to sort out an estate agent – get it valued. I've been in a living hell all week. Someone's blackmailing me. You must know about the photograph, the one of me and Simon.'

Andrew sighs heavily down the phone. 'Luccccy,' he says softly and my eyes fill. It's been ages since he's said my name so tenderly.

'Don't believe Simon's lies.' I sniff, wiping my nose with the back of my sleeve. 'He kissed me, launched himself at me before I had a chance to push him off. No one believes me, Andrew, apart from Teddy.' I look around the car park desperately, hot tears sliding down my face. 'Whoever is blackmailing me wants me out of the picture. They're even threatening to hurt my mum.'

I pause but he doesn't comment. Unlike him to be so quiet. Andrew has an opinion about everything. Is Teddy right? Has Andrew been blackmailing me? I brace myself then blurt out, 'If it's you, Andrew, if you're the one who took that picture of me and Simon and sent me those texts and flowers, I'll understand. I promise. People do strange things when they're desperate for money. If you're in trouble, Andrew, got yourself into serious debt. Just tell me. We'll sort it out.' Silence.

'I won't go to the police,' I promise. 'I'll do everything in my power to help you overcome your difficulties. We can put the flat up for sale next week. Ask for a reasonable price. You could have your money in no time at all. Just please don't do anything you might regret. You know how panicky my mum gets and she's not getting any younger.' More silence. Oh, God. It is him. I've only known him to go silent when he's up against the ropes. 'Please, Andrew, I'm begging you, don't go to my mum's. Andrew? Hello?' I look at my phone – screensaver. Shit. I quickly ring him back as I hurry along – *'I'm sorry, but the number you're calling is busy. Please leave a message...'* Fuck. FUCK!!

Traffic roars in my ears as I weave through a sea of parked cars, mouth dry, heart pounding in my throat and ears. God, have I just made matters worse? What did Andrew mean by Brighton and M4? I don't think he's following me. Is he on his way to my mum's? I've got to ring her, tell her to stay indoors and not to answer the door to anyone until I get there. A white car swishes by, turning into a parking bay, and then I hear a door slam and then a voice.

'Lucy, wait. Don't walk away from me. We need to talk.'

'Get away from me, Teddy. We're done.' I up my pace then break into a run. A red car swerves as I cross in front of it. The driver, a burly skinhead man, presses the horn relentlessly, setting off other drivers behind him. A cacophony of car horns scream in my ears, but I don't break my stride. I don't even look over my shoulder. Where the hell is the exit? Taking a sharp left, I tear down a clear path, blood pounding in my ears, eyes darting around for the Way Out sign. I've got to get out of here. Ring my mum. Get away from Teddy.

Spotting the blue exit sign, I quickly change direction, tripping in my haste, and then I hear the stomp of heavy footsteps behind me, getting closer and closer, the sound of heavy ragged breathing, and then he's standing in front of me, wheezing, hands on hips.

'Lucy, please…' Teddy bends forward, gripping his kneecaps. 'Shit. I can't believe how out of shape I am since…since… Oh, never mind,' he gasps, exerted. 'Let me…let me… Please. Don't do this.'

'We've got nothing to say,' I pant. 'Go back to your wife.' I go to bypass him but he shields me each time I move, blocking me like a security guard. My eyes dart around the secluded car park. 'If you don't let me past I'm going to scream,' I warn, catching my breath. I glance up hopefully at a man in jeans and a green t-shirt with a campervan printed across his chest, who doesn't even bother looking in our direction as he unlocks his car and climbs in.

'Not until you hear me out.'

I roll my eyes, exasperated.

'I can't leave it like this. I need to explain. Five minutes, that's all. Then I promise I'll leave you in peace.'

'I don't want to hear any more lies, Teddy.'

'I won't lie.'

'Five minutes?'

'Yes, I promise.'

'The truth?'

'I swear, I'll tell you everything.'

I'm tired and I'm fed up and I don't even know where I am. I follow him to his car.

Chapter 25

'Mind if I smoke?'

'Whatever. It's your car,' I say absently, punching out a text to my mum:

> *Running late. Will ring u as soon as I know what time I'll be there. Don't answer the door to anyone. XX* heart emoji

I press send and within seconds Mum's reply buzzes through:

> *Sounds ominous. Should I worry? X*

Christ, why did I say that? Mum'll start panicking now. What was I thinking? I quickly type:

> *Everything's fine. Will explain later. Luv U. XX*

I look at the screen – Mum – *typing*:

> *Ok, love. Luv u 2. Xxx*

The window buzzes down, there's a click of a lighter and then the mist of tobacco, curling towards me like a snake. I bat my hand in front of my face. The passenger window buzzes down. 'Thanks,' I murmur, stifling a cough. A phone pings, his. I snort as he pulls it out of his pocket. Another message from his wife, no doubt. It pings again.

‘It’s my mum.’ Teddy sighs, reading it. Bloody liar. I roll my eyes at a couple walking by. The dad has a toddler on his shoulders. I can barely see her eyes beneath her pink plastic helmet. She’s squealing with delight, little hands wrapped around her father’s forehead, squashing his eye. Mum follows behind in long grey oversized coat, head down, texting. A normal happy family on a Saturday afternoon. How I ache for a bit of normality in my life.

‘Look, if you don’t believe me.’ Teddy shoves the phone under my nose and I can’t help but quickly read the message.

Mum

Are you there yet, sweetie? Phone me.

Don’t forget to get me a stick of rock. #Brighton. Hashtag Brighton? She’s not on bloody Twitter.

‘Whatever,’ I huff, picking at a fingernail. ‘I need to get going soon. So, if…’

‘Okay, I did lie to you,’ Teddy says abruptly, 'and I’m sorry.’ My eyes close. I knew it. He’s married. ‘But it’s not what you think.’

‘Really?’ I say sardonically at a black 4x4 pulling up next to us in the parking bay. ‘You could’ve fooled me.’ Car doors clank followed by the thud of central locking.

The tip of Teddy’s cigarette crackles as he takes a long lug, then blows the smoke out of the window from the side of his mouth. The driver of the 4x4 gives him a look as she shepherds her children along the narrow gap sideways. Teddy offers her a gormless grin, takes one final lug and chucks the cigarette out of the window. Jesus, I hope it doesn’t start a fire. ‘I lied about Lydia taking the kids to the party,’ he admits, exhaling smoke from his mouth and nostrils. ‘Lydia didn’t ring me this morning, or text a week ago to cancel. I rang her. But it went straight to voicemail so I stupidly left her a message, explaining that I couldn’t make it today, but she obviously didn’t pick it up.' Come on, Teddy Fallon, is that the best you can do? Really?

'Are you STILL saying you're not married?' I shake my head. He must take me for a bigger fool than I clearly am.

'I'm divorced. Please, don't. Wait.'

I pull the metal lever. 'Open the fucking door.'

'I swear on my children's lives.'

I swing round in my seat sharply. 'Teddy, I saw the messages Lydia sent you,' I say quietly, and his hands stiffen around the steering wheel. 'I wasn't prying,' I add, guilt creeping into my voice. 'They… um… flashed up on your screen. I couldn't help but look.' God, why am I even explaining? Why do I suddenly feel like the guilty party?

His fists loosen. 'Okay, so you read the messages. And?'

'And? AND? They were from a frustrated wife waiting for her husband to come home.'

'No,' he says smoothly, 'they were from a frustrated ex-wife waiting for her ex-husband to pick up their kids so she can go on a weekend away with her new bloke,' he corrects, and I don't miss the hint of vitriol in his voice.

I narrow my eyes. Another lie. 'Whatever,' I spit, glancing at my watch. Three minutes to go.

'You don't believe me.' He runs a hand over his face tiredly. 'I don't blame you. You've got every right to be angry. Why did I lie? I'm such an idiot.'

I squeeze my lips between my fingers again, he taps his fingers against the steering wheel, exhaling loudly, and then he says, 'What if I can prove it to you?' Pulling out his phone, he jabs at the screen. 'I'll call Lydia now and put her on loud speaker.'

I jerk my head up. 'What?'

The ringing phone resounds in the car. *BrrrBrrr…BrrrBrrrr.* 'Then you'll believe me, won't you?' *BrrrBrrr…BrrrBrrr.*

Adjusting my hoodie in dissent, I throw him an incredulous glance. If he's calling my bluff, expecting me to stop him then he really doesn't know me at all. The phone rings and rings and then a woman's husky, frustrated voice says, 'What now?'

'Lydia, it's me.'

'I know it's you. So–'

'Before you say anything,' Teddy cuts across her. 'I'm sorry about before. I'm sorry about leaving you a voicemail instead of speaking to you, about not picking the kids up today, and I shouldn't have shouted at you. It wasn't fair, but it's just that you kept talking over me.'

'What did you expect? You've screwed up our weekend. We were meant to be in Canterbury an hour ago. Mum will be climbing the walls.' Teddy tries to respond but she just talks over him. 'It's the kids I feel sorry for. All you ever seem to do is let them down. And to think you–'

'Lydia, please…'

'All that crap with the solicitors and visitation–'

'Lydia, just let me speak, will you?'

There's a brief silence and then, 'Go on. But I've only got a few minutes. We're already running late. Because of YOU.'

'This won't take long. I thought you'd picked up the voicemail. I shouldn't have assumed but there you are. My bad.'

'My phone has only just alerted me of a voicemail,' she groans, sounding put out. 'You should've texted too. This was important.'

'I know. I didn't think. I'm sorry. And I'm sorry about ruining your weekend away with your new fella,' Teddy says, watching me steadily. 'I'm sure you wanted to spend some quality time alone.'

Lydia hisses loudly down the phone. 'He has got a name, you know. You can say it, it won't give you genital herpes.'

I cover my mouth. I want to laugh. I like her.

Teddy shakes his head at me, his expression depicting – see what I have to put up with. 'I'm sorry about ruining your weekend away with Joseph.'

'We're only staying with my parents, for fuck's sake.' Oh, she swears too. I love her now. 'It's hardly a romantic weekend away. Besides, Joe loves the kids. He's fine about it.' There's a pause and then, 'It's you messing with their heads, making promises you can't keep. If you'd just agreed to…' There's a scuff and a whir and then, 'No, Max, Daddy's not coming today, sweetie. He's…' There's a brief but powerful pause. 'Busy. We're all going to Grandpa's and Nanna's. Go up and get ready, we're leaving in half an hour, and tell Liam to get off the PlayStation too.'

There are muffled voices and then a boy cries in the background, 'Five more minutes.'

'Now!' Lydia yells and Teddy's face reddens.

'I mean it, Lyd. I didn't do it on purpose. Something came up.' Swallowing hard, he looks at me. 'Something important.'

'More important than seeing your own kids? And what about the maintenance money you promised me. I suppose we won't be seeing any this month either. That'll make it three months on the trot. It's not on. I can't cope, so…'

Teddy closes his eyes and raises his hands. 'Okay, okay, calm down. I told you I've got the money,' he says through gritted teeth, and I can see he's trying hard to keep his cool. 'I'll give it to you next week. All of it.'

'Yes, well,' she huffs. 'I'll believe it when I see it.'

'I told you. I've got work now, Lydia. I promise. I'll make it up to the kids too,' he adds hastily, giving me a sideward stare.

A doorbell shrills in the background, a child's voice calls out, 'Muuuum, someone at the door.' There's shuffling, a hiss and a scrape as she covers the mouthpiece, and then hushed voices. 'I'm going to have to go.' Her amplified voice bellows in the car again like surround sound. 'Do you want to have the kids next weekend then?'

Teddy's face brightens. 'Yes, of course I do. Thanks, Lyd, and I'm really–'

'I'll text you,' she cuts across him and then the line goes dead.

'Now do you believe me?' he asks as his screen blackens.

I hesitate for a moment. Did that really just happen? I was almost certain he was still married, was hiding something from me. 'So, what *was* more important than seeing your kids, then, hmm?' I say quickly. 'Why didn't you pick them up as planned?'

He tilts his head back and fills his lungs. 'I've known about the Canterbury thing for weeks. Lydia wanted to take the kids but I said no. It was my turn this weekend. I'd made plans. They're my children too, you know. I've got rights,' he demands, as if I objected. 'In the end she gave in. She's good like that. But when I saw the police at your flat this morning and how scared you looked, and then those flowers from Andrew, or whomever they're from. I panicked. Rang Lydia and cancelled. I wanted to make sure you were safe. You're being threatened, Lucy. I was worried about you, okay? I didn't want to leave you alone.'

I frown at him. 'What do you mean *whomever* they're from, are you saying you don't think Andrew's the blackmailer now?' I wish he'd make his mind up.

He rubs his face tiredly with both hands. 'I don't know, Lucy. I'm not psychic and I'm not a detective either. It's all guess work, isn't it? Speculation. Probability.'

There are a few moments of silence as I mull it all over, and then I say, 'So are you saying you did all this for me? Let your kids down at the last minute, for me? Messed things up for your ex-wife?' I want to believe him but I can't ignore the little voice inside my head saying he did it to rattle Lydia's cage. I wonder if she knows about me. If Teddy showed her that selfie we took in the club on that first night we met. The thought makes my skin crawl. I was sloshed, eyes half-open, arms slung around Teddy's neck like a letch. She probably thinks I'm a pathetic drunk. 'Why would you put me before your kids anyway?'

'Because I care about you,' he yells suddenly, throwing a hand out, and I jump. 'Is that really so hard to believe?' Actually, yes, it is after knowing me for just a week. 'They wanted to go to the sodding party anyway. Max and Liam are safe with their mother, whereas you.' He pauses. 'I'm not like Andrew, or your dad. I want to be there for you. Look after you. I...' He trails off.

I swallow hard. No one's ever put me first before. But I'm still not convinced. Why would he let his own children down to escort a woman he barely knows to Brighton? It just doesn't ring true. I give him a sideward stare as he slips the phone into the inside pocket of his jacket, and just then I remember the grubby handset I found in the glove compartment earlier and my mind reels again. Could my instincts have been right? Is Teddy involved in all this somehow? Did Alison rope him in? Offer him a wad of cash to follow me, so she can find out if I was having an affair with her husband?

In my mind's eye I trace over the last few days. He's never been around when any of the anonymous texts have come through, yet always manages to show up at the right moment in his superhero cape. Did I leave the backdoor open last Monday when the intruder paid me a visit and left that photo, or did Teddy have a key cut and let himself in? Teddy was there that night I had that dream of being smothered with hands that reeked of sandalwood. Was it a dream, or did it really happen? Did Teddy try to suffocate me? Terror marches along my spine and I sit up straight. *Stop it, Lucy. Alison has not hired a hitman to do you in. Teddy is a lovely, decent ordinary man – he is NOT an assassin. This isn't Killing bloody Eve.* Unless…

I jerk my head up and look at him. 'What about the other phone?' I bark, heat prickling my face.

He bobs his head back, confused. 'What other phone?' He knows damn well what I'm referring to. He's just trying to buy time so that he can cook up another lie.

'The one you said belonged to Max.' He looks at me, stumped. 'Promise me that it wasn't you. That you didn't send me any of those threatening texts from that phone.' Because money would be a motive, wouldn't it? Lydia said he's three months behind with the maintenance. Alison might've been suspicious of me and Simon for ages for all I know. She did insist that he drove me home that night, even though I was happy to ring a cab, even though Simon had had a few drinks and couldn't be bothered. Maybe she had her reasons. Maybe Teddy Fallon was waiting for me in the wings, waiting for something to happen. And it did! 'That…' I hesitate, 'that Alison didn't pay you to follow me.'

'Whoa.' Teddy puts his hands out. 'Talk about an active imagination. You can't be for real?' He looks at me, horrified, but I don't flinch.

'Why not? You said yourself that Alison thinks I've been having an affair with Simon for months.'

'You're joking, right?' He throws his head back and laughs but my face is deadpan. 'Jesus, you really are serious. Wow. Do you really think I'd do something like that to you, threaten you? When all I…' he falters. 'Okay, okay.' Shaking his head, he laughs as he rummages in his pocket for Max's phone, switches it on and holds it aloft. 'Call the number.' I tilt my head to the side. 'Go on,' he dares. 'Call it.'

I quickly find the texts from Unknown Sender on my phone. It rings and rings and rings but his phone doesn't light up. It's not him. A mixture of guilt and relief spins in my stomach like a whirlpool. I feel sick. My head feels like it's about to implode. I cover my face with my hands. Nothing makes sense anymore. Nothing seems real. 'I'm sorry,' I say, feebly. 'I don't know what came over me.' But I do know one thing – using Teddy Fallon as a scapegoat isn't the answer. 'I'm just so stressed out.'

'Right, I see,' Teddy snaps. 'I don't like being accused of being some kind of crazy crook. You obviously don't trust me.' He starts the engine, face like thunder. 'This isn't going to work, is it? You're not ready. I'll drop you off at a station. You can make your own way to Brighton.' He slams the car into reverse.

'You did lie to me, Teddy.'

'Okay, I lied to you. If I'd told you I was going to cancel on my kids today so that I can stay and look after you, would you have been all right with that?' I shake my head. Of course not. 'Is it my fault that Lydia didn't pick up my voicemail?'

'You should've told me the truth from the beginning.'

'Yes, well, hindsight's a wonderful thing, isn't it? Have you never told a lie, hmm?' My face twitches – the ring. Although, technically I haven't lied, I just haven't told him about it.

'That's not the point.'

'Okay,' he huffs, 'Fine.' He releases the handbrake.

Shit, am I being hasty? Everything was going so well between us up until now and he does seem genuinely contrite. I don't even know why I suspected Teddy of being the blackmailer. I don't think he is. I told you I always find a way to mess up all the good things in my life. And he's right about people lying. I've lied. To him. We all lie sometimes, don't we? But if the lie is to help someone, to protect them, or to make them feel better about themselves, then that cancels it out, right? Teddy's supported me through this nightmare – stood by me. He even put me first today, rowed with his ex-wife, missed seeing his kids – all for me.

We start moving. 'Wait.' The car whines. 'Teddy, please. Stop!' Teddy hits the breaks and looks at me, annoyed. 'Andrew called me.' Teddy's eyebrows rise and fall knowingly, lips a thin line. 'Just now when I was outside the service station. Jasmine is still missing and…' I hesitate, take a breath. 'And he thinks I'm involved somehow. That I had something to do with damaging her car. He mentioned Brighton too, which was weird. I think you're right. I think Andrew's got himself into a lot of trouble and needs the money from the flat to bail himself out. I'm sorry I said those horrible things to you. I don't think you've got anything to do with this. I don't even think Jasmine's involved, to be honest. I think Andrew is the blackmailer. I'm really scared, Teddy.'

Teddy looks as if he's seen a ghost. '*God.*'

My eyes fill. 'I don't know how much more of this I can take. I feel so…' I whimper, 'Alone. Frightened.'

Teddy pulls me to him, wordless, and I sob into his chest. 'It's okay, I've got you,' he whispers, squeezing tight. I inhale his scent, a weird concoction of tobacco, Dior Sauvage, campfire and sweat. 'And you've got me.' He kisses the top of my head.

I look up at him, face wet with tears. 'Have I?' I sniff.

'Yes,' he says, softly, wiping my wet cheeks with his thumbs. 'God, we're a right pair, aren't we?' I lay my head back on his chest, feeling his heart thudding against my cheek – lubdub, lubdub, lubdub. 'I wish I'd met you years ago.'

'Me too,' I blub, inhaling phlegm, because it seems the right thing to say.

'Still, we're together now. Two lost ships in the night, eh?' He sighs. 'Wouldn't it be great if we could sail away together? Start somewhere new, somewhere fresh – somewhere warm and sunny?'

'We could go to Spain,' I hear myself say, snuggling against him. 'Can you imagine that?'

'Buy a little derelict house, do it up. Run a beach bar.'

I laugh at the silly dream. 'My sister and her boyfriend would drink us dry.' Pulling away from him, I wrench the sun visor down and dab at my swollen eyes with my fingers, pleased that I decided not to wear any makeup today, apart from my signature lip gloss, because my dry lips would never forgive me if I didn't. 'I'm sorry about before, Teddy.' I do a little involuntary shiver and fold my arms. 'I am grateful, you know. For everything. And I'm glad you're still here.'

'I'm not going anywhere,' he promises, turning the key in the ignition. 'I'm all yours.'

Chapter 26

'What did she say?' Teddy asks, smiling contently, as we thunder along the M25.

'She said yes, of course,' I reply and he grins stupidly.

'You sure you don't mind me staying? I'll be fine at the B&B.' Reaching over, he takes my hand and links his fingers with mine. 'It's only a few miles away.'

'Definitely,' I confirm and he brings my hand to his lips, kisses it, then lets go to change lanes, eyes not leaving the road.

I asked Teddy to stay with us in Brighton. We're a couple now, aren't we? Sort of. I know what you're thinking, it's early days, I don't really know him. But what is there to know? I knew Andrew for five years and look where that got me. You know when you've met the right person. We're perfect strangers – kindred spirits. My sister told me that she knew Matteo was the one after their second date. Within the month she chucked in her job and moved to Spain with him. Mum was appalled – like me, she's more of a glass is half-full kind of person. She said it was too soon. It won't last. Impulse decisions never end well. But, six years on, Kate is still there, a mother, a partner, happy, settled. Not that I'm going to do anything as drastic as that. Kate is the risk-taker in our family, not me – takes after our dad. Besides, what's the point in forking out for a B&B when there's a spare room going begging at Mum's?

I glance at Teddy. 'And she said she's glad we're stuck in traffic because it'll give her time to change the bedsheets and do the hoovering.' I smile at my screensaver, as if she's still on the line, as if she didn't hang up moments ago with strict instructions that Teddy would sleep in the spare room and I'd kip in with her – she doesn't want any jiggy-jiggy in the middle of the night – she's a light sleeper (she is) – the walls are thin (they're not, it's an old building, strong, sturdy) – we'll have plenty of time for sex once we get to know each other properly (too late, that ship has sailed.)

I recline in my seat, holding the phone with both hands against my chest, and Alison slips into my mind. She hasn't called again, or texted. Maybe the urgency is over. I go to put my phone in my bag when it tinkles with a new message. Mum's right, I have got Aunt Stella's witchy gene. I look at the screen – Andrew. I read it quietly and then laugh.

'Mum again?' Teddy smiles as we slowdown in traffic.

'What? No,' I reply, distractedly, rereading the message. 'It's Andrew. I can't believe it. Listen to this.' I recite the text out loud. *'Lucy, am sorry, can't pick u up. Still in Clacton-on-Sea. Bloody shit coast. Jas and I having a break.'*

I frown at the traffic ahead. A break? Jasmine didn't mention anything about a break. Mind you, he looked a bit rough yesterday morning and she was a little out of sorts. I thought it was the shock of seeing me on her doorstep but perhaps they'd had a row. No wonder she didn't tell him that I've agreed to sell the flat. I carry on reading excitedly. *'She lied about baby, btw – not pregnant.'*

'I could've told you that. I counted her contraceptive pills in your bathroom cabinet.' Teddy looks nonplussed. Bloody hell, did I just say that out loud? He's going to think I'm some sort of freak now. 'Oh, you're going to love this next one, Teddy – *Jas gone AWOL. Not picking up phone or replying to texts. Last*

I heard from her was when she texted yest after u left telling me you'd been round there looking 4 me. Police contacted me about car. Practically accused me of chucking acid over it. Busy body neighbours said they heard loud voices yest morning.' So I was right, they did have an argument. *'They'll be saying I killed her and buried her in the garden next!!!'*

Teddy's eyebrows rise and fall. 'I wouldn't be at all surprised.'

I shake my head, snorting. 'Not even Andrew would go that far. Do you think it was him who vandalised her car? I mean, if she lied to him about being pregnant, they might've had a blazing row. Andrew has got a temper, you know, and Jasmine's no doormat. They've both got loud voices. No wonder their neighbours were concerned.' I twist my lips to the side. 'He did let down the tyre of that couple in St Albans who refused to pay him, didn't he?' Teddy nods, says I told him the story. 'It would've been a clear run for him – he knows the CCTV isn't working.' I pause, narrow my eyes, then say, 'No, I'm being ridiculous.'

'No, you're not. In fact it's very plausible given his track record. Have you ever considered a job in the police force? You'd make a great detective.' Teddy reaches over and strokes my thigh.

'Yeah, right,' I scoff. 'Imagine me as a copper, I'd arrest everyone.' We both laugh. Something rattles under the car. 'Must be the exhaust again,' I offer, and he agrees, says he'll check it at the next service station – we'll need to refuel soon anyway, it's on the red, didn't expect this much traffic. My phone pings again. 'Oh, you're not going to believe this next text.' I sit up straight in my seat like an excited child.

Ali went to our flat. Looking for you. 'Note the OUR,' I say, then carry on reading the message aloud. *'Spoke to Xenia. Know ur on way to see mum. Hope ur safe now. Still care about*

U.' I pause and make a hissing sound through my nose. 'Oh, and look,' I say, voice laced with sarcasm, 'he's put little heart emoji. Bless.' Curving my lips down in mock sadness, I throw a glance at Teddy and he rolls his eyes, then I carry on reciting the message. *'That bloke ur with is a psycho.'* I was wondering when the name calling would begin. Sorry, Andrew, Teddy's ten times the man you'll ever be. 'Can you bloody believe it?' I yelp. 'Now he's split up with Jasmine he wants us to break up too. Idiot.'

Teddy snorts, shakes his head, but his jaw is tight, face dark. The exhaust tap, taps, taps. Something's wrong. His tempo has dropped. Maybe I shouldn't have mentioned the psycho part. It is a bit of a sore subject at the moment, given that I accused him of stalking me. I look at his sad little face. I've hurt his feelings.

Another message buzzes through:

< Glad you ditched him. Stay safe. Text me when u get to mum's. need to talk. X

I narrow my eyes at the screen then quickly close the app. He doesn't sound like a man who is blackmailing me – a man who is out to hurt my mum. He just sounds like… like Andrew.

'Him again? What did he say?'

'Nothing,' I sigh.

Teddy's face twitches. 'Can't be nothing, or don't you want to share?' Changing lanes swiftly, he puts his foot down.

I press my fingers against my lips. I obviously can't tell him what Andrew really said, not after offending Teddy with the last message. I've already overshared.

'He just said, to take care, that's all. Oh, don't take any notice of Andrew,' I insist, trying to defuse the tension, 'he's the bloody psycho. He can't bear to see me happy now he's split up with Jasmine.'

I gaze out of the window at the greenery flashing by – questions buzzing around in my head. Why did Jasmine lie to

Andrew about being pregnant? Was it to keep him? Is she seriously that desperate? God, I wonder when their problems started and if he really is behind all this in some twisted, jealous way. He was blasé about Mum though, and didn't even mention selling the flat. And what was Alison doing round mine, anyway? Couldn't she just have texted me? Mind you, Teddy did say she's convinced I'm the other woman. Maybe what she has to say can't be conveyed in a text message.

There's only one way to find out, Lucy, ring her back. I glance at Teddy and decide very quickly to ring Alison when I get to Mum's. He looks totally fed up and tired and I don't want to piss him off any more than I already have.

'Aren't you going to text him back?' Teddy asks smoothly, eyes not leaving the road. 'I can see you're preoccupied. Are you thinking about him?'

'God, no,' I retort truthfully. 'He's the last person on my mind.' I snuggle in my seat, thoughts of calling Alison dissolving like a snowflake 'I've got nothing to say to Andrew.' I sit upright. 'Why are we turning off? It says Brighton straight ahead.'

'The sat nav is redirecting us, because of traffic. This is a quicker route, I suppose.'

We drive in silence through woodlands for the next fifteen minutes listening to Magic FM, then as I'm about to dose off, Teddy shouts, 'SHIT! Shit!'

My eyes snap open and I sit upright, heart in my mouth. 'What is it? Why have we stopped?'

'We're out of bloody fuel,' he says, staring at the petrol gauge as if it's to blame. 'SHIT!' He bangs his fist on the steering wheel and my stomach stings. I raise my eyebrows, heart playing squash against the wall of my chest. I didn't think he had a temper.

I tell myself that it's okay, everyone loses it sometimes; he's just tired. It's been a long day. Swallowing back a ball of unease, I say, 'I thought we'd hit a deer, or something. Are you with the AA? Teddy shakes his head. 'RAC?'

'Can't afford bloody breakdown cover,' he groans.

'Jesus, what are we going to do now?' In the distance, I see a flicker of light, green and yellow and white. 'Look. Just there.' I point at the BP petrol sign and Teddy's eyes sparkle. 'Do you think we could push it there?'

'It's at least a quarter of a mile away.' He glances at his watch then unbuckles his seatbelt and it flies across his body. 'It'll be quicker if I jog up there. They're bound to sell Jerry Cans.' He looks around him. 'Not sure if we can park here though.'

'I'll stay in the car,' I offer. 'You go.'

'You sure? I shouldn't be longer than twenty minutes.'

I pull my red Gap hoodie around me. Actually, I'm not sure that I will be okay, not on this spooky deserted lane, but it doesn't look as if I've got much choice. 'Of course,' I lie, eyes flicking to the creepy woodland. I look at my watch. It's only seven fifteen but the clouds have darkened the early evening and there isn't a glint of life in sight. But I'm sure I'll be fine…won't I? 'Go on.' I shoo him away. 'Go. I'll be fine.'

'Okay,' Teddy says. The door swings open. I watch silently as he shrugs out of his jacket, grabs his wallet and phone from the inside pocket, then opens the back door. There's a hiss of fabric, a low thump, then the thud of the door closing. 'I'll be as quick as I can,' he promises, leaning across and puckering his lips. 'Ring me if anything happens.'

I watch as he jogs along the deserted road, phone in the back pocket of his jeans, wallet in hand. I wonder why he didn't take his jacket. Perhaps he thought it would slow him down.

The next five minutes go by slowly and eerily. A few trees rustle in the light wind. A car swishes by. Jesus, I feel as if I'm on a film set of a horror movie. Any moment now, someone will leap out of the bushes holding a shiny twelve-inch kitchen knife and stab me to death. I do a little shiver. I need distraction. I look at the little white battery on my phone – 23%. No point in firing up any apps. I'll just have to wait it out, and then it lights up with a message from Teddy.

>*You ok? xx*

Aww…how thoughtful. He's only been gone a few minutes. I fire one back right away.

> *Yes, thanks. No one has abducted me.*

> *Yet!*

> *Hurry back. X* I look at the message, then delete the big kiss and put a lower case one.

Teddy: < *Will do. And don't even joke about that. Miss u.*

I smile at that. It's our first bit of proper romantic banter. > *Miss u 2.*

Teddy: > *No going back to Andrew now. Ur stuck with me.* I had a feeling that's what upset him earlier. Perhaps he thinks now that Andrew and Jasmine have split up I'll go running back to him. But I won't. I can see a bright future for me and Teddy. He does need a bit of reassurance though. He's far more sensitive than Andrew. I text back.

> *No way. Like being stuck with U.*

Teddy*:* > *I like it that U like it.*

> *I like it that U like it that I like it.*

Teddy*:* > *Good cos I'm urs.*

I quickly type, grinning stupidly.

> *My teddy bear.* I chew my nail, waiting for him to reply but nothing comes. I hope he hasn't taken that in the wrong way – as if he's fluffy and weak. I'm about to follow it through with something more virile when my phone pings with a new message.

> *Always. XX*

Sighing with relief, I'm typing again when my phone buzzes in my hand – *Alison Calling.*

Chapter 27

I stare at my phone aghast as it continues to buzz in my hand – Alison. *Brrr.* I'm going to have to answer it. *Brrr.* My finger hovers over the handset. Swallowing hard, I go to tap Accept Call, then hesitate. What if she shouts at me again? *Brrr.* Blames me for the breakdown of her marriage? *Brrr*. I'm not sure I can cope with that right now, not with this…this thing, which began as some sort of emotional ransom but has quickly escalated into something darker, or dare I say, sinister, hanging over me like a hungry wolf; not without Teddy here. *Brrr*. I take a deep breath. *Come on, Lucy, stop being such a wuss and answer the bloody phone. You're going to have to speak to her sooner or later.*

'Hello,' I say with trepidation, as if a hand is about to burst through the phone and squeeze my throat.

'Jesus, Lucy, where the hell have you been?' Alison asks anxiously. 'Why aren't you answering your phone? I must've rung half a dozen times. I've been going nuts here. Mum and I are sick with worry.' I frown. Not the greeting I was expecting from a woman who thinks I'm shagging her husband. 'Xenia and Spiros are having kittens.'

I gasp audibly at this but she's too busy blabbing to notice. Didn't they find the note I pushed through their letterbox? I go to speak, then Alison says, 'Are you okay?' Blimey, she sounds frantic. 'I was going to text you but Andrew told me he'd already spoken to you; you got cut off or something, said he was going to text you with the news. Did he?' she asks, hopefully. 'He hasn't bothered to phone back here or message. Typical bloody Andrew. Are you okay? Do you want me to pick you up? Are you still stuck on the motorway?' A lift? From Alison? And then it dawns on me – she knows.

'Has Simon told you the truth about kissing me?' I blurt, without preamble.

A few moments of silence hang between us and then, 'Yes,' she says faintly, and my entire body slumps with relief. I've been vindicated – at last. 'He didn't have much choice. I'll tell you all about that in a minute. Did Andrew fill you in on everything else?' Alison presses on.

I shake my head. 'Yes, he did.' I'm not sure why Alison thinks that Andrew and Jasmine's temporary split is breaking news, but I don't say anything. Instead I drink in her excitement, 'Alison, I…' There's so much I want to say but I'm suddenly stumped for words. 'I was in a bit of state earlier, when Andrew called, but I'm fine now. Well, apart from running out of–'

'Simon and I are getting divorced,' Alison interrupts. 'I've thrown him out. I think you should know. You've every right. I can't begin to tell you how sorry I am for what I've put you through, for blaming you. He's been screwing around for months, Lucy, probably years. I found some texts from his tart on his phone.' I close my eyes – thank God she no longer thinks it's me. 'Stuff on his computer. Dating sites, porn – hard core.'

I'm about to tell her that I know about the texts, the dating sites and porn, that Teddy has filled me in with her news too, when his voice reverberates in my ears – *If Alison calls, let her do the talking. I don't want to lose my job, not with winter around the corner.* 'I'm sorry to hear that, Alison,' I say stiffly, 'Are you okay?'

‘I will be,’ she says immediately. She’s being stoic but I know that inside she’s breaking. Simon was the love of her life – her hero.

‘That’s good,’ I say simply. ‘Time’s a great healer.’

‘Good?’ she replies, and I press my fingers to my lips. ‘Is that all you’ve got to say?’ No, I’ve got lots to say, actually, but my hands are tied. ‘Don’t you even want to know how I discovered it was Simon who came on to you that night?’ I stay silent, anxiety seeping into my bloodstream.

Alison breathes heavily down the phone. ‘I know I can apologise until I’m blue in the face and it still won’t make any difference. I wrongly accused you of having an affair with my husband. You. My lovely, lovely sweet friend,’ she admits, voice breaking. ‘You probably hate me now, anyway.’ Silence, and then, ‘I’ve been a right cow to you. But I really *am* sorry, and I promise to make it up to you if you give me a chance.’

I think about her apology as she continues to rant about Simon – he’s a rat, a pervert, she doesn’t know what she ever saw in him. Alison’s wrong. I don’t hate her. I am bloody annoyed with her for putting me through this, for not believing me. But hate? No, that’s too strong a word. Any woman would’ve reacted in the same way. Picture it. One day, out of the blue, a multimedia message pings through on your phone. You open it, full of anticipation, and see your best friend and husband snogging. What would be your first reaction? Shock? Horror? Disbelief? Probably all three condensed into one blinkered, seething ball of fury. In your mind’s eye you’ll trace recent events. Question everything. That look she gave him last Christmas when he complimented her on her clingy outfit, the way she touched his hand when he said something funny at the summer barbeque, how they belted out ‘We Will Rock You’ at your birthday bash, arm in arm, as you stood in the audience watching, wishing you loved Queen as much as they did, wishing you loved karaoke; his hand lightly touching her back as they walked out the front door on that fatal night when he gave her a lift home at your insistence. All innocent gestures at the time but now? Evident signs of betrayal.

'It's okay, Alison. I'd have thought the same if I were in your shoes.'

'Oh. Right. I don't expect you to–'

'Alison, listen,' I interrupt, 'we definitely need to talk about this but…' I'm dying to find out what happened but I've got to keep my phone free in case Mum calls; in case Teddy needs to get in touch. I wish he'd hurry back. 'But…um… my battery is low and–'

'Lucy, Andrew did tell you about Teddy Fallon, right? Because you sound pretty calm to me.'

I snort. 'Tell me what?' Then I quickly replay Andrew's texts in my mind. 'Oh, you mean about the psycho comment?' I pause, wait for her to chuckle at the absurdity of it, tell me how ridiculous and jealous Andrew is, but instead I'm met with an eerie silence. 'Andrew's name calling like a bloody child, Ali. He's just bitter because there's trouble in paradise. I mean, he's only seen Teddy once, he's hardly in a position to judge.'

I hear a long crackly inhalation of breath and then, 'Did Teddy tell you about what happened at my mum's this morning?' I frown. Apart from Karen going out for a run and moving pots around, all he divulged was that she tried paying him twice for that fence. But I'm not sure if I should disclose this information to Alison. He was taking the piss out of her mum. Not that I approved of his piss-taking, but I don't want to get him sacked. *Come on, Teddy, where the hell are you?* And then I look up and spot him ambling back – a tiny dark figure in the distance. 'I'm sorry, Ali, I don't know anything,' I mutter absently, eyes not leaving Teddy. The figure disappears into a parked car and my heart sinks. It wasn't him.

'Lucy, I know you're trying to protect him, but I really need you to be honest with me. This is serious.' I pull a face. Serious? 'Did he say anything about me? Anything at all?'

Yes, I want to say, he told me that you found out Simon was seeing another woman and you thought it was me, your best friend. Again. I swallow the words and they trickle down my throat like acid. 'No, he hasn't mentioned you at all,' I lie, and then a thought enters my mind. 'Oh wait, he did say that you called him last night to cancel a gig for Monday, but that's all.' I squeeze my eyes tight, cringing. *I won't say anything else. I won't say anything else.* Oh, fuck it. 'Actually, yes, he did say something else. He told me you'd found out Simon had another woman on the go and you claimed it was me. In fact, you were certain of it.'

There's a long unbearable silence and then she says. 'Lying fucking piece of SHIT.'

I drag my bottom lip along my teeth. Gosh – what've I done? Alison's furious. Teddy's going to lose his job. He won't be able to give Lydia the child maintenance he promised – might lose visitation rights. 'Hang on, Ali, I might've…'

Alison's sigh is loud and desperate, and I have to move the handset away from my ear. 'Did he tell you about our altercation this morning at Mum's?' she asks, exasperation sliding into her tone. 'And, for the record, I didn't ring him to cancel Monday's "gig." *Jesus.*' She pauses, blows loudly. 'Teddy called me yesterday evening to confirm our appointment for Monday. But I was in the middle of an explosive row with Simon. Yes, I might've mentioned Simon's tart but that was mainly for Simon's benefit, to humiliate him, but I didn't say the texts were from YOU. That you were the other woman. *Christ!!!*'

I look at the deserted street again, nonplussed. Teddy definitely said Alison thought I was the other woman. And I'm positive he told me SHE phoned him last night. I narrow my eyes at a plastic carrier bag caught on a tree branch, billowing in the wind. He obviously misunderstood, either that or something is very wrong here. 'Look, Alison, I'll double check with Teddy as soon as he gets back, but you must've got your wires crossed. He shouldn't be too long now. I…'

'You're not still with him?' she asks, voice so cold that it sends an arctic trickle along my spine. 'Andrew said you'd had a fallout, ditched him at the service station.'

'No, that was a misunderstanding. Alison, it's fine. Teddy and I are–'

'Jesus Christ, Andrew,' Alison cries. 'I don't fucking believe this.' She sounds manic. What has Andrew told her?

'No, you don't understand,' I say smoothly, trying to placate her. 'Teddy and I had a bit of a disagreement earlier. Well, it was more of a full- blown row, to be fair. I thought he was still married. Anyway, we're fine now.'

'Fuck sake, Andrew,' Alison yells, ignoring me. I've never heard her swear so much. I hear the scuffle of movement, a crackle and a hiss, and then, 'If you…do…it…' She's cutting out. 'Where… bloody…keys?' she yells. God, what's wrong with her? Is she drunk? 'Okay,' she says, voice clearer. 'Obviously, Teddy didn't tell you what happened this morning when he came to secure Mum's fence. The fence he bodged up yesterday because he hasn't got a bloody clue.'

'Alison, you're not making any sense. I don't understand.'

'Okay, hear me out and please try to stay calm. You know that mother at the school gates who told me about her gardener just before the summer break?' I tell her that I do. Teddy came highly recommended. 'I saw her yesterday; the kids are back at school and she said Teddy Fallon is still waiting for me to phone him about mowing my lawn.

I pull a face – she's totally lost me now. 'You did phone him, Ali,' I say carefully. Alison's obviously confused. This thing with Simon has hit her hard. I must admit, I was a bit spaced out when Andrew left me but I was completely compos mentis. 'Alison, he's been round to mow your lawn several times.'

'Lucy, I'm not bloody senile. I didn't…he isn't…' she falters. I can almost see her running a hand over her face. 'Teddy Fallon, the gardener I was meant to hire, is a sixty-seven-year-old man from Hertfordshire.'

'A sixty-seven-year-old man?' I repeat. I look up at the deserted street again, tiny headlights sparkle in the distance. 'That can't be right.'

'Lucy,' she pauses, and then, 'the man you're with is not Teddy Fallon,' she says quietly. 'I got the number wrong, lovey. I scribbled it down on the back of a Sainsbury's receipt at the school gates and wrote eight instead of three. I wrote three but I wasn't wearing my glasses. When I read it back it looked like an eight. You know what my handwriting is like sometimes.' Not sometimes, Alison – always. It's like hieroglyphics. We all joke about it.

'Wait. Slow down.' I put a hand out. 'You're scaring me now. You got the number wrong and called someone else called Teddy Fallon who's also a gardener?' I know it's random, but I'm desperate for her to be wrong, confused, drunk, anything but this.

'That would be one hell of a coincidence, wouldn't it?' Alison says gently. She stays silent, giving me a few moments to process it all. But I can't think straight. What the hell is happening? Everything's fuzzy. All I can hear is a whirring buzzing sound in my ears, like a lawnmower whizzing around in my head. 'He's a liar, Lucy. An imposter.'

'What?' I gasp. 'No… how?'

'When I rang him that first time it went straight to voicemail. I left a message, saying something like, "Hi, this is a message for Teddy Fallon. I'm Alison, a friend of Sandie's from Orpington Road. I'm desperate for a gardener. If you've got time, please give me a call back on this number." He rang back within five minutes. He was nice, friendly, he even told me he'd give Sandie a discount for the referral if I hired him. After a brief chat about prices, I gave him my address and the rest is history. He's a chancer, Lucy, a phony. I know more about flipping plants than he does.' I clamp a hand over my mouth, sealing in a silent scream. No, no, NO. It can't be. She's got it all wrong. 'He's been winging it. After my conversation with Sandie, I googled him and, surprise, surprise, no Teddy Fallon of his description. I mean, what professional hasn't got a profile online these days? I confronted him with Mum this morning and he just turned, got into his car and sped off, without a word.'

I suddenly feel faint, lightheaded. I think I'm going to pass out. I go to speak when I hear a string of knuckles rapping against my window – bang, bang, BANG! Snapping my head round, I gasp loudly, heart in my mouth, as I stare into watery, bloodshot pale-blue eyes.

'Lucy, what's wrong? Lucy, talk to me?' Alison's little voice cries out from the handset.

I open my mouth to speak but my tongue feels like lead. The man continues to glare at me – late-sixties, with dough-like features and a huge veiny nose. 'You can't park here,' he snaps in a West Country accent.

I open the door and he takes a wobbly step back in his muddy dark red wellies. 'We've broken down, sir,' I manage, catching my breath. 'I'm sorry if we're trespassing. My…my friend has just gone to get petrol.' I point at the BP sign.

'Aye, just warning you, Miss,' he says, displaying a set of yellowing teeth. 'You'll get a hefty fine if a copper turns up.' With this, he touches the rim of his filthy flat cap and hobbles off, limping with each slow step. I watch in silence as he clambers onto his aging four-wheeled scooter and zips off. A harmless stranger warning me, not an axe murderer.

'Lucy!!!' Alison's voice again. 'Lucy, can you hear me? LUCY!!?'

'Sorry, some stranger just accosted me about parking here. He's gone now.'

'Why didn't you ask him for a lift?'

'Um…let me think, because he looked like a serial killer?' I say, unable to keep the cynicism out of my voice.

'There's no need to be sarky.'

'Are you positive that the man I'm with isn't Teddy Fallon? I mean, he might be. It might all be one big coincidence. Stranger things have happened.'

'I'm sorry, Lucy. You need to get as far away from him as possible.'

I look up at the glowing BP sign feeling numb, wishing I'd hopped onto the back of that well-meaning serial killer's moped after all. 'Are you telling me he's dangerous?' I ask, lips trembling.

'I'm not sure if he's dangerous, per se, but we think he's the one who sent you that picture message.'

'WHAT!!?' I blurt, blinking wildly. Teddy can't be the blackmailer. NO. He can't be. This is insane. Unreal. I thrust a hand through my hair, face on fire. This type of thing only happens in those psychological TV dramas that Andrew loves to watch, not in real life. 'But he can't be.' My mind races. 'It's impossible. I got the first threatening text on the day I met him. That photograph was taken over a week before.'

'Don't get in a tizz but…'

'But what?' Silence. 'ALISON!!!?'

'Please try to stay calm, Lucy, freaking out isn't going to help anyone.' Her deep inhalation crackles down the line. 'I showed him your photograph, which he loved, by the way, because his pupils dilated and he went a bit red, about a week before you met him.' Jesus, why is she telling me all this now? 'An hour later, I caught him reading my address book in the hallway. When I questioned him he told me he knocked it off the side table bringing a plant through. I believed him, why wouldn't I? It was feasible. But…'

'Go on,' I urge, blinking furiously at the empty road ahead. 'I haven't got much time. He'll be back soon.'

'The page was open on the initial L and your name, address and phone numbers were on that page.'

'That doesn't prove anything.' Maybe Teddy Fallon is a liar and a cheat, an opportunist, but he isn't the blackmailer – he can't be. 'Next you'll be telling me he's the one who took the photograph of me and Simon that night.'

'No, he didn't.'

'At least we agree on one thing.'

'No one took a photograph of you that night. The image was–'

I tut. 'Alison, someone has been blackmailing me with a picture message,' I interject. 'It exists. You've seen it.'

'If you just let me finish,' Alison says firmly.

I glance at my watch. Teddy's been gone eleven minutes. 'Go on,' I say impatiently.

'Remember that night Simon dropped you off home in Mum's car?' I nod, even though she can't see me. How could I forget? Simon used Karen's VW Golf, because his was in the garage and Alison's insurance had expired. 'Mum had a dashcam fitted recently, which none of us knew about, by the way. She kept finding random scratches on her car and Trevor, her new bloke, suggested she invested in one. Once it was installed, she forgot all about it. It's tucked behind the rear-view mirror. Anyway, the day after she got back from that yoga retreat in Devon, she noticed a small dent on the back wing.'

There's a pause, a shuffle, the mutter of voices. I think she's covered the mouthpiece. 'Sorry, Oscar's just come in. Anyway, Mum wasn't sure if it was a hit and run, or if it was one of us.' She lowers her voice. 'You know Oscar's got his provisional licence?' I tell her that I do, he's had it a few months. Karen gives him lessons in her car because Ali's Lexus is too big and Simon's is a company car. 'Mum didn't want to start pointing any fingers until she was sure, then she remembered the dashcam, but had no idea how to use it. She couldn't ask one of us, for obvious reasons, and didn't want to ask Trevor, because deep down she suspected it was Oscar.'

Alison pauses and I picture her rolling her eyes. Poor Oscar's always blamed when something breaks or goes missing. Let's say, he's a bit heavy handed. 'So she called Teddy in from the garden, asked him if had any idea how the thing works.'

I listen in silence as she goes on to tell me how Karen had paid Teddy thirty quid to upload the footage from the dashcam SD card on to her computer and check it for any discrepancies. She made him a cup of tea, then left him to it while she went up to clean the bathroom; about ten minutes later, he called up to her from the bottom of their stairs, told her he'd skimmed through it and it was all clear, the dent must've already been there, and no, there was no need for her to come down – he'd see himself out and see her next Friday to jet wash her patio.

'Poor Mum took his word for it,' Alison continues. 'You know how trustworthy she is. But as fate would have it, last night Mum tried to upload some photos onto her computer. A few had vanished, so she checked her recycle bin and that's when she stumbled across the dashcam video file. Once she realised what it was she sat there and watched it all – frame by frame and then bingo, there you both were.'

'Oh my God.' My stomach tightens. 'It recorded the whole thing?'

'Yep – stupid sod left the engine running when he got out. Mum rang and told me right away. She wanted to call you but I managed to persuade her to wait until morning to give me a chance to see it first.'

'Oh, God,' I utter, raking a hand through my curls. 'Karen's dash cam. I can't believe it.'

'I watched it all, Lucy. Simon jumps out of the car, meets you at the bonnet, hands you something – your phone, I think, and then…' Alison hesitates. 'And then.' Another pause. God, this must be so hard for her. 'And then he kisses you. It's all on film. You pushing him off, everything,' she admits, voice breaking. 'We even saw you wiping your mouth in disgust and spitting on the ground. I can't believe I fell for his lies. I've been such a bitch to you.' Another pause and a sniff. I think she's crying. So that's how Simon Maxwell got caught out – he didn't finally develop a conscience. The snake.

'Okay, but how is Teddy involved in all this?'

'Teddy saw it all, obviously.' Alison pauses, blows her nose loudly. 'Took snapshots with his phone, deleted the video clip, probably thinking that an old biddy like Mum would never find it, then lied to her about his findings. That way he'd have access to the footage if he needed it again, probably to blackmail Simon.' Shit, is that how he intended on paying Lydia the maintenance arrears? I can't breathe. 'And he'd also have something on you if you rejected him. A bit of security in case things went pear-shaped. It's how these psychopaths think.'

'Psychopaths!!?' Is she serious? Hot tears blur my vision. 'But why would he do such a thing?' I cry. 'It doesn't make sense.'

'I think he's got a fixation on you. I'd go as far as saying that he fell for you from the photo stage, followed you, pursued you, with the aim to alienate you from everyone and everything, so you'd end up relying on him completely. Think about it, Lucy, he knew there was nothing going on between you and Simon because he saw the footage. Your first date didn't go well, did it? You told me and Mum that you didn't want to see him again.' That's right. I didn't. He wasn't my type. 'He must've picked up on it, knew he wasn't going to get a second date, so he sent you the threatening text and then the picture message, to weaken his prey, make you vulnerable, powerless.'

A feeling of dread tears through my guts. 'When he saw you breaking, he forwarded it to me to end our friendship. That's when you fell for him, wasn't it, when you were all alone and needy?' My insides sink. She's right. It was. 'He's a very clever and calculating man, Lucy. He lied to you about what I said too, about me ringing him to cancel, about me saying you're Simon's bit of stuff. Why would he do that, hmm? I think you've got yourself a stalker.'

I quickly kick the door open and vomit onto the grass footpath. Gripping the doorframe, I retch again but nothing comes out. I wait out another bout of nausea, hair in my face, spittle drooling from my lips, before collapsing back onto my seat. Alison's tinny voice drifts from my phone. I lift my hand up weakly and press it to my ear. 'Alison, how could you have set me up with a madman?' I ask, wiping vomit from my lips with my sleeve. 'I'm stuck in the middle of god-knows-where with him now. I can't get away. What am I supposed to do?'

'Oh, God, I know. I'm sorry! He seemed so normal. Nice. Decent. Where are you now? I'll come and get you. Phone the police.'

'I don't know,' I whimper. 'Parked up on a country lane somewhere. We've run out of petrol.' I swing my legs round, carefully avoiding my vomit, eyes darting around for a road sign, for someone to help me. 'Alison, I'm going to have a quick scout.' Tiptoeing around my puke, I round the car, then cross the road, craning my neck for a better view, but all I can see is stretches of tarmac and the BP petrol sign.

'Oh, Ali, I can't see a thing.' I scan the isolated street wildly. 'I don't know what to do. I could make my way towards the petrol station but I might meet him on the way back. What do you think?'

Silence.

'Alison?' I hope we haven't been disconnected. I look at the black screen on my phone.

Shit. I'm out of fucking juice.

Chapter 28

I try to steady my breathing but each breath feels as if it'll be my last. My phone was my only ally, my only way out, and now it's died on me. And it's all my fault. Why do I always leave the battery until it's on its last legs before charging it? I know it's old and decrepit. Everything inside me pounds. My stomach feels as if a butterfly is trapped inside it, desperate to get out.

I take a few awkward steps towards the car, like a drunk staggering out of a pub. This can't be happening to me. Any moment now I'm going to wake up and it'll all have been a dream. I squeeze my eyes tightly shut. A flock of crows squawk above me and my eyes snap open. Not a dream – very real.

Swallowing hard, I steady myself against the bonnet of the car. It's still hot. And then, closing my eyes, try the controlled yoga breathing Karen taught us when she got back from her retreat in Devon – *in one-two, out one-two, in one-two, out one-two. Come on, Lucy, you got this.* Okay, Teddy isn't who he says he is but he must have a good reason for concealing his identity. He's a good man. Alison got it wrong. He's not a psychopath. *In one-two.* Isn't dangerous. We've had sex. I'd have noticed if he were – seen the signs. *Out one-two.* Alison said she thinks he's the blackmailer, thinks he's been stalking me – THINKS, isn't certain.

In one-two. It's all speculation. Other people have access to Karen's computer. *Out one-two.* What about that new bloke of hers, Trevor. How long has she really known him? Didn't Alison tell me at the pub last Saturday, when Karen slipped off to take a call from Trevor, that he'd been suspended from the police force, then took early retirement? Alison didn't get a chance to fill me in with all the juicy details because Karen appeared, all sparkly eyed and loved up. But it must've been something serious. Sexual harassment perhaps, or money laundering – Karen mentioned that he was in the drugs squad. Theft, blackmail, or even stalking. Bent coppers are capable of anything. I run a hand over my face, berating myself for sounding like a paranoid idiot. Who am I kidding? Teddy Fallon has lied to me from the get-go. I've got to get away from him – fast.

A tiny sound fills my ears and I realise that it's raining. I round the Ford Mondeo as the rain spits against it like pins, cogs in my mind turning wildly. The pins turn to nails as I reach the passenger side, splattering on my hair, face, shoulders. A low rumble echoes in the distance. Brilliant timing, thunderstorm, thank you. I pull the hood of my top over my head, wild curly hair splattering from the sides like lined fur, and just then I get a flashback of Teddy chucking his phone charger in the glove compartment. I could try that, it must be a universal fit, then I can call Alison back, or the police. They're bound to be able to trace my call. But what if that takes too long, what if Teddy gets back before it's even on 1%. I decide very quickly to get back in the car and wait for him to return, pretend that everything is normal, then at the first set of red traffic lights, I'll jump out and make a run for it. But as my hand closes around the door lever, a thought tears into my mind, his car has auto central locking. I hear them clank whenever we set off. What if that means I can't get out?

Stepping away from the suffocating car, I hold my head in my hands and turn full circle. There's no way out. Bending slightly, I hold my thighs and take a few deep breaths. 'I'll be fine. He's not going to hurt me, he's not going to hurt me,' I mumble like a mantra, because the more I say it, the more I'll believe it, right? That's what Alison always said. It's a technique she often uses on her clients, to help them gain confidence. The rain peters out but the grey slate clouds hang in the sky, darkening the evening. Okay, there's only one thing for it, I'm going to have to get back in the car and keep my cool, pretend that everything is normal, then ring the police when we get to Brighton. We can't be that far away. The blue road sign on the motorway read – Brighton 15 miles – before we turned off earlier.

I snatch the door lever again, now slippery with rain, then as I look up I see the beam of flashlights and my heart flips. I leg it into the middle of the road and flay my arms, screaming for help. The car thunders towards me, as if I'm a target, but instead of getting out of the way I just stand there – frozen. For a horrible moment I see Teddy Fallon behind the wheel, face tight with anger. I always wondered how I'd die but I never envisaged being mowed down by my stalker. A cacophony of blaring horns and screeching wheels scream in my ears and I have to raise my forearm to block out the dazzling headlights. It's only when the driver hits the breaks, just feet away from me, that I come to my senses and dive out of the way.

Cowering by the pavement, I watch as the white 4x4 swerves and skids before screeching to a halt a few metres away. Blinking, I focus on the silhouette of a female driver, hair in a bun, narrow shoulders, hooped earrings. She's waiting for me. She's going to save me. Clambering to my feet, I break into a sprint, surprised that nothing aches. But as I reach the car, I hit a puddle, immersing my right foot in rainwater. The driver sizes me up in her rear-view mirror, eyes like discs, then the engine rumbles and the car starts moving. 'No wait, please! Don't go.' I manage to reach the back door and pull on the lever but it's locked.

Stumbling forward, I chase after her but she puts her foot down. 'You fucking BITCH.' I cry. I watch in dismay as the car soars into the evening, leaving only an imprint of its wet tyres on the tarmac in its wake.

Hobbling back to the car, foot squelching in my trainer, I catch sight of my reflection in the darkened windscreen of Teddy's Ford Mondeo – an unrecognisable hooded figure with sunken features and grubby clothing, soiled from the impact of the fall, stares back at me. The driver must've thought I was a druggie, a down and out. Didn't want to get involved. Didn't want me in her precious car.

I fold myself into the passenger seat, haul off my trainer and squeeze out the rain from my sock, heart aching with grief, and as I slide my foot back into my shoe, I remember Max's old phone, the one Teddy put in his jacket pocket. My eyes widen. It was definitely working because he made me call the number, and although it didn't ring, I did see it flash with icons when he pressed the home button.

I'm on the backseat, checking the pockets of his brown corduroy jacket – a blue pen and a red one, a pencil. Half a packet of Polo mints. His breath always smells fresh. A blue plastic lighter. A pair of reading glasses, which I've never seen him use. A neatly folded handkerchief with the initial S on it. S? Is that a clue? Simon, or Stephen, or Sean, perhaps. No he doesn't look like a Sean, he looks more like a Stephen. My hands are shaking. I slide my hand into the other pocket, keeping an eye on the road ahead. 'Come on, come on,' I groan, 'where is it?'

My hand closes around something smooth and heavy. I pull it out hurriedly – a pocketknife. I turn it around in my clammy hand. It's big and red and shiny with multiple tools. Isn't it illegal to carry a Swiss army knife these days? I decide very quickly that there's no time to psychoanalyse Teddy Fallon. Slipping it back where I found it, I plunge my hand into one of the inside pockets, eyes darting to the street ahead, and instantly feel the familiar edges of a mobile phone. I pull it out hurriedly and with it flies a plastic card. It falls between the passenger seat and the centre armrest. An oyster card? A credit card? Sliding my hand in-between, I locate it with two fingers. I turn it around in my hand, eyes wide. An ID card. I flip it over and start reading – Name: Solomon Oakley. Occupation: School Teacher. My eyes flit to the thumbnail imprint on the left-hand side. Teddy Fallon's face stares back at me. Fuck, fuck! Alison was right – he's an imposter, a phoney.

Oakley? That name rings a bell, and then it hits me – his MP mother. Teddy's voice rings in my ears – *Fallon has more of a ring to it that Oakey, particularly as her first name is Carrie.* I thought he said Oakey. I must've misheard. I wonder if she really is an MP, or if that's another fucking lie.

I fire up the phone, no passcode, thank goodness. Although a bit careless of him, given he's got so much to hide. Please, please, please let there be 4G, or even 3G. The moment 3G appears on the top left-hand side of the handset, I swipe left, locate the Google app and type his name in the search field with tremulous fingers – Solomkon Oakley – and hit search.

Showing results for Solomon Oakley

I start scrolling –

Solomon Oakley Consultancy Limited

Solomon Oakley (1738 -1812)

Family Tree for Solomon Oakley

I hit the Images tab and run my thumb along the screen, flicking through unknown faces – none of him. Right. I'm going to have to be a bit more specific. My thumbs fly over the screen, eyes darting from the phone to the road – *solomon oakley school tea4her lodnon.*

Bingo! A Facebook profile with his photograph, albeit taken several years ago. Nothing unusual. I'm used to seeing old profile photos of friends, or filtered ones. People want to look their best, impress. I tap onto the link and a bigger picture of his face appears, along with an update posted six months ago. Damn, he's got it set to private, including his list of friends. I go back to 'search' and scroll and that's when I spot it.

Obsessed school teacher sacked for stalking mother of two|Surrey...*https://www.surreygaz/.../obsessed-teacher-sacked-for-stalking-mother-stu-col...*
31st April 2020 – Solomon Oakley / KNP / 48730. Picture Desk 0387265 A *TEACHER stalked* a student's mother at a comprehensive *school* by ...

I tap the link, blood pounding in my ears, breath ragged, and wait and wait and wait for the page to load. 'Come ONNNN!' I growl impatiently. The page opens. I glance at the road. It's empty. I start reading.

A local 46-year-old school teacher was sacked after allegedly harassing a mother of a fifteen-year-old student by bombarding her with text messages and sending her gifts, refusing to believe that she was in a happy relationship with colleague Mr Tom Norton, an employment tribunal heard. Teachers said Oakley would stalk the mother outside Wingdale Comprehensive School when she picked up her son and she showed no signs of reciprocating his advances. Obsessed Solomon Oakley continued to pester Melanie Stuart – who was ultimately given police protection during the year-long ordeal. Oakley was linked to an arson attack on Mr Norton's home when neighbours raised the alarm of a fire. A petrol bomb was later found in Mr Norton's house. Oakley was also questioned in connection with a violent attack on his ex-wife, Lydia Oakley, 41, causing bodily harm by pushing her down a flight of stairs in their family home in Surrey. Mrs Oakley, who spent a week in hospital, later dropped the charges, it was said.

My skin tingles. 'Oh, no, oh no, oh no, no, NO,' I cry. The phone almost drops out of my quivering hands as I open the photo app. I scroll through his album, expecting to find the photograph of me and Simon kissing, which Solomon took from the dashcam footage and blackmailed me with. But all I see is pictures of his kids, a posh plate of burger and chips, a photograph of a school football team, a pint taken at a pub, nothing suspicious.

I'm about to give up when I swipe left and my blood runs cold. There's a picture of me going into my flat. I swipe again – me asleep in my bed on the first night we met. I swipe again, I'm getting into a cab outside my flat, Spiros and Kiki, his nephew, photobombing the shot. Another swipe – I'm hiding behind the bushes outside Jasmine's house, then outside her door – the picture was taken from the side. He must've been on the premises, followed me there. How did I not see him? I swipe again and again – several photos of me and Jasmine outside her house – me getting into a taxi – Jasmine waving me off.

On my next swipe a video appears and every hair on my body stands on end – the dashcam footage. He must've copied it to his phone. I go to tap play and that's when I hear it. The faint sound of ringing. *Brrr brrr…brrr brrrr…brrr brrr.* Dropping the phone, I follow the sound to the back of the car. Bending down, I press my ear against the boot, listening. Nothing. Perhaps it was my imagination, or a sound coming from another parked car. I go to move away and then I hear it again. The sound amplifies as I open the boot. I move things out of the way, frantically – a rake, a shovel, a turquoise sponge in the shape of a wave, a blue centrefeed roll, a tub of patio cleaning detergent.

Sweat trickles along my forehead and curves around my nose as I heave up a bag of compost – nothing. I can't find it. The ringing stops and then starts again. Pushing everything out of the way haphazardly, I follow the sound, and then, using both hands, haul up the gunmetal-grey boot carpet and there it is – nestled against one of the spokes of the spare tyre. That's what the rattling sound was. The phone must've been knocking against the metal.

It stops ringing as I pull it out. It has a large screen and is quite heavy. I press the home button. Again, no passcode. Perhaps his brain can't store more than one passcode. It lights up with a bright blue and yellow background – three missed calls.

I immediately open the photos app, and almost throw up in the boot of the car. There it is. The photograph of me and Simon – kissing. 'Oh, Alison,' I whimper, 'why do you always have to be right?' I fire up the messages app and read all the texts he sent me one by one, eyes wide, breath shallow, mouth dry.

'I don't fucking believe it,' I whisper.

'Quite frankly, neither do I.'

Chapter 29

'What the hell are you doing?' Teddy asks coldly. 'And what's happened to you?' He takes in the length of my body. 'You look a mess.' And then, flicking his eyes to the phone in my hand, he says, 'Where did you find that?'

I should keep my cool, not let on, play it safe, because, according to that newspaper report, he's dangerous. But I can't. I point the handset at him as if it were a loaded gun, anger sweeping through my veins. 'You,' I spit, 'it was you all along.'

He frowns, red petrol can in hand. 'What are you talking about?'

'Don't try to deny it. I've seen it all.' I jab at the screen on the phone. 'On here.'

Teddy pulls a face, concerned, then drops the tank by the side of the car. 'Seen what?'

'The photograph.'

'Photograph?' he asks, mystified.

'Oh, come off it,' I say, sounding bolder than I feel. 'You know what I'm talking about.'

Studying me carefully, Teddy stuffs a hand into the pocket of his jeans and scratches his five o'clock shadow. 'Sorry, you've completely lost me now.'

'Don't act all innocent. I know you uploaded Karen's dashcam SD card onto her computer, don't deny it.'

He frowns at the footpath for a several moments, bottom lip jutted, and then he says, 'Oh yeah, that's right. She found a scratch on her car, thought it might've been her grandson, or that oaf son-in-law. Is there a crime against helping old ladies out these days? Wait, how did you…' A pause and then, 'Oh, I get it. You rang Alison while I was gone, even though you promised you'd wait until we got to Brighton.' My stomach clenches but I stay silent. 'Brilliant. I did warn you about ringing her, didn't I? I knew she'd fill your head with nonsense. Bloody therapists. They're all the same. Fucking know-it-alls. I suppose she told you she didn't think you were Simon's mistress, that I lied.'

God, he's really thought all this through. 'That's exactly what she said,' I exclaim, 'because it's the truth.'

Teddy shakes his head. 'Absolute rubbish. I thought you were smarter than that, Lucy. Can't you see what she's doing?' I twist my lips to the side in disdain. 'She's trying to split us up because she's jealous.' Jealous? Next he'll be telling me she's obsessed with him, wants him for herself. 'Where was she when you were being blackmailed and threatened, hmm? Taking Simon's side and believing his lies, that's where.' I want to cover my ears to block out his words. He points his finger. 'I'm the only one who stood by you. The only one who believed you.' *No, stop it, stop it.* 'And now you want to believe her lies.'

Teddy goes to pick the can up when I yell, 'You saw what happened in that footage, saw me pushing Simon off yet lied to Karen. Told her it was all clear.'

'No,' he says simply, palms up. 'I just uploaded the thing onto her computer then left.' Then his face pales. 'God, what was on it? Did someone–'

'LIAR.' I pull a strand of hair out of my mouth. 'You know damn well what's on it.'

Pressing his fingers to his lips, he regards me carefully. 'Okay, you're right. I've been rumbled. I did lie to Karen about the dashcam footage.' At last. I brace myself for a confession, even though I've got no idea what I'm going to do with it. 'I told her that I watched the whole thing and didn't find anything, that the scratch must've happened in a car park, people are always parking so close. But…' He scratches his top lip, leaving a black mark on his skin from the dusty can. 'Between you and me, I only flicked through the first few minutes.' My heart sinks. Not a confession, another lie. Another attempt to manipulate me.

'Oh, come on, Lucy, it's a two-hour recording. I've a business to run.' Some businessman he turned out to be. The fraud. But I'll get to that later. I don't want to overload him. 'I mean, she probably scratched it herself. Have you seen her parallel parking? People over a hundred shouldn't be allowed on the road.' Disrespectful prick.

'You're lying. I've seen it all on here.' I wave the phone at him.

'So you keep saying. Seen what exactly? What am I supposed to have done?'

'Okay, I'll spell it out for you, shall I?'

'Go ahead. Knock yourself out.' He folds his arms.

'Karen's dashcam recorded Simon kissing me that night. There was no one lurking behind a tree with a long lens camera – no jealous ex-husband with a cocaine habit – no twisted new girlfriend.' Teddy's eyes widen. If I didn't know better I'd believe his incredulity. 'But you know all that, don't you, because you paused the dashcam footage and took a photo of Simon kissing me with your phone,' I exclaim.

'I've never heard such bullshit in all my life.'

I inch closer. 'You then blackmailed me with it and forwarded it to Alison, so we could fall out. You sent me those threatening texts. YOU.' I hold up the phone. 'It's all on this. Those lilies I received, those "death flowers" as you put it were from you, weren't they?'

'Hey, back up,' he barks. 'Firstly, that phone isn't mine. I swear on my kids, and secondly–'

But I don't want to hear any secondlies, or thirdlies, or any more of his lies. 'Then why was it hidden in the boot of your car, hmm?'

'I don't know!' he exclaims, throwing his hands out like a music conductor demanding emphasis from his orchestra.

'Did it get in there by magic?'

'You tell me. You're the one who found it.' He bobs his head back. 'Apparently.'

'Stop trying to be clever. You've been blackmailing me.'

'Hang on a minute,' he says, hands on hips. 'I don't think I like your tone. Why would I blackmail a person I've only just met? *Christ*, why would I blackmail anyone?'

I hesitate for a moment. That was my first thought when Alison suggested it to me, and, although I loathe to admit it, he does look innocent. Clearly, he's a brilliant actor. An Oscar performance, no less. 'For revenge.' I squeeze the words out through gritted teeth, holding onto my resolve.

'Revenge for what? We'd only just met.'

'Rejection. You took the photo for security in case I didn't want to go out with you again.' I realise how childish and pathetic it sounds the moment it leaves my lips. 'I must've told you in the pub that night, in my drunken state, that I didn't want a relationship with you, so you went ahead with your plan. Ruined my friendship with Alison and Karen. Made me paranoid, vulnerable, powerless. Terrorised me until you brought me to my knees and then…and then…'

Teddy looks at me as if I'm insane, a small smile playing on his lips. 'And then what? Took advantage of you?' he scoffs. 'I think you'll find that you're the one who wanted to have sex with me. You're pathetic.'

'You groomed me, so that I'd enter into a relationship with you.'

'Jesus,' he mutters, shaking his head, 'you don't know how crazy that sounds. What are you, twelve?' And with this, he picks up the petrol can and unscrews the cap, completely unperturbed. 'I really don't know what's got in to you today, Lucy. I do know, actually. Alison bloody Maxwell. Silly cow. I knew she'd fill your head with ludicrous ideas.' More head shaking. 'You do realise she's lost it, don't you?' He fits the nozzle into the tank and pours. 'She's unstable. Discovering your partner has been cheating on you is bad enough, but imagining it's with your best friend is enough to send anyone over the edge.'

How dare he insult Alison. I want to punch him so hard that my knuckles will bleed and take a week to heal.

'Look, you've been through a lot this week. You're stressed out. I get it.' He pauses, and then. 'This is what's going to happen. Let's forget we had this conversation.' I look at him as if for the first time. I can't believe I trusted him – let my guard down – slept with him. 'Oh, come on, don't look at me like that.' He glances up at the gunmetal sky. 'I'll drive you to your mum's because it's getting late, but then I'm going straight to the B&B in Hove as previously planned. Give us both a bit of space. We can talk again tomorrow. Once you've had a good rest.'

'I'm not getting in the car with you.' I say defiantly, sliding my hands into the pockets of my hoodie.

He shrugs. 'Suit yourself.' The pungent smell of petrol drifts to my nostrils as he empties the last dregs into the tank and my stomach spins. *Come on, Lucy, this is no time to be sick.* 'I'm quite disappointed in you, actually.' Teddy's voice again. 'Taking Alison's word over mine.'

That's it. I've heard enough. I lean against the car and brace myself to deliver my trump card. 'I know who you really are, Solomon Oakley.'

For a moment he pauses, jaw clenched, and then, to my surprise, his shoulders start shaking.

'What's so funny?' I demand.

'You are.' He throws me an approving glance. 'Okay, you had a dig around. I knew you would. So now you know who I really am. Great. We don't have to pretend anymore,' he says matter-of-factly. 'God, Lucy, it's such a weight off my shoulders.' He stretches his back and winces. 'You don't know how hard it's been lying to you. I tried to tell you so many times but–'

'You can't seriously think we can carry on after this?'

Nudging me out of the way, he puts the petrol can in the boot. 'Why not? I love you. More than I've ever loved anyone. And I know you love me too.' I stare at him in horror as he tears strips of blue paper towel off a huge roll and wipes his grimy hands. I want to tell him that I loathe him. That I curse the day I set eyes on him. That he's made my life a misery. But instead I swallow the words and they sting my throat like thorns. 'Okay, maybe I'm being premature, but you can't deny you've got feelings for me,' he says, wagging a finger.

Taking a pace back, I look at him agape. This man is completely insane and now I'm stuck in crazyville with him. But despite it all, I press on. I need answers. 'Why did you lie to Alison about who you are, about being a gardener?'

Scrunching the paper into a ball, he tosses it onto the pavement. 'I was out of work. Desperate for money. Alison rang me and offered me a job. What was I supposed to do?' he says all cocky, 'You can't look a gift horse in the mouth. Lydia wants her pound of flesh every month, or else. I busted my balls to get visitation rights. I wasn't going to give her a reason to kick off again, stop me from seeing my boys. Besides, I can't live off fresh air.'

'Alison thought you were someone else,' I say, defending her, 'that's why she hired you. Jesus, any normal person would've said, "Sorry, wrong number."'

He shoulders past me. 'Stop being so sanctimonious. I saw an opportunity and took it. I mean, how hard is it to mow a lawn and do a bit of weeding and digging? Alison and Karen are loaded. No harm done.'

'No harm?' I stand behind him as he opens the back door and grabs his corduroy jacket. 'You stole someone else's identity, swindled people out of money, and you've been following me.' His jaw tightens as he slides an arm into his jacket. I've hit a nerve. 'Yes, I've seen the photos you took of me on Max's old phone.'

Following my gaze, he frowns at Max's handset, which I dropped in my haste on the backseat earlier. If he grabs and smashes it, all the evidence will be lost. My heart thuds hard as he continues to stare at the phone, but then he blinks, almost as if he's awoken from a trance, turns and folds himself into the driver's seat, lips a thin line. 'I've just had to jog over half a mile and back. I'm knackered. So, if you've finished with the interrogation. Can we please get going?'

Finished? I've only just started. He turns the key in the ignition. It doesn't start. He turns it again and again, face pink. 'Come ON,' he moans. On the next turn, the engine roars. 'What do you want from me, Lucy?' The truth would be nice. 'I really don't understand you,' he says, anger slipping into his voice. 'Don't you want to be happy?'

'Er…hello,' I scoff, curling a hand around the doorframe. 'I want to know why you've got photographs of me on Max's phone.' He revs the engine, eyes on the dashboard. 'Why you've been lying to me about your identity.' More revving, I can barely hear myself think. 'Why you stole that image from Karen's computer and blackmailed me with it.'

The engine dies. 'All I wanted to do was look after you,' he says at the bleak street ahead. 'I didn't want to be like all the rest – like your dad, like Andrew.'

'You've been stalking me,' I quiver, unable to control the tremor in my bottom lip.

He shoots me a look. 'That's a bit harsh, isn't it? I took a few photos of you. So what?' he admits, clambering out of the car and dusting himself down. 'People take photographs of their girlfriends all the time.'

'Not while their unaware.' I follow him briskly to the back of the car. 'Not covertly.'

'I just wanted to make sure you were safe, that's all. Someone was after your blood. Still is. *Jesus, Lucy!!!*' he yells, rummaging around in the boot. 'I can't believe I put myself at risk for you.'

'What risk?' I hit back.

He straightens up and I follow his gaze to the patio cleaning tub. It was facing the other way around when I picked it up. The words, in thick red marker, swim in my vision – PAINT STRIPPER. 'Oh, my God.' I whisper, clamping both hands over my mouth. 'Jasmine's Porsche.' Terror slices through me like a knife and I have to steady myself against the car. 'I swear, Teddy, if you've hurt her.'

'Oh, come off it. I'm not a murderer. And I'm not a stalker either. You've got it all wrong.' I wish I could believe him more than anything but I can't. I think he's hurt Jasmine. I think he's the reason she's missing. 'Okay, you've had your outburst. Can we go now? Please!?'

I shake my head to and fro, to and fro. 'You're a sociopath.'

He snorts in disgust. 'Do you even know what that means?'

Anger burns through me like wildfire. Yes, I do know what it means, I want to scream, I've got a bloody Masters in English Language. But I say nothing. 'What about the school mum?' My eyes flick to a sharp-looking pair of shears in the boot, blades glistening under the streetlight. If I'm going to get out of this in one piece I'm going to need protection – a weapon. I inch closer to the boot. 'The one that took out an injunction on you? Did you love her too, want to protect her?'

'You're being ridiculous,' he says smoothly, as my eyes flick back to the shears. I'm about three feet away. I take a few tentative steps forward. It's almost within reach. 'How did you find out about me and Mel, anyway?' he asks, as if she's just an ex-girlfriend, as if he didn't stalk her for over a year, as if he didn't try to burn down her boyfriend's house. 'Oh, never mind.'

Straightening up, he reaches for the lid of the boot. *Please don't close the boot, please don't close the boot.* The boot closes with a loud thud and every part of me sags. The only chance I had of grabbing something to protect myself with – gone. 'I'm quite flattered that you're jealous.' He grins, and as he slips his hand into his jacket pocket my heart stops – the penknife. That's why he put his jacket back on. I shouldn't have confronted him. I should've just kept quiet until I was somewhere safe.

I press my lips together hard, sealing in a scream. The trees, lining both sides of the street, rustle in the wind, a gate rattles and squeaks in the distance. I've riled him. He's angry, getting defensive. My mind races. I've got to try a different approach, try to placate him until I find a way to escape. Other motorists use this road. The serial-killer-lookalike on the moped was definitely a local. He might ride through again. A car is bound to show up sooner or later, and when it does I'll throw myself in front of it if I have to, anything to make them stop.

'Look, Teddy…I mean…Solomon.'

'Sol,' he says coldly. 'Everyone calls me Sol. Or you can carry on calling me Teddy, if you like. I've become quite fond of it. I love the way it sounds on your lips.' He looks at me intently, then drops his gaze to my mouth then breasts. I pull my hoodie around me self-consciously. 'I love everything about you. Your infectious laughter. Your husky voice. The way your head rocks slightly when you're nervous.'

What? It does not. I tuck my hair behind my ear nervously.

'Your beautiful smile and lovely straight teeth – small but perfect. The way you tie your hair back when it gets unruly.' I rarely tie my hair back. He could only know that if he's been watching me for ages 'I even love how messy you are.' I frown when he says this. I'm not that bad. 'And God, those blue eyes. I could lose myself inside them forever,' he whispers. 'You're just amazing.' Reaching out, he brushes my cheek with the back of his fingers and I cringe.

'Thank you.' I swallow, folding my arms, and he lets his arm fall by his side. Up until this moment I held my own, but he's really starting to frighten me now. 'Um…Teddy,' I say, and he smiles, likes it that I'm still calling him Teddy. I'm moving in the right direction. 'You're right.' I lean my back against the car and push a hand through my hair. 'I'm stressed to the hilt. Alison caught me off guard earlier. I believed everything she said but I don't anymore. I think you're right, she is unstable.' I nod furiously. 'I wouldn't be surprised if she's back on Sertraline,' I lie, and he frowns. 'They're antidepressants.' His frown intensifies. 'What I'm trying to say is I do really like you. A lot.'

I watch him steadily but his smile doesn't quite reach his eyes. He's no fool. I'm going to have to try harder. 'You're the only one who stood by me, Teddy, and I'm truly grateful for that, but surely you can see how I got sucked in.' Squaring my shoulders, I look him straight in the eye, feigning confidence, even though I'm breaking inside, even though I want to wet myself. 'I'm not promising anything, but if you explain it all to me, from the beginning. In your own words. I think we might be able to get through this.'

He stares at me for a few moments, face unreadable. I can see his knuckles moving against the corduroy fabric, turning the knife around in his hand. I don't think he believes me. A lump forms in my throat. He could kill me now and bury my body in the woods – no one would know. It could be weeks, maybe months, before anyone found me. He could be out of the country by then, with a new life and a new identity. I go to speak, lie about how much he means to me, when his hand flies out of his pocket, weapon in hand, and everything around me sways.

Chapter 30

I shudder, eyes squeezed shut, arms wrapped around my quivering body. This is it. I'm going to die. Blood pounds in my ears, breathing ragged, and then I hear a shuffle followed by a few clicks. 'Okay,' Teddy says cheerfully. My eyes snap open. Teddy is sucking on a Marlborough Light, head dipped. Not a knife. A lighter. The penknife's in the other pocket. Relief sluices through me and I do a little shaky sighing noise. Grateful that I dodged a bullet.

'I don't want any more secrets between us,' Teddy says, blowing smoke from his nostrils. 'I'll tell you everything.' He takes a long inhalation on his fag. 'I'm a teacher. Science. Mel's son, Dylan Stuart, nice lad, bit dim, was in my class. We first met at a parents evening. I liked her. She wasn't snooty like the other mothers. She was fun, chatty, ordinary. No airs and graces. The kind of woman you could have a laugh with. Enjoy a pint with down the pub.' He gestures at me, fag in hand. 'A bit like you.' He smiles, flicking ash off.

'Summer before last, she started coming to rugby practice, you know, to pick Dylan up, or so she claimed. I was the school coach. Played rugby all my life. Considered going pro when I was younger, but Dad wouldn't have it,' Solomon complains bitterly, face darkening with resentment. 'Mel and I got on – had a lot in common. One evening, I bumped into her at our local – she was having a drink with a friend. One thing led to another and we ended up in bed together. When her boyfriend got wind of it, she cried wolf. Made up some crazy story, said I was harassing her. Got me the fucking sack, the bitch.' With a final drag, he flicks the cigarette onto the ground and points a finger at me. 'I had nothing to do with that fire at her pesky boyfriend's house, by the way. He tried to stitch me up because I slept with his girlfriend. I was never charged, you do know that, don't you?'

I swallow hard, dread coursing through every fibre of my body. I think I need the loo. *Come on, Lucy, you're a strong woman, you can do this.* 'Okay, that makes sense.' I shake my head furiously. 'What a bitch though – getting you sacked,' I lie, and he gives me a small smile and a nod. 'But what about Lydia?' I press on. 'You told me she pushed you down the stairs, but I read online that it was the other way around.'

He laughs, stuffing his hands into the pockets of his jeans. 'Good old Google, eh? Don't believe everything you read online. Newspapers want to make money. They destroy people's lives.' That's true, but not this time. On this occasion the reporter was spot on. 'Lydia did push me down the stairs. I went to A&E. You can check if you like. The Royal Marsden.'

I watch wordless as he opens the passenger door, sits in sideward, then emerges with a half-filled bottle of mineral water. He unscrews the cap, takes a swig then offers it to me. With a slightly tremulous hand, I take it and drink thirstily, mainly because I'm parched but also because I want to keep him onside.

'What you read about me online is fiction. Lydia dropped the charges, and do you know why? Because it was all a pack of lies.' I almost choke on my final gulp. Poor Lydia must've dropped the charges because she was petrified of him, afraid of what he'd do to her. 'I promise you,' he pauses, takes the empty bottle from my hand and hurls it into the woodland. Good throw. He must be telling me the truth about being the school rugby coach. 'I didn't lay a finger on her. Yes, she did have a spell in hospital, that's where that cock of a reporter got his story from, but that was on a separate occasion, when she got blind drunk and fell down the patio stairs in the garden. Smashed her face on the concrete.'

His face reddens. 'There was blood everywhere. Poor kids were terrified. That was the last straw. I told her I'd had enough and was going to leave with the children. The next thing I knew the police were knocking on our door. She gave them the domestic abuse line, played the victim, so that I wouldn't get custody of the kids. They believed her, of course, took me in for questioning but then let me go. She kept changing her story, couldn't remember a thing the next day. Ask the police if you don't believe me.' He stares at me darkly, challenging me. 'It's all on record.'

I shake my head, yes, trying not to show my disgust. Poor, poor Lydia. 'One more thing, Teddy.' I close my eyes briefly, breathe in. 'How long were you following me for, was it days, weeks?'

'Not long,' he says simply.

'But why?' I press.

'To make sure you were safe,' he answers, as if it's the most natural thing in the world.

'And the photos? Why did you take them?'

His demeanour changes in an instant and he stiffens. 'Can I ask a question, please?' he says in a clipped tone. 'Because I've had enough of being cross-examined.'

I nod, heart picking up speed. 'Yes, of course.'

'Why did YOU lie to me?' He taps his chest with two fingers. 'Why did YOU lie to the police?'

The hairs on the back of my neck prickle. 'What? No…I…'

'Last night you told me that you were going to take a shower and go to bed, right?'

'I…'

'Is that right?' he demands, face tight with anger.

'Yes,' I say quietly.

'But you didn't, did you?' Silence. 'Instead you took a cab in the middle of the night and went to Jasmine's.' He slips his hand into his jacket pocket, the one with the penknife, and I feel my knees give a bit. 'Can you please tell me why?'

'I didn't…' I begin. My eyes dart to his pocket. I could lie about what I did, but what would be the point? He knows I was there. Of course he does. He's been following me. I'm going to have to come clean. Even if it means going down for it. 'Okay, I lied to you,' I admit. 'But only because I didn't want to get you involved,' I add truthfully.

I lean my back against the car and fold my arms. 'When I went to see Jasmine yesterday morning, I stole her engagement ring. Well, it was mine, Andrew nicked it off me and gave it to her.' I give Teddy a thin smile but his face is deadpan. 'It was a moment of pure madness. I shouldn't have done it. I felt awful afterwards. Later that night, I showered and went to bed. But sleep wouldn't come. I kept tossing and turning. Technically, I knew I'd done nothing wrong. I was only taking what was mine. What Andrew stole from me. But I felt like a criminal. I knew it was only a matter of time before Jasmine would discover that her ring was missing, and then she'd put two and two together and call the police.'

I start pacing, wringing my hands. 'I had these images of courts and judges and prison cells. I couldn't rest – couldn't get it out of my mind. In the end, I got dressed, jumped in a cab, went round there and pushed the ring through her letterbox.' The relief of my confession is instant, like kicking off an uncomfortable pair of heels I've been walking in for hours.

'And then I left,' I say, candidly. 'I was hoping, praying she'd find it in the hallway and think she'd just dropped it. But then she disappeared. God, I hope her housekeeper doesn't hoover it up. You do believe me, don't you?' I ask, and he gives me a small nod. 'You followed me there last night, didn't you?'

Another little nod, face slick with sweat. 'I had to make sure you were safe. I didn't know why you were going back there in the middle of the night, drunk. So I…' he falters. His left cheek and neck is covered in red blotches. I can see his heart beating through his fitted shirt. He's weakening.

'Go on,' I probe gently. 'It's okay.'

I watch as he squats against the car, head in hands. 'You said someone had to teach Jasmine a lesson. I thought you were going round there to do something stupid.' What, like pour paint stripper all over her car, I want to say. 'I didn't know you'd found your ring there, taken it back. You should've said,' he says irritably. 'When I saw you leaving a few moments after you arrived, I thought you'd bottled it. I couldn't just stand by and do nothing. You were hurting.'

'So you took the paint stripper out of the car…'

'I was only going to drench one of the headlights, teach her a lesson, but a fox shot across me and it went everywhere.' A confession. Why am I not recording this? 'All over the bonnet, all over me. I had to burn my clothes.' That's why I could smell campfire in his hair. He slowly gets to his feet and rubs his eyes with his knuckles. 'Wow.' He puffs out his cheeks and blows. 'This is a first. I can't believe I told you all this. No other woman has had this effect on me.'

I take a tentative step towards him. 'So, where's Jasmine now?'

Confusion flashes in his eyes. 'I don't KNOW,' he says, his anger returning. 'Why do you always have to think the worst of me, eh? I've just bared my soul to you and all you can do is scoff. The damage to the Porsche was an accident. Give me a break, I'm just a normal guy who fucked up.'

His outburst startles me but I press on. 'You photographed me in bed asleep on the first night we met.' I close my eyes briefly, inhale. 'How is that normal?' But he has an answer for everything – he took it after my nightmare – was looking for marks on my face and neck because I said I'd been smothered, and he believed me, thought someone had come in through the open French doors and attacked me while I was asleep – wanted to gather evidence in case the intruder returned.

'And the blackmail?'

'Oh, not that old chestnut again. Come on.' He glances at his watch. 'We can continue this ludicrous conversation in the car. His hand closes over mine. It's hot and clammy. 'Christ,' he mumbles, 'we're going to miss the crossing at this rate.'

'Crossing?' I holler. 'Where are you taking me?' For a moment I have visions of being gagged and tied and taken abroad in the boot of a car. I go to move but my legs feel like lead. I look up at him and his face sways in my vision. Oh God, the water, what was in it? Has he drugged me? But no, he drank some too. Did he swallow? Panic powers through me like a Japanese bullet train. I'm not sure. I think he might've just pressed it against his lips, and then I feel his hand around my wrist. 'No, please, wait. I can't.' I drag my feet, squatting to break the impact. 'Let go, Teddy, you're hurting me.' I try but fail to prise my hand out of his tight grip, and then, fuelled with adrenalin, I lean forward and sink my teeth into his flesh.

'OUCH!' Letting go, he glares at my teeth marks on his palm. 'You fucking bitch.' I barely have time to process what I've done when his hand comes down and everything spins. I'm on all fours, grit piercing through the skin of my hands, face throbbing, and then I taste something metallic in my mouth – blood. I think he's broken my jaw. I'm about to get up when I hear the crunch of feet, then his legs swimming in my vision. Looming over me, he hauls me up by my hair. The pain is unbearable, almost as if my hair is being pulled out of my skull. 'Get in the fucking car,' he spits, eyes bulging, hair slick with sweat.

'Please, Teddy,' I whimper, 'if you let me go I promise I won't say anything about this. You have my word. I won't go to the police…'

I kick and scream and plead with him as he drags me back to the car and opens the boot. 'No, no, *nooooo*! Somebody help me, PLEASE!'

But my words fall on deaf ears. No one can hear me. No one can save me. In the distance, I hear the sound of a siren. Oh, please let it use this lane. PLEASE. The wail grows louder and louder, until it's screaming in my ears. Blue and yellow lights flicker in the darkness.

Swinging me round, Teddy pins me against the car, face so close to me I can feel the heat from his breath. 'You stupid fucking witch,' he cries, one hand on my throat. 'Our first row and you go running to the police.'

'I didn't,' I croak, truthfully. His hand tightens. I can't breathe. 'Please, don't hurt me,' I squeak, the words mangled. The lights are blinding. I'm backed against the car, hot tears blurring my vision. I hear the screech of wheels, the siren stops wailing but the lights are still flashing, and then I hear the clank of doors and hurried footsteps against tarmac. Releasing me, he staggers back. I drop to my knees, choking, holding my neck.

'Miss,' says an officer, 'Miss, are you okay?' I try to speak but my mouth is too dry. The back of my head feels numb, my throat burns. Every ounce of me aches. 'Can you please tell me your name?'

Tears spill from my eyes as they throw him against his car. Then I hear a male voice, strong and loud. 'Can you trace vehicle registration number Roger eighteen, Whiskey, Foxtrot, Lima, over and out.'

'Lucy,' I stammer, looking into the police officer's kind gentle brown eyes. 'Lucy Harper. How did you find me?'

'I'm Rula, and this is PC Herodotou.' I look up at the male officer but he's too busy trying to restrain Teddy to acknowledge me. 'Someone reported a distressed woman on the road fifteen minutes ago,' she answers kindly. The driver of that car that sped past. The one I hurled abuse at. She saved my life. 'An ambulance is on its way, Lucy, try to stay calm.'

'I haven't done anything!' Solomon yells. More flashing lights as an ambulance pulls up. 'It was just a lovers' tiff. Tell them, Lucy, don't do this to me. Haven't you people got real criminals to catch?'

'Come on, love,' Rula says, as PC Herodotou cuffs Solomon and reads him his rights. 'Let's get you home.'

Chapter 31

'All set, ladies?' Karen breezes into Alison's lounge smelling and looking gorgeous. She's wearing a black and white Chanel suit, with matching kitten heels. 'Oh, is she still upstairs?' Karen groans. Rolling her eyes, she flicks back her signature blonde bob whilst dropping her black Birkin onto an armchair. I didn't hear her let herself in but I'm glad she's here. I've been sitting on my own for twenty minutes, killing time on social media. There's only so much tweeting you can do.

'That you, Mum?' Alison calls from upstairs. 'Pour me and Lucy a glass of fizz. There's a bottle in the fridge. I'll be down in a minute.' Karen and I glance at the Roman numerals skeleton clock hanging above the Victorian cast iron fireplace, then smile at each other knowingly. Who really drinks prosecco at nine thirty on a Friday morning? Apart from an overexcited Alison who can't wait to go on a weekend luxury spa in the Lake District, that is.

Abandoning my phone, I quickly get to my feet, sidestep our heaving suitcases, and envelop Karen in my arms. She feels warm and safe and snuggly. We cling to each other for a few moments and I inhale the aroma of her freshly blow-dried hair and perfume, an amalgamation of coconut shampoo, hairspray, and YSL Opium. Karen always looks so smart and elegant, like a Greek goddess.

It's the first time I've seen her since Solomon Oakley's arrest a month ago. I've been meaning to, but you know how life gets in the way. Most of my weekends have been spent in Brighton with Mum. When something as traumatic as this happens, everything shifts – your priorities, your outlook, your values; and Karen's been busy too – weekends away with Trevor, yoga retreats with her neighbour. I really think she's getting in to all that Om stuff now. Yoga's a gentle exercise, perfect for her heart condition.

This luxury spa break in Windermere was Karen's idea. She even booked it all online for us, volunteered to look after the kids and keep an eye on Oscar. Poor Oscar has become a bit withdrawn lately. The breakup of his parents' marriage has really hit him hard. Leah and Barney seem to be taking it a lot better – perhaps it's because they're younger, or maybe because Simon's their biological father. Simon's dropping them off after school, Alison told me earlier, then going back to his bedsit in North Finchley.

'So, I hear you're staying put at your flat,' Karen says as she deposits a bunch of keys the size of a prison warden's on to the Indian-inspired sheesham wood coffee table.

'Yes, that's right.' I curl a strand of hair behind my ear. 'Mum is releasing equity on her house in Brighton to help me out, bless her, and she's helping Kate too.' One good thing that's come out of this is that it's brought our family back together. Kate rang Mum when she couldn't get ahold of me on the day I was almost kidnapped by alias Teddy Fallon. Mum was first to find out that Kate had left Mateo. They'd drifted apart, she'd said. He was spending all his time in the gym or drinking at the bar with his mates, and she'd fallen in love with someone else. Gemma, a holiday rep. I've seen photographs of them together. Jacob, my nephew, is in every single one of them. I haven't seen Kate this happy in…well, ever, actually.

Mum and I can't wait to see them all when they come over for Christmas.

'I refused her offer at the beginning, of course,' I say to Karen now. 'But you know what Mum's like.'

Karen smiles. 'Good old, Mum, eh? I'd have done the same, mind. I'd do anything for our Alison. Coffee?' Karen suggests, and I nod, following her into the kitchen.

'I hear Jasmine has sorted her car out,' I say as Karen fills the kettle at the sink. I was wrong, by the way, Teddy Fallon didn't abduct and kill Jasmine. She was on a silent retreat in Hampshire. According to Andrew, she went there to get over their split – left her car at home and switched her phone off. 'Can't believe Teddy…I mean, Solomon, destroyed her lovely Porsche.'

'A crime of passion,' Karen says, spooning coffee into two mugs. 'Isn't that what he told the police? That you made him do it, or something?'

'Yes,' I sigh, 'but they didn't believe him, thank God.' Teddy denied vandalising Jasmine's car at first, which didn't help his case because, as fate would have it, next door's CCTV caught it all on their camera. 'And he's still denying the blackmailing charge. Tosser.'

Karen pulls a face, incredulous. 'Alison said they've charged him with assault and harassment.'

Karen hands me a white Vilroy mug and we mosey back into the living room, taking a seat opposite each other. 'Yeah,' I say, taking a sip from my cup and scalding my top lip. 'He's awaiting trial.'

'I hope they lock him up!' she says bluntly and I smile at her over my cup.

'They've put a restraining order on him too,' I explain, crossing one leg over the other.

Karen blows on her hot coffee. 'He seemed like such a lovely man – kind, gentle. Couldn't do enough for me, if I'm honest.' She shakes her head incredulously. 'Pulled the wool over all our eyes.' We sit in silence for a few moments, sipping our drinks, then a sudden thud of grime music filters through the ceiling. 'Oscar must be up.' Karen smiles and we both look up at the ceiling. The volume increases. Karen winces, then leans forward and whispers, 'So, how're things?'

'Okay,' I admit, 'slowly getting back to normal.'

'Good. It'll take time, love.' Karen leans closer and points at my tummy. 'What about the baby?'

The room grows dim and I have to put my cup down on the coffee table. 'Baby? What baby?' Karen gives me a knowing look. My stomach stings. 'How…?' Jesus, how could she know? I only found out this morning.

Karen winks, points at my bag, and the bangles on her liver-spotted wrist rattle. Shit. I left the pregnancy test in full view. I knew I should've asked the pharmacist for a bag.

'I did a test this morning,' I say quietly, visualising the long plastic tube with the word '*pregnant*' on it in my mind's eye. 'I'm going to do another one when we get to Windermere, to be on the safe side. I'll tell Ali when I'm sure.'

Karen nods slowly. 'Is it his?' she asks softly, and I nod, looking at my feet. 'Are you going to keep it?'

I jerk my head up. 'It's all I've ever wanted,' I hear myself say. 'I'll be thirty-eight next month. This might be my only chance of becoming a mother.' I've been going nuts since I missed my period. After ten days of agonising, I plucked up the courage and took a pregnancy test this morning, expecting it to be negative. I read online that stress can make you miss a period. I almost fell into the toilet bowl when the word 'pregnant' flashed up on the white stick, a mixture of joy and fear swirling in my stomach. Questions flew around in my mind. How could I have Teddy Fallon's baby inside me after having sex with him once, yet nothing with Andrew for years? It wasn't possible. What if the baby looks like him? Takes after him? But no, it'll have my genes too, I conceded, my values, my ethics.

'At least something good has come of all this,' Karen says warmly. 'Are you going to tell him?'

'No,' I say immediately, and then, 'I don't know. Not yet.'

Karen half stands, picks up a blue toy rabbit and tosses it into the play box. 'You don't have to, lovely.' She pulls a tube of hand cream out of her bag. 'It's your baby. Congratulations,' she whispers, glancing at the stairwell. 'There's no love greater than that of a mother's for her child. You'll soon find out, Lucy.' We grin at each other as she squeezes cream onto the top of her hand. 'I would do time for my Alison,' she admits, nonchalantly, massaging the cream into her hands. 'If anyone touches a hair on her head, upsets her, I'll go after them.' I nod again knowingly. I've heard a lot of mother's say they'd kill for their child. 'Alison and the kids are my world.'

Karen gets to her feet, stretches her back and tells me that yoga is making her backache worse rather than better, and then she ambles towards me, squats and puts one hand on my bare knee, peeking from the tear in my jeans, more for stability, I think, than affection. 'You, my little one.' I can feel the warmth of her touch radiating through my pink floral frill sleeve blouse. 'Are one lucky little boy or girl.'

I smile down at her. What a lovely thing to say, and then she cups her hands around my face. They're warm, soft, familiar. The grime music has stopped and in its place Lewis Capaldi *is liking the way you numbed all the pain*, and as the heavy scent of Karen's hand cream dances under my nostrils, nausea stirs in my stomach, ascending to my chest like a rocket. 'Oh God,' I cry, 'I'm going to be…' I bolt to the loo as fast as my legs can carry me and vomit violently into the bowl.

A few minutes later, I stagger back into the lounge, wiping a bit of spit from my lips with the back of my hand. Karen is pacing up and down, turning the tube of hand cream around in her hands nervously. The moment she sees me she rushes over and throws her arms around me. 'God, Lucy, are you okay?' I hear a puff and I realise that she's plucked a tissue from a box on the side table behind me. 'Was it my fault? I'm so sorry,' she says, scrunching the tissue in her bony hand. Then she lowers her voice. 'I was like that with my Alison. Couldn't keep anything down.'

I swallow back another bout of bile to the kerfuffle of Alison thumping around upstairs, then the sound of footsteps clambering in the hallway, a fist against a door and her loud voice telling Oscar to turn off the music and make sure he has a shower. 'I'm sorry, Karen.' I can still smell the faint scent on her hand as she tenderly wipes the side of my mouth with a tissue. 'It's that…that smell…is it…' Karen looks confused. 'Your…um…hand cream.'

'Oh God, was it this?' She stares at the tube in her hand in horror. 'It's Molton Brown,' she says, as if their products are made by angels. Then she puts her glasses on and starts muttering to herself nervously. 'Coco and sandalwood,' she clarifies, looking at me over her oblong glasses.

Of course it is. It had to be. I'm about to tell her that it's not her fault, she couldn't possibly have known that the scent of sandalwood makes me want to throw up my entire intestines, when a thought shoots into my mind and stands there defiantly. Solomon Oakley still denies the blackmail charge. Surely, Karen…

I fix my eyes on her as she continues to read the label, and then I say, 'Karen.' She snaps her head up. I can see the fear in her eyes – like a deer in headlights. 'You didn't–' But before I can finish, Alison thunders down the stairs in a red A-line dress and matching pumps, dark hair tumbling over her shoulders, blue eyes shining with excitement.

'What do you think, Lucy?' Alison says, throwing me intermitted glances in the mirror. 'Is it too loud for the Windermereians?'

I look at her reflection agape. What do I think? I think that my hormones are giving me sick thoughts about your mum, that they're trying to convince me that she blackmailed me and, quite possibly, breezed into my flat as if she were *Roz* bloody *Huntley* out of *Line of Duty*, and almost smothered me to death with those soft hands of hers that reek of bloody Sandalwood. I lick my dry lips, eyes darting between Alison and Karen.

'Lucy? What's wrong?' Alison asks. 'You've gone pale.' Rushing over, she pulls me to her, then looks at Karen, worriedly. 'Mum, get her some water, for crying out loud.'

'She was just sick,' Karen explains, anxiously. The veins in her neck have enlarged, her blue eyes are wide. 'I think it was because of something I did,' she admits, voice shaking. Looking down at the hand cream she says, 'I put this bloody thing on and then she just…' Karen holds up the tube and I notice that her hand is visibly shaking, lips pursed. And in that moment she looks so old and tired and frail, as if she'll snap in two. *Oh, stop it, Lucy. STOP IT. Solomon Oakley is the blackmailer. He's been charged. His fingerprints are all over the phone he used to blackmail me with. He photographed my every move, took photos of me while I was sleeping. God, stop!!!* I blink rapidly, batting the thought away.

'Mother!' Alison's loud voice makes me jump. 'I've been looking for that hand cream all morning.' Alison snatches the tube from her mother's hand and my mouth drops open. *No, no. It can't be. It wasn't Alison. Sandalwood is a popular scent. I need to get a fucking grip.* 'Oscar bought it for me for mother's day with his pocket money. Bless his cotton socks. A charity find.' A pause and then. 'Brand new,' she clarifies. 'Great for carrying around in your handbag. What I'd like to know is how it found its way into your handbag, Mum.'

'You left it by my bathroom sink yesterday, dear,' Karen says dryly. Poor Karen. I can't believe I almost accused her of being a psychotic maniac. 'Lucy's obviously got some sort of allergy to the ingredients.'

Alison turns it around in her hand and frowns at it. 'Aww, really? Well, if it upset your stomach, Luce, I…oh shit, Sandalwood. Of course. The stuff makes her puke,' Alison explains to a bewildered-looking Karen. 'I'm sorry, Lucy. I won't bring it with.' Alison drops the hand cream onto the Mahari dark wood sideboard. 'Are you okay? We can cancel if you're not feeling up to it – go another time.'

I tell her that I'm fine now, of course we're still going, I've been looking forward to it all week, and then I look at Karen's frightened little face and hate myself for upsetting her, for making her blame herself, for having such dark thoughts about her.

Swallowing hard, I sit back down. 'It's okay, Karen, it wasn't your fault,' I say softly, one hand over my tummy, feeling grateful that she didn't share my pregnancy news with Alison, that she respected my privacy, kept my secret. 'It's probably the after-effects of that bug I had.' I say to Alison dismissively, and I almost see Karen's tense muscles loosen.

Satisfied, Karen straightens her back, her Greek goddess persona returning and tells me to take care of myself, I've had a tough time. Then, tugging her sleeves up a fraction, she shepherds her daughter back to the mirror, all the while showering her with compliments – she looks stunning, she's lost a bit of weight, it suits her, that dress shows off all her curves, we'll have an amazing time in Windermere, she wishes she was going too. Alison laps it all up, turning this way and that in the full-length mirror against the wall.

Sitting back, I smile as Karen fusses over her daughter, pulling an invisible thread off her dress, fastening a loose strand of dark hair behind her ear. Karen's a good mum. One of the best. If I'm honest, for a crazy nanosecond I was hoping that Karen, or even Alison, was the blackmailer, because that'd let the father of my baby off the hook.

It'd mean that he had nothing to do with terrorising me, that he was just looking out for me, like he said, was having some kind of emotional breakdown on the day he almost kidnapped me, onset from the stress of losing his family and job in such a short space of time; it would make me question whether Lydia did drop the assault charges against him because they weren't true, if Mel, the school mum who accused him of stalking her, did have a one-night-stand with him then regretted it when her boyfriend found out, that my baby's dad had nothing to do with the arson attack on Mel's boyfriend's house, that it was all just one big coincidence. It'd make me believe that he did love me, in his own peculiar way. But, of course, I know that's all a load of wishful-thinking bollocks.

A car horn beeps. Taxi's here.

Alison wheels her case loudly towards the door, all the while giving Karen a list of things to do, while Karen groans in protest, asking how she could possibly forget when she's reminded her a hundred times.

Outside, wheels grind against stone slabs, an engine rumbles, and as I extend the handle of my suitcase, squinting up at the October sun, a warm glow washes over me. Yes, my baby will have some of Solomon Oakley's genes, but it will also share some of mine. I'll bring her up (yes, I think it's a girl) to have morals and values and ethics. I'll love her unconditionally, but will teach her right from wrong, because this miracle that is growing inside me, this faceless, nameless baby whom I am already in love with – is mine.

Epilogue

They say the camera never lies. When I first saw that image of you and Simon kissing, I thought you were guilty as hell. A classic case of divorcee falls for best friend's husband. I read about it all the time, see it in movies. It's everywhere. I felt sick. You were just dating other men to take the scent off your sordid affair. Taking us all for mugs. No one deserves that.

I light a cigarette and blow the smoke high into the air, visualising your innocent face in the mist. I don't know if I'm sorry for what I did to you. Actually, yes, I think I am because you were innocent, weren't you? But you must take some responsibility for your actions, Lucy Harper. If you'd spoken up sooner, said what'd happened with Simon from the get-go, I could've spared you so much pain. But your silence sealed in your guilt, like hot tar in a crack. I didn't deliberately go out to hurt you, you know. I'm not a maniac. But I couldn't just sit back and let you get away with it either, not when so many people were involved, not when there was so much at stake.

I take another lug on my cigarette, the tip crackles and glows. I don't even know why I started smoking again. It was probably because of you. I must stop. I chuck the ciggie onto the stone slabs and watch it roll into a puddle and fizzle out – dead – like the end of a tragedy. Closing my eyes, I see you and Simon in that clip again but this time I don't feel rage, this time I feel contentment.

A friend once told me that everything happens for a reason, that life is a chain of events. I wonder what would've happened if I'd worked out how to upload that dashcam footage myself and played it all back, frame by frame, instead of relying on that lying, cheating bastard; if Oscar hadn't discovered it in my recycle bin while he was using my computer, before I did; if he hadn't panicked when he heard me on the landing, paused the frame of you and Simon kissing under the street light and snapped it with his iPhone, without seeing the entire scene play out, without knowing the truth; if he hadn't sent it to you anonymously from a pay-as-you-go phone in an effort to get you to confess without implicating himself, without being responsible for the breakdown of his parents' marriage; if I'd not walked in on him that Friday evening while he was sending you that dreaded text, confronted him, threatened to tell his mother if he didn't fess up; felt sorry for him when he broke down and begged me to keep quiet; and better still, if I'd been savvy enough to dismiss Oscar's claims about an affair and how he'd been suspecting it for months but needed proof; dismissed his ludicrous story about how he snuck out of the house the night Simon gave you a lift home, hitched a ride off a friend, followed you back and took the photograph of the pair of you having a goodnight kiss outside your home. If only I hadn't been so full of rage that I took over from where he left off – finished the job myself. If only…

I hear footsteps along the side of the house and then my name. I quickly get to my feet and, amble towards you, smiling. Folding you in my arms, I tell you that you're late, traffic will be building; and you apologise, explain that you missed the bus then had to wait twelve minutes for the next one. I scold you for refusing a lift as you climb into my VW Golf, even though I know you did it because you didn't want to inconvenience me.

With a wry smile, I buckle in, ask if you're comfortable, if you'd like me to open a window, I don't want you to be sick all over my car. I've only just had it valeted. I'm about to confess that I almost drenched myself in sandalwood body lotion this morning, the one that Trevor bought me on our second date, but remembered in the nick of time how violently ill it makes you; but then you pat your tummy, tell me that the morning sickness has subsided, and I decide against it. I don't want you to feel as if you've put me out and I know you will. Just like I know you acted on impulse on the night that Simon kissed you, because you are a bit impulsy, Lucy, aren't you, especially when you're under pressure. But no matter, we're all keepers of secrets, tellers of lies – if needs must.

Perhaps you kept quiet to save Alison's marriage, or perhaps you felt sorry for Simon when he broke down and cried, as I did my grandson. I kept Oscar's secret to protect him. My lovely, lovely boy. Seventeen is a tricky age, Lucy. He's a good lad, really, and, like you, he thought he was doing the right thing. Simon kept his secret so that he could continue to get his leg over without jeopardising his marriage. I think it's called cakeism, isn't it? When you want your cake and eat it. He hates it at that B&B, especially now he's lost his job. It didn't take long to find out he was screwing the wife of the Head of Finance. It was instant dismissal.

Teddy Fallon, or whatever his name is, kept his secret to deceive us all, to swindle us out of money, trap you into a relationship. The trouble with arrogant people is they take the rest of us for idiots. I was looking for a scapegoat. How easy he made it for me. The call from Alison came early that morning, she'd found out he was an imposter and wanted to question him, to be one-hundred-per-cent sure. The timing was perfect – he was in my garden trying to secure a fence he'd bodged up. When Alison told me to hold the fort until she arrived and not let him out of my sight, I thought all my Christmases had come at once. It gave me just enough time to hide the pay-as-you-go phone in the boot of his car – the phone I handed to him in my marigolds so he could show me how to use Zoom, the phone covered in his fingerprints, the phone that was used to blackmail you. I don't feel an ounce of guilt for framing him. I'm glad he got sent down. He had it coming – terrorising women, stalking them, setting people's homes on fire, cheating innocent people out of their hard-earned cash, without so much as a slap on the wrist. He thought he was so clever. He thought he could get away with murder, but not on my watch, Teddy Fallon, not on my watch.

The engine growls and I put you through the drill before we set off. I'm so glad you accepted my offer of driving lessons. It's the least I could do after everything you've been through. Leaning forward I turn up the radio as we pull away from the kerb with a jerk, a small smile playing on my lips. You're not a bad person, Lucy Harper, and I know you probably meant well, but I meant what I said too, if anyone touches a hair on my Alison's head, upsets her, I'll go after them.

Note from the author

Thank you so much for reading Mine. I really hope you enjoyed it. If you did, I'd be grateful for a brief review or star rating on Amazon. Reviews and ratings help readers discover new books and make the author smile. They sometimes even make them do a little jig around the coffee table!

About the author

Kelly Florentia was born and bred in north London, where she continues to live with her husband Joe, and where her novels The Magic Touch, No Way Back, Her Secret and her psychological thriller, Mine, are set.

Kelly has always loved writing and was a bit of a poet when she was younger. Before penning her debut, she wrote short stories for women's magazines - To Tell a Tale or Two is a collection of her short tales. In January 2017, her keen interest in health and fitness led to the release of Smooth Operator - a collection of twenty of her favourite smoothie recipes.

As well as writing, Kelly enjoys reading, running, drinking coffee, gyming, watching TV dramas, and spending way too much time on social media. She is currently working on her next novel.

Website: www.kellyflorentia.com

X: @kellyflorentia
Facebook: @kellyflorentiaauthor
Instagram: @kellyflorentia
TikTok: @kellyflorentia
Threads: @kellyflorentia

S
A Stylo Publication

Printed in Great Britain
by Amazon

39924861R00202